THE WANDERER

Based on a True Story

THE WANDERER

BIGAMY, DECEIT, AND MURDER

James Keene

The Wanderer

Copyright © 2024 by James Keene. All rights reserved. Printed in the United States of America. For information, address Silly Goat Media, PO Box 2594, Beaver, UT. 84713.
No part of this book can be used or reproduced in any manner without written permission except in cases of brief quotations in articles or reviews.

To protect the privacy of individuals when required the names and identifying details have been changed.

Some of our authors do participate in speaking arrangements. If interested, please visit the website below.
www.sillygoatmedia.com

ISBN: 978-1-961181-21-2

ACKNOWLEDGMENTS

This book is dedicated to the brave women who allowed me to tell your stories. In return, I hope it gives you some sense of closure.

For the one woman whose story we will never hear in her own words, I dedicate this book to you and your family. May you rest in peace.

And to all those who have experienced domestic abuse, you are not alone. Please, speak up. Your stories deserve to be heard.

National Domestic Violence Hotline (USA): 800-799-7233

The Wanderer is a thriller mystery based closely on true stories. A such, it contains certain depictions and themes that may not be suitable for all readers. These include the following: domestic violence, threats to children, death/murder, suicidal ideation, substance abuse, strong language, and allusions to sex work. Reader discretion is advised.

This book involved domestic abuse, sexual assault, suicidal ideation

PROLOGUE

Blackbirds flapped their wings and called ominous warnings to one another, hopping around the gravel as they searched for scraps. The chilled wind didn't bother them as much as it did the detective, who had turned his head from the gray-colored landscape to watch the birds.

The morning was rotten, the kind that twisted in your gut before things got worse. He took a slow breath. The air was sour, as if carrying the stench of whatever hell they were about to throw themselves into. He scanned the trail up and down, imagining what eyes could view him from where he stood. Further ahead, his partner, Blair McCoy, spoke on the phone while she routinely shot him serious looks suggesting he should come closer to hear.

But he wasn't paying attention to her phone call. She would summarize it well enough for him later. Instead, he imagined trying to grab Blair from where she stood and dragging her up the path, kicking and screaming, all the way to their SUV. He wondered who would see, how far her cries would carry in the thick air. How hard would she struggle?

Perhaps, if done early enough, it could be possible. Especially with the cold of autumn creeping closer and closer, he couldn't imagine too many people would be anxious to leave their homes. No witnesses had come forward. It was likely none would.

"Myers!" Blair called to him, perhaps for the second time. She never called him by his first name. "Traffic light clocked his license plate over the state line." She put her phone in her pocket, determination written across her face. "Interstate kidnapping. We're officially on the case."

Only just beyond, white, red, and blue lights flashed. They warned everyone who looked at them—something bad had happened here. Uniformed officers stood uneasily around, their faces unreadable at this distance.

"Myers!" Blair called to him again, her arms gesturing her annoyance. "Let's go."

She was right. Their suspect was on the run, and time was against them. They needed to talk to the local detective and get debriefed.

The black birds cawed at Jack as he passed, flapping their wings aggressively, yet another force driving him toward his quarry.

The hunt for Cayde Miller had begun.

CHAPTER 1

AUTUMN

"**G**rab it!"

Autumn's arm shot forward, fingers curling around the red disk as it sailed through the air. She almost toppled over, momentum pushing her off balance. She only had seconds before Tania would close in. Morgan waved from the distance, arms up behind a wall of opponents. Autumn flung the frisbee toward her, wincing at the sloppy throw. Still, Morgan chased after it, outpacing her defenders.

A gust of wind rustled the trees as Morgan caught the awkward pass. Kathy stood poised behind the end line, focused as the frisbee whipped in her direction. The moment she snatched it, Autumn and her teammates erupted in cheers.

Tania groaned but flashed a playful smile. None of them were upset—how could they be? The park was too perfect, the weather too beautiful. A full day of celebration stretched ahead. Finals were over, and with no more deadlines or professors to stress them out, Autumn and her friends were basking in the freedom of finishing their first year at Lipscomb University.

The teams reset for the next play. Autumn edged toward the boundary, eyes trained on the frisbee as it darted from player to player. She readied herself near the end zone.

"Autumn!" Justin's voice broke through the noise. The red disk floated her way, but this time she fumbled. It bounced off her fingers and sped across the grass. She chased it, but the frisbee rolled past the sidewalk, stopping at a stranger's boots. The man picked it up, eyes on the girls.

"Throw it back!" Morgan called out.

The man raised an eyebrow, grinning. "Which team?"

Everyone laughed, voices mixing in playful demands for the frisbee.

"I'll take it." Autumn's face felt hot. She brushed auburn hair from her eyes and held out a hand.

"Hope I didn't mess up your game." He extended the frisbee toward her.

"You didn't." She grabbed it. He didn't let go.

"Know any good steakhouses around here?" he asked.

"Steakhouses?" She almost laughed. "This is Nashville. Take a drive, and you'll find one in any direction."

"But I want *your* favorite," he said, locking eyes with her. His gaze was sharp. She was about to decline when he added, "I'm Cayde."

"Autumn." Her name slipped out before she could stop it.

His hair was hidden underneath a cowboy hat, but she could see jet black locks peeking out. Dimples appeared in his handsome smile.

"You've got the most beautiful blue eyes I've ever seen, Autumn. How about dinner?"

A nervous laugh burst from her. She glanced back at her friends. Tania, Morgan, and Kathy wore identical grins, silently urging her to go for it.

"I don't know," Autumn hedged. Cayde was charming, sure, but he was a stranger.

He still held tight to the frisbee. "How about just your number?"

Autumn hesitated. "Fine." She took his phone, entered her number, and handed it back.

"Thanks," Cayde said with a wink, finally handing the frisbee over. He strolled toward a sleek black Corvette, waving to the girls. They giggled in response.

"Wait!" Autumn called out as he opened the car door. "I didn't give you the name of a steakhouse!"

"You can tell me when I take you out," he replied. He shot her another grin, and then took off.

Laughter erupted behind her. Her roommates rushed up, teasing expressions plastered on their faces—except for Justin, who stood with his arms crossed.

"What's wrong with you?" Morgan nudged her. "You should've said you'd go out with him."

"He's a stranger," Autumn shot back. "For all I know, he could be a murderer."

"Handsome, charming, and friendly—classic killer traits," Tania deadpanned.

Justin cut in, "So, are we redoing the play?"

"Doesn't matter," Kathy smirked. "She still scored."

"Knock it off!" Autumn's face burned as the group laughed, returning to the game. But Autumn couldn't shake the butterflies in her stomach. Her smile lingered.

To hell with her doubts. She wanted Cayde to call.

CHAPTER 2

CLAIRE

Ugly holes marred the walls of Claire's home where family photos had once hung. At first, she thought it was just about getting used to not seeing Zach every day, even in a still image smiling at her from the hallways. But after a few weeks, those holes started to feel bigger. Gaping. They seemed to swallow her up every time she passed, a constant reminder of everything she'd lost.

Claire sighed. She stood in the hardware aisle of the department store. Even trying to fix up the walls reminded her of Zach. He'd always been the one to handle repairs.

"You look a little confused," a man's voice interrupted her thoughts. Browsing only a few feet away, he offered her a sympathetic expression from beneath a cowboy hat.

"Probably because I am." She forced a laugh. "I'm just grabbing a few things to fix some nail holes in the wall."

"You don't need much." He grabbed a small bucket of spackle and a scraper off the shelf. "Plannin' to repaint?"

"No, just patching up a few things." She tried to sound casual, but her voice felt tight in her throat.

"Good to get ahead of it," he said. "Before you know it, the list of things to fix gets longer and longer. My two daughters are nearly as wild as boys. My own walls could use some love."

Claire smiled faintly. "I teach English at a local school. The kids in my class have endless energy. They're more destructive than animals sometimes."

The man raised his eyebrows. "At East Junction? My girls go there. You don't happen to have any Millers in your class, do you?"

"I actually teach at a high school," Claire replied, "but my friend teaches there. She might know them."

"Cayde, by the way." He extended his hand.

"Claire." She shook it, feeling a little more at ease. They chatted briefly, mostly about school and his daughters. He seemed proud of them, and Claire was grateful for the distraction from her own thoughts. But eventually, the conversation dwindled, and Cayde handed her the supplies.

He pulled a small card from his pocket. "You know, if you'd like, I'd be happy to fix the walls for you. Free of charge." He handed it to her. "Teachers do a lot for the community. Consider it a small way of givin' back."

Claire glanced at the card. *Cayde Miller. Private Investigator.* She opened her mouth to respond, but Cayde just gave her a nod, like the decision was already made.

"Well, take care," he said, walking off.

When Claire got home, she sat on the stairs with her German shepherd, Tank, lying at her feet. She scratched him behind the ears absently as she stared at the holes in her wall. She got the feeling Tank was bored without Paige and Zach around to play with him. It made her feel guilty she didn't have more time to spare, but they were a comfort for one another and had bonded a lot since the divorce.

The supplies was sitting on the counter. It was an easy job, one Zach would've handled in no time. But standing there, staring at the damage, she realized how little energy she had for it. She reached for her phone and dialed her friend, Jessie.

"Do you know any Millers? Their dad offered to fix my walls for free," Claire asked once Jessie picked up. "I just want to know if he's safe."

Jessie's response was sympathetic. "Finally took the photos down, huh?"

Claire swallowed. "Yeah."

"Well, I don't know much about *him*," Jessie continued, "but his youngest girl is in my class. They're pretty popular. Smart, well-behaved. But, Claire—I think he's married."

"Oh." Claire raised her hand, as if to ward off the thought. "I wasn't asking because I'm interested. I just want to make sure it's safe to let a stranger into my house."

Jessie laughed. "Fair. But let's be real—any repairman you call would be a stranger too, and probably overcharge you."

That was true. Claire hesitated, then sighed. "Maybe you could call me while he's over? Just in case?"

"I can do that. Always good to have backup."

After their call ended, Claire stared at the black holes again. She fished Cayde's card out of her pocket and dialed his number.

CHAPTER 3

JACK

The chatter from police radios buzzed in and out, garbled words Jack couldn't quite catch. He and Blair moved down the dirt path, eyes scanning the scene. Time wasn't on their side; Cayde's last known location was seventy miles away, and they had no luxury of delay. They needed to speak to the head detective and go.

Everyone stood outside, near the area where the victim had been staying. Multiple police cars were parked, and caution tape roped off the entry.

The local detective, looking worn and slightly harried, approached with a file in his hand. "This is everything we've got on Cayde Miller so far. His records, statements from the victim's family, and past charges. We've sent out a few requests, so more are coming in, but I'll email you whatever else you need as it comes."

Blair took the file, tucking a strand of mousey brown hair behind her ear. "Appreciate it," she said, flipping through the papers. "Jesus, this guy's been busy. Long record."

"The record alone gives us all the more reason to catch him as soon as possible." The detective looked genuinely sad. "This girl is in trouble." He offered up a little evidence bag, his hands still gloved. "We found this about ten paces away. It was probably the exact spot he got her."

Jack and Blair examined it, tilting their heads to catch the glint that shone through the plastic. A silver-chained necklace—broken. A small diamond in the shape of a heart was at its base.

"This belonged to the victim?" Jack asked.

"It's been confirmed, yes."

"It may have come off in a struggle." Of course, he couldn't know for sure, but he'd met this man before. Not Cayde Miller, to be exact. But an abuser. Someone who would stop at nothing to keep their control over someone. Jack eyed the scene like it would cough up another clue if he stared hard enough. "Does the media know?"

The detective sighed and rubbed the back of his neck. "We let 'em run the story," he admitted, shifting his weight like he regretted the call. Jack could see why—it was a gamble. The media could help, sure. But it could also make things worse. Panic the suspect, make him desperate. Or worse, spook him enough to start wiping away the evidence, leaving them chasing shadows.

"What else did he leave behind?" Jack asked.

"We got tire tracks. They're documented, and we'll see what we can get off them. You'll have the results as soon as we get 'em."

"What about witnesses?" Blair interjected.

The detective's frown deepened. "None so far."

Jack's jaw tightened. "If he grabbed her here, he had to be armed. Someone should've heard or seen something. You don't just take a girl off the street without a struggle."

"Maybe he picked her up somewhere quieter. Somewhere out of sight," Blair said, her head swiveling as she looked around. "But it doesn't matter where he got her. What matters is where he's going."

She was right. They weren't here to clean up the mess, they were here to prevent a bigger one. Time was ticking, and every second wasted brought Cayde and his kidnapped wife closer to disappearing for good.

Blair looked back to the detective. "Keep us updated on anything else. We'll take whatever you get."

With a quick handshake, they headed to their SUV, footsteps crunching against the gravel. The road stretched out before them, long and winding. Jack glanced up, spotting a few black birds circling overhead before flapping off, their hunt for scraps just as futile as theirs had been so far.

CHAPTER 4

KATE

Kate drummed her fingers on the café table, annoyed she'd agreed to meet here in the first place. Twenty minutes late. No messages. No apologies. Just her, sipping on a lukewarm coffee, watching baristas scramble around delivering orders. The guy had been relentless on the dating app, firing off texts like it was a race. And now he couldn't even show up on time?

Cursing under her breath, she mentally kicked herself for getting her hopes up. She should have just stayed home with Bella, her Yorkie. The little dog often made for better company than men anyway.

Maybe she should just walk out. She stared at her phone, considering sending him a message that made it clear she didn't appreciate being stood up. After two failed marriages, she didn't need another excuse to ban dating. If he made her wait another minute, she'd delete the app for good.

A black Corvette rolled into the parking lot, catching her attention. The guy who got out was clean-cut, wearing a polo shirt, cowboy hat, and sunglasses. He twirled his keys like he owned the place, scanning the café until his eyes landed on her. He took off his sunglasses and flashed her a Hollywood grin.

Kate stopped drumming her fingers. She tried not to smile, but there it was—he'd made it. Finally.

"Kate?" He didn't wait for her answer, just sat down across from her.

"That's me," she said. He was handsome, she had to admit. A cowboy-coded Heath Ledger, with dark hair and striking brown eyes.

"I gotta say, you look way better than your profile photos." He leaned back, eyes trailing over her.

She fought the blush creeping into her cheeks. This was ridiculous. She wasn't some lovestruck high schooler. "Thanks," she said, more out of habit than anything. He too was more put together than she'd expected from his blurry profile pics. She'd let the lateness slide—for now.

"Nice car," she said, nodding toward the black Corvette outside.

"Thanks. I practically live in it. My job keeps me runnin' from place to place."

"What is it you do again?" His profile had been vague.

"I run a few businesses in Nashville. I have guys to manage most of it, but it still keeps me busy."

Kate raised an eyebrow. "That's impressive. What kind of businesses?"

"Finance and sales, mostly," he said.

Kate glanced down at her half-empty coffee. Her work seemed modest in comparison. "I work at a bank in Virginia Beach, but I love it."

He gave a polite nod. "It's good to like what you do. I run a lot of stuff, but that's not where my real interest is."

"Oh yeah?" She leaned forward. "What's that?"

His eyes lit up a bit. "Private investigatin'."

She almost laughed but caught herself. "Seriously? Isn't that dangerous?"

"Yeah," he said, dimples creasing in his cheeks. "I work with the police a lot."

"Okay, so what's the wildest case you've worked on?" She crossed her arms, curious despite herself.

Cayde's grin widened. "Most of it's classified."

Kate rolled her eyes. "Come on. You don't have to share names. Just one story."

He leaned in, lowering his voice like they were in on something together. "All right, but you can't tell anyone."

"Scout's honor," she teased.

He launched into a wild story involving hunting down a drug runner for the police, and before she knew it, two hours had passed. She laughed more than she expected to. He had a way of making even the boring parts of his life sound interesting. He complimented her a few more times, and the way he looked at her each time made her feel... noticed. It had been a while since anyone had looked at her like that.

When they stood to leave, Cayde helped her with her jacket. He walked her to her car, putting his cowboy hat back on.

"Look," he said, and there was a pause, almost like he was second-guessing himself. "I'm headin' back to Nashville soon, but I'd really like to see you again before I go."

Kate looked up at him, her heart kicking up a little. "I think we can make that happen."

CHAPTER 5

SOPHIE

Carnival music blared, blending with the shrieks of kids hopped up on cotton candy and parents doling out cash for overpriced tickets. A coaster whooshed by, dropping riders close to the ground, then swinging them up just in time to send them spiraling through the air, feet flailing as screams echoed—half terror, half thrill.

"Mom, can we go on that one?" Noah yanked Sophie's arm, pointing to the behemoth of a ride.

"Absolutely not. We're sticking to rides closer to the ground."

Charlie, a few years younger, pouted. "I'm not scared."

"Then we're sticking to the kiddie rides for me," Sophie said, tousling his hair. "If a carnival can build it in a day, it can collapse in a minute." She snapped her fingers for emphasis. "Besides, we only have enough cash for a few more games."

Charlie swung the rubber hammer at the strength test, but at nine, he barely sent the puck halfway up. He frowned, disappointed.

"I'll win you something," Noah said, determination in his eyes. "What do you want?"

Sophie let her boys lead the way, watching them dash from booth to booth. After months of stress, it felt good to see them act like kids again.

They stopped at a shooting game where players aimed air guns at cardboard targets. Noah handed over his last tickets and took his place next to an older man, who took his time lining up his shots.

As Charlie cheered, Noah fired off shots like he was in a hurry, hitting the rabbit figurine only four times.

"Sorry, Charlie," Noah grumbled, putting the fake gun down.

"I wanted the giraffe!" Charlie said, eyes glued to the stuffed animals.

"Care to try again?" the game runner asked.

Both boys looked up at Sophie, who shrugged. "Sorry, kiddos, we're out of tickets."

They turned their attention to the man beside them, who calmly took aim and knocked down target after target. He never missed once.

"Eight out of eight!" The booth runner clapped. "Claim your prize."

"I'll take the giraffe," the man said, glancing at Charlie, whose eyes lit up. He handed it right to him, and Charlie squealed with joy.

"What do you say?" Sophie prompted.

"Thank you!" Charlie shouted, hugging the giraffe.

"Anytime," the man replied, tipping his cowboy hat. Then he turned to Sophie. "I wouldn't have much use for it anyway." His eyes sparkled under the carnival lights.

"Thanks again," Sophie said, and turned to her boys. "Are you ready to head home?"

"No!" they protested.

"You wouldn't want the rest of my tickets, would you?" The man pulled out a stack of at least fifteen.

"Oh, we couldn't!" Sophie interjected.

"Thanks, mister!" Noah said, glancing at Sophie for approval.

She relented with a gesture, and Noah took them. "Come on, Charlie!" The boys took off for another game booth, ignoring Sophie's calls.

"Are you sure?" she asked the man. He was handsome, and something about him drew her in. "That's really kind of you."

"I'm sure," he said, extending his hand. "I'm Cayde Miller, by the way."

"Sophie," she responded, shaking his hand. "Nice to meet you."

"Your boys remind me of my daughters. Happy to help."

"Are your daughters here?" she asked, falling in step with him as he followed her toward the boys, who were now bouncing from booth to booth.

"No." Cayde shook his head, following beside her. "I was supposed to meet them here, but I guess something came up." He shrugged. "Or my *ex-wife* had something come up."

Sophie nodded, feeling the weight of shared experience. "It's the same with my kids," she said, glancing at her boys. In the middle of a divorce and battling for custody, she understood how precious moments like this could be.

Cayde's eyes flicked to her, but he didn't pry. "Did your boys eat yet? There's a good hotdog stand over there." He pointed east.

THE WANDERER · 29

"No, we were planning to head home for dinner," Sophie replied.

"I want hotdogs!" Charlie shouted from a distance.

Cayde chuckled. "I'd be happy to treat them. I was going to eat with my girls, but—" He shrugged, the air turning somber.

Sophie hesitated. She didn't exactly want to eat with him but felt bad turning him down after his generosity. "Okay, sure," she said, a hint of reluctance in her voice.

"Right over there." He pointed the boys toward the hotdog stand lit up with bright lights. "You can't miss it."

The boys bolted ahead, and Sophie called after them to stay close, but they were already lost in the excitement.

"Of course," Cayde added, giving her a charming smile, "you can grab one too. I'll pay."

Sophie thanked him, the strangeness of the situation settling in, but the sight of her boys' faces beaming warmed her heart. Besides, she couldn't remember the last time someone treated her to anything.

It wasn't like she was committing to a date or anything—just a meal at a carnival with her boys and a kind, admittedly handsome man.

CHAPTER 6

WENDY

Two lines. Faint, pale things. Yet they had the power to dismantle everything. Wendy stared at them, her hand steady, almost like her brain hadn't caught up to reality yet. Maybe she'd already known before taking the test.

She placed the pregnancy test beside the two others. All the same. Pregnant. Pregnant. Pregnant. With a sudden swipe, she sent them clattering into the trash, along with a tube of lip gloss and an old blush brush. She pressed her hands to her face, but no tears came. Somehow, that felt worse than crying.

"Fuck," she moaned, the curse drawn out.

She bit her lip, cycling through every possible outcome, trying to figure out how this would play out. Normally, she was good at this—seeing ahead, planning her next move. But now? The future felt like a fog, thick and unforgiving. How the fuck was she supposed to have a baby?

Instinctively, she wanted to call her mother. No, that idea was dead on arrival. All it would accomplish was a fight. Besides, her mother didn't even know she was married.

She groaned inwardly, the weight of the past few months sinking in. Things had been good, better than expected. She didn't want to think about what Cayde's reaction would be.

They hadn't exactly planned this. A few months of dating, a reckless trip to Vegas, and now she was tied to him. Permanently. Eloping was one thing. Having his baby was another. Was he really the man she wanted forever?

Forever. The word sat heavy in her mind.

Wendy dropped her hands from her face, her eyes falling to the trash. She fished out the makeup, leaving the tests buried beneath. No tears, no laughter, just numb confusion.

The front door clicked open. Cayde was home. She heard him call out, the sound of grocery bags hitting the counter. And then his voice, casual, carefree.

"Picked up some flowers," he said, not even noticing her hesitation as she stepped out of the bedroom. "I'll put 'em in a vase in a sec. But first—grilled cheese." He flashed her that easy smile, like everything was fine. Normal. Wendy managed a weak smile back, hovering near the kitchen, her thoughts spiraling.

"They're beautiful," she said, watching him.

Cayde moved around the kitchen like he always did—charming, effortless. But now, every small gesture felt loaded, like the weight of the next twenty years was crushing her. He didn't notice. He was too busy buttering the skillet, slicing cheese.

"Met with a new client today. He wants me to investigate an ex-business partner." Cayde chuckled. "This is one case that should be wrapped up quickly. These wealthy businessmen always have somethin' to hide."

Wendy sat down at the three-stooled bar that served as both her counter and table. He continued talking about his work, but she could barely hear. Instead, she imagined him in the kitchen, years from now, making both her and a small child grilled cheese sandwiches.

And then it hit her; if she was going to be pregnant with anyone, Cayde wasn't the worst option. He'd been nothing but kind, generous even. He had money, a job as a PI Sure, he had his secrets, but didn't everyone? She could've done a lot worse.

"Cayde," she said, cutting through his monologue. "I'm pregnant."

He froze. The grilled cheese sizzled in the pan, forgotten. "You are? For sure?"

She nodded, bracing herself.

Cayde crossed the room in seconds, pulling her into a tight embrace. "Wendy, that's amazin'!" His grip was so strong it almost hurt.

A laugh slipped from her, more disbelief than joy. "You're not upset?"

"Upset?" He pulled back, staring at her like she'd said something ridiculous. "Why would I be? This is great news."

"Cayde." Her voice dropped, serious. "This is huge."

"I don't care." He smiled again, and this time she wasn't sure if she could trust it. "When I met you, I knew you were it for me. This baby? It's just... I don't know, a blessin'. It's gonna bring us closer."

Wendy broke. The tears finally came. "I'm scared," she whispered.

"Don't be," Cayde said, his voice soft, but there was something in his eyes—determination. "I've got this. I'll take care of you. *Both* of you. Just let me handle it."

He held her tighter, promising things she wasn't sure anyone could fulfil.

CHAPTER 7

JACK

"You know, I was supposed to be on vacation right now," Blair muttered, barely looking up from the mess of papers scattered across her lap. Outside, the city blurred past, but she was too buried in notes, names, and half-finished phone calls to care. The dashboard and floor were drowning in files. Her open laptop sat at her feet, awaiting emails. Jack had the wheel, as usual. He preferred it that way. Blair had a better knack for pulling the right info and, frankly, she was better at talking to people.

"Vacation?" Jack raised a brow, keeping his eyes on the road.

"To Wyoming," she said, almost wistfully, but not without a hint of sarcasm. "Mountains, geysers, bison. My sisters and I had it all planned out—cabins and everything." She gave him a sideways glare. "Instead, I'm here with you."

Jack didn't bite. "Guess we'll have to wrap this up fast. Get you back to your bison." His voice stayed flat, noncommittal. He didn't feel like playing along with her antics today.

"Cayde Miller." Blair sighed and flicked through the stack of papers. "His timeline's a disaster. I can't figure out who he's legally married to. He's got marriage certificates all over the place, but only a few divorce papers. The earliest marriage I've got is Lacey Miller."

"That's not the name of our victim," Jack said.

"No, it's not."

"So, we've got a bigamist on our hands?"

"Hasn't been charged for it yet." Blair pursed her lips. "Bet we're missing half the records."

"Maybe it's just a domestic gone sideways. One wife finds out about the other, things get ugly," Jack said. But he knew better.

"It's worse." Blair's voice hardened. "Restraining orders, fraud, abuse charges—domestic and child, you name it. It's a fucking laundry list, and it keeps getting worse the closer you get to the current date."

Jack's grip tightened on the wheel. Men who liked control. The kind who kept everyone around him scared, off-balance. That was the kind of man that haunted his thoughts, even after all these years. He swallowed, trying to push away memories. "What's he do for work?"

"Private investigator," Blair said, barely looking up. "Licensed out of Tennessee."

Jack snorted. He didn't need to hear more. Guys like that weren't playing investigator—they were playing hero, thinking they were smarter than everyone else. And sometimes, they were.

"Stalking charges?"

"Complaints," Blair corrected, flipping more pages. "But nothing that sticks."

"For every restraining order, every complaint, there's probably a dozen more things he's gotten away with." Abusers like him didn't just stop. They learned to hide it better.

Blair's phone buzzed. She pulled it out, her eyes narrowing as she answered. "Agent McCoy," she said, her tone snapping from weary to razor-sharp. "Yes, I called earlier." She tapped the speaker button, the line clicking.

"You wanted to speak with me?" It was a woman's voice.

"This is Agent McCoy with the FBI," Blair said, all business. "We're calling about your husband, Cayde Miller."

"*Ex-husband*. I haven't seen him in years. And I've remarried since."

Jack glanced at Blair, mouthing, "Lacey Miller?"

Blair shook her head, holding up a couple of fingers. Wife number two.

Jack almost snorted. With the trail of women this man had left, it might be easier to refer to them by number. Unprofessional, sure. But easier.

"I see. Mrs...?"

"Armstrong, now."

"Mrs. Armstrong, we need to ask you a few questions."

There was a pause on the other end, but when she spoke, her voice was cold, certain. "This is about the woman he took, isn't it? I can't tell you where he's gone. I don't know. But I can tell you what you're dealing with."

So, in the hours Jack and Blair had left the scene, the news outlets had run the story. If luck was on their side, a witness would call in about Cayde's car.

Blair leaned forward in her seat. "Anything you can share could help."

A deep breath on the other end, the kind that sounds like resolution. Then Mrs. Armstrong's voice cut through the line, sharp and certain. "The first thing you need to know? He's going to kill her."

CHAPTER 8

CLAIRE

Cayde opened every door for Claire, polite in that old-fashioned way that felt out of place in a world too fast to notice such things. She found herself enjoying it, surprised by how long it had been since she'd spent an evening outside the four walls of her own thoughts. She had to admit it—his attention was flattering. He paid for dinner without hesitation, helped her slip into her jacket, and suggested a walk along the city streets. For a first date, it had gone surprisingly well.

Their conversation had started polite the first time he came by to fix the holes in her walls. But after a few patches and a couple of glasses of lemonade, they were talking about life. He mentioned he was divorced—amicable, or so he said. He still lived with his ex-wife, for their daughters' sake. That's why Jessie thought he was still married. By the time the last hole was patched, he'd asked her out. She hadn't been expecting that.

"It's nice to get some fresh air," Cayde said now, hands in his pockets, eyes tracing the glow of city lights reflected on the sidewalk. He seemed easy, content. Maybe, like Claire, he felt lonelier than he let on. "Makes me think about bringing my girls out here sometime."

"Mine lives with her dad," Claire replied, a sad smile flickering on her lips. "Her name's Paige. She'll be a junior in high school next year."

"What's she like?"

Claire's face lit up, the way it always did when she talked about her daughter. "She's amazing. Probably the kindest person you'll ever meet. And she's so smart."

"Sounds like she takes after her mom."

Her cheeks warmed at that, and she glanced away, too shy to hold his gaze. "What about your kids? Do they volunteer like you? You're involved in so many things." During dinner, he'd listed off an expanse of activities and programs he lent a hand to in his free time.

"I try to get them interested when I can," he said, a trace of pride in his voice. "I hope they pick some of it up in school. You know, learn to care about something bigger than themselves."

"I only teach writing," Claire said with a shrug.

Cayde looked at her earnestly. "That's important. You give kids a way to express themselves. They need that more than you think."

For a moment, they walked in silence. Then Cayde reached into his pocket and pulled out a small black box. "I want you to have this."

Claire's fingers hesitated as she opened it, revealing a delicate diamond heart necklace that sparkled under the streetlights. Her breath caught. "Cayde, I can't—"

"Yes, you can." He cut her off, voice gentle but firm. "There's something about you, Claire. Even if you don't want to see me again after tonight, this is yours. You deserve it."

He took the necklace from the box, motioning for her to turn around. She hesitated but obliged, feeling the cool metal against her skin as he fastened it. The gesture, the gift—it was all too much, and yet, she found herself unable to refuse. She thanked him quietly, and they began walking back to the car.

How long had it been since anyone had made her feel like this? Claire realized, to her own surprise, that she did want to see him again. Maybe it would be fun to date around this summer, just for the experience. It was too soon to think about anything serious—her divorce from Zach was still fresh, the wound still tender—but there was something comforting about having someone beside her, even if only for now.

Cayde wasn't Zach. Maybe that's why she liked him. He was a different kind of man, more direct and assertive, charismatic. And maybe that's what she needed. She still missed her ex-husband, in ways she couldn't admit, but she'd heard somewhere that if you want a wound to heal, you have to stop picking at it. That was what got her to take down the photos of Zach. Maybe that was what had brought Cayde to her.

The wound wasn't healed yet. But for tonight, Cayde was enough of a distraction to dull the pain.

CHAPTER 9

AUTUMN

When Autumn opened the door and saw Cayde standing there with a bouquet of roses, her stress over the upcoming semester seemed to vanish.

"These are beautiful," she said, standing on her toes to kiss his cheek. He'd been bringing her flowers every week since they started dating.

"You're beautiful," he replied, then turned toward Morgan, Tania, and Kathy as they wandered into the room. "And for you." He handed each of them a single flower. Autumn liked how he always made an effort with the people close to her. Though she didn't need to flaunt their relationship, there was a certain satisfaction in watching her friends experience Cayde's charm firsthand.

After the flowers were passed out, he still had a bag hanging off his wrist. "I want to take you out to dinner, but first, I've got somethin' for you."

There was a playful look in his eyes as he handed her the bag, taking back the roses while she pulled out a small black box. Inside was a heart-shaped diamond necklace. Autmn let out a small sound, somewhere between a sigh and a gasp.

"Let me." Cayde gently took the necklace from its box. "Turn around."

She did, and he clasped it around her neck, his fingers brushing against her skin. When she looked in the living room mirror, it sat just below her collarbone. "I love it."

He stepped back, looking her up and down, and whistled. "It suits you."

She hugged him, feeling the weight of the necklace against her chest. "Thanks, Cayde. Really."

He smiled and offered his arm. "Shall we?"

"Bye, you two! Have fun!" Morgan called out with a wink as they left.

As they drove, she glanced over at him. "We should invite the girls sometime. They'd love the food."

Cayde cringed. "Maybe not."

"Why?"

"It's nothin'." He hesitated, then sighed. "It's just... Have you ever noticed how they treat you?"

Autumn frowned, unsure where this was going. "What do you mean?"

"They make little comments here and there. Rude. Jealous, even."

"Jealous?" The idea didn't sit right with her. Sure, her friends could be blunt at times, but she never thought they were envious of her.

Cayde shifted in his seat. "Look, I'm just sayin' I see things you might not. Maybe it's because I'm on the outside lookin' in. They don't always seem to have your best interests in mind. Maybe take a step back. You're more mature than they are. That's why I was drawn to you from the start."

Autumn didn't respond immediately. She wasn't sure how to feel. On one hand, it was flattering to hear Cayde talk about how different she was from her friends. But on the other, his words left a strange taste in her mouth. Her friends could be a bit immature, sure, but they were still her friends.

Cayde reached over, resting his hand on her knee. "I'm just lookin' out for you, Autumn. You know that, right? I care about you. I'll always be there."

CHAPTER 10

JACK

"The first thing you need to know? He's going to kill her." Both Jack and Blair took a moment to let Mrs. Armstrong's words sink in.

"Why would you say that?" Blair asked. It wasn't accusatory.

"There were several times in my marriage to him when I thought I wouldn't make it out. In the beginning, he was charming—always giving me lavish gifts or showering me with affection. He knew the right things to say, and then one day he just... flipped." Her voice cracked on the last word. "He is *evil*. Please believe me when I say that."

"I do," Blair said. Whether she was telling the truth or not was unclear to Jack, but it was undoubtedly the best thing to say to coax more information from Cayde's ex-wife. "Is there any possibility that Cayde convinced his current wife to go with him willingly?"

"I did a lot of things against my will that appeared otherwise. He knows how to make a woman do that. Even if he got her to leave without a fight, I promise you she doesn't want to be there. You have to rescue her, and fast."

That was the goal. Jack could curse a thousand times over about the lack of leads. It seemed that Cayde had taken his wife, picked a random direction, and disappeared. He could still be on the highway, or maybe he'd tucked himself away in a small town, waiting for the watchful eyes of the law to glaze past him before he made his next move.

"We're doing everything we can—"

"It's been years," Mrs. Armstrong interrupted Blair. Her voice was laced with contempt. "He should have gone to jail for what he did to me. He should have gone to jail for what he did to the other women after me. But the law didn't help."

Jack frowned. In the deeper, more private recesses of his memory, Jack could see police lights filtering through the window of his mother's home, casting blue, white, and red shadows on the walls. He could hear his mother crying.

"I'm sorry, Mrs. Armstrong." This time, Blair sounded sincere. "I assure you, while I'm on this case, I will do everything I can to ensure Cayde Miller is brought to justice."

"I hope you mean that." Mrs. Armstrong's tone softened, like a scared child's. "After all this time, I still look over my shoulder."

"Can you think of anything that might help us locate him?" Blair asked.

"He was a private investigator. He probably knows a thing or two about hiding from the law. I wouldn't put too much faith in easy, conventional methods."

"Do you think he's a danger to anyone else?"

"He used to threaten my family a lot. It scared me. He would beat me—and he loved it. I think he'd hurt anyone who got in his way. I saw it in his eyes a hundred times." Her voice quivered slightly. "When things were bad, they were really bad."

Well, shit. Jack and Blair exchanged a glance. He was a ticking time bomb—confirmed.

"Do you have any numbers he might try to contact?" Blair asked. "People he knew, places he might go?"

"I have a few names you could look into, and the numbers for his mother and his first wife, Lacey," Mrs. Armstrong listed them off, and Blair wrote each one down in her notebook. "Please," she said, desperate. "He's gotten away with so much already. Don't let him get away with this too."

"He won't," Blair said. "I promise."

CHAPTER 11

KATE

Raindrops tapped against the windshield, the sky overhead thick with clouds. Kate glanced down at the engagement ring on her finger. Even in the dull light, the stones sparkled, almost too bright.

Cayde leaned in, smirking as he admired it. "It's perfect," he said, his voice low.

Actually, the ring was a bit too tight around her finger, but Kate didn't mention it. Cayde looked happy, and that was enough. She was trying to feel the same way. It was fast—six months, barely enough time to catch her breath. But after all her second-guessing, her doubts and overthinking, she figured maybe she needed to stop questioning everything and just go with it. Overanalyzing hadn't exactly saved her with the last two husbands, had it?

Both Kate and Cayde made the long-distance thing work. He'd flown out, driven miles just to see her. They'd even taken a camping trip with her daughter, Zoey. Kate had wanted Zoey's opinion on the relationship, though she wasn't sure what she was expecting. Zoey didn't warm up to him, but she didn't freeze him out either. In the end, she shrugged and said, "I'm happy if you're happy, Mom."

That was it. The blessing Kate hadn't realized she needed until Cayde dropped to one knee. On the way to the airport, out of nowhere, he pulled out the little black box and asked her to marry him. If Zoey had shown any discomfort with him, Kate might've turned him down.

"Should we call my parents?" Kate asked, breaking the silence.

"Yeah." Cayde nodded, pulling out his own phone. "Gotta make a quick call before I head through security. Tell her without me." He stepped out of the car before she could stop him.

"Wait, Cayde—" But he was already out, pacing in the rain. She glanced at her phone screen as her mother's face appeared. "Hi, Mom," Kate said, forcing a smile as she looked past the window. She watched Cayde pace, phone to his ear, already agitated. "I've got some news." She lifted her hand, flashing the ring.

Her mother's face lit up in surprise. "He proposed?"

"About half an hour ago."

"Congratulations, honey!" The words sounded a bit forced. "Is he there?"

Kate shifted. Cayde's voice was muffled through the glass, but the tension was hard to miss. "Yeah, but he had to take a call. He's outside the car."

Her mother paused, then leaned closer. "Are you sure about this? I mean, I like him, but it's... fast."

Kate nodded, expecting the question. "I know. But I've prayed about it." Maybe not as much as she should have, but she knew it was something her mother would've wanted to hear. "It feels right."

"When do you think you'll have the wedding?"

"Cayde wants it soon, maybe before Zoey's."

The logistics were already grinding in her head. Zoey's wedding was around the corner. She wasn't up for throwing more money into a celebration other than her daughter's. Something small and quick would suit Kate better. But Cayde—he was all about the big talk, the money, the success. He might push for something over-the-top. She chewed her lip, hoping he wouldn't.

Cayde's voice outside had risen into full-on shouting. Whatever was happening on his phone call, it wasn't good.

"I've got to go, Mom. It's time for Cayde to head to security."

"Alright, honey. Call me back later. I love you."

When Cayde slid back into the car, the air was heavy with tension. Kate had seen his temper flare once or twice while they were dating, but not like this.

"Fucking bank," he muttered.

Kate frowned. She hadn't heard him use that language before. It wasn't exactly the type of vocabulary she liked to have around. "What's wrong?"

"One of my employees screwed up an account tied to the business. The bank froze everythin'."

Kate stared. "What? What did they do?"

"Doesn't matter," Cayde snapped. "I need fifteen grand to cover payroll tomorrow."

Kate blinked a few times before she understood he was genuinely asking her for that much money. "Cayde—"

"I'll pay it back. Everythin's locked up until Monday. You won't even miss it."

She let out a sharp laugh, but when she saw the look on his face, it faded. She sighed. "There's a branch inside. I can pull out ten thousand. Legally, that's all I can take."

Cayde's mood flipped. He pulled her in for a rough kiss, his lips pressing too hard. "Ten's perfect. Let's go."

Kate stepped out of the car. Her hair whipped loose from its bun in the sharp autumn wind. The trees bent, leaves torn free and scattered into the air. She pulled her hair back, watching as the green and yellow specks flew off, swallowed by the dark clouds creeping closer and closer.

CHAPTER 12

SOPHIE

Cayde stepped into Sophie's apartment, dragging in the last box. "This is it," he declared, scanning the room.

Sophie raised an eyebrow as she shut the door behind him. "That's all you're bringing?"

"Most of it's back at my mobile home." He shrugged. "Just some remnants from my first marriage. That place is just a storage unit now. Besides—" He leaned in, planting a kiss on her. "—I like bringin' less. Fresh start, right?"

Sophie blushed; the excitement was still there after months of dating.

His phone rang, cutting the moment short. He answered it, striding into the kitchen.

Cayde was between homes and had asked Sophie if he could move into her apartment. Technically, it was Tanner's apartment. Her brother owned several units in Nashville and had allowed her to stay in one for free while she sorted things out in her divorce.

Sophie had hesitated about letting Cayde move in, but the sadness in her boys' faces weighed on her. She'd do anything to bring back their spark. Maybe having a man around would help. Cayde had showered them with presents, and she ran her fingers over the small diamond heart pendant resting against her collarbone—a gift that felt just right, simple and unassuming, but still valuable.

"No!" Cayde's voice cut through the air, rising in anger. "She's makin' that up. It's ridiculous." He paused, waiting for a response. "Well, figure it out. I've done my part. I'll call you later, okay?"

Something about his tone sent a chill through her. Sophie fished out a hair barrette from the box he'd brought in—pretty, but too young for her taste.

"Who was that?" she asked after he hung up.

"Veronica," he said, and tossed his phone aggressively on the coffee table.

"*Veronica*?" She held the barrette up like evidence. "Is this hers?"

"No," he laughed, taking it from her. "Veronica is just a friend from work. Helping me deal with my ex. She's got my back on some legal stuff."

"Oh," Sophie replied, not entirely convinced.

He changed gears, the mood shifting. "We need to talk about the campin' trip this weekend."

"What about it?"

"Can't go. Got a new case."

"You're kidding, right? The boys were so pumped!"

"I know, but there'll be other trips. A lifetime of 'em."

"A lifetime?" She smirked, skeptical.

"I'm serious." Cayde took her hand. "I wanna take care of you, Sophie. Make you happy, every single day." His thumb brushed over her lips. "I wanna marry you."

"What?" she blurted, glancing toward the boys. "Marry me?"

He smiled and kissed her. "We're in the same boat, and I think we could help each other out."

"Cayde, I'm still married. The divorce isn't final."

"I can wait."

"That isn't the problem." She ran a hand through her fine blond hair, feeling the weight of it all. "It's too fast. I love you, but—"

"Take a chance, Sophie. Don't you wanna be happy again?"

She locked eyes with him for a moment, his sincerity cutting through her doubts. "I do."

"Then say yes!" He scooped her up, kissing her fiercely.

Sophie bit her lip, heart racing. "Then... yes!"

He spun her around, laughter spilling from her. But over his shoulder, she caught sight of his phone buzzing on the coffee table—Veronica's name glared back at her. And despite the happiness she felt, something in her gut twisted.

CHAPTER 13

WENDY

Wendy's mother had insisted on throwing a reception. In just two weeks, she'd transformed her backyard into a venue for family and friends, pulling off the whole thing with a force that bordered on manic.

It was a bit ostentatious; canopies, endless champagne, silks, and over-decorated tables, but Wendy and Cayde hadn't been asked to chip in, so they went along with it. They'd also agreed not to mention Wendy's pregnancy to anyone. Cayde figured if people found out, they'd push for an annulment, and he wasn't taking any chances. When Wendy's own doubts crept in, he was quick to shut them down, insisting that it was best for the baby.

"The ceremony was gorgeous!" Lisa said, holding a bouquet that matched the dress Wendy's mother had paid for.

Wendy forced a smile at her oldest friend—and only bridesmaid. "Thank you for helping."

"How are you holding up?" Lisa asked. Other than Wendy's mother, Lisa was the only one who knew about the midnight run to Vegas.

"Honestly?" Wendy checked over her shoulder to make sure her mom wasn't within earshot. "I'm glad it's over. Somehow, my mother managed to turn one of the most exciting events of my life into the most stressful."

"Well, it's nice to see her putting in some effort for you."

Wendy shook her head slightly. "I don't know half of these people. The effort isn't for me."

Wendy's mother had always been the picture of propriety—the perfect wife, the perfect mother. Even after Wendy's dad died, she kept up appearances. Of course, she couldn't just let Wendy's elopement slide. Not when she had an image to maintain.

"Really?" Lisa leaned in, scanning the groups of middle-aged guests clustered around the yard, complimenting the decor and congratulating Wendy's mother. She was soaking it up, all smiles and handshakes. "I thought some of these were Cayde's family."

"Actually, Cayde's family didn't come." Wendy glanced over at her husband, who was deep in conversation with some woman. "He doesn't talk about them much, and the wedding was too short of notice for his friends."

Lisa looked hesitant, like she was weighing each word before speaking. "Have you… met any of them?"

"No," Wendy admitted, the unease she tried to bury bubbling up again. "But I will. Soon."

"Wendy, we've been friends forever. You know you can tell me anything, right?"

"Of course."

Lisa took a breath. "Then, is there anything you want to tell me?"

Wendy felt calm looking into Lisa's face. Maybe confiding in one more person wouldn't hurt. After all, she was her rock. "Lisa, I'm—"

"Wendy!" Cayde's voice cut through, smooth and confident as he walked up, the woman he'd been talking to trailing beside him. Long black hair, low neckline—too revealing for a wedding. She smiled, but her eyes raked up and down Wendy. "This is a friend from work," Cayde said, gesturing to the woman. "Veronica."

"Pleasure," Veronica said, holding out a perfectly manicured hand. "I work for the police department in Nashville. Cayde's helped us out on a few cases."

Wendy shook her hand. "Good to finally meet one of Cayde's friends." Her tone came out sharper than she'd meant, but Wendy had never been good at hiding her emotions.

"Well." Veronica glanced at Cayde, then back at Wendy. "I have to run, but it was great to celebrate with you."

"I'll be in touch," Cayde said, watching as Veronica sauntered away.

Lisa gave Wendy a look that spoke volumes. Neither liked Veronica, despite her polite words. Call it women's intuition.

"Cayde?" Wendy took his arm. "There's something I want to give you." She tugged him toward the house, throwing Lisa an apologetic glance. They'd have to finish their conversation another time.

"It's inside?" Cayde asked.

"It's not the kind of gift you give in front of a crowd," she said, shutting the door behind them. "It's something for work."

She led him over to a stand in the entryway, where she'd placed a small case inside a drawer. "I didn't wrap it."

He shot her a curious look, flipping up the latches. Inside was a nine-millimeter Glock. He paused, fingers hovering over the weapon, then lifted it out, turning it slowly in his hands.

"Do you like it?" Wendy asked, biting her lip.

Something shifted in his eyes, and a slow smile tugged at his lips. He nodded, still studying the gun.

"Good," she sighed, relieved. "We can test it out later, maybe go shooting. But right now—" She gently took it from him, placing it back in the case. "—we've got guests to entertain." The words dripped with sarcasm.

"Your *mother's* guests."

"She paid for all this," Wendy said, "and she offered to cover a year's rent on the apartment to start us off. The least we can do is keep up appearances."

"Before we do..." Cayde reached into his jacket pocket. "I've got somethin' for you too."

He pulled out a small jewelry box and flipped it open, revealing a diamond necklace. "It's a heart," he said, draping it around her neck. "I hope you like it."

"I do." Wendy grinned. It wasn't something she would have picked for herself, but it was from him, and that made it special.

Cayde followed her out, but his eyes flicked back to the stand where she'd hidden the case. Wendy felt a small surge of pride. She'd gotten him exactly what he wanted.

"There they are!" Wendy's mother raised a glass of champagne as they stepped outside. "A toast to the couple."

"To Cayde and Wendy!" the crowd echoed, glasses lifted.

Cayde kissed her cheek for show, and Wendy laughed, catching her mother's eye.

Her mother smiled, but there was something off in her expression—a tightness Wendy couldn't quite place. "May you two be blessed with happiness," she said.

Amid the cheers and celebration, Wendy locked eyes with her mother. While everyone else shouted and the music started back up, the two women just stared at each other. If she didn't know better, Wendy would've sworn the look on her mother's face was a warning.

CHAPTER 14

CLAIRE

Summer break came and went, and Claire was back to the grind at the elementary school. Her workload didn't slow down her new social life. Cayde made sure of that. What started as a casual fling had turned serious. Three months in, and it felt like a whirlwind.

"Next time we go shopping, you should bring your girls," Claire said as Cayde drove them to a strip mall in Nashville. "I'll buy them some jewelry or makeup sets."

Cayde's smile tightened. "I'm not sure they're ready to meet anyone yet. My ex and I are still keepin' the divorce on the down-low for the girls. They wouldn't understand. And I don't want them to hate me for being with someone who isn't their mom."

Claire winced. Her split with Zach had been rough, but their daughter, Paige, was old enough to see through the mess. No games. No manipulation. She couldn't imagine having a child turned against her.

"Maybe start small, then?" she offered. "It's not just your girls I want to meet. What about your friends? Your family?"

"Honestly, Claire?" Cayde's thumbs drummed the steering wheel. "I've been wrapped up with you, my girls, work, volunteering... My friends? I don't know where they are these days. As for my family? We haven't talked in years." His voice was flat, so casual it stopped her from asking more.

They pulled into the lot. He stepped around, opening her door, hand steady as he helped her out.

"Look at that!" Claire nodded toward a shiny Mercedes parked in the mall entrance. Flashy boards surrounded it, tempting passersby to enter a drawing. "Maybe we would win it!"

Cayde squeezed her hand. "I could see you in a Mercedes. Why not buy one?"

"Yeah, right," Claire scoffed. "On a teacher's salary? By the time I could afford that, my sedan would have broken down a dozen times. I need new brakes as it is."

* * *

That week, Claire was sorting stacks of papers on her desk when a knock came at the door. The principal leaned in, a grin stretching her face.

"Oh, Claire," she sang, "someone left a present for you."

"A present?"

"Outside. In the parking lot."

Claire followed her to the east exit. The halls were empty, school out for the day. Her heart nearly stopped when she stepped out.

Cayde stood beside a brand-new Mercedes SUV, a giant red bow across the top. He held up the keys, grinning. "Want to take it for a spin?"

"You didn't!" Claire shook her head. "Cayde, I can't accept this." A few months ago, she'd been hesitant to accept a diamond necklace. Now a car?

"*You can*." He pressed the keys into her hand. "Go on. Give it a try."

Claire shook her head again. "I really can't take something this big. Even if it's beautiful."

"Relax. Before I met you, I sold one of the homes I own. Car's paid off, no strings attached."

She bit her lip, then laughed, excitement bursting out of her. She threw her arms around his neck, kissed him, and slid behind the wheel.

The car drove like a dream. At dinner, Cayde insisted she order whatever she wanted. Claire felt like she might burst from happiness. He spoiled her. After her divorce, she never thought she'd feel this way again.

"Claire," Cayde started, their plates almost empty. "I wanted to talk to you about somethin'."

"Uh-oh," Claire teased. "Did you buy me a motorcycle, too?"

"I want to marry you."

She froze. That wasn't on the menu.

He took her hand. "I love you. You're smart, beautiful—everything I've ever wanted."

The words knocked the wind out of her. It was way too soon. But... she'd been so happy these last few months. She didn't want to be alone, and here was a man offering something real. The dates, the attention, the car, the ring. He made her feel wanted.

"Yes," Claire whispered, breathless. "Yes, I'll marry you."

They celebrated with champagne. But when Claire got home, the thrill was gone. She lied in bed, staring at the ring on her finger. She should be happy, but something felt off. Her gaze shifted to the empty spot beside her. She thought of Cayde... but Zach's ghost lingered in her memory.

She closed her eyes and turned her back to the place where he used to sleep.

CHAPTER 15

JACK

Blue, yellow, and green sticky notes were plastered across the dashboard, the inside of the passenger door, and even one or two on the car radio—all in classic Blair McCoy fashion. They flapped lightly in the breeze from the air vent. Her handwriting wiggled as the car rattled down the road. They were nearing empty on the gas tank.

Their conversation with Mrs. Armstrong had confirmed the type of man they thought they were dealing with. Not only that, but the request for a records search had yielded even more marriage certificates. Cayde Miller wasn't just a bigamist; he was a serial one. The fact that Tennessee hadn't nailed him yet was shocking, considering several marriages had occurred there.

Mrs. Armstrong wasn't the second wife, as Jack, Blair, and she herself had thought. There had been two more marriages before her.

Blair absentmindedly chewed on her nail, occasionally plucking a sticky note and relocating it elsewhere.

"Don't leave me in the dark," Jack said, glancing her way.

"I'm not sure it's all that dark," she replied, leaning back and crossing her arms. "He's a baser kind of man."

"Start with the big picture, then."

Blair shuffled through the paperwork, pulling out a list of names. She counted down. "Mrs. Armstrong, who thought she was wife number two, is actually wife number four. We've now got records confirming eight marriages in total, eight children between them all, and reports of a dozen affairs linking to lawsuits for lost money and property, accompanied with battery charges. All this ranges throughout Tennessee and almost every state around it."

Jack let out a low whistle. "How much money against him?"

"For the lawsuits? It's almost two million."

"Fucking hell." It wasn't something to laugh at, but Jack did. If they did their jobs well enough, Cayde Miller would owe more than that—some time behind bars.

They were still heading north. Another hour and they would hit the light that had caught his plates. But nothing else had come in since—gathering all the information they could on him wasn't helpful enough. They needed to know where he was going, and they needed to know now. They still had plenty of women they needed to call. They hadn't talked to every wife yet. The thought was ridiculous.

"Eight wives?" Jack huffed in disbelief. "That can't be right."

"It's right, even if it's not legal. That's the tricky part."

"We'll worry about legalities later," Jack said. "How many have you talked to so far? Four? Five?" The car ride had been long, and the many, many phone conversations Blair had engaged in were blurred together.

"I've called five of the women he was entangled with. Not all of them were married to him. Three answered, and only two were willing to talk, including Mrs. Armstrong." Blair tapped her fingers on the paper, frustrated. "Zero had any clue why he's heading north."

She scanned the list of names: Autumn, Claire, Sophie, Wendy, Kate, and more. Jack glanced over at her paper. His eyes lingered on the victim's name. Jack pressed harder on the gas, though he knew they were running low.

He shook his head. "He's hurt a lot of people, Blair." It seemed stupid to say.

Blair didn't seem to hear him. "His records are a damn mess, and we don't have time to sift through it all. But we know he's got a pattern."

"And a type," Jack added.

"Yeah," Blair said. "Gullible."

Jack flashed her a stern look. "Don't say that. He's a manipulator. A textbook abuser. Guys like him know exactly how to worm their way into someone's life and control everything before they even know it." He pulled off the next exit, heading for the nearest gas station.

"Yeah, I know," Blair said. "I just don't get how that many women fell for it. I wouldn't."

"What do you mean, 'fell for it?'" Jack parked beside the pump.

"I mean, how could you let someone treat you like that?" Blair unbuckled her seatbelt, her words laced with frustration. "Why stay in a situation like that, knowing it's only going to get worse?"

The words dumbfounded Jack. "You're seriously questioning their decisions?"

"Aren't you?"

"No." His tone was curt, definitive. He got out of the car. "Victims stay with their abusers for a million reasons—reasons we both should understand." Jack could list them. Fear, finances, children, love. They'd been trained to know the reasons inside and out—and even if they hadn't, Jack knew firsthand what that kind of situation was like. Fucked would be sugar-coating it.

"I get it," Blair said, stepping out of the car. "I just don't understand it. Would you stay with someone who hit you? Knowing they'd do it again?"

Jack grabbed the gas pump. "You sound like you're blaming these women for their abuse."

Blair sighed. "No, I'm not blaming—"

"That's exactly what it sounds like," he said cooly.

"I'm just saying I don't–"

"Understand." He looked at her over the top of the car. "No, I guess you don't."

Her nostrils flared as she took a deep breath. Her voice was tight. "I'm going to get us lunch. We need to keep moving."

Now they'd done it. The last thing they needed was an argument between the two of them. They needed to be a united front if they were going to catch Cayde Miller.

"Blair," Jack called, but she was already marching toward the gas station's food mart, ignoring him. "Damn," he hissed. "Well done, Jack. Well done."

CHAPTER 16

AUTUMN

Autumn loved hymns, especially when Cayde sang them. He'd been going to church with her for a while now, always showing up in a crisp three-piece suit. Today, they were at her parents' church, doing the whole Sunday family thing.

The chapel was bright and warm, sunlight streaming through the windows. It lit him up. He looked like an angel. *Maybe*, Autumn thought, *he was.* Maybe God had sent him just for her. She offered up a silent prayer, thanking Him for this godly, kind man who seemed to be everything she'd ever hoped for.

When the service ended and people started trickling out, Autumn exchanged smiles and greetings with old family friends. One familiar face lit up when she saw her.

"Kailey!" Autumn wrapped her old friend in a tight hug.

"How are you? How's life in the city?" Kailey asked. Her eyes darted to Cayde. "And who's this?"

"This is my boyfriend." Autumn couldn't keep the grin off her face.

"Nice to meet you." He offered his hand. "I'm Cayde."

Kailey's expression shifted as she shook it. "I feel like I've seen you before."

"No, I don't think so," Cayde replied, not letting go of her hand, his eyes narrowing just a touch.

"Didn't you used to live up the street?"

"No."

Kailey's face went pale as she looked him in the eye. "Oh." She yanked her hand back, a little too quickly. It was almost like she'd been trying to pull away for a few seconds, and he'd just now let go. "Right. I... I should go."

"Wait, we didn't catch up!" Autumn protested.

"Another time." Kailey frowned. She rubbed at her palm. "See ya."

Autumn shot a confused look at Cayde. "What was that about?"

"What do you mean?" Cayde asked, still smiling, as if nothing odd had happened.

Autumn furrowed her brows. "She was acting sorta... strange."

"Probably just embarrassed she made a mistake." Cayde shrugged, unbothered. "Hey, since we're all dressed up, why don't we go out for a bit?"

They walked along a stream near the church, enjoying the summer air and each other's company. He pressed a kiss to her temple. "I love you, Autumn." She smiled, but he grabbed her shoulders, making her face him. "I really do."

"I love you too, Cayde."

"When I think about everythin' I want—my future, starting a family—it's always with you." He dropped to one knee, reaching into his pocket. Time seemed to freeze, yet everything was moving too fast. He pulled out a ring. The diamond caught the light, brilliant and flawless. "Marry me." His grin widened.

Excitement, happiness, and a rush of adrenaline all hit her at once. But doubt clawed at her gut. She was only nineteen. He was twenty-four. And yet... "I want to marry you. But I think we should wait a year."

"A year?" He blinked, looking caught off guard, maybe even hurt.

She nodded. "I do love you, but—"

"Then why wait?" His grip on her hand tightened. "When two people find somethin' this good, they shouldn't put it off. I can take care of you. You'll never have to worry about anythin'."

Autumn swallowed. He had a point. It would all make sense if it weren't for the tiny voice in the back of her mind saying she should slow down. But maybe that was just fear talking. Maybe she was being too cautious.

"If you mean it," she said softly, "then let's get married."

Cayde's smile returned, his eyes glittering with satisfaction as he slid the ring onto her finger.

CHAPTER 17

KATE

Kate punched the off button on the car radio. The song that had played at her and Cayde's wedding had started, and as much as she loved it, Kate couldn't think about him right now. He'd moved to Virginia after they'd tied the knot. The current plan was to get them both settled in Nashville. But it was a month in, and nothing was happening. No calls to realtors, no property listings. He was just... sitting there. Kate didn't get it.

He should be eager to get back to work, back to his businesses. Hell, she wanted it too. Maybe then he could pay her back the money she'd loaned him. All of it. So far, every dollar she'd handed over disappeared like water down a drain. There had been multiple instances after she'd loaned him ten grand at the airport.

She shook off the thought as she stepped into the bank, heading to her desk. Emails, paperwork, and client meetings filled the first hour. Everything was routine until Mr. Rodriguez poked his head out of his office.

"Miss Moore?" he beckoned.

Kate forced a smile, stepping in and shutting the door behind her. She'd changed her name to Miller, but no one at the office could shake the habit after all these years. It was fine. Easier that way.

"Just wanted to check in," Mr. Rodriguez said, his face set in an awkward frown. "And see if you were able to handle the issue we discussed last week?"

Kate took a breath. "I talked to my husband. I promise it won't happen again."

"That's what you said last time." He adjusted his tie. "I'm just concerned about your performance. I want to make sure your work isn't being affected."

"I understand," Kate said, forcing the smile wider. "You don't need to worry."

Rodriguez nodded, visibly relieved. "Alright. Let me know if you need anything."

"Of course." She backed out of his office. Her head was already throbbing by the time she reached her desk. Just as she sat down, her cell phone buzzed. She snatched it off the desk, lowering it out of sight. Cayde's name glared up at her.

She nearly cursed. Cayde's foul language had been rubbing off on her lately. With a sharp jab, she declined the call. Dropping it into her purse, she turned back to her computer. *Focus, Kate.*

Then her work phone rang. She felt every head in the office swivel her way.

Kate grabbed the receiver. "Hello, Kate Miller speaking," she said.

"Kate! Did you just decline my call?"

Her voice dropped to a hiss. "Cayde, you can't call this phone, remember? We talked about this."

"I wouldn't have to if you picked up your cell."

"What do you need?" She rubbed at her temple.

"What did your boss want?"

Her hand tightened around the receiver. "He wanted to make sure I spoke to you about not disturbing me at work. I told him I did. And that it wouldn't happen again."

Silence. Then, "Have you been sleepin' with him!"

The question was the most ridiculous thing she'd ever heard. Kate let out a sharp laugh. She instantly regretted it.

Cayde exploded, his voice blasting through the phone. Kate yanked it away from her ear, but it was too late—he was yelling so loud, the whole room could hear. A few coworkers turned in their seats, eyebrows raised.

Flushing red, Kate slammed the receiver down. The phone rang again. She snatched it up, dropped it back down, and then took it off the hook entirely. Her hands were shaking. Her cell buzzed again. She reached down and shut it off completely.

Sweat beaded on the back of her neck. She knew ignoring him would set him off, but he was making it impossible to get anything done. She couldn't do her job with him breathing down her neck every second.

A question crept into her mind. How did Cayde know she'd spoken to her boss? She looked around the office and glanced outside at the tinted windows. Was he in the area? Was he watching her? For an hour she worked, the stress debilitating her almost as much as Cayde's phone calls.

She heard the phone in her boss' office ring.

Please, God, no.

Rodriguez picked up. "Hello?" He paused, then laughed softly. "Yes, I've got all the materials right here."

Kate let out a breath. She couldn't keep doing this. And it wasn't just about her—it wasn't fair to her coworkers either. Her gaze drifted to the phone on her desk. It was still off the hook. She reached over, placed it back—

It rang.

Something inside her snapped. She stood, spine stiff, and marched to Rodriguez's office.

"I thought about what you said," Kate said, voice as steady as she could manage. "I've decided to formally submit my resignation."

"I'm really sorry to hear that, Miss Moore."

Kate stiffened. "Yeah, me too. I was hoping for a transfer, but under the circumstances, I think this is the best option."

"I understand," Rodriguez said gently. "And I'll gladly write you a letter of recommendation."

"Thank you."

"You've been a star employee for years. I'm sorry to see you go."

Kate swallowed. She used to be a star. But Cayde had blown all that up. Everything she'd worked for was trashed in a matter of months. Her fingers curled into fists.

"I'll wrap up my work and pack up my things."

Rodriguez's brow furrowed. "Kate... can I ask you something?"

She braced herself. "What?"

"Are you alright?"

Her smile wobbled. "Of course," she said. "I'll be just fine."

She turned away before he could see the tears gathering in her eyes.

CHAPTER 18

WENDY

Little Archie screamed until his tiny face turned purple. Wendy had tried everything—feeding him, changing him, bouncing him, swaddling him. Nothing worked. He just kept screaming.

"Archie, please!" Wendy begged, holding him up as if he might finally answer. "What is wrong?"

Cayde had been gone all weekend, off on a case he claimed was too sensitive to share. Lately, it seemed like he was always off on one case or another since Archie was born. At first, Wendy didn't mind. But now, with each passing day, he was more absent, more distracted. She was drowning, stuck alone with a newborn.

Out of options, she dialed her mother, forcing herself to sound calm. Heaven forbid she show any weakness. "He's been crying for over an hour," Wendy said, swallowing the frustration in her voice.

"All babies cry, Wendy," her mother shot back, dismissive as always. Her southern drawl was stronger when she had an attitude. "You just have to let them."

"No!" Wendy snapped. "Something's wrong. Can you just come over and see if—"

"Wendy," her mother cut her off, her voice flat, "I've already helped you with the apartment, paid for most of Archie's things, and told you a thousand times that having a baby takes gumption. If I run over there every time you can't handle a little crying, how will you ever toughen up?"

Wendy clenched her teeth, fighting back tears. She'd thought she'd be able to handle this. That was back when she figured Cayde would be around more. Now, she was lucky if he showed up at all. But she couldn't tell her mother that. It'd be like handing her a loaded gun.

A sigh crackled through the line, her mother's irritation practically humming. "It's probably gas."

"I already burped him—"

"Pump his legs and massage his stomach. Go on. Do it now," her mother ordered.

Wendy stared at Archie, his face scrunched and furious, every muscle tight with rage. "His… legs?"

"Just do it." The line went dead.

Wendy dropped the phone, biting back a curse, and turned back to her child. "Okay, Archie, let's see if Ma knows what she's talking about."

She pumped his chubby legs and gently pressed her thumbs along his belly, repeating the process a few times. To her shock, Archie passed more gas than Wendy knew a baby could hold in one tiny body. The cries turned into little grunts and then, finally, blessed silence. Exhausted, he sucked on his pacifier and drifted off to sleep in his rocker. Wendy flopped on her back beside him, letting out a sigh of relief.

The front door clicked open. Cayde stepped in, dropping his briefcase in the entryway. He scanned the room, his nose wrinkling in disgust. "Fuck, Wendy, the place is a mess."

"Shush," Wendy whispered, getting off the floor. "You're back. Good." She placed a hand on her hip. Now *her* southern drawl came out. "We need to talk."

"Can it wait? I've been workin' all weekend, and—"

"*I've* been working all weekend," she shot back. "I can't keep this up, Cayde. Something's gotta give."

He huffed. "Why don't you start on dinner, and I'll wash up. We'll talk after I get a hot meal." Without waiting for a reply, he turned toward the bedroom. "And seriously, Wendy—this place is disgustin'."

Wendy clenched her jaw to keep from hurling insults. She yanked a pot out of the cabinet, filled it with water, and slammed it onto the stove. She cringed at the noise of her miniature tantrum, but Archie didn't stir. Cayde wanted dinner? Fine. He'd get dinner. By the time he came out of the shower, she was stirring sauce into a pot of pasta, rummaging through the cupboards for spices.

Cayde wandered into the kitchen, glanced at Archie—barely sparing a second look—and made a face. "He needs changin'." Instead of following his own suggestion, Cayde folded his arms and approached Wendy in the kitchen. "You're not gonna make any garlic bread?"

Wendy froze. The spoon clattered onto the counter as she whipped around. "Cayde, if you make one more damned comment, I'm going to lose my fucking mind."

He narrowed his eyes, almost like he was daring her. "It's just bread, Wendy."

"No," she hissed. "It's not. It's the cooking, the cleaning, the changing—everything! I'm doing it all by myself!"

"Because I'm out workin'."

"You're not bringing in any money!" she snapped. "We're living off my savings and the money my ma gave us to help with Archie! You're not contributing." His face flushed red with anger, but she kept going. "You promised me you'd handle things, that I'd have help. You took over the bank accounts, and now all you do is drain them dry. I feel like I'm raising two babies!"

"That's enough!" he roared.

Archie startled awake, his cries piercing through the room.

Cayde's chest heaved as he glared at her. "I've tried to hold my anger back, but you've gone too far, Wendy. You're ungrateful. Spoiled. You have no idea what I've sacrificed to be here."

"You're right," Wendy spat back. "I don't know. I can't imagine what a struggle it must be having a wife who takes care of your food, your house, and your baby. Must be so difficult for you."

Cayde's hand shot out, shoving her hard. Wendy crashed into the stove. Her elbow caught the handle of the pot, sending it toppling over. Hot pasta splattered across the floor and onto her legs, causing her to cry out. She stared at Cayde in shock.

"Fuck!" he cursed, looking at the mess. Archie's cries turned into screams, shrill and frantic. Cayde pushed past her, grabbed his briefcase, and stormed out, slamming the door behind him.

Wendy backed away from the stove, shaking. Her legs burned where the sauce had splashed. She crossed the kitchen, scooped up Archie, and held him close, pressing his face to her shoulder.

"It's okay," she whispered. For Archie, she kept her voice strong. "Daddy didn't mean it."

Her gaze drifted to the door. What the hell had gotten into him? Maybe he was right. Maybe she'd pushed too hard and brought out a side of him he didn't mean to show. Or maybe, she thought bitterly, that was the real Cayde—the one she'd never seen before.

And the man she married? He was just a lie.

CHAPTER 19

SOPHIE

Both Charlie and Noah stayed up long past their bedtime. Sophie wanted one last movie night before they went to their dad's for a few days. Despite the late hour, they were still bouncing off the walls. Charlie was practically doing acrobatics on his bed, throwing kicks and punches at invisible enemies.

"Did you brush your teeth?" Sophie asked, turning on the nightlight. Charlie insisted he didn't need it. Sophie knew he did.

"Yes," Noah said, already half buried under his blankets.

"Watch this, Mom!" Charlie tried a strange sort of cartwheel on his bed, kicking his feet out awkwardly.

"Very good," Sophie said, pretending to look impressed. "But could you fight against *this*?" She scooped Charlie up and gently slammed him onto his back, pinning him under the covers. He burst into giggles.

"Goodnight. No more ninja stuff." She kissed Charlie's cheek and moved to Noah, but he wrinkled his nose and scooted away. "Too old for a goodnight kiss now, huh?" She ruffled his hair. "Say your prayers," she reminded them, closing the bedroom door.

Sophie joined Cayde on the couch. He hadn't watched the movie with them, even though it was an action flick. Now, with the remote in hand, he flipped through channels aimlessly.

"After I drop the boys off tomorrow, we can rent something else. Maybe one you'll like?" Sophie sifted through the popcorn bowl. The good pieces were gone. Only half-popped kernels remained.

"Are you going to see Mark?" His tone was sharp.

Sophie stiffened. "No, I'm just dropping them off. I'll let them out on the driveway and make sure they get inside."

Cayde didn't respond, which only set her more on edge.

"What else can I do?" she pressed. "You won't let Mark come here to get them. Now you're mad when I drop them off?"

"Aren't you worried about 'em spendin' so much time with your ex?" His voice was cold.

She blinked. "I don't understand."

"The more time they spend with him, the more chances he has to win 'em over. You're in a custody battle, Sophie. Shufflin' 'em back and forth is just gonna confuse 'em. Do you have any idea how fast a kid can turn against a parent?" He fixed her with a hard stare. "Take it from me. Every minute he has is a minute he's makin' himself look like the good guy—and you, you're the villain. You won't even realize it until they stop showin' up for things. Until they start lookin' at you different."

Sophie's stomach twisted. She thought of Noah shying away from her kiss. He'd been silent all night. She'd chalked it up to him getting older, wanting his own space, hanging out with friends instead of her. But what if it was more than that? What if one day Charlie glared at her, refused to even let her into his room? What if Noah told her not to come to his games anymore? That he didn't want her there? A special kind of fear only reserved for mothers settled deep in her chest. A poisonous seed. Sophie knew it would grow.

"No," Sophie said. "Mark wouldn't do that. We promised we wouldn't speak badly about each other, especially in front of the kids."

"I'm just tellin' you what I know." Cayde shrugged, turning back to the TV. "You keep lettin' 'em get close to Mark, they'll turn on you. Sooner or later, they'll turn."

Sophie refused to look at him. Then, abruptly, she got up and left. Cayde didn't even glance her way. She stopped outside the boys' room and pressed her ear to the door. Silence. No whispers. No sneaky sounds of hidden game consoles. They must've fallen asleep.

She wanted to open the door, just to see them. Time had become a slippery thing. What used to be hers every day was now split in half. It could stay that way forever, depending on how the court ruled. What if Mark got sole custody? What would she have left?

Her eyes burned. She squeezed them shut, but the tears spilled anyway. No matter what, she couldn't allow that to happen.

CHAPTER 20

CLAIRE

Claire found herself watching the clock more than the kids in her class. Fall break had finally arrived. Everyone buzzed with anticipation. Even the teachers. Jessie was taking her out for dinner tonight. Convincing Cayde had taken all morning. He'd relented but insisted she text him where they'd be. He always wanted to know where she was, who she was talking to. A few times, he'd blown up at her for going somewhere without telling him first, even when it was just a coworker's birthday party. She wondered if his ex-wife had cheated on him before, but he never wanted to talk about her.

When the final bell rang, the kids exploded from the classroom, chaos in their wake. Claire tidied up what she could and straightened her desk. She met Jessie, who'd driven over to whisk her away for food. Cayde had taken her sedan to get her brakes replaced, but it had taken ages for some reason. He'd been dropping her off and picking her up in the Mercedes.

"A friend's joining us," Jessie said. Her tone was low. "She'll meet us at the restaurant."

Claire frowned. She hadn't told Cayde another person was coming. What if he walked in and saw them together? How would he react? She hoped he'd just call when he arrived.

They pulled into the restaurant. A woman with blond hair waved at Jessie. Friendly enough. She had a work bag slung over her shoulder. "I'm Donna," she said, shaking Claire's hand. They settled in, ordered drinks, and waited for their food.

"Donna works for the state," Jessie started, glancing at Claire. "She has access to public records."

"Public records?" Claire echoed, confusion knitting her brow.

"Jessie asked me to look into your fiancé," Donna said. She rummaged through her bag, pulled out a file, and handed it to Claire with a frown.

"You looked up Cayde?" Claire felt a mix of anger and curiosity. Jessie had gone behind her back. But the urge to see what was inside outweighed her irritation. What could warrant such secrecy and a dinner invitation?

Inside were multiple documents, but their meanings blurred at the shock of it all.

"I'm sorry," Jessie said, her voice a low whisper. "I just had this awful feeling."

"He's been married before. Many times," Donna explained, her tone heavy with revelation. "We found divorce certificates, but not for every marriage. He's still technically married to Lacey Miller—the mother of the girls in Jessie's class."

A folder of Cayde's lies sat before her. Emotions wrestled for dominance. Blame ricocheted inside her—blame for herself, then Cayde, and back and forth. She should've seen it coming. He'd wormed his way into her life, spun webs of deception with practiced ease.

Claire pressed her palms against her eyes. "Oh, God," she groaned.

Jessie reached across the table, laying a supportive hand on her shoulder.

Then her phone vibrated, startling Claire. She grabbed it instinctively but knew it was Cayde. With a quick tap, she declined the call.

"What am I going to do?" Her thoughts spiraled—Zach, the divorce, the crushing loneliness, Cayde's lies, her daughter. "I was getting married," she whimpered, the weight of it crashing down as tears spilled over.

The waiter delivered their food, glancing at her with concern before walking away. Everything looked delicious, but Claire's appetite had vanished along with her composure.

"We'll help you with whatever you need," Donna reassured her.

"We'll get you out of this," Jessie added, determination in her voice. "If that's what you want."

Claire wiped her eyes. Embarrassment mingled with a strange sense of relief. Had she been wrestling with cold feet all along? Maybe she never wanted to marry Cayde. Maybe she'd only craved the past she had with Zach. Or maybe she simply couldn't bear the thought of being alone.

Her phone rang again—Cayde. Hesitation gripped her as she glanced at the two women. With a deep breath, she answered. "Hi, honey!" she chirped, forcing a smile she didn't feel.

"I'm comin' to pick you up. Why didn't you answer my first call?"

"We were ordering. Didn't hear it. I'm sorry," she lied. Claire looked at Jessie and Donna. "We haven't eaten yet—"

The phone clicked. He'd hung up on her.

"What are you going to do?" Jessie asked.

Claire wiped her eyes once more. The tears had stopped. "I have no idea."

* * *

Cayde arrived fast. Even if Claire had been hungry, he would have only given her about half the time it took to eat before showing up. Almost instantly, he could tell something was wrong.

He shot her a double-take as he drove onto the main road. "Were you cryin'?"

Her eyes were undoubtedly swollen. "Yes," Claire admitted. She wasn't sure it was wise to spill everything now. But the weight of the truth felt too heavy. Her brain was too loud to be quiet. "I know everything."

"Excuse me?" He sounded defensive already.

"I know, Cayde.!" Her voice rose to a shout in the car. "Your divorce didn't finalize. I know you don't have all the businesses you said you did. How did you even pay for the Mercedes?" God knew what else he had been lying about. For all she knew, he could have been a drug dealer.

"The fuck, Claire?" Now Cayde was shouting too. "Where are you hearin' this? Is this what that cunt Jessie told you?" He made a sharp turn. Now they were headed in a different direction than Claire's house. "Unbelievable. You're gonna believe her over your own fiancé? I'm the one marryin' you, Claire. Fuckin' bullshit."

She inched away from him, squishing herself against the door. The car sped up, weaving recklessly through traffic.

Honks and shouts followed. "Take me home!" she ordered, fear lacing her voice.

"I'll prove it to you," Cayde growled. He drove some time, then pulled off the main road into a series of neighborhoods. Suddenly, he braked hard.

Claire's body slammed forward, then back against the seat. The back of her head hit the door. She wiped her hair out of her face. "Where are we?"

"That's the house I sold." He pointed aggressively near her face, gesturing to a home outside the car window. "After the divorce."

Claire furrowed her brow, shrinking away from him. It seemed obvious he'd just stopped at a random house. With a slam of his foot, the Corvette peeled away. Her heart raced as the reckless driving continued. She reached up to where her head throbbed. A small amount of blood wet her fingers.

Cayde started to ramble about everything Claire had confronted him about. More excuses. Obvious lies. She didn't say a word. His anger felt relentless. Anything she said would only fan the flames. Instead, Claire closed her eyes against the onslaught of car lights whirring past. She hoped an officer would pull them over. Just to escape. Police lights never lit up behind them.

Eventually, they pulled into Claire's driveway. Silence enveloped them for a moment. "I don't want to marry you anymore," Claire said, too nervous to look at him.

An explosion of shouting erupted next to her. Insults mixed with excuses. Claiming her friends were liars. Cunts. Homewreckers. Claire fled from the car. She wouldn't dare run inside her house. He had a key. He'd made one right after they'd gotten engaged. Instead, she ran up the street, ignoring him as he demanded she come back. He followed her in the car. She ran faster.

It was then she realized her purse was still inside, stashed on the car's floor. Her keys. Her wallet. Her phone. She had nothing. No way to call for help. Where would she go?

"Claire!" he bellowed. The car roared and sped up behind her.

She bolted off the road, cutting through neighboring yards. Cayde was forced to stop the car, still screaming out of his window.

Eventually, she crossed enough yards to lose sight of him. But she knew he'd be waiting at home. Instead of turning back, she trudged forward and knocked on the door of a random house.

A polite, older couple welcomed her inside. She asked to use their phone to call a ride. Claire dialed Jessie, her hands shaking so hard she almost couldn't press the buttons. She explained everything, doing her best to keep her voice level. Quiet. She didn't want to alarm her hosts. "Please come and get me," she whispered.

"Donna and I will be there as soon as we can," Jessie said. It sounded like they hadn't left the restaurant yet. Claire gave them the address and hung up, waiting.

She kept away from the windows, sitting still on the couch. The older woman offered her tea or water. Claire politely declined, grateful yet apologetic for imposing.

"It's no trouble at all," her host said.

That was where she was wrong. Claire had just broken up with Cayde. Instead of feeling relief, or even heartbreak, she was terrified. She was in more trouble than ever before.

CHAPTER 21

JACK

Jack could feel the tension in the air between them. Blair hadn't said much since they'd left the gas station, but the quiet was heavy. He wasn't used to this kind of silence from her. Especially not on a case. Usually, she filled the gaps with ideas or small observations, anything to keep their focus sharp. But now, her eyes were fixed on the road ahead, her thoughts clearly somewhere else.

She'd hit a nerve earlier. Jack was professional enough to keep it together, but he couldn't tell what she was thinking. They'd been partners long enough that he could usually read her, but today, everything felt off. If he wanted to rectify the tension between them, it was better he do it sooner than later.

"Blair, about earlier—"

Blair's phone buzzed in her lap, and she grabbed it, glancing at the screen before quickly answering. "This is Agent McCoy," she said, putting the call on speaker.

"Hello," a woman's voice crackled over the line, clear but worn. "This is Lacey. I'm Cayde Miller's wife. You called?"

Jack glanced sideways at Blair. *Wife.* One of them, anyway. It was hard to keep track of how many women Cayde had strung along, but from what they now knew, Lacey was the third.

"Hello, Lacey," Blair said, keeping her tone calm. "I'm calling on behalf of the FBI involving a case with your husband."

Jack wasn't even sure Cayde could be called that, considering the mess of marriages and affairs trailing behind him. Lacey might still be married, but there were plenty more chained to him after her.

"I know," Lacey said, her voice steady but carrying an edge. "I've seen it all over the news. Still looking for him?"

Blair leaned forward, her attention fully on the call. "We were hoping you might be able to share any information about Cayde. Has he contacted you recently? Any idea where he might be heading?"

"No, I haven't heard from him in months," Lacey replied, with a bitterness that wasn't hard to miss.

Blair's pen hovered over her notes. "We understand you're still in Tennessee, correct?"

"Yeah, still here. Same place."

"We have reason to believe Cayde's headed north. Do you know of any reason why he would be going that way? Any connections?"

There was a pause on the other end before Lacey spoke again, her voice colder now. "With the woman, you mean? The one he took?"

Blair stayed quiet. A tactic to get someone to reveal more information in the silence.

"He's done his fair share of forcing women into cars. This time doesn't sound all that different."

Jack exchanged a look with Blair, but she didn't take the bait. Instead, she shifted her tone, trying to draw Lacey in. "We're trying to find both of them as quickly as possible. If you know anything about where he might be heading, it could help us."

There was a long sigh from Lacey, a mix of frustration and resignation. "There's a woman he used to know. Lives up north, where the media says he's headed. She said they were just friends, but I'm not stupid. Cayde didn't have female friends. He had affairs."

Jack's hand tightened on the steering wheel, feeling the pull of something tangible in her words. This could be it—the connection they'd been looking for. He glanced at Blair. She was already writing furiously.

"Do you know this woman's name?" Blair asked.

"Veronica Webb," Lacey said. Her voice held bitterness. "She worked with him back in Nashville. She was a sheriff at one of the local stations. Some kind of 'professional relationship.' That's what they called it. But he's been having an affair with her for years."

Blair's pen stopped moving. "Veronica Webb," she repeated. "Was she involved in any of his other legal issues?"

"Not that I know of," Lacey replied. "But Cayde's good at keeping his secrets. He's had a lot of practice. And Veronica is one of his better-kept ones."

There was a pause, a heavy silence filling the car as the weight of Lacey's words sank in.

"Thank you, Lacey," Blair said. Her voice had a hint of excitement. "We may need to contact you again as this investigation continues. If Cayde reaches out to you or if you hear anything—anything at all—please let us know."

Lacey's voice hardened again. "He won't call. But if he does, I'll let you know."

Blair was about to end the call when Lacey added one more thing. "If you find him—and the woman—see if she's wearing my wedding ring."

Blair frowned. "A wedding ring?"

Lacey's voice had a bite to it. "It's mine. My wedding ring. He gave it to every single one of them after me. I just want it back."

Blair hesitated. "I'll... make a note of it."

"He won't call me," Lacey said again, as if convincing herself. "But if he does, I'll let you know." Then, with a soft click, the call ended.

Jack exhaled, loosening his grip on the wheel. "That's the best lead we've had."

"Veronica Webb," Blair murmured. She flipped through her notes again. "She's come up before. I saw her name in a few legal matters tied to Cayde, but nothing that screamed 'affair.'"

"Maybe she's more than that," Jack said. "He's used women before. Webb could be helping him now."

Blair didn't respond right away. Instead, she stared at her notes, her expression clouded with doubt. Jack could feel it too. The conversation with Lacey had been revealing, but it also carried a dark undertone. Time was slipping through their fingers, and with every minute that passed, the odds of finding Cayde's latest victim alive grew slimmer.

"We need to move fast," Jack said, pressing down harder on the gas. The SUV roared forward, eating up the miles. "We've passed the area where he was last seen now. Call Veronica. She's our best chance at a lead now."

But there was something unspoken between them now, a tension that had nothing to do with the case and everything to do with the argument that still hung in the air. Jack glanced at her again, trying to find the right words to smooth it over, but he couldn't bring himself to say anything.

CHAPTER 22

WENDY

Lisa scooped up Archie, bouncing him until his gummy smile appeared. Little teeth were starting to peek through. "I've missed you!" she cooed. "Yes, I have!" Archie kicked his legs and let out a giggle. Lisa whipped her head toward Wendy. "He laughs now?"

"Only when he's not throwing tantrums. His mood swings are worse than my mother's."

"I'm not much better," Lisa admitted, rolling her eyes. "I've been cramming for med school, filling out applications, and writing letters. It's giving me the biggest highs and lows you've ever seen."

"Any good news yet?"

"Maybe." Lisa's smile hinted at excitement she couldn't hide. "I might have gotten into a school nearby. But we'll see."

"No one's worked harder than you." Wendy picked up a few toys and Archie's tummy-time blankets. "Your application must've been flawless."

Lisa glanced around the house, her voice dropping. "You're sure Cayde isn't coming back soon?"

"Oh, I'm sure." Wendy gave her a serious look. "He said he needed the weekend for a case." She hadn't told anyone about the kitchen incident. Or how his temper had kept flaring up since Archie was born. Lisa didn't like him—and the feeling was mutual. During Wendy's pregnancy, Cayde had suggested Lisa stop coming around. And Lisa started asking Wendy to hang out without him, which he rarely allowed. The strain had made it hard to stay close.

But they were still close enough for Lisa to drop everything when Wendy called, asking for help.

"I just need to do some deep cleaning," Wendy said, her eyes drifting to the ceiling where the attic hatch was. "And... go through some of Cayde's stuff."

Lisa stopped bouncing Archie. "You mean, like, dejunking?"

"More like investigating." Wendy hesitated. "I think he might be having an affair."

Lisa's eyebrows shot up. "Are you serious?"

"Come on, Lisa. He's hardly been around since Archie was born. He's always away 'for work'—but he never brings in any money. We're living off my savings and help from Ma."

"Maybe he's got a separate account?"

"I don't know why he would. We merged our money."

"You what?" Lisa's expression was a mix of shock and disbelief. Wendy could only nod, feeling the weight of regret.

"Right after I got pregnant. He insisted I focus on myself and the baby and not worry about finances. He'd handle it and gave me one of his cards for groceries and bills."

Lisa's jaw tightened. "But your savings—"

"I know." Wendy felt the stupidity of it all sink in. "But I still have access to the money. Right now, I just want to check the attic. Can you watch Archie while I go through a few boxes? And make sure the ladder doesn't fall?"

"Wendy, are you looking for proof as an excuse to leave him?" Lisa asked. "Because you don't need a reason if you want to go."

Wendy set up the ladder beneath the attic hatch. She didn't answer. Maybe she didn't know.

Dust rained down as she pushed the hatch open and poked her head inside. The first box she could reach was heavier than expected, so she lifted herself into the attic and sat on the edge.

"Can you grab the flashlight from the counter?" she called down, directing Lisa. "Let's see what we've got."

The first box was random junk—hair clippers, some broken tools, a few old files. The next one was weirder. A framed picture of Jesus—since when was he religious?—a woman's shoe, and a journal. She flipped it open and saw notes, times, and dates. But none of it made sense. It looked like a schedule for someone else. A woman. Had he been following this person? Maybe it was for his investigative work.

Maybe it wasn't.

Disturbed, she set the journal aside and dug deeper. More junk. Then her fingers brushed over something smooth and glossy. Photos. Wedding photos. She pulled one out, her heart stalling. The picture was a little blurry, taken from a distance, but she knew it was Cayde. The bride beside him, pale and expressionless, was a complete stranger. Red cursive across the back read, "Mr. and Mrs. Miller."

"What the hell?" Cayde had been married before her. *Married.* Who the hell was this woman? She glanced at the journal and shoe. Perhaps a better question: What had happened to her?

"Find anything?" Lisa called up, Archie babbling in her arms.

"Plenty," Wendy muttered under her breath.

Lisa had been right. Wendy *did* want a reason to leave Cayde—and now she'd found one.

CHAPTER 23

AUTUMN

Autumn's happiness was impossible to miss. Anyone could see it in her face, the lightness in her steps. And when Cayde looked at her like he was now, she hoped he knew he was the reason. They were parked at Centennial Park—the spot where they'd met. The wedding was just six weeks away, and the excitement drowned out the worries of life. Tonight, after a cozy dinner and a drive through Nashville, all she felt was peace.

Cayde leaned across the console and kissed her. She wrapped her arms around his neck and kissed back, the rush of affection taking over. "Soon," she breathed between kisses, "we won't have any of the wedding stress. Just… this."

"God led me to you," he whispered. His eyes had that focused, intent look. He kissed her again, harder this time. His weight shifted, sliding across the console, almost on top of her.

She laughed, a little awkward. "What are you—"

He cut her off, mouth moving down her neck, hands gripping her shoulders. He was on her now, pressing her into the passenger seat.

"Cayde," she murmured, pushing lightly against his chest. "Maybe we—"

"Shh," he muttered, lips still on her skin. His weight doubled. She pressed harder, but it didn't do anything. He was too strong. Too heavy. Panic shot through her, the moment turning ugly in a blink.

"Cayde, stop!" Her voice came out in a desperate whine.

But he didn't. He kept going. His hands roamed, pinning her in place. Her heart hammered. This was wrong. All wrong. She twisted under him, trying to shove him off. "No, Cayde, please—"

But he ignored her. He didn't even look at her. Just kept moving, kept taking. Her chest tightened, breath caught in her throat. Her vision blurred with tears. The world shrank to the small space between them, the cold, hard feel of his body crushing her down.

This wasn't how she'd imagined their first time. She'd pictured tenderness and warmth. But this was ice. Brutal. Nothing like she'd dreamed. Nothing like she'd wanted.

It felt like forever, though it couldn't have been more than a few minutes. He finished with a shudder, breath harsh in her face, and shifted off her. Immediately, Autumn grabbed the door handle and hastily toppled from the car.

"Why?" she gasped, sobbing. But she didn't stick around for an answer. She staggered away, retching onto the park grass, choking on her cries.

He was behind her in an instant, grabbing her shoulders, pulling her back. "Come on—"

"Don't touch me!" she shrieked, but her voice was raw, useless. She tried to shove him off, but everything hurt. The world tilted. She went limp, body trembling, the tears and pain merging into one throbbing ache.

"Get in the car, Autumn," he murmured, voice low and calm like nothing had happened. Like he hadn't just—

"Why?" she gasped again, but it was a broken sound.

"Get in," he ordered, firmer this time. He grabbed around her waist and hauled her away.

This was supposed to be love. But now...she didn't even know what it was anymore. Or what she was supposed to do.

He shoved her back into the passenger seat, then circled around to the driver's side. The ride home blurred. She was numb, barely processing what had just happened. When the car finally stopped outside her apartment, Cayde turned to look at her. "You know I would never hurt you."

Autumn wanted to run, wanted to disappear, but her body wouldn't listen. She looked down, staring at her dress. She could tell he'd finished.

He leaned closer, grabbing her face in his large hands. Autumn flinched but didn't dare pull away. He studied her for a moment, and a smile split his lips. It wasn't sadistic, or even taunting—Autumn knew it to be genuine, and somehow that was worse.

"A man and woman bein' together is a blessin', Autumn," he said. "It brings children. They're gifts from God. He put a baby in you tonight. He wants you to be a mother."

No, please, don't let that be true, Autumn prayed. She let out a soft moan and her chest seized with an uncontrollable sob. Talking about God's will in the mix of the trauma only made her head spin more. Why would God want this for her? This pain, this terror? Convulsions started racking her body. She would be sick again.

"I love you, Autumn," he continued, ignoring her distress as his thumbs caressed her lips. "The only way I would ever make love to you is if you'd wanted me to."

She shuddered. She had been holding him, clinging to him until everything went wrong, but that wasn't what she'd meant. This wasn't what she wanted.

His smile faded, as if he'd noticed the words didn't calm her, and a flip seemed to switch somewhere in his head. "No one will believe you if you tell them what happened," he said flatly. His fingers dug into her cheeks, no longer gentle. "And if they did? Imagine what they'd think of you. I'll tell them the truth—that you wanted it."

He leaned in, voice dropping lower, his eyes turning dark. "And don't even think about goin' to the police. I have friends on the force. People who know me, who trust me. They'd never believe you."

His words were knives, cutting deep. Her lips trembled under his grip. He let her go.

She bolted. Threw herself out of the car and sprinted for the door. Her roommates' laughter drifted from the kitchen, cutting off the second she slammed the door behind her. She stumbled into the bathroom, barely locking the door before she was retching again. Everything came up—dinner, bile, every bit of pain and fear she couldn't hold back.

There was a knock on the door. "Autumn, honey? Are you okay?"

Morgan. How long had it been since they'd actually talked? Autumn hardly saw them anymore, not since Cayde convinced her to take the semester off.

"I'm fine," Autumn choked. She wiped vomit from her mouth and fought to keep her voice steady. "Dinner didn't agree with me."

"Can I get you anything?"

"No," she rasped. Autumn wished she'd just go away. What would they think if they knew? What would her parents think?

"I just…need to shower and go to bed."

Silence. Then a hesitant, "Okay. Let us know if you need something."

"I will." It took everything in her not to break. "Goodnight."

"Goodnight. We love ya."

She smothered a sob, waiting until Morgan's shadow faded from under the door before moving. She stripped off her clothes, fingers trembling so badly she could barely pull them free. Her underwear was torn. There was blood. She wrapped them in toilet paper, shoved them deep into the trash can, and turned on the shower.

Scalding hot. As hot as she could stand. She scrubbed her skin raw, until it burned red and angry, but it wasn't enough. She couldn't wash him off.

After what seemed like ages, she got out of the shower, wrapped her wet hair in a towel, and crawled into bed. Even in the comfort of her blankets and pillows, she couldn't stop crying. Even with the scent of conditioner in her hair, the smell of floral soap against her red and scoured skin, she knew this night would leave a mark on her forever.

CHAPTER 24

CLAIRE

Claire stared at the McDonald's arches from inside Jessie's car. Her friend had been generous enough to lend the vehicle to her. She'd stayed at Jessie's house, talking for hours. Crying. Hugging. Planning.

Claire would meet Cayde in a public place to get her purse back. The Corvette was in the lot. He was already inside. She'd arrived on time but couldn't bring herself to get out of the car. Why had she chosen this place? Unhappy memories lingered in every corner.

Reluctantly, Claire stepped out and went inside. Cayde sat in the same booth where she'd last met Zach. Where they had discussed what was best for Paige after the divorce. That conversation had gone smoother than the one ahead would. The moment felt like a lifetime ago. If she were being honest, she wished she was meeting Zach instead.

She huffed at the irony and approached the booth. Doing her best to look confident, she sat down across from Cayde. He already looked agitated. But he wouldn't fly off the handle again. Not in front of so many witnesses. Children and parents flowed around them, shouting and munching on their grease-covered food.

"Are you gonna listen to me this time?" Cayde asked. "Or are you still gonna believe those jealous friends of yours? I have all the proof you need. We could—"

"I'm not interested in any of that, Cayde," Claire cut him off. "I'm only here to get my purse and phone back."

He slid her cell phone across the table. She took it. "And the purse?"

"You can have it back if you come to the house with me."

"No." Her answer was firm. "It's my purse, Cayde. Give it to me, or I will have to call the police."

"The police?" He laughed. Claire suspected it was fake. "I have friends in the police. They ran the number you called me from. I know exactly where you stayed last night." Cayde leaned over the table, lowering his voice. "If you don't want anythin' bad to happen to that lying bitch Jessie, you'll come back with me."

Claire's heart pounded. His threats were unsettling. But it was the sincerity behind them that scared her most. The man she'd been with since summer had been a façade. Now it was all too clear. "No." Claire swallowed her nerves. She had to play this firm and cool. "Give me back my purse."

"Come with me now," Cayde growled. "Or I'll call my friends to pay a visit to Paige." Icy terror crept through her. "Don't you know how dangerous it is for young girls to be on their own? How easy it is to rape them on the way to their cars—maybe while she's out for a late study night at school? A young girl wouldn't stand a chance against a man like that."

The fear overtook Claire completely, and she abruptly stood. Cayde watched, a satisfied smirk creeping across his face.

"I'll be back in a second," she breathed, marching into the bathroom. Her hands trembled as she called her daughter, but Paige didn't pick up. She called again. Nothing. Claire took a deep breath, trying to convince herself everything was fine. Cayde was just angry. Empty threats. But she couldn't shake the feeling he knew what he was talking about.

She reached for the door handle, but it opened before she touched it. Cayde slid in, rounding himself so Claire backed against the door, shutting them both in. Her hair stuck to the grime. The bathroom was long overdue for a deep cleaning, but she preferred the cold, slimy tile to the feel of Cayde pressing up against her. One of his hands slammed next to her face while the other locked the deadbolt. She was cornered.

"You're comin' back with me. You can either do it the easy way—" He leaned forward, inches from her face. "—or the hard way."

He meant it. She saw it in his eyes. They shifted back and forth, wild and dark. Like a hungry wolf. He would assault her right here, in the McDonald's bathroom, if she refused again. She gave a few weak nods. Complying. He unlocked the deadbolt and grabbed her arm, dragging her out and heading for the doors.

Claire knew she couldn't get to a second location with him, even if it was her own house. She would grab the purse and jump out of the car if she had to.

They walked outside. He practically threw Claire into the passenger seat and slammed the door behind her. She sat quietly while Cayde walked around to the driver's side. She scanned his seat, the floor, behind the back seat; the purse wasn't in sight. Cayde sat down and turned on the car.

"I want the ring back." He glared at the jewel on her hand.

"Fine." Claire slid it off her finger, the cogs in her mind planning the next move. "Take it. I don't want it."

She held it out. As he reached for it, Claire let it go prematurely. It bounced off the gear shift and fell at his feet. Cayde unleashed a string of curses as he bent over to grab it, but she wasn't listening. Her hand shot toward the ignition, and she ripped the keys out. Before she could fully turn and jump out of the car, Cayde grabbed her arm, ignoring the ring completely. A small struggle ensued, and the keys fell from both of their hands. Claire didn't care. She burst from the car and bolted toward Jessie's, fishing for the key in her pocket. She jumped in as fast as she could, locking the doors behind her. But Cayde wasn't there. He'd started his own car.

Claire peeled out of the parking lot, not missing Cayde pulling out behind her, cutting off several cars in his haste. The light ahead was yellow—then red. She slammed her foot against the gas, scrunching her face as she blew past the intersection unscathed. Cayde, undaunted, followed through. Now Claire was the one cursing. "Fucking man is insane!"

Cayde's Corvette easily caught up to her. He swerved next to Claire, trying to run her off the road. She stomped on her brakes, and Cayde's car shot ahead. A flurry of honks surrounded her. She turned down another road, the light ahead turning red again. Claire slammed on the gas and blew through it, apologizing out loud to the two cars that had to brake, though they couldn't hear her.

She turned erratically a few more times, constantly checking to see if Cayde had found her. After ten minutes, she slowly turned into a public park. Her car eased along the parked ones until she found a spot out of sight from the main roads. She sat, trembling with adrenaline. While she tried to catch her breath, her phone rang. Paige!

"Honey!" Claire flipped open the phone and answered it. "Are you okay?"

"I'm fine! Sorry I didn't answer. I was in class." Her daughter sounded confused. "What's going on?"

"I want you to stay inside tonight. Don't go anywhere without your dad or Seth or someone else, okay?"

"What? Why?"

"I just want to make sure you're safe. Promise me?"

"Mom, are you okay?" Paige sounded upset. "Want me to come over and—"

"No!" Claire insisted. "I'm fine. You just focus on your schoolwork and be safe, okay?"

Hesitantly, Paige agreed. If Claire had told her the details, nothing she could have said would stop her daughter from returning. She ended the conversation with, "I love you," and promised to see her for the holidays. Zach would take care of her. And her boyfriend, Seth, was a good kid.

She called Jessie. "Plan didn't work," she said, unable to hide the fear in her voice. "And we're both going to need to find another place to stay tonight."

CHAPTER 25

WENDY

Thanks to Lisa's help, the apartment was clean. Archie was asleep for the night. The green digital numbers on the clock changed to eight—the time Cayde said he'd be home. Wendy sat on the couch, waiting. Not looking too hard at the photograph she'd brought down from the attic. It lay on the coffee table as she watched the door.

Fifteen minutes later, it opened. Cayde walked in, his expression shifting to mild curiosity at the dark mood in the house. He saw Wendy on the couch and carelessly dropped his briefcase on the floor.

"It's clean," he remarked. "It'd be better if there was a hot meal waitin'. I've been drivin' all day."

Wendy narrowed her eyes. "You expect me to cook a meal this late after spending the day cleaning and looking after our child?"

His demeanor shifted at her tone. She'd avoided trouble by watching what she said, but now she was done walking on eggshells.

"You want the perfect little housewife, Cayde. I can't be that for you anymore. I won't. If you don't like it, then leave.

Your perfect ideal doesn't exist. You'll just keep bouncing from woman to woman to find it."

Cayde bunched his fist. A warning, but Wendy pressed on. "And I won't tolerate this hostility in my home any longer. For Archie."

"I'm a workin' man, Wendy. I handle the bills and the finances. I make sure you and Archie are cared for. I'm the husband." He marched closer. "That means you do what I say."

"And if I refuse? Will you leave? Pretend our marriage didn't exist the same way you pretended your first wife didn't?" That stopped him in his tracks. Wendy pushed the photograph toward him. "Maybe you didn't leave her. Maybe she had the good sense to leave you."

His eyes flicked up from the picture to her, dark and menacing. Something horrible lurked beneath them. Wendy realized she was afraid. She'd pushed him past the point of anger. Now deep rage simmered beneath his words. "Don't ever go through my things. Did someone put you up to this? Was it Lisa?"

Wendy's anger flared despite her fear. She picked up the picture and threw it at him. It drifted away across the floor. "That's all you have to say? You lied about having a wife! You lied to me. I don't want to hear about your rules or the way it should be. You don't provide this family anything!"

Cayde picked up the photograph and pointed a finger at her, the implication behind it far more terrifying than the gesture itself. "Do not poke into my past affairs. Or you'll regret it. Lisa, too."

Wendy stared at him. "You don't have to worry about that, Cayde. I don't care about your past or your future. I'm done with you. I'll pack up your things this week and bring them to wherever or whoever it is you disappear to. So get out."

Cayde's only reaction was a laugh. "I'm not goin' anywhere. But if you're so set on distance, why don't you sleep on the couch tonight? Or maybe the attic since you're so keen to be up there? I'll be in the bedroom."

He walked down the hallway. Wendy marched after him. "No, Cayde! This is my apartment. I want you to get out. Now!" She should have changed the locks while he was away. She pulled down a suitcase from their shared closet and opened the dresser, pulling out his clothes unceremoniously. "If you won't pack, then I'll do it for you."

"Wendy, stop," Cayde growled. He grabbed her arm and harshly tugged her away. She aggressively pulled free and shoved him back. Cayde, a fire behind his eyes, cracked his hand across her face.

Wendy gasped, holding a hand to the mark. Shock coursed through her. "Don't you ever hit me!" His palm slammed into the other side of her face, her lip splitting from the impact of his wedding ring. "You can't—"

Another slap. She fell into the dresser. Cayde pinned her to it in an instant. His fingers tangled in her hair and pulled her scalp. He gave her skull a measured hit into the wood.

"Yes, I can," he hissed. She stared at him, stunned. "I can," he repeated, then backed away, releasing his hold on her. "Pick up the suitcase."

Wendy sank to her knees, cleaning up the mess of clothes, her mind reeling and her face throbbing. She sucked on her lip, blood filling her mouth.

"I tell you to stop, and you shove me away," Cayde said. His voice was calm, logical. "If you don't want me to defend myself, you can't put your hands on me."

Wendy trembled. Is that how he really saw it? She hadn't attacked him. At least, not in the way he had her.

Cayde knelt to get eye level with her, but she wouldn't meet his gaze. "I know the law." Wendy recalled the black-haired woman at their wedding but said nothing as he continued. "It takes one call, and I could send you to jail. Would you prefer a cell to being here with me? Is that what you want?"

Her heart skipped a beat. Not because she was afraid for herself, but because she was afraid to leave Archie here with Cayde overnight. Slowly, she shook her head, tears dripping down the red marks on her face.

"Okay then," Cayde spoke softly and stood up. Apparently, he was unbothered by the whole situation. With trembling hands, Wendy folded and put away the rest of the clothes, then placed the suitcase back in the closet. When she was done, she backed out of the bedroom into Archie's nursery. She half expected Cayde to follow. He didn't.

She locked the door behind her, listening for footsteps. Instead, she heard the shower start in their shared bathroom.

She looked back at Archie, who thankfully hadn't woken during the argument. His cries irritated Cayde so much, she wondered with growing dread what he would have done if Archie had started screaming. Sliding her back against the door, Wendy fell to the ground. She thought about weeping. She thought about calling the police. Instead, she remained silent and detached. She wasn't panicking or angry anymore.

She was trapped.

CHAPTER 26

SOPHIE

The apartment had three rooms: one for the boys, one for Cayde and Sophie, and an office Cayde had completely taken over. Sophie was on the hunt for work. Cayde's clutter made it hard to focus on her laptop. She'd never shaken the habit of tidiness from her military days. Even in her early thirties, with two rambunctious boys, Sophie did her best to keep the house clean.

Frustrated, she got up from her desk and moved to his side of the room, where files were dumped everywhere. He'd said over and over not to touch them—cases he was currently working on or had worked on before. She wasn't going through them. Just organizing.

Sophie straightened up the piles, shaking her head. How did he keep his cases straight in this mess? Then again, Cayde's mind never seemed to look far ahead. He sorted out the chaos as it came.

As she lifted a few folders, a couple of envelopes slipped through her fingers. She bent down to grab them but froze. The mail wasn't for Cayde. It was addressed to her.

What she read turned her blood to ice.

An hour passed. Then another.

Sophie was glad the boys were at Mark's for the week. So far, Cayde had been a dream come true, but all couples fight, and it appeared this would be their first. She waited, patient and calm, until he walked through the door.

"Hey, Sophie." Cayde leaned down for a kiss, but Sophie held up a hand to stop him.

"Don't." She smacked the letters down at his feet. They'd been opened and read. "You hid *court summons* from me?"

Cayde looked at the letter and then back at her. His face was blank, void of emotion. He stepped over the letters and entered the kitchen, shaking his head. "I'm not in the mood for this."

"Cayde!" She wasn't one to raise her voice, but a few years in the military had trained her to use a commanding tone when necessary. It worked on her boys, but she'd never had to use it on a grown man before. Not even Mark. "Don't ignore this."

He opened the fridge and pulled out a sandwich from the day before. Grabbing a knife from the counter, he began cutting it in half with an aggressive sawing motion. "I don't even know what you're talkin' about."

"My letters, Cayde! You hid legal summons meant for me! I could go to jail for this." She rubbed her face. "I'm going to have to call Mark and explain. Why didn't my attorney call me—"

"You're not callin' Mark." Cayde pointed the knife at her, then continued to saw his sandwich. "I told you I didn't want you talkin' to Mark."

"A jealous streak is one thing. This is bigger than that. This is about my children, Cayde. I'm in the middle of a divorce. You don't get to hide things like that from me. Do you understand?"

Sophie pulled out her phone. "I've got to clear this whole mess up, now."

"I said don't fuckin' call him!" Cayde snatched her cell phone from her hands so fast she didn't know what happened. It smashed against the wall on the other side of the room. He was inches from her face now. Sophie leaned back, aware of the knife in his hand, but he advanced. His nose brushed against hers, his wild eyes boring into her own. "I've packed up my life, moved in here to be with you. I've gone out of my way to befriend another man's children—"

"They aren't another man's children. They're *my* children!" She fought to raise her voice over his.

"You continue to disrespect me—"

"How have I disrespected you? You come into *my* home, rent-free, hide things from me, lie, and now you claim I'm the one disrespecting you?"

He shook his head violently, a roar escaping him. Sophie hadn't realized he'd shoved her until she tripped backward over the coffee table. She gasped, flailing her arms behind her as she crashed down, her legs kicking up. Cayde stepped over the table and was on top of her before she could lift her head, the knife still in his hand. He pressed her shoulders down, the tip of the blade poking behind her ear.

"Don't you raise your voice to me, Sophie." His voice was low and deep, the false calm in the middle of a tempest. She thought it sounded like the devil. "Or you and your boys will regret it."

Silence fell between them. The mention of her children sent a shock of fear through her sternum. She felt the weight of his words as much as she did his hands, pressing her hard into the floor.

And then, all at once, Cayde got up, leaving Sophie behind.

She sat up, lifting two fingers to examine behind her ear. A streak of red stained them. He'd actually cut her skin. Sophie looked up at him in disbelief. He returned to the kitchen, gave her a look that told her the conversation was over, and took a bite of his sandwich.

CHAPTER 27

KATE

"Are you still angry with me?" Cayde glanced over from the driver's seat.

Kate flipped down the passenger sun visor and peered at her reflection. "No," she coolly stated, fluffing her hair and rummaging in her purse to reapply her lipstick. "I just want to make sure everything goes smoothly today."

"I know," Cayde frowned. "I said I was sorry."

Kate's house had been sold. Ideally, she'd hoped to find a place in Nashville before the move, but Cayde had dragged his feet. After quitting her job, packing, and helping Zoey plan her wedding, time slipped away. The house went on the market and sold quickly. Before Kate knew it, her belongings were in a storage unit, and she and Cayde were road-tripping to Nashville. But first, they were heading to Claudville for Zoey's wedding. Both she and her fiancé attended the university there.

Yesterday, before the final boxes were packed, Cayde had yelled at one of the movers. It caused a massive argument between him and Kate, and Cayde had pouted the rest of the night, leaving Kate feeling guilty. He'd cooled things over by granting her a diamond necklace in the shape of a heart. She loved it, but no matter how shiny, the diamonds couldn't distract her from her rising unease.

"Please be on your best behavior, Cayde." She brushed a bit of lint from his suit. "This wedding is in a church. We need to be respectful."

Kate had been religious most of her life. Christianity shaped her upbringing and her daughters'. It was one of the things she liked about Cayde. He was religious, in his own way. Not a church-goer, but he respected God. That was enough for her.

A small bark came from the back seat. Bella, Kate's Yorkie, ran back and forth, her paws stepping over road trip snacks, Kate's mystery thrillers, and a few boxes that didn't fit with their suitcases. Kate reached back, scratching Bella's ears to quiet her. Once they arrived, Bella would have to be tied up outside the church. After the ceremony, they'd head straight to Nashville.

They arrived at the church a bit early. Family and friends were there, introducing themselves to Cayde and remarking how much they'd miss Kate when she moved to Nashville. The children played with Bella, oblivious to the grass stains streaked across their church clothes as they rolled around in the field. Most of the guests were Zoey's friends. While Kate liked her fiancé, Will, it reminded her too much of how young she'd been when she married Luke. Kate had been eighteen, the same age as Zoey, and almost immediately got pregnant. She hoped things worked out better for Zoey and Will than it had for Kate and her first husband.

As usual, Cayde charmed everyone as easily as he charmed her. She watched him smile in his wry, charismatic way, telling the same stories he'd entertained her with when they'd first started dating. Once, she might have beamed with pride. Now, she only sat and frowned. Something about his manner unsettled her.

Kate took a deep breath. She needed to relax. When he was on his best behavior, things were good—really good. But that hidden temper, sparked by jealousy, turned things sour. Luckily, Cayde was in a good mood today, enjoying the attention. He chatted with cousins, aunts, even hugged Kate's parents.

"Where is Zoey?" Kate asked her mother.

"She's still getting ready with the bridesmaids."

Kate wanted to find her, help her with hair or makeup, hold her close, and wish her well on one of the biggest days of her life. But she couldn't dare leave Cayde, especially with her ex-husband just pulling up.

Luke smiled as his eyes met Kate's. He walked up, adjusting his coat, and hugged her. "Hey, Kate!" He held fast. "It's good to see you."

Kate pulled away, giving a polite smile. "How are you?"

Luke's smile flipped into an exaggerated frown. "Our baby is getting married."

"I know," Kate shook her head. "Time just flies."

"Hello." Luke extended his hand to Cayde. "I don't believe we've met. I'm—"

"I'm Cayde Miller. Kate's husband," he cut him off.

Something shifted in their handshake. Kate felt it more than saw it. Cayde was rough and firm, asserting dominance. Luke, confident as ever, seemed to find this funny. Amusement flickered across his face, and Kate inwardly cringed. Nothing sparked Cayde's temper more than mockery.

Luke's eyes slid to Kate, unspoken communication passing between them. *Really?* his eyes said. *This guy?*

Anxious and embarrassed, Kate grabbed Cayde's arm. "Oh, look! Zoey's fiancé is just over there. I want you to meet him." She practically dragged him away from Luke. Beside her, she felt Cayde bristle with annoyance. They talked briefly with Will, the groom, and then found their seats at the front of the aisle.

The music began. The bridal party made their way down, smiling and happy. Then Zoey appeared in the back, arm linked with Luke's, her white dress modest and timeless. Tears sparkled in her eyes as she looked at her future husband. So much hope and promise in their gazes. Kate's hand drifted over, gently grasping Cayde's.

Zoey reached Will at the end, and they took each other's hands. Luke, no help to Kate's nerves, sat on her other side. It was appropriate for the wedding, but her heart pounded. She prayed Cayde's temper would remain in check. She held his hand for the remainder of the ceremony.

Tears were shed. The ceremony was beautiful, and Kate felt an overwhelming mix of emotions. She was truly happy for her daughter, but she knew she would miss her dearly. Nashville wasn't so far away. She wondered if the love and affection she saw on her daughter's face would ever become reality in her own relationship. She had taken a chance on Cayde and his charms, but now she wasn't sure how deep their connection really was. What she thought was fine now paled in comparison to the obvious love Zoey and Will held between them.

It made her think in ways she wished it hadn't.

Immediately after the ceremony, the photographer—a young blonde woman who looked like she attended Zoey's university—swooped in with a smile. "Now is the best time to take photos!"

She started with the bride and groom, inviting the groom's family to join. Cayde pulled out his phone and took a photo of Kate. She laughed awkwardly, inwardly cringing at the angle he shot from.

"Here," she stepped beside him. "We'll take one together." After the selfie, Cayde kissed her and snapped another. It was more than a polite kiss for public display. Perhaps a level or two above that. When he pulled away, Kate saw Cayde's eyes dart to Luke, who stood off to the side, waiting for the photographer.

The smirk on Cayde's face irritated Kate. She stepped out of his embrace, uncomfortable with the kiss, and even more so that he snapped a picture of it. Whatever pissing game Cayde and Luke were playing, she wished they would stop.

"Okay," the little blonde photographer glanced at her list. "Bride's family. Let's start with parents, then we'll add in grandparents, and then extended."

Kate walked over, grinning with pride at her beautiful daughter.

Zoey's smile faltered as her eyes slid to Kate's left. She was looking at Cayde. "Just my mom and dad," she said, her voice awkward.

Both Kate and Cayde stopped in their tracks. Her heart could have weighed a thousand pounds with how fast it dropped. She hadn't expected Cayde to follow her, nor did she have any idea how he would react.

"I'm the stepfather," Cayde said, looking at the photographer as if she were in charge.

Luke stepped in, placing himself between Zoey and Cayde. His voice was calm but had tones suggesting he was placating Cayde. "It's really just up to Zoey."

Kate shook her head in tight movements, not directed at Luke or Cayde. An inner protest bubbled up. She could see the storm brewing.

"Kate will stand next to me in the photos," Cayde said, his handsome features contorting into something threatening. "I'm her husband."

Luke wasn't impressed. Maybe, Kate thought, it was because he didn't know. Luke didn't understand what Cayde's outbursts looked like. What he saw before him was a man who might look good but didn't amount to much else. That's why he found Cayde's jabs at dominance funny. But now, defending his daughter, Luke wouldn't hold back. Kate knew this about her ex-husband. All of it was about to reach a boiling point. She looked at Zoey, her daughter's eyes wide with anxiety at the subtle confrontation.

"I'm the bride's father." Luke tilted his head. "You don't need to feel threatened—"

"I do not feel threatened!" Cayde stepped closer. A warning.

"Cayde, don't," Kate hissed under her breath. People were starting to look.

Cayde's hand lifted, jabbing a finger in the air toward her. "You shut up."

"Hey!" Luke snapped. He moved between Kate and Cayde. "You don't talk to her that way." The tone in his voice shifted to genuine anger.

The expression on Cayde's face morphed into bewilderment. He couldn't comprehend that this man, who no longer had any responsibility for Kate, would step in on her behalf and tell him what to do. "Step back, buddy," Cayde said.

"No, Cayde, we're leaving." Kate reached for his arm. "Let's go."

She didn't care about the alpha-male game unfolding before her. All she saw was Zoey's face, horror etched in her features, as anger spilled onto the church lawn—right in front of friends and family on the happiest day of her life. Removing Cayde was all Kate could think of to fix this mess. But Cayde smacked her hand away. A little thing, really, but it triggered something in Luke.

"That's enough." Luke braced his hands against Cayde's shoulders. Not a push—more like forcefully guiding him out of the chapel. "You need to leave."

Cayde dug in, gripping Luke's shirt. "Get your hands off me," he growled.

"Leave!" Luke insisted, pushing harder. Maybe he didn't think Cayde would fight back. Maybe he underestimated how far this would escalate. But when Cayde reared his fist back, surprise flickered across Luke's face.

He hit Luke square in the nose, sending him stumbling into the church pews. Luke reached out to catch himself but completely missed the bench. He crashed to the floor. Zoey screamed. Her hands covered her face, and her bouquet hit the floor.

Luke looked up, blinking in shock. Then blood streamed from his nostrils, carving trails over his lips and down his chin, dripping onto his white dress shirt.

Will stepped forward, anger flaring on his face, but Kate held up a hand. "Cayde, let's go!" She tugged at his sleeve.

Cayde shot Luke one last furious look before turning on his heel and storming out. Kate glanced back. Tears welled in Zoey's eyes as she watched them leave, her mouth open in shock.

"I'm sorry," Kate mouthed, her own tears spilling. "I'm so sorry."

Cayde headed straight for the car. Kate followed partway, then remembered Bella tied up in the shade. She doubled back, trying to ignore the judgmental stares from onlookers filtering out of the chapel. Their faces were marred with disdain. At least it made leaving easier than it should have been.

"Cayde!" Kate yelled as soon as the passenger door slammed shut. "What is the matter with you? This is my daughter's wedding!"

Cayde peeled out of the parking lot, tires squealing in protest. "Shut up, Kate!" He shot her a wild-eyed look. "You're gonna defend Luke? You want me to sit there while my wife cozies up to her ex-husband?"

"That is not at all what happened!" She was practically screaming now. She'd never been this angry, not even after quitting her job due to his interference. "Luke and I split on good terms. He's Zoey's father. I'm not going to be at his throat like you and I are." The truth sank in. "I don't like the way we are now."

He glared. "What?"

"I don't like us!" Kate admitted, her voice rising. "You used to treat me better than any man ever had, but now? You're so jealous and controlling—" She paused. "I don't want to go to Nashville with you. I don't want to be your wife anymore. I want you to pay me back the money you owe me. I want a divorce."

Cayde slammed the brakes. Boxes, suitcases, books, and snacks flew forward, spilling onto the seats and floor. Even Bella, who had been secure on Kate's lap, yelped as she tumbled to the floor beneath the dashboard.

Before Kate could check to see if Bella was hurt, Cayde's hand shot out, gripping her neck. Kate's head slammed into the window, freezing her in terror. Not from his grip, but from the look in his eyes—a darkness and rage she hadn't seen before. His charming smile seemed like a distant memory.

"You're not goin' anywhere, Kate. Do you want me to go back to the church? I will if you even think of gettin' out of this car. I'll finish up with Luke, and then I'll move on to Zoey's husband and beat him senseless."

The anger in those last words sent chills down her spine. She raised her hands, surrendering, and Cayde finally released his grip.

"We're just angry." Her voice wavered. "We're both saying things we don't mean."

Oh, but he did mean it. Her bones shook with the certainty of it; her blood ran cold. She looked at the man beside her, and he wasn't the same man who had showered her with gifts and sweet words. The ring on her finger felt tighter now, a vice biting into her skin.

What had she done? What had she gotten herself into?

Kate glanced back at the church as it shrank into the distance, along with her family and the life she once knew.

CHAPTER 28

JACK

The phone rang, each buzz cutting through the silence in the car. Jack had pulled over on the side of the road, engine idling, knowing this was a conversation that demanded his full attention. They were running out of leads, and if Veronica Webb knew anything about where Cayde Miller had gone, this could be their breakthrough. If Cayde was headed north while on the run from the law, it wasn't a stretch to think they might have already crossed paths.

The ringing abruptly stopped mid-tone, the sudden silence signaling someone had picked up. "This is Veronica Webb," a soft, lilting voice said on the other end.

Blair's eyes sharpened as she spoke. "Hi, Veronica, my name is Blair McCoy with the FBI. I'd like to ask you a few questions, if you don't mind."

"Of course," Veronica responded with ease. "Regarding what, exactly?"

"Do you know Cayde Miller?" Blair's voice was calm, almost friendly, mirroring the tone Veronica had used.

"I knew him back when I lived in Nashville," Veronica answered casually. "We worked together a lot. He was a private investigator, and we helped each other on cases."

Blair nodded to herself, her tone gentle but probing. "Would you say the two of you were close friends?"

Jack smiled. Blair was good at this. She knew better than to ask directly if Veronica and Cayde had been romantically involved—too blunt, too easy to deny. But framing it as a friendship? That opened the door, whether Veronica wanted to admit more or not.

"Yes," Veronica said smoothly, "we've known each other for many years."

Blair kept her tone steady. "Are you currently aware of Cayde Miller's situation?"

"No," Veronica said. "Not at all. Is he okay?"

Blair glanced at Jack. "We believe he's in the area, and we were hoping that, as old friends, he might have reached out to you."

"No, ma'am," Veronica said, her voice carrying just a touch of curiosity. "So, the FBI is looking for him?"

Jack felt the hairs on the back of his neck prickle. Something about the way Veronica asked that question was off. It wasn't just idle curiosity. It was more—like she was probing them back, trying to find out what they knew. He glanced at Blair, who had clearly picked up on the same thing.

Blair stayed professional, playing along with the charade. "When was the last time you had contact with Cayde, Miss Webb?"

Veronica hesitated, then answered, "Oh, I'm not sure. It's been a long time. Since I moved, I've maybe talked to him two or three times."

Blair scribbled something in her notebook. "Have you been in contact with his wife at all?"

There was a shift in Veronica's tone, slight but unmistakable. "His wife?" she repeated, her voice tight with barely concealed bitterness. "No. But in the time Cayde and I have worked together, he's been with several women. He's a friend and a coworker, but with the rate he goes through them, it doesn't do me any good to try and befriend them. I'm surprised to hear he still has a wife. Last time Cayde and I spoke, she wasn't behaving as she should in a relationship. I'm surprised he didn't leave her ages ago."

Jack's eyes met Blair's. The bitterness, the past-tense reference to Cayde's wife—Veronica wasn't just a coworker or an old friend.

Blair took the bait. "They were having problems?"

"She was insane," Veronica said bluntly. "Always accusing him of things, acting out. It's a wonder they stayed together for so long."

Jack tensed. Blair's face remained impassive, but he could tell she'd caught it too. Veronica was giving away more than she intended. And she was lying.

"What sort of things did she do?" Blair asked, her voice still friendly, like a woman settling in for a gossip session.

"Oh, she was disrespectful," Veronica continued, clearly on a roll. "Always going behind his back, never helping him as a wife should. Flat-out lying to the police about things he'd done, just to make him look bad. Most of the time, the cops saw right through it. Trust me, they know a liar when they hear one."

Blair stayed calm, but Jack thought Veronica was right. A good detective *did* know when a suspect was lying. They both knew now. And she was defending Cayde, likely still loyal to him, even after all these years.

"So, Cayde often confides in you about his relationships?" Blair pressed, keeping her tone neutral.

Veronica hesitated again. "Yes," she answered shortly, the earlier ease in her voice gone. "At least, he used to. Like I said, we haven't talked in months."

"Veronica," Blair said, her voice serious but calm, "are you aware that Mrs. Miller is missing?"

The line went quiet for a beat. Then, in a voice much flatter than before, Veronica responded, "No, I didn't know that."

Blair pressed on. "If you have any information about where Cayde might be, or if he's contacted you recently, we need to know. This is a critical situation."

"As I said," Veronica replied, her voice cool and detached, "we haven't spoken in months. But if he does call me, I'll let you know."

"I'd appreciate that," Blair said, her tone polite but firm. "Thank you for your time, Miss Webb."

"Of course. Bye-bye now." The call ended with a sharp click.

Jack leaned back in his seat, shaking his head. "She's lying."

Blair sighed, tapping her fingers against her notebook. "We can't prove it. Not yet."

Jack shrugged, glancing at the road ahead. "So, what now?"

Blair didn't hesitate. She tapped another contact on her phone, waiting as the line connected. "It's me," she said when someone picked up on the other end. "I need everything you can send me about Veronica Webb—especially her phone records and recent transaction history. I want to know who she's been talking to and when. Send out a subpoena. And get me her current address."

CHAPTER 29

AUTUMN

The familiar church was the only place that brought Autumn any peace since Cayde had hurt her. She hadn't left her room for days, feigning food poisoning. She ignored every call from Cayde, shut out her friends, and hid under her blankets. Only when her mother called, asking if she wanted to join them for church this Sunday, did she finally drag herself to her feet and get ready. She craved the music, the light, the comfort. In the darkness, she was desperately reaching for God. The service couldn't start soon enough.

A familiar form in a three-piece suit slid into the pew beside her. Autumn tensed. From the corner of her eye, she saw her mother lean forward, whispering a welcome to her fiancé. The hymnal books opened, and the congregation began to sing. Autumn remained silent.

As the music swelled with the chorus, Cayde leaned so close to her ear that his nose pressed against her skull. "You haven't been answerin' my calls. You're not reconsiderin' anythin', are you?"

She couldn't look at him. Wouldn't. Silence was her only response.

He leaned in again. "Especially when God's seen what we did. Not when you could be carryin' my child."

No! She squeezed her eyes shut against the thought. They couldn't know for sure.

"Do you know what these people will think if you don't marry me? They'll see you as a pregnant whore. Your own brother, your parents—they'll know what you really are." He sat back a little, confident no one would hear him over the singing. "The weddin' is planned, the invitations sent. You can't back out now, Autumn. No other man will want you once they all know what you've done."

A crushing wave of darkness washed over Autumn. The church no longer felt bright. All sense of comfort dissipated. She suddenly felt isolated from everyone in the room, cut off from light and hope.

Cut off from God.

Because he was right. If she was pregnant, everyone would know.

She pictured her parents' cruel disappointment if she told them she didn't want to marry Cayde after all. Especially after all the money they had spent on the wedding. They'd also loaned a hefty amount toward his practice as a private investigator. And now, on top of that, she could be pregnant. The shame overwhelmed her. She couldn't do that to her parents. She wouldn't.

Tears burned her eyes as fear coiled like a snake inside her, slowly squeezing the air from her lungs. She sat silently through the rest of the service. There was no other choice.

She would marry Cayde.

CHAPTER 30

CLAIRE

Something had to change. Hiding at Donna's wasn't cutting it. Guilt gnawed at Claire for dragging Jessie and Donna into her mess. Paranoia had all three of them losing sleep. She couldn't take it anymore—it was time to return home and face her ex-fiancé.

"Ready?" Jessie asked, parking a few houses down from Claire's.

"As ready as I'll ever be." Claire had already called Cayde and told him she was coming home. "You'll call me in ten?"

"I'll check in. If you say 'fine,' I'll know you're okay. If you say 'okay' or don't answer, I'm calling the police."

Claire shot Jessie a look that said it was now or never. She got out and approached the house, anxiety bubbling in her stomach. The door was locked. Her irritation flared as she knocked, waiting for Cayde to let her into her own home.

Cayde opened the door and stepped aside. Claire's palms began to sweat as she slid through the entryway, never turning her back on him. Cayde stared intently at her, locking the door behind him. They sat at the dining table, tension thick in the air. Claire scanned the mess. She hadn't heard Tank's familiar barks. "Where's Tank?"

"He's safe. For now." The threat in his tone was clear—Tank was Cayde's hostage for this meeting.

"I want my purse."

"You'll get it back if you talk to me." He leaned forward, elbows on the table. "You need to calm down and listen."

Claire's anger simmered, but she held back.

"I want to get back together," Cayde continued. "I don't want to call off the weddin'. Everythin' your friends told you was a lie." He rambled on, spewing excuse after excuse. Each minute stoked Claire's anger. The insults aimed at Jessie, the threats against Paige. "Don't do anythin' you'll regret. If you're smart, you won't push me anymore."

Claire's phone rang. She glanced at it, knowing it was Jessie. "I have to get this. Hello?"

"How's it going?" Jessie wasted no time.

"I'm okay. We'll talk later." Claire hung up, steeling herself. She would need the police to handle this after all.

"Who was it?" Cayde asked.

"It doesn't matter. I just want my purse back. And my dog."

"So, you still won't listen?" He leaned in, venom dripping from his words. "They're lying—"

"Oh my God! It's not just about what you told me, Cayde! It's the lies, the manipulation, your temper." She lowered her voice. "You threatened my daughter. How can I trust you?"

"You're not listening!" Cayde yelled, his face flushed with anger. Claire gripped the chair, recalling how he cornered her in the bathroom. They argued back and forth like this, going nowhere, for over ten minutes. She could see Cayde's rage rising to a boiling point as he stood and leaned over the table, gripping the edge with white knuckles.

Just as she braced herself for him to unleash on her, a knock on the door made Claire's heart race. Cayde stormed to the door, and she held her breath, hoping for a miracle. When three police officers greeted him, relief flooded her.

"Got a call from your friend?" one officer said, approaching Claire.

"Yes. This is my ex-fiancé. He's been threatening me and won't leave me alone. I want him out of my house and my things returned."

The officer's face was stone. "Has he hurt you in any way?"

Claire hesitated. He'd tried to run her off the road, but admitting she'd been reckless too felt like a gamble. "No."

Cayde chatted casually with the two other officers, painting her as the irrational one.

"I can't force him off the premises," the officer said.

"What?! Why not?!" Confusion and anger caused her tone to come out sharper than she'd intended. "I'll change the locks."

They looked at her like she was crazy. "You can't do that either."

"But the house is mine! Why can't I change my own locks?"

"Ma'am, calm down." One officer raised a hand, trying to soothe her like a wild animal.

This was spiraling out of control. Cayde and the officers exchanged quiet laughs. The friendly sound made Claire's stomach twist into a knot.

"We're not escorting him out," one officer said loud enough for her to hear. "And she can't change the locks."

It suddenly dawned on Claire that Cayde's seemingly exaggerated threats about his police friends might be real. Did this officer know him?

"None of that would be necessary," Cayde said smoothly. "I'll leave for the night so she can calm down."

"Best for everyone," the officer agreed.

"What about my dog? My purse? My car?" Claire pressed.

"Tank's in the garage." Cayde opened the door, revealing the Mercedes parked next to his Corvette. Tank barked, tail wagging as he bounded inside. The dog sniffed the officers, blissfully unaware of the tension.

"She left the purse at my place. I can grab it, but it'll take a while," Cayde said.

The officers exchanged annoyed glances. "We can't wait around for this. Can you get someone else to stay with you?"

Claire felt disbelief wash over her. "You're just going to leave me here? With him?!"

"Cayde, go get that purse," the officer said, looking at Claire. "Work things out amicably next time. We don't want to come back."

"Yeah, I'll go get it." Cayde's familiar smugness returned. "I'll see you guys later at poker night."

Claire's heart dropped. Damn it all. They did know each other. She wanted to scream curses at the four men in her house, but she knew better than to give the officers any reason to take action against her.

As Cayde drove off and the officers left, anger and despair mixed within her. Jessie walked in, eyes shining with triumph, but her expression fell when she saw Claire's face.

"What's wrong?" she asked.

"They thought I was making it up," Claire replied. "They thought I was being dramatic."

"Did they say that?"

"They might as well have. Cayde left because he wanted to, not because they forced him." Claire relayed everything that happened.

Jessie wrapped her up in a much-needed hug. "I'll wait while he comes back," she offered. "I don't care how long it takes."

Claire melted into the embrace, grateful at least for her support. She only realized then how isolated Cayde had made her feel. His control on her life was debilitating. Jessie had done so much for her the past few days, and Claire's guilt again rose to the surface in her flood of emotions. "Thank you," was all she could manage.

When Cayde returned, both Claire and Jessie felt the full force of his anger as he threw open the front door. But he didn't drive the Corvette back—someone dropped him off. Claire's gut tightened with unease.

"Claire!" he yelled, storming in. "What the fuck did you call them for?"

Claire and Jessie stood. Tank barked at Cayde, sensing the tension.

"Pull something like that again, and you'll regret it!" Cayde growled, ignoring Jessie's presence completely.

Jessie stepped in front of Claire. "You need to leave—"

"Don't you say a word to me, you cunt," Cayde rounded on Jessie, taking a threatening step toward her. "I know whose fault this is." His face twisted into something murderous, silencing both women. He stormed toward the garage. "If you don't appreciate what I've done, I'll take it all back." A moment later, Claire heard the Mercedes peeling out of the garage and down the street, leaving her empty-handed.

Claire sank back down, defeated. "What do I do now?"

Jessie's brows were knit with concern. "He's dangerous, Claire."

"I know." Frustration laced Claire's voice.

"I'll stay here tonight."

"Don't go out of your way," Claire said, though she had no strength to argue. She was terrified to be alone. "If he comes after you, I don't know what I'll do."

"I can handle it."

By dinner, the calls started pouring in. Cayde, again and again. What more could he say? The same excuses and threats repeated ten times over. Eventually, she turned off her cellphone just to find some peace.

"I'm exhausted," she admitted after barely finding the strength to eat several-days-old leftover pasta. She hadn't slept in her own bed for so long.

"Go on to bed," Jessie offered. "You need some rest."

"I can make up Paige's room for you—"

"Oh, I won't be sleeping." Jessie's tone turned serious. "I'll stay the night, but I'll be keeping watch."

Too exhausted to argue, Claire dragged herself upstairs, collapsing into bed and sleeping for twelve hours straight.

CHAPTER 31

SOPHIE

Sophie's phone screen was cracked, but she could still see Mark's name listed in bold as she waited for him to answer.

"Now you call." Mark's voice was gruff.

"I'm sorry, Mark. I thought you'd gone radio silent."

"What? I've tried calling and texting you dozens of times in the past month! Even the attorney couldn't get ahold of you."

"My phone was broken," Sophie lied. "And some things came up."

"You missed court."

"I know."

"What's going on?" Mark asked. "Don't give me the broken phone excuse, either. We both know that's a lie.'"

The truth was that Cayde at one point had gotten into Sophie's phone and blocked the numbers of Mark, his attorney, and her attorney.

"I'm just—" Her fingers moved up behind her ear, to the small scratch now scabbed over. "I'm under a lot of pressure right now. You could have sent a message with the boys–"

"No," he said firmly. "We promised to never do that. We'd never drag the boys into our shit."

"Please, don't use that language, Mark." Sophie closed her eyes.

"I'll say what I want, Sophie. And some things have to be said."

She knew what was coming.

Mark sighed. "Noah and Charlie say you're engaged?"

"Yes."

"You understand our divorce isn't finalized, right?"

"I know." Sophie rubbed at her temples. She was still shaking from the earlier incident with Cayde. She wasn't sure what she felt anymore—other than tired. "Look, about custody—"

"What do you want me to say, Sophie? I don't know anything about this guy. The boys hardly talk about him. I don't feel comfortable backing down from this. They're my children, too. And I don't think replacing me with the first cowboy you come across is going to be good for them."

"That is not what happened!" Sophie argued, but even in defense, her voice was soft and reserved. "Are you jealous?"

"No. I'm concerned. You used to always put the boys first, and now you're... you're slipping. Something is *wrong*. And I'm sorry. But I'm going to fight to get my boys out of there."

A feverish chill swept across Sophie. "Nothing is wrong with me. Mark, please—"

"I'll see you at the next hearing."

"Mark!"

"Take care, Soph." The line went dead.

Sophie's hand trembled as she lowered the phone. Her mind felt heavy, as if she were wandering through fog just to find a comprehensible thought. She bit back her tears and threw her cell phone.

    This time, it did break.

CHAPTER 32

KATE

Kate Miller had spent most of her adult life believing that after the age of thirty, you had finally settled into the person you were going to be for the rest of your life. Sure, small changes may happen, like opinions being swayed or values shifting slightly. In the younger years of a person's life, especially in teenage years, a person is entirely different every few years. As for the elderly, they tend to be exactly what they have been for quite some time, having used up all their tolerance for change, even building a resistance to it. It is in the years of middle-age adulthood that it begins; the need to change one's person fades, as change is happening all around, in the world, in politics, in work, and in relationships. It's overwhelming.

Yet here she was at thirty-seven, a stranger to herself. If the woman from a year ago stood before her now, Kate wouldn't recognize her reflection. Too much had changed, too much had altered her. The bright hazel of her eyes, once warm and kind, was now shadowed by dark circles creeping beneath them. Bruises marred her arms and hands, her ribs and back, even her neck. A year ago, she had a stable job and a home. Now she bounced between extended-stay hotels and truck stops, crammed in with a haphazard collection of items meant for life on the road in Cayde's SUV.

With a sigh, she slid deeper into the bubble bath she'd drawn for herself, careful to keep her book dry. When she wasn't walking on eggshells around Cayde, she lost herself in the pages of whatever novel she could snag from thrift stores. Sometimes she devoured two in a day.

She heard Cayde enter their hotel room, the jangling of keys announcing his arrival. Bella barked in alert.

"Kate?" he called.

"In the bathroom," she replied, her eyes glued to the page. Today's read was about a woman on the run from a small-town killer—a familiar trope. She'd seen the same plot unfold in at least five other stories, yet it still held her captive. It was the thrill of the chase that kept her turning pages. Death was certain; it was all about discovering which character would meet it first.

Cayde opened the bathroom door and leaned against the sink, rubbing a weary hand over his face. His boot nudged the blow dryer resting on the floor. "The bathroom is a mess."

"I'll clean it up when I'm done," she said, her gaze still on the book.

"I just finished my meeting," he said, probing for her attention. Kate didn't have it in her today. "Talked to a realtor about buying a house."

She managed a polite smile, then returned her focus to the story. A year ago, that news would have thrilled her. Now, after hearing it time and again, it meant very little. He hadn't talked to a realtor. He hadn't even looked at a house.

Time has a funny way of forcing you to settle into your circumstances. She had resigned herself to her new life. It dawned on her very soon after the move that she had not married a millionaire after all. The businesses he boasted about likely didn't even exist. And that dream of buying a house in Nashville? It felt as distant as the stars. No. All she had now was this.

"Are you ignoring me?" Cayde's voice pierced through her thoughts.

"I'm not ignoring you," she replied slowly, finally meeting his gaze. "I don't feel well, and I just want to relax."

"You're always relaxing. I'm on the phone all day with clients and business partners while you just read."

She swallowed the retort that burned at the back of her throat, reminding him that they were living off the proceeds from the sale of her house. He was the one without a job, but she didn't dare voice it.

"Tell you what," she said, her voice measured as she channeled her patience. "I'll finish this chapter, clean up the bathroom, and then we can watch a movie or something."

Cayde grumbled but offered no further argument. She returned to her book, racing toward the climax where the protagonist was fighting for survival, chased by the killer closing in behind her.

Then the blow dryer roared to life. Kate glanced up, puzzled. Cayde was inspecting it. His eyes slid to her, and a horrible grin spread across his face. He swung the dryer by its cord, stepping closer to the tub.

"Cayde," she frowned, clutching the book to her chest. She was so alarmed by the expression he wore she no longer cared about suds coating the old pages. "What are you doing?"

"Think I'll drop it?" It appeared he found this amusing. His hand reached out, and the blow dryer swung back and forth over the water.

"Take it away!" she shouted, pointing to the door. "Get out!"

This only made him laugh.

Fear masked as anger coursed through her, and she shrank back into the water. "Please, don't," she whispered.

Cayde let the cord slip, and the dryer plunged toward the water. Kate screamed, bracing herself against the tub and splashing water everywhere, soaking the pages of her book.

Cayde's grip tightened on the cord, halting it inches from the surface. Hot air sprayed foam and bubbles around her. He laughed, then pulled back. The moment he moved it away, Kate flung herself from the tub, water cascading off her body as she snatched a towel from the rack and backed into the corner behind the toilet, wrapping it around herself.

"Kate!" he spat, annoyed at the mess she'd made. The water had soaked his pants. His glare bore into her. Then his gaze fell to her ruined book, sunk beneath the bubbles. The corners of his mouth twitched. "Guess you're done with the book now."

He switched off the dryer and tossed it on the counter, waving at the water pooling on the floor. "Clean this up. Fuck. I have to change."

He slammed the bathroom door behind him.

Kate trembled, catching her breath. Her heart raced as she wrapped the towel tighter, a desperate attempt to shield herself from the dread. She drained the tub and fished her book out.

Her heart sank as the pages fell apart in her hands. She laid it out on the counter, hoping it would dry enough to salvage. She needed to know if the heroine escaped the killer.

    Kate really, really hoped she did.

CHAPTER 33

WENDY

Wendy cracked the eggs into the pan, watching them sizzle. The smell of burnt toast filled the kitchen. She didn't check her reflection in the kitchen window. Didn't need to. She knew her face was still a mess. The toast popped, and she grabbed it, slapped on some butter, shoved it next to the pile of eggs, and slid it across the counter just as Cayde walked in.

He sat. He ate. He didn't say a word about last night. Didn't glance at her bruises. Just sipped his coffee, sitting like a king on his throne. Wendy moved around, careful not to clatter a dish or scrape a spoon, afraid even the smallest sound might set him off. Archie squirmed in his highchair, hands slapping at his empty bowl, a wail building. She quieted him by slipping a spoonful of mush into his mouth. Anything to keep him from screaming.

Cayde set his fork down and watched. Eyes on her. "Breakfast this mornin', keepin' the house straight, lookin' after the kid. Not so hard, right?" He smiled, that calm smile she hated. "All I ask is that you do what I say. Take care of our son, take care of the home, and things can go back to normal."

She nodded. "Okay, Cayde."

"Good girl." He stood and picked up his keys. "I'll be back at six." A demand for dinner disguised as a promise.

Wendy held her breath, waited for the front door to click shut, then ran to the window. His car pulled away. Gone. Her façade fell, and she chewed on a fingernail. *Think, think.* She grabbed her phone from their bedroom where she'd left it overnight.

Her hands shook. Who to call? Not the cops. He'd said she'd end up in jail. She couldn't risk losing Archie. Couldn't have some social worker tearing him out of her arms. There was one person she could talk to—even if she hated it.

"Hello?" the familiar voice said.

"Ma?"

"Wendy? What do you want?" Her mother's tone was sweet, despite the accusatory words.

Wendy took a deep breath. "I need some help."

Her mother laughed, a high, lilting noise. "Well, I know that."

"No, Ma. This isn't about money or advice with Archie—it's about Cayde."

"Relationship advice isn't really my strong suit. And none of my business. It's best for couples to work things out between themselves."

"Did Pa ever hit you?" Wendy asked.

The line was silent for a moment. "Why?"

"Cayde hurt me last night—"

"Did he touch Archie?"

"No, but—"

"Wendy." Her mother sounded exasperated. "I don't have time for your dramatics."

"Ma!" Wendy's voice became stone hard. "I'm not making this up. I don't know what to do. Should I call the police?"

"The police? For God's sake, Wendy, that man is your husband and the father of your child."

"I know." She pinched between her eyes, feeling less comforted than before she'd called.

"Why did he hit you?"

"We were arguing. I was packing a suitcase for him, ordering that he leave."

"You were trying to remove him from the home? You've been married all of what, a year and a half, and you're already kicking him out?"

"You don't understand, Ma." Wendy was growing increasingly frustrated.

"No. I don't understand why you married a man that quickly in the first place. Despite everyone's warnings not to—despite *my* warnings. And now you don't want to deal with the consequences of your decision. Well…" Her mother clicked her tongue in annoyance. "You got yourself into this mess. It's up to you to figure it out. Maybe if you weren't so headstrong and stubborn, you wouldn't anger him so—"

Something snapped within Wendy, and she hung up with a loud curse. She should have known better than to call her mom, but it hurt deeper than she realized to be so dismissed at her lowest.

Archie had been startled by the sudden shout and now looked at Wendy with big, sad eyes and a frown that threatened to turn into a cry. She lifted him out of his highchair and wiped his mouth with his bib.

"I'm sorry." She kissed his cheeks. His toothless smile and grunt of happiness lifted her spirits a little. "I'm not giving up yet, okay?" she promised him.

She got Archie dressed for the day and decided to walk him in his stroller. A hefty process, as she lived on the second story of the apartment complex. She had to walk the folded stroller down the stairs, set it up, go back up to the apartment, grab Archie, and carry him down while juggling her keys and purse.

Wendy walked to the gas station with her shoulders tight and her jaw clenched. She felt as though everyone on the street and every driver passing by saw the bruises on her face and the truth behind them. A wife beaten by her husband. She gripped Archie's stroller until her knuckles turned white. She hadn't been told she couldn't leave, but that didn't mean Cayde wouldn't be mad if he caught her. Every car that passed made her nervous.

The gas station's ATM blinked up at her, waiting. Wendy yanked open her purse, fingers tearing through the mess of baby wipes and pacifiers until she found her wallet. She opened it and froze.

The cards were gone. All of them.

Her license and some useless gift cards were still there, but the debit cards—every single one—had vanished. She knew she'd put them back last time, knew they were there yesterday. No, he'd done this. Cayde. That bastard had taken them.

Heart hammering, she shoved the wallet back into the purse and turned, pushing the stroller back to the apartment as fast as she could without breaking into a run. She bundled Archie into his car seat, didn't bother with the stroller—just threw it beside the apartment complex stairs—and slid into the driver's seat, tires screeching as she tore out of the parking lot.

Fine, no cards. She'd get the cash. They couldn't stop her from pulling her own money. She still had her ID. She'd walk up to the teller and take every dollar out if she had to.

The bank was quiet. She carried Archie in, glaring at anyone who looked at her funny. She slapped her license onto the counter. "I need to make a withdrawal."

The teller looked up, polite, like they always were. "I'll need the last four digits of the account."

Wendy swallowed. "I don't have the number, but it's a shared account with my husband."

The teller glanced at the ID, typed a few things on her computer, and then looked up again, eyes wary. "I'm sorry, ma'am, but you don't have an account here under your name."

"What?"

The teller squinted at her screen, leaned closer, and then frowned. "It says here the account was closed last year."

Wendy laughed, the sound dark in the quiet lobby. "No, that's not right. I merged it with my husband's. Cayde Miller. We talked to someone here. My name should still be on it."

"Hold on a moment." The woman left, conferred with another teller, and then a manager. When she came back, she had a stack of papers. Wendy's stomach sank. "You signed a closure notice last year," the teller said, handing over the stack.

Wendy's fingers trembled as she flipped through them. Her name, her signature, right there. Closure notice. "No," she whispered. "This wasn't a closure. It was supposed to be a merge." She could barely hear her own voice over the rush of blood in her ears. "He *told* me—he said we were merging."

The teller's face softened. She sounded genuinely sympathetic. "It was a transfer of funds to your husband's account."

Wendy stared at her, brain spinning. A transfer. A setup. He'd dragged her out of bed that morning, insisted they go to the bank, and yammered about merging accounts while she sat there, sick, half asleep, and extremely pregnant, signing her own future away.

"Legally," the teller continued, her eyes flicking to the cut on Wendy's lip, "the funds belong to your husband. You don't have access anymore."

Wendy swallowed hard. He'd led her in like a handler, sat her down, and smiled the whole damn time. She signed away every dollar she had.

"Ma'am?" The teller leaned closer, voice gentle. "Is there anything else I can help you with?"

Wendy's throat closed. She couldn't speak. Couldn't breathe. "No," she finally rasped. "Thank you."

She staggered back to the car, buckled Archie into his seat, and laid her head on the steering wheel. Gone. Every dollar. Every penny she'd saved. Gone. It was all his now. Her whole world felt like it was underneath his boot.

Wendy gripped the wheel, knuckles white, a furious scream rising in her throat. She swallowed it and looked at Archie in the back seat, his bright eyes on her, babbling happily to himself. She envied his attitude.

Wendy straightened, wiped her eyes, and started the car. He'd taken her money. If she had to fight for every scrap, claw her way through every barrier, she'd find a way.

It made sense now that she thought about it. She had access to Cayde's debit card, but he always went over receipts and spending with her. What she thought was a man with a good sense of business, who planned for the future, was a controlling narcissist ensuring she hadn't spent more money than she needed to. More for him—to do whatever he wanted with.

Without money, she had nowhere to go and no way to help herself. She started wondering what she could do to get some cash. Odds were she'd have to call her mother again. To add salt to the wound, her car was nearly out of gas. She had enough to get back to the apartment, but if she wanted to travel any further, she'd have to fill it up. Great.

"Broke, beaten, and stranded," Wendy whispered to herself, pulling under the carport designated for her apartment. She got Archie inside, placing him in his highchair while she went to get the stroller. Once it was put away, she fed him a warm bottle, changed him, and settled him in for a nap.

He fell asleep without any fuss, and Wendy was grateful for it. Now, it was time to consider her next step.

First, she needed money. That was the most important thing if she really wanted to be rid of Cayde. It was unfair he'd taken all of hers, let alone denied her access to it, but maybe that could all be settled in the divorce. Maybe thinking of divorce was too far ahead. She needed to distance herself from him. And to do that, she had to be independent. It was almost laughable how carefully he'd planned all his moves to ensure that she would rely on him. She'd given him all the control and hadn't even realized it.

She would have to call up her mother again. Fuck. She'd have to beg. *Fuck.*

Biting back her disdain, she fished her phone out of her pocket. She'd missed a call from Lisa. Strangely enough, Lisa had left a voicemail.

"Wendy!" Her voice was harsh. "Call me back, *now!*"

Alarmed, Wendy did. She had no idea how to explain to Lisa the events of last night. Not only had she failed to kick Cayde out, but he'd also physically hurt her and cut her off from their finances. Yet there was something urgent in Lisa's voice that told Wendy something else had happened.

"Wendy," Lisa's voice snapped on the other line.

"Lisa? What's wrong?"

"What's wrong? My application to the medical school in Nashville was denied. Apparently, early this morning, an investigator asked to meet with the counselor over my file and explained he was investigating me due to malpractice and abuse at the assisted living complex where I work."

"Oh, shit." Wendy covered her mouth. Cayde. They both knew it. "Can't your counselor call your workplace? Check the facts?"

"The '*investigator*' claimed to be hired independently by the family of a resident. He warned my counselor that my workplace was trying to sweep it under the rug. Obviously, my boss would cover for me, as they didn't want to ruin their reputation."

"That's not fair! They have no proof—"

"You don't need proof to deny an application, Wendy. I'm cut from the list, and with this kind of sabotage, who knows what connections have been lost to me now?" There was clear hurt in her voice. "Did you tell Cayde I was with you yesterday?"

"I—" Wendy stuttered over her words. "—didn't think he would do something like this. I'm sorry. What can I do?"

"Nothing. I've been rejected." Lisa was quiet for a moment. "Did you kick Cayde out?"

"I tried, but he's still here." Considering Lisa's crisis, Wendy couldn't find the words to explain what had happened.

There was a laugh that sounded more incredulous than anything else on the other end of the receiver. "Of course he is. Look, Wendy, I don't know how to say this but, until you figure things out with Cayde, I think it's best if we take some time apart. After what he's done, I don't ever want anything to do with him again. If you really need me, I'll be here for you, but until then…"

"I understand." Wendy was fighting tears. She'd been strong enough not to cry up until this very moment. How could she tell Lisa that she *did* need her? She couldn't, not after what Cayde had just done. In truth, it was best that Lisa stay far away. She wouldn't call her mother for help either—this was about more than just sabotaging Lisa. This was a threat from Cayde. Anyone helping Wendy would suffer a similar fate.

"Lisa, I'm sorry."

"So am I." The line went dead.

Wendy put the phone down and sat on the couch. She considered eating since she'd skipped breakfast, but she felt too nauseous. The truth was that Wendy and Archie were trapped. Until Wendy could find a way to make money, and then save enough to get them both far away, she was stuck with Cayde.

So be it.

She didn't care how long it took or what dedicated act she would have to play; Wendy made a promise then and there that she would get her and Archie out.

CHAPTER 34

CLAIRE

One by one, Claire skimmed the forms to fill out an emergency protective order. Pen scratched against paper. Somewhere between the signatures was the key that would keep him out for good. Jessie had taken her to the courthouse to collect everything, but without her purse and license, Claire couldn't fill everything out. Cayde never had returned to bring it back. So Claire took the papers and returned home to finish—where she had access to her files and sensitive information—but not before telling Jessie to go home.

"Enjoy fall break. Don't worry about me," Claire had said.

Now she wondered if that had been the right decision. She didn't like being alone in the house. And her sedan still hadn't been fixed. She was stranded.

Then the front door crashed open.

"You cunt!" Cayde's voice filled the room, loud and raw. "The fuck did you go to the courthouse for?" He stormed in, briefcase slamming onto the table. His eyes locked on the papers. "What's this?"

Claire froze. He knew? Had he followed her? Had he been watching, waiting for Jessie to leave? He grabbed the forms, his eyes sweeping over the pages, expression darkening. Then he ripped them to shreds. Torn bits of white fluttered around them like ash.

He reached into his briefcase and pulled out a gun.

Claire's world narrowed to that single point. A click—the safety flipped off. He leveled it at her chest, eyes blazing. "You even think about goin' back to the courthouse, and I'll blow your fuckin' brains out. Do you hear me?"

She stared, pulse hammering. *He'll do it,* she thought. *He'll kill me.*

"Do you *hear me*?" he shouted.

"Yes," she whispered, barely moving, barely breathing. Her body screamed for her to run, but there was nowhere to go.

"Maybe," he murmured, tilting his head, gaze thoughtful. "Maybe I should pull the trigger now." His finger twitched, ever so slightly. "Give me one good reason why I shouldn't."

Claire's mind blanked. *Maybe he should,* she thought, hollow and numb. *At least then this nightmare would be over.* But then she saw Paige's face—Paige laughing, chasing Tank across the yard. No. No, she couldn't give up.

Cayde lowered the gun slowly, lip curling. He smirked. "Maybe I'll start with your little friends instead. Jessie. Paige. Your ex." He ticked them off like a grocery list. "And you can watch every second of it." He leaned closer. "You can't run from me, Claire. No Mercedes. No sedan. No way to escape."

"You wouldn't dare!" Claire shouted.

"Wouldn't I?" Cayde reached into his pocket and pulled out his phone, his other hand still on the gun. He tapped on it for a moment, then flipped it around. Paige was on his screen—at lease, a photo of her was. She was hunched over a desk in a room. Her room at Zach's. The photo had been taken outside of her window. He swiped his thumb. The next photo was her at school, leaning against lockers and talking to friends. "It was easy enough gettin' these. You think I couldn't do more if I wanted to?" He shook the gun a bit.

The floor seemed to tilt under her feet. He'd thought of everything. She had no car, no access to money, no police who'd listen. And now, with the barrel of a gun inches from her face, no way to call for help. Jessie was gone. Her daughter was out of reach. She was alone.

How did it comet to this? This wasn't the Cayde she'd met. The man she'd known wouldn't be standing here spitting threats, finger twitching on a trigger. But maybe she'd never really known him at all. She placed a hand over her chest, the diamond necklace cool against her skin.

The gun lowered. "You want me out of your life?" he asked, voice soft but cruel. "Fine. One hundred thousand dollars. That's what it'll take. Pay me back for the Mercedes and everythin' I spent on you, and I'll disappear."

She blinked. *One hundred thousand dollars.* He might as well have asked for the moon.

"Cayde," she said softly, trying to keep her voice steady, "I don't have that kind of money. "

He smiled, teeth bared. "You do. I know what's in your savin's, Claire. And that four oh one K of yours? I know all about that, too."

Her stomach churned. She'd never told him. Never once shared that information. He'd known this whole time. He'd planned it.

"I don't have access to my retirement," she tried, voice shaking. "You can have the Mercedes, Cayde. I don't want it."

The gun came up again, steady. Closer now. "I bought that car for you. You pay me back, or we have a problem. Or maybe I'll go and pay your daughter a visit—"

Claire swallowed. "Alright! Alright."

He watched her for a long moment, then flicked the safety back on, tucking the gun into his waistband. He ran a hand through his hair, casual now, like this was just business. "I'll be stayin' indefinitely. To make sure you pay up and don't play any tricks."

What tricks could she possibly have up her sleeve? Her hands were tied. Cayde had set everything up perfectly. For the sake of her friends and family, she had to be rid of him.

* * *

Day after day, it was the same. A waking nightmare. Cayde's shadow stretched over every hour. He was always there—when she woke, when she ate, when she made a phone call. Breathing down her neck, watching, controlling.

Getting the money had taken time. But she didn't care. She would've handed over twice the amount if it meant being free. Anything to crawl out of this hell. She'd taken out a second mortgage on her home and waited every morning for the bank's approval for the rest. Her stomach tied itself in knots. But Cayde didn't care about the delay. He just hovered, snapping at anything that set him off. A passing glance from another man, a word about Zach—it all lit his fuse.

He constantly accused her of scheming, plotting a way out. And she had to lie. Smile. Promise him she wasn't, even as his eyes drilled into her, dissecting her every word. Fear wrapped around her like a second skin. She memorized his routine, crept through her own home like a ghost, anxious every time she dropped a fork or let a cabinet door close too hard. Cooking under his gaze became torture. She barely ate. Barely slept. Work was no sanctuary either. He'd call once a day to check in, make sure she hadn't vanished. Coworkers asked, Jessie asked. Claire brushed them off. What could she say? She was afraid. And embarrassed.

But then, the approvals came. She felt the first flicker of hope. Maybe this nightmare was almost over. She gave him everything in cash, just like he'd demanded. And for the first time in weeks, Cayde almost seemed… happy.

"Once I get the title for the Mercedes, it's yours," she said quietly. "That was the agreement."

"The papers are in the sedan. I'll hand them over when the car's done."

Her stomach twisted. Liar. He'd never let her have it. She thought about tearing up the check then and there, but he'd threaten her with the gun again, and still walk out with every dollar. Maybe more.

"Take it, then," she said softly. *Please. Go.*

"Not just that." His eyes gleamed. "I want what's left in your savin's. And the account for your mom."

Claire blinked. "My mother's account? No," she said, voice shaking. "That money's for her care. It's not mine to give."

He smirked, and his hand drifted toward his briefcase. "You know what'll happen if I don't get what I'm owed."

"When do I get my sedan back?"

"It's not ready," he said, gaze dropping to the check again. "Parts are still bein' shipped."

Still being shipped. It'd been months. "You have your money," she snapped, pointing at the door. "Get out. Take it, and go. You don't get my mother's money." Her mother was disabled and declining. Claire had that money strictly to ensure her medical and residential bills were paid on time.

Cayde's eyes darkened. "I'll leave when I get the rest."

"Cayde—" her voice broke, anger crumbling into something manic. "Leave. *Now!*"

His hand shot out. The force of his shove sent her stumbling into the wall. "Don't you raise your voice to me!" He shoved again, pinning her there. Breath hot against her ear. "Don't you ever tell me what to fuckin' do."

She just stared at him, blood rushing in her ears, heart hammering. She should fight. Scream. Push back. But she didn't.

Cayde leaned in, voice dropping to a growl. "Like I said, I'm stickin' around. Until everythin's sorted out."

CHAPTER 35

JACK

There wasn't much they could do for the rest of the day. Blair and Jack found a nearby hotel, deciding to settle in for the night. Veronica's house wasn't more than ten miles away, and local law enforcement had been briefed to do extra patrols in the area. Everyone knew what car to look for, but that didn't offer much comfort. Until they got the records for her phone logs and recent purchase history, they'd have to play the waiting game.

Blair was visibly frustrated. A night without an arrest wasn't just another delay, it was another day lost for the victim. Jack could tell she was wound tight, and he couldn't deny that he felt the same.

After checking in, they received keycards for side-by-side rooms on the third floor. The hotel wasn't terrible, but the faint smell of mildew hung in the air, making the place feel a little more run-down than it probably was.

"Guess you get your vacation after all," Jack said. It was his best attempt at being funny. Blair just blinked at him, so he offered, "Are you going to grab dinner or...?"

"I'll probably just order room service." She gave him a smile that really just looked like a tight line across her face. "Well, I'll let you know if anything comes up. Goodnight, Myers."

"Blair." Jack stepped toward her. He wasn't sure what to say—he'd never been good at this sort of thing. He sighed and lowered his voice. "I can't stand it when things aren't right between us."

She looked down at her feet, her shoulders shifting uncomfortably before she met his gaze again. "Neither can I. Maybe it's the case. You've always told me that we can't let things get personal. In this line of work, we have to detach, but some cases hit harder than others. If you let it get in your head, it's going to mess with how efficiently we can solve this."

Jack scoffed and shook his head. "That's exactly the kind of attitude that's really pissing me off, Blair. I'm not weaker because I can relate to the victim. The emotions this stirs up inside me don't make me a liability—they make me more determined to catch this guy."

Blair paused, his words sinking in. "Relate? Myers, have you… have you experienced something like this?"

He crossed her arms over his chest, his expression hardening. "My dad. All growing up."

Blair's eyes closed in regret, briefly. "Myers, I had no idea."

"You don't know what it's like until you're in their shoes—living with that kind of fear every day. Not everyone can just leave." He thought of his mother. The bruises on her face, the smiles she wore to cover them up.

"Your dad… He's still alive, right? You still see him?" Blair must have recalled him mentioning something.

"He's my *dad*," Jack said quietly. His shoulders slumped in defeat. "And it's amazing how much you can love the person who hurt you the most. Even while it's happening."

She met his gaze, her expression softening just a little. Maybe Blair would never fully understand what Jack had been through, but that didn't mean she couldn't respect the depth of his feelings. She was kind and resilient. Despite the uncomfortable vulnerability, he knew she would understand.

"I'm sorry, Myers," Blair said. Her tone was gentle. "For earlier."

"That's all right, Blair. I'll see you bright and early."

She turned to go to her room, but Jack gently grabbed her arm. "Hey, why don't you ever call me Jack? When it's just us?"

A smile pulled across her face. "*Goodnight*, Myers," she said, slipping away as she scanned her keycard and disappeared into her room, leaving him standing there alone in the hallway.

CHAPTER 36

AUTUMN

Over a hundred guests packed into the church for Autumn's wedding. Laughter echoed through the pews. Voices mingled. Everyone admired the flowers, the decorations. All her friends. All her family. No one had shown up for Cayde. And no one seemed bothered enough to ask—other than her family. Whatever excuses Cayde had crafted with his silver tongue, they were satisfied.

Morgan tugged at Autumn's dress, fluffing the train and smoothing the veil. "You're beautiful," she murmured, stepping back. "Should I go find your dad?" She was to walk down the aisle any minute.

Autumn bit her lip. Peeked out again. Her pulse hammered in her ears. Could she really do this? Commit her life to him? He'd been so perfect in the beginning. So sweet. But after? Would it still be that? The perfect man, the perfect life? Or would it be more like the other night? The night he—

No. She swallowed hard, eyes flicking to where Cayde stood. Laughing. Hugging guests as they filed in. All of them congratulated him. Kissed his cheek. Shook his hand. Those same hands—hands that held her down, pinned her while he—

"Autumn?" Morgan's voice cut through the memory, pulling her back. "You okay?"

Autumn turned and gave a tight grin. "I'm just nervous!" She gripped the bouquet, knuckles white.

"You know...you don't have to marry him."

"What?" Autumn's eyes went wide.

Morgan leaned closer, face serious. Then a mischievous grin. "My car's just out back. We can still make a run for it."

Autumn swatted her with the flowers. "I thought you were serious!"

"I was!" Morgan laughed. "We could ditch this whole thing and go to Florida!"

"Stop it!" But Autumn smiled. "Go find my dad."

"Fine, fine." Morgan lifted her hands, grinning, but her gaze lingered. "You sure you're okay, though?"

Before Autumn could answer, a voice called out. "Sorry—I'm here!" Her father appeared with his arm outstretched. Autumn took it, gripping it tight. She forced herself to breathe.

"I'll go tell them to start," Morgan said softly. Then she slipped inside, disappearing into the crowd.

The music started. The doors swung open, and suddenly, every eye was on her. Watching. Seeing. She wanted to shrink back, to hide. It felt like they knew. Like they could see everything. But she forced herself forward. One step. Then another. Each one dragging her closer to Cayde. To a life that loomed like a shadow at the end of the aisle.

Her father kissed her cheek and let her go. She stepped up beside Cayde. Numb. The ceremony blurred around her. The words. The vows. The rings. It all ran together.

"I now pronounce you man and wife!"

And so it was done.

Applause exploded around her. Cayde grinned, pulling her close. He leaned in, whispering in her ear. "Man and wife. You belong to me now." He kissed her cheek, gentle for the crowd, for the cameras.

The celebration passed in a blur. Faces. Smiles. Congratulations. Her brothers clapped Cayde on the back. Her parents hugged him, tears of joy in their eyes. All Autumn could do was smile. Nod. Try to breathe. But everyone swarmed around her. She felt like she was going to choke.

Then she saw Justin, her and her brothers' childhood friend, through the crowd. He broke through and wrapped her in a hug. Brief. Warm. His arms tightened around her, just for a moment. "Congratulations, Autumn." His voice was soft. "I wish you the best."

And then he was gone. Vanished into the sea of people.

She trembled. She didn't want him to leave. In his arms, she'd felt safe. Safer than she'd ever felt since Cayde had raped her in the park.

There it was. The word she hadn't been able to say, even to herself. She wanted to deny it, make up excuses and reasons for him, even when she knew the truth. Sickness settled again in the pit of her stomach.

Had she done the right thing? Or was this the biggest mistake of her life? The music swelled. The dancing began. Photos were taken. But even in the church full of family and friends, she'd never felt so alone.

CHAPTER 37

SOPHIE

Two weeks after her phone call with Mark, Sophie's divorce was finalized. She thought she'd feel relieved. She didn't. Just... numb. And then, the very next day, Cayde dragged her to the courthouse. He insisted they get married right away. She'd been second-guessing everything since the kitchen incident. She told herself it was just a one-time thing. But Cayde had proved her wrong—there were many instances after that.

And now, she was his wife.

She'd asked Tanner and her parents to come. Her brother and father signed as witnesses. Then they all drove back—Charlie and Noah included—to Tanner's place. He and his family had put out drinks and desserts. Even with the short notice, they were able to throw Sophie a celebration.

"Congratulations, little sister!" Tanner wrapped her in a hug, pulling back when she winced. "You okay?"

"Yeah." She forced a laugh, hand drifting to her ribs. "Just sore."

"From what?"

She froze. Caught herself. "I started working out again."

Tanner frowned. "You always worked out."

"I stopped for a bit." She turned away, brushing it off.

Tanner's eyes narrowed, but he didn't push. "Well, guess you must like the guy if you married him. Wish I'd met Cayde sooner."

"Me too." The words she spoke didn't sound like her. To Sophie, it felt like someone else was using her voice, saying all the right things while she wailed and screamed on the inside. The conflict within her was so intens,e she didn't understand what was right or wrong anymore.

"But thanks." Tanner smiled softly. "For including me today. I'm glad I could be your witness."

"It's me who should be thanking you," she said quietly. She gestured to the table, loaded with cookies and brownies. "You did all this for me."

Tanner's wife, Melissa, swooped in with plates. "We're happy to do it. Wish you both the best."

"Thank you," Sophie murmured.

Tanner slipped a hand on her back, gently steering her away from the noise. Lowering his voice, he said, "Hey. By the way, you and Cayde can use one of my properties for a weekend getaway. Honeymoon, you know?"

"Any of them?"

"California, New York, Illinois—your pick."

Sophie smiled. Hollow. A weekend away. Right. She'd take him up on it. Just without Cayde, if she could.

"Everybody," Cayde's voice rang out, loud and commanding. "Before we dig in, let's take a moment to bless the food. Give thanks to God for bringin' Sophie and me together."

Their dad nodded, eyes shining. Her mother pressed a hand to her chest, blinking back happy tears.

But Sophie? She just felt empty. God. Faith. It meant everything to her. When she'd met Cayde, she thought she'd found someone who felt the same. But now? Now she wasn't sure who he was at all. She glanced down at her wedding ring, but Tanner took her hand. Her mother took the other. Everyone linked together as Cayde began to pray.

Noah and Charlie stood off to the side, eyes lowered. Silent.

Cayde's voice rolled through the room. Strong. Smooth. Gentler than she'd ever heard him. He prayed for their future. For the kids. For everything she thought they were supposed to be. But Sophie didn't bow her head. Didn't close her eyes. She just stared at her boys.

She'd always known what was best for them. Always been so sure.

But now? She didn't know a damn thing.

She looked at Cayde. The man she'd married. The man she thought she knew. But standing there, his eyes shut tight, lips moving in practiced reverence—she realized she didn't know him at all.

All she did know was that she would do whatever it took to protect her boys.

CHAPTER 38

CLAIRE

The lights of Nashville excited Claire. After months cooped up inside her home, she'd convinced Cayde to allow her to go out with her Bunco club friends. Since calling off the wedding, she hadn't seen them. She'd convinced Cayde to let her join them for a night out to celebrate Christmas before the holiday packed their schedules.

Claire had hoped Cayde would leave for Thanksgiving, but he hadn't. In fact, he remained all throughout the holidays. Claire, too afraid for Paige to come home to Cayde, suggested she celebrate the holiday with Zach. The conversation was sad, and Paige hadn't completely understood why her mother didn't want her to come over for the holidays, but Claire thought it was for the best.

She'd strategically chosen an outfit that wasn't too tight or revealing, to avoid setting him off. And she'd been forced to wear long sleeves for some weeks now to hide the bruises he'd given her. Most of the time, he only grabbed her harshly to make a point, and other times he shoved her around if she got too snappy with him. She didn't want anyone to see—they'd try to get involved, and that was the last thing she wanted.

"I'll be coming too," Cayde said, pulling into the parking lot.

"You won't feel out of place in a group of women?" she asked. "I can't imagine what you'd contribute to conversions about children and housework. Oh, I know! Maybe you can talk to them about your volunteering!" The last bit might have been too sarcastic, and she reminded herself to hold her tongue. She was lucky enough he was letting her out at all. But maybe he'd gotten just as stir-crazy, constantly watching her every move in the house.

Cayde glared at her. "No. I've invited two of my buddies in the police force, so we'll sit on the other side of the bar to make sure you don't get into any trouble."

"We're just going to have a bit of fun," she said, unbuckling her seatbelt. What wrongs could she do in a place like this? They were bowling, for fuck's sake.

She got out of the car and marched inside, leaving Cayde to follow behind in the chilly air. She couldn't get inside fast enough, anxious to see her friends, drink a little, and not care about anything else.

Everyone welcomed her with smiles and laughter. Somehow, it made her feel worse. If they knew what was happening to her behind the walls of her home, would they still be so happy? Would they believe the smile she shot back at them?

As they caught up and updated one another about their lives, Claire spotted Cayde on the other side of the bar where he said he would be, chugging back a beer. He finished it and said something to two men next to him. Claire wrinkled her nose. His cop friends, she assumed.

Laughter erupted in the circle, and drinks were passed around. As the night continued on, Claire's spirits dampened. She wanted to have fun, to enjoy herself, but instead, all she could think about was Cayde watching her, drinking beer after beer. He was supposed to be her ride home.

Eventually, they made eye contact, and he waved her over. She didn't want to anger him in front of her friends or cause a scene, so she walked toward the men.

"This is Rick, and that's Jacob," Cayde introduced them. "They're both off-duty cops." The two men pressed their lips together in half smiles and nodded politely, but didn't say much after a small, mumbled greeting. Cayde dismissed her with a wave of his hand. "You can go back to your girls, now."

It took everything in her not to roll her eyes at him.

"Why don't we go next door and get some real food?" One of her friends, Jade, suggested after an entire game of bowling finished up. "It'll be quieter there."

Immediately, Claire knew Cayde wouldn't like her leaving out of his sight. She moved toward the bar, but only the two cops were there. "Will you tell Cayde we've moved next door?"

The two men looked confused for a second. "Oh, right. That guy. Sure."

Claire blinked at them. It dawned on her that these men had never met Cayde before tonight. They were strangers. There was a good chance they weren't even off-duty cops, and he'd gotten them to play along. They eyed her, clearly uncomfortable.

A bit unnerved, and slightly embarrassed, Claire went back to the group as they returned their bowling shoes and got ready to head out. She spotted Cayde making his way through the crowd to get to them.

"I'll meet you guys there; I just have to check with Cayde."

"Okay." Jade eyed her a bit suspiciously. "We'll grab a table."

Claire turned around and barely stopped before colliding with Cayde. He looked flushed, drunk, and upset. "You were goin' to leave?"

Claire looked back at the group, already making their way out of the building. "We were just going to the restaurant next door. I was coming to tell you."

He didn't believe her. "We're leavin'." He put his hand on her shoulder and began to guide her to the door and back toward the car. Claire looked back with dread. She could see her friends entering the restaurant, laughing.

With a sinking feeling in her stomach, Claire felt she had no choice but to leave with Cayde.

CHAPTER 39

KATE

With winter's chill creeping in, Kate welcomed the warmth of the Nashville Airbnb. More than that, she welcomed the tiny face nestled in her arms. Her grandchild. So small. So helpless. Untouched by the darkness lurking in the world. Kate traced a gentle finger down the newborn's nose. A miracle.

Zoey, sitting close, hummed softly. "She's healthy, Mama. Happy." Her eyes shone with pride. "Since she was born, all I wanted was for her to meet you. So you could see her beautiful blue eyes. Too bad she's asleep now."

"Little Alice," Kate cooed. She looked down, heart swelling. "Oh, Zoey... there aren't any words."

"I know," Zoey whispered.

Kate had missed the birth. When Zoey went into labor, all she wanted was to be there. To support her daughter. Cayde refused. Said work kept him in Nashville. Then it was the cost of gas. One excuse after another. She'd put up with a lot—beatings, public humiliation, living in hotels and parking lots—but she'd never begged. Never got on her knees.

Until that night.

He didn't yell. Didn't scream. Just looked at her. Almost… sympathetic. Even then, he gave no apology. He just wrapped his arms around her as she cried, trying to console her. But nothing could make up for missing that moment.

Even if she'd tried to leave, there was no way out. She hadn't touched the keys to the SUV since they'd moved south. Cayde kept them on him at all times—sometimes even in the shower. And money? Forget it. He'd drained her accounts. Maxed out her credit cards. Kept every scrap of financial control in his wallet.

So Zoey did what she could. Rented an Airbnb for the weekend and brought Alice to her. It was the first time Kate had seen her daughter since the wedding. That was over a year ago. She'd missed the whole pregnancy. Zoey called often, asking for advice, but Kate knew what it really was. Zoey was checking in. Making sure she was okay.

Kate never admitted to what Cayde did. She couldn't lie, so she danced around the questions and laughed it off. He talked about his promises of buying a house someday. But Kate didn't believe him anymore. There was no money for hotels, let alone a home.

It was just another lie.

When Zoey called, saying she and Will were coming down, Cayde didn't have much of an excuse. Zoey insisted Kate stay with them for the weekend. But Cayde? Banned. He wasn't to go near them. Not after what he'd done at the wedding.

It led to a fight. A big one.

"After what you pulled, you can't blame them," Kate had tried to reason.

"You can't go," he snapped.

"If I don't, Zoey said she'll call the police." That shut him up. "She needs to see I'm okay. It's just a couple of nights."

"One night," he growled. "That's it."

So he dropped her off, told her he'd be back in the morning, and left. But she knew—he wasn't far. He never was.

"Mom, there's something you need to know," Zoey started softly.

The front door swung open, and Will stepped in, grinning, arms full of takeout. Kate's stomach growled at the smell.

"You're here!" He looked genuinely happy to see her.

"Will!" She handed Alice back to Zoey and hugged him tight. "How are you?"

They chatted and laughed, Kate soaking in every detail of the pregnancy, the birth, their life back in Virginia. Alice slept peacefully, her tiny face relaxed. By the time they finished dinner, Kate leaned back, staring at the ceiling, heart aching. She wished she could stay forever—not in the Airbnb, but with them. With her family.

But in the morning, Cayde would come. Drag her back.

"Mom?" Zoey's voice cut through her thoughts, sharp with concern. "What is that?"

"What is what?" Kate blinked, sitting up.

"In your hair." Zoey reached forward, fingers brushing through Kate's strands right along her hairline. "Is that a bruise?"

Kate jerked back. "It's nothing."

"Mom." Zoey's eyes scanned over Kate's body, searching. But it was winter. Sweaters, long pants, socks—everything hidden. No bruises on display. Makeup covered any trace left behind on her face.

Will's expression darkened, gaze shifting between the two women. "Did he do this?"

"No!" The lie shot out, followed by a nervous laugh. "I hit my head getting in the car the other day." She hated lying.

Their silence was louder than any accusation. They didn't believe her. And she could feel herself unraveling. "You know me," she babbled weakly. "Always clumsy. I never pay attention." But their faces stayed hard. The room went cold.

"Mom, I need to talk to you," Zoey said again. "It's about Cayde's past."

Kate's head twitched. "His past?"

Suddenly, loud knocks thundered through the Airbnb. All three of them turned. Will stood, jaw set, and moved to the door.

"Hon—" Zoey started, but Will cut her off with a raised hand. He opened it.

"Hey, buddy." The voice sent ice through Kate's veins.

"Cayde," Will replied evenly, blocking the doorway. "What can I do for you?"

"It's cold out here. Mind lettin' me in? I just need to see Kate." He was probably flashing that charming smile. His too-perfect grin that only made Kate feel sick. She used to find it endearing. Now, she hated it.

Kate stepped into view. Will glanced back, eyes wide with concern—a beacon of warmth. But behind him, lurking in the dark, Cayde's smile looked more like a snarl.

Will hesitated—just a second. It was all Cayde needed. He stepped through the threshold, brushing past. A chill washed over Kate.

"Cayde," Will said, voice louder now, bracing himself. He towered over Cayde, muscles tense. But Cayde turned, gave him a look that froze Will mid-step.

His gaze swept across the room, from Zoey—standing protectively by Alice's bassinet—to Kate. "Have I interrupted?"

"We just finished dinner." Kate forced a smile. "Did I forget something?"

"No," Cayde said, casually. "Just wanted to say hello before we leave. Maybe meet the baby?"

Zoey's eyes narrowed.

"Leave?" Kate echoed, frowning. "I just got here."

"I'll bring you back tomorrow."

"She isn't going anywhere," Zoey snapped, stepping closer. Will moved in beside her, after closing the door. "I want you to go. Mom is staying with us."

Kate felt trapped. Stuck between her family and the man she feared. The man she was married to. Her vision blurred. "Now, Zoey..." The words came out weak, almost pleading. She couldn't let her daughter talk to him like that. Not when the consequences could be so much worse.

"He's married, Mom," Zoey spat. "He's got kids. A record. Charges against him. Especially for abuse."

Something changed in Cayde. The smile vanished. The charm drained away. His eyes—cold and burning—turned on Kate. "Come on, now."

"Married?" Kate shook her head, voice trembling. "No... You said you'd been engaged once."

"He's married," Zoey pressed, relentless. "And he's got child abuse charges, too."

The room spun. Kate felt the blood leave her face. "Is this true?"

"Kate," Cayde growled, voice low and dangerous. "Get in the car."

"Mom, please!" Zoey begged. "Stay with us."

"Bella's in the car," Cayde warned. That did it. Kate couldn't leave her dog with him. "Let's go."

Will stepped forward, standing tall. "You need to leave. Now." His tone was steady, his stance defensive. "Or I'll call the police and have you charged with trespassing."

"The police?" Cayde's face twisted, anger warping into a sneer. "I work with the police! There isn't a precinct down here that doesn't know who I am."

"I don't care!" Zoey shot back, moving to the table where her phone lay next to empty takeout boxes. "I'll call them anyway."

It was like a switch flipped. Zoey's lunge for the phone triggered Cayde's advance. Will stepped forward, hand raised like he was trying to calm an enraged bull. Kate moved without thinking, heart pounding in her ears. She had to stop him. Had to protect her daughter. He couldn't get to Zoey—couldn't lay a finger on her. The bruises on Kate's body throbbed, screaming at her, *Not Zoey! Not my daughter!* Images exploded in her mind—Cayde's fists, his rage, the pain—and all she could see was Zoey taking those blows.

Her hand caught his shirt, yanked hard, spinning him around. She struck. Hard. "Don't you touch her!" The words tore from her throat, raw and savage.

Shock flashed across his face—she'd never hit him before. But it vanished in a second, replaced by rage. His fist slammed into her nose. Bone crunched. Light exploded behind her eyes.

Blood sprayed as she hit the floor, pain radiating through her skull.

The room blurred. Zoey's scream sounded distant, filled with fury. Will's form shifted, solid and protective, a human shield between Cayde and his wife and child. But the world was spinning, tilting, and Kate's vision darkened at the edges.

I can't let him hurt them. Please, God, not them!

It all sounded muffled. Like the world had been dunked underwater. Once, in a cheap extended-stay motel, after a brutal beating, she'd drawn herself a bath. Cayde had been in the other room, raging at a client over the phone. A missed payment, as usual. So he'd taken it out on her. She couldn't bear the sound of his voice, couldn't stand being in a world where he existed. So she'd slipped under the water, eyes open, staring up at the wavering surface. The world had seemed far away then. Just like now.

She wanted to be back there. Underwater. Gone.

A sharp cry cut through the fog. Alice.

Kate lifted her head, body trembling. She spotted the baby through Will's legs, still tucked in her bassinet. Tiny, pink fists clenched tight, face scrunched, gums bare as she screamed. Fear. Innocent, unblemished Alice was afraid. The commotion had touched her.

Kate's hand shot up to cover her mouth. Not to stop the blood. Not from the broken nose, not from the shouting, not even from Cayde. It was because Alice, that little miracle, had felt fear. And it was Kate's fault. A low, guttural moan escaped her.

"I'll go," she rasped, forcing herself to her feet. Her vision swam, blood dripping down her lips.

Zoey, phone in hand, stared at her, pale as a ghost. The yelling stopped.

"Kate," Will said softly. His face—so full of pain—made her heart clench. "You don't have to." His posture screamed he'd fight Cayde right here, right now, for her. But Kate just shook her head.

"I want to go." Her voice snapped like a whip. Tears mixed with blood, soaking her shirt. "I want to leave."

"Mama, no," Zoey's voice cracked. "I've called the police."

The dispatcher's voice echoed over the phone, asking for details. Demanding answers.

"I'm going. *We're* going." Kate glared at Cayde. "I don't want to be here when they arrive."

Cayde stepped forward, eyes locked on hers. He glanced at Zoey, at Will, at Alice's shrieking little form, then grabbed Kate's arm and yanked her toward the door.

"Don't go!" Zoey cried, rushing after them, face crumbling. "Please—stay!"

Kate turned, eyes hard. "Don't come over here."

Zoey froze, shock flooding her features. Then the door slammed shut. Cayde shoved Kate into the car, cursing at the mess of blood she'd made. He climbed in, hit the gas, and tore out of the driveway. Kate didn't sob. Didn't scream. But the tears didn't stop. As they sped away, it hit her—she'd never got to see little Alice's eyes.

CHAPTER 40

WENDY

Archie pointed at everything as they moved through the grocery store, naming the items he knew, and making up words for the ones he didn't. He waved at every person who passed, repeatedly greeting the strangers. Most smiled and waved back, delighted by the happy, talkative toddler. Wendy kept her head down and pushed the cart forward. At two, Archie was more curious and observant than ever.

Smiling politely at the cashier, she paid for the groceries with Cayde's debit card, asked for the receipt, and loaded the bags into the cart. Then she headed straight to customer service. The older woman behind the counter glanced up and smiled. A face Wendy knew well. Holly-Anne Brown. The one person Wendy could rely on. She'd timed every shopping trip to match Holly's shifts.

"I'm so sorry to be a bother," Wendy said, adjusting her sunglasses and reaching into the cart. She pulled out a case of lightbulbs and some cleaning supplies, placing them on the counter. "I forgot I'd put these in the cart until after I checked out."

"No worries, hon." Holly's eyes crinkled warmly. "Want it back on the card, or cash?"

"Cash, please."

Holly nodded knowingly, glancing at the receipt before counting out the exact change. She handed over the money, and Wendy reached for it, but her sleeve slipped, exposing a faint blue mark on her wrist. She pulled back, a bit too fast, heart thumping as she grabbed the cash and shoved it into her pocket. "Thanks, Holly." She meant it.

"Take care now." Holly's soft, withered hand rested briefly on Wendy's. "Bless your heart."

Most places wouldn't give cash back on a card return. But Holly bent the rules for her. Just a little. Just enough. It was an old-fashioned trick. One that could only be pulled off in a local grocery store like this. It had let her build up an emergency stash—slowly, steadily.

Wendy made her way back to the car. After strapping Archie into his seat, she glanced at her watch. She was running late. She needed to be home before Cayde got back. The gas gauge dipped below a quarter, the needle nearly resting on empty. It'd been like that for over a year. Cayde only let her put in five, maybe ten dollars' worth of gas at a time. Just enough to get around town. Never enough to go farther.

That had been her second trick: to use half the money, and pocket the rest. Take the receipt back to the clerk, ask for the remaining balance in cash. Just a few dollars at a time. But it added up.

She pulled into the apartment complex, rushing Archie inside. Groceries in hand, she quickly took him up to the apartment. The first thing she did was head for the pantry. She opened it and reached for a plastic canister of dried prunes. Prying off the lid, she revealed not wrinkled fruit but rolls of cash, tightly wound and packed inside. She fished in her pocket for the change from Holly and tucked it into the stash. Every little bit helped.

For a year and a half, she'd been saving. Scrounging. Getting just enough to have something—anything—set aside. When Cayde started trusting her again and let her use his card for groceries, she'd come up with the idea of returning unnoticed items for cash. Something small, something he wouldn't notice missing. And every time he got suspicious or threw a tantrum, he'd tear through the house, turning everything upside down in search of evidence.

She couldn't hide the money in a sock drawer. Couldn't stuff it under the couch cushions. So she chose a spot in plain sight—somewhere she knew he'd never think to check. Somewhere he'd never touch.

Wendy replaced the lid to the dried prunes canister.

The front door swung open, making her jump. Cayde stormed inside, briefcase dropping to the floor as he kicked off his shoes. Wendy's stomach clenched, but she forced herself to smile.

"I went shopping," she said quickly. "Dinner's running a bit late." She set the canister on the counter, heart hammering. She needed to keep him calm, keep his temper in check. She grabbed the receipt and slid it toward him as casually as she could.

Cayde sniffed, sitting down. He took the receipt, glanced over it briefly, and tossed it aside. Not interested. Wendy turned, intending to put the prune container back in the pantry, when Archie started fussing in his highchair.

This was always the hardest part: keeping Archie quiet, calm, controlled whenever Cayde was home. She quickly prepared a small bowl of cereal and a plate of fruit to keep him busy while she finished unloading the groceries.

But her eyes kept drifting to the canister—dangerously close to Cayde. *Don't be obvious*, she warned herself, pretending to stay busy. But the urge to snatch it up and shove it out of sight was overwhelming.

"Why do you buy those anyway?" Cayde's voice made her freeze.

Wendy turned slowly, gripping a loaf of bread. "What?"

"Those." He pointed to the prune container, wrinkling his nose. "What's the point?"

Her pulse roared in her ears. She forced herself to shrug, placing the bread on the counter. "They're good for constipation," she said lightly.

Cayde scoffed, wrinkling his nose. "Gross. I'm goin' to shower. Have somethin' ready to eat when I get out."

He got up and left the kitchen. Wendy waited, heart pounding until she heard the shower turn on. Only then did she let out a long, shaky breath.

That was too close. There'd been more and more close calls lately. She glanced at Archie, watching him stuff Froot Loops into his mouth. *There's enough,* she told herself. *Enough money.*

She looked at the pantry. The canister. Then back at her son.

We'll leave tomorrow. She'd take Archie and the cash.

And they'd be gone.

CHAPTER 41

AUTUMN

Autumn never thought she was claustrophobic. But living in Cayde's cramped mobile home was changing that. Days trapped inside, nights alone in the dark. Unable to block out the music blaring from parties next door or the dogs barking endlessly. She didn't know the neighbors. Cayde didn't either. She wasn't allowed to leave without him. Auutmn the place more than she feared the consequences of what she was about to ask.

Cayde sat on the bed, unlacing his shoes after another graveyard shift. Autumn sat on a chair nearby, brushing her hair, eyeing him. He didn't seem angry.

She swallowed. "Cayde?" She kept brushing, pretending it was casual. "All my stuff's crowding your space. I was thinking maybe I could stay with my parents until we find somewhere bigger?"

She braced herself. For the explosion. For him to call her stupid. Say a husband and wife living separately was ridiculous. But he just shrugged.

"Good idea."

She froze. Heart racing. She kept brushing and smiling at the vanity mirror. "I could see you after work in the evenings," she offered sweetly.

"Of course." He stood, stepping toward her. "But you won't leave the house without my permission. I need to know where you are." His fingers brushed along her arm. Up her neck. Toying with her hair.

Autumn nodded. "Of course." It made no sense, but she didn't care. She'd be out of this hellhole. Back home. Maybe after some time apart, Cayde would return to his old self.

"If you're gonna be out of my sight," he murmured, "I want to make sure other men aren't lookin' at you."

She laughed lightly. "What men, Cayde?"

His hand tightened. Tugging her hair. Pulling her head back. "There's that neighbor of yours. What's his name? Justin?" Cayde dropped down to his knees. Eyes level with hers. His hand still gripped her hair. "I know how he looks at you."

"What?" A chill ran through her. Panic flickered. What was he talking about?

"I know just how to make him stop." He yanked hard.

Autumn yelped, hitting the floor. Cayde was on her in an instant, pinning her down. "Cayde, wait—"

But he didn't touch her pants. Didn't lift her shirt. Just yanked her head up, pulled something off the vanity, and— *snip.* Red strands floated around her.

"Cayde!" she screamed. "Stop it!"

"Shut up." His voice dropped to a growl. "You want to live with your parents? This is my condition."

She bit her lip, sobbing into the carpet as he hacked at her hair. Wild. Jagged. Chunks fell around her face. She cried and cried. But she never stopped him.

* * *

When she arrived at her parents' house, suitcase in hand, they gaped.

"Oh, Autumn!" Her mother's eyes went wide, a horrified look sweeping across her face. "Your hair!"

Autumn managed a smile and made sure it reached her eyes. "I should've gone to a salon, but—" She shrugged. "I just couldn't stand it. I'll call Morgan to help me fix it later."

It was practically a pixie cut. Once, her auburn hair had brushed past her waist. Now it barely skimmed her jawline. The reflection in the mirror reminded her of the worn Raggedy Ann doll her mom still had hidden in a closet somewhere. But seeing her old home—the porch, the familiar door, her parents waiting inside—she didn't care. For the first time in weeks, she felt safe. Warm. Loved. So what if she'd had to sacrifice her hair?

Her dad took her bag inside, and her mom pulled her into a tight hug. A hug she leaned into, body sagging. Letting go of the tension that had wrapped itself around her like a noose. In that embrace, she felt herself unwind. The first moment of peace since the wedding.

In her old room, staring at the walls she'd grown up with, she thought about the life she'd left behind. The apartment she'd shared with Tania, Kathy, and Morgan. She'd dropped her classes to marry Cayde. They'd found a replacement for the lease almost immediately. Autumn wondered if they liked whatever girl had moved into her room more than her.

Dinner was harder than expected. Her parents and brother asked question after question, eager for details. How was married life? What was the honeymoon like? Was she adjusting to life in the trailer?

She danced around the truth. Smiled through the lies. Because the problem wasn't that Cayde was angry all the time. Sometimes, she caught glimpses of the man she'd fallen for. He loved her. Didn't he? Why else would he have married her?

Drained from too many sleepless nights, she changed into pajamas and crawled into bed early. There was a soft knock. She looked up as her younger brother, Jeremiah, slipped inside.

"Can we talk?"

"Of course!" She patted the bed beside her. He'd grown so much in the past few months.

He sat down, shifting awkwardly. "I was at the park today," he said slowly, "with some friends."

Autumn frowned. "Okay?"

"I saw Cayde there."

Her heart skipped. "Cayde?"

"Yeah. He was talking to a woman, and..." He trailed off, glancing away.

"What?" Autumn's pulse pounded. "What is it?"

"He looked like he was flirting with her."

The words hit like a punch to the gut. She shook her head. "No. Cayde wouldn't—"

"I'm just telling you what I saw," Jeremiah insisted. "Thought you should know."

Her head spun. Flirting? Nothing would surprise her anymore. But she didn't want anyone to know. Not her family. Not him. She'd swallow the shame before admitting it.

"No, it's just..." She forced herself to sound calm. Even. "Cayde's just like that. He's... charming. Sometimes it comes off wrong, but he doesn't mean anything by it. He even brought flowers for all my roommates when we started dating."

Jeremiah's frown deepened. "If you say so. It's good to have you back, Autumn. Goodnight."

"Night," she whispered, watching him close the door behind him. She buried her face in her hands. Why would Cayde flirt when he was married to her? If he was acting like his old self with someone else, why had he turned so cold toward her? What had she done? What was wrong with her?

She pressed her face into the pillow, wrapping herself in her childhood blankets, and tried to forget through sleep.

CHAPTER 42

CLAIRE

Cayde was drunk. No doubt about it. He tore through the streets after they left the bowling alley, swerving like he had something to prove. Claire tightened her seatbelt, stealing glances at his face. His eyes barely stayed on the road.

"I could see what you were doin'." Cayde's voice was low. Snarling. "I saw it all."

"See what?" What did it matter what she did or talked about with her friends? She and Cayde weren't together. Not anymore. But she knew better than to say that out loud. Reasoning with him sober was bad enough. She turned her gaze forward, praying he'd get pulled over and arrested for a DUI.

His words kept tumbling out. Faster. Louder. He wasn't even talking to her—just rambling. Muttering. Arguing with himself.

"My buddy in Cross Plains owns a rock quarry. You know how many people go missin' every year in Tennessee? Bodies never found?" He laughed, slurred and hollow. "Easy. Crush 'em under rocks. Bones blend right in. Blood dries like clay."

Her stomach twisted. He blew past the exit toward her home, foot pressed harder on the gas. He took the off-ramp. The one leading to Cross Plains.

Panic flared hot in her chest. She fumbled with the seatbelt, unbuckling and scrambling into the back seat. He grabbed for her, and the car lurched left. She swatted his hand away, shrinking as far back as she could, curling up like a cornered animal.

"Claire," he snapped, gaze flicking to the rearview. "Get back up here!"

"No!" she shouted. "Turn around."

"Just—"

"Around, Cayde! Take me home!"

It broke through the shroud of drunken rage that had wrapped itself around him. He slowed the car and pulled off onto a side street. He headed back toward her place, muttering under his breath.

Claire huddled in the back seat, shaking. Eyes locked on his reflection in the mirror. He looked calmer. Tired. Like the fight had drained out of him.

"You need help," she murmured. "You need to see someone for your anger."

"I do not need therapy." He bristled, jaw tight.

She didn't argue. Just watched his face slowly relax. His shoulders dropped.

"If I did..." He looked at her again. His voice softened. "If I went... would you put the ring back on?"

"Maybe." A lie. But she'd say anything. Anything to keep him from turning back to that quarry.

Silence filled the car. The rest of the drive passed in tense quiet. When he finally pulled into the garage, Claire jumped out and bolted inside. She heard his heavy footsteps trailing behind.

"Where are you goin'?"

"To bed," she threw over her shoulder. "I'm through with tonight."

"You're through when I say you are!" His shout echoed off the walls. "Don't forget how much you owe me. We're only in this mess because of you. Because you haven't paid!" His eyes darted around wildly. "You know what I'll do if you try to outsmart me? I'll put a bullet in your fuckin' face, Claire."

He glanced around. Scowling. Looking for something. His briefcase. Claire realized it wasn't there. No briefcase—no gun. She took the chance and bolted up the stairs.

"Get back here!" he roared, stomping after her. "Get back here or I'll kill myself, Claire! I'll do it. It'll be your fault!"

She sprinted, heart hammering, taking the steps two at a time. Then a heavy *clunk*. A thud. A crash. She whirled, eyes wide. Cayde tumbled down the stairs, landing face-first at the bottom.

She froze, staring. He didn't move.

She took a step down. Then another. *God,* she hoped he didn't get back up. Hoped his neck was broken. Hoped he was—

His fingers twitched. A groan escaped him. Slowly, he pushed himself up. Blood and drool dripped from his lip as he looked up at her. Swaying.

"Claire." His voice was thick. Heavy. He reached for her, trying to steady himself.

Claire's pulse pounded. She backed up, then turned and bolted to her room, slamming the door shut behind her. She pressed her ear to the wood, listening. When she didn't hear the sound of his footfalls coming after her, she breathed a sigh of relief and locked the door.

It took her half an hour to stop shaking. Even longer to change for bed. And even after that, sleep didn't come easy. When it did, her dreams were twisted. Dark. Violent. Sheets coiling around her like vines, pinning her, trapping her. Crawling up to her throat.

They were—*heavy*.

She jerked awake. Blinked. Cayde's face hovered above her. Eyes burning. He'd sobered up. No longer drunk. Just furious. It wasn't the blankets that had been heavy. It was him.

"You think a lock can stop me?" he hissed, leaning close. "If I want to come in, I'll *come in*." His hands moved. Something tight was tugging at her neck. A belt.

Claire's pulse hammered. She swallowed, but it cinched tighter. Her breath hitched, coming in small, desperate gasps. She tried to scream, but nothing came out. Gagging and choking, she clawed at the leather cutting into her skin.

"If I want you," he growled, tightening the belt, "I'll have you."

The world started to blur. Black splotches danced across her vision. Pressure built behind her eyes. Blood pounded in her ears. She thrashed weakly, vision narrowing. Everything faded. Her lungs burned, fighting for air that wouldn't come. She saw him—face red, veins bulging in his neck, teeth bared like some rabid beast.

He leaned closer, spitting fury. "There's nothing you can do to keep me out."

The room started to tilt. She was slipping. Fading.

Then, it stopped.

The belt slackened. Air rushed in, sharp and jagged. She coughed and gasped, yanking it off her neck, chest heaving.

He tossed the belt aside and stood over her, watching. Enjoying her fear. She curled up, still gasping, shuddering.

"You piss me off again," he whispered, voice low and dangerous, "and I won't stop."

He grabbed her face, fingers digging into the soft flesh under her eyes. Pinning her head in place. "Understand?"

Claire nodded frantically, tears spilling over. He held on a second longer. Squeezed. Then let go. He stood up and walked out. The knob dangled uselessly, snapped clean off.

Claire rolled onto her side, her hand clutching her throat. Her heart hammered under her ribs. She breathed in and out, ragged and shuddering breaths. Again. And again. And then she cried.

CHAPTER 43

JACK

A few police officers gathered outside the dingy gas station, their quiet conversation barely audible over the hum of traffic from the highway. Jack and Blair pulled up, the tires crunching on loose gravel as they parked. The strong scent of gasoline wafted through the air. Introductions were quick and businesslike. No unnecessary chit-chat, just facts.

A call had come in at four in the morning. Someone had spotted Cayde Miller *and* the victim seventy miles north. Jack and Blair had practically flown up the highway to get there.

The gas station, isolated and worn down by years of neglect, had the kind of atmosphere that made you want to get in and out as quickly as possible. It hadn't seen a decent cleaning in a decade at least. It was dressed only with cracked asphalt in the lot and a faded neon sign that flickered intermittently. Grime smeared the windows. The doors creaked under the weight of never-replaced hinges.

Blair led the way inside. The fluorescent lights buzzed overhead. An unflattering yellow glowed over everything, making the store feel even more claustrophobic. Behind the counter stood the clerk—a heavyset man with an uneven, patchy beard. His stained T-shirt stretched over his large belly, and his skin had the pallor of someone who hadn't seen sunlight in far too long.

"Did Mr. Miller come into the store?" Blair asked, her voice cutting through the stagnant air like a knife. She'd set the introductions up fast, and immediately both her and Jack knew who should ask the question; the clerk's gaze lingered on Blair much longer than Jack.

The clerk nodded slowly, wiping his hands on his jeans. He didn't look particularly nervous, but there was an uneasiness in the way he shifted from foot to foot, like he wasn't used to being the center of attention. "Yeah, he came in. Paid with cash." His voice was gravelly, like he'd spent his life inhaling cigarette smoke. His mouth pulled into a thin, uneven line. "I only knew to call 'cause I saw his face on the TV. Y'all been lookin' for him." He jerked his thumb toward a small, boxy television perched high on a shelf in the corner.

"And the woman?" Blair pressed, her eyes narrowing slightly as she leaned in.

"Yeah, I saw her," the clerk said, his hand scratching absentmindedly at his beard. His gaze flicked nervously to the parking lot, as if expecting the car to still be there. "She stayed in the car. Didn't come in."

Jack stepped forward, sensing something off in the clerk's tone. "Did she look okay?"

The clerk hesitated, his lips tightening as he thought about it. "I think she was asleep," he finally said, but there was uncertainty in his voice, like he was still trying to convince himself.

Jack's gut twisted, the tension in the air growing thicker by the second. He exchanged a glance with Blair.

"What time did this happen?" Blair asked, her voice still calm.

"Last night, maybe 'round seven or eight," the clerk answered, still scratching at his beard, his eyes darting nervously between the agents. "I didn't call it in 'til this morning when I saw his face on the news." He glanced at the clock. "I was supposed to get off at five."

Blair narrowed her eyes. "Did you notice any other details?"

The clerk cleared his throat. "There was someone else, too. Another car."

Jack's attention snapped to the clerk. "Another car?"

"It pulled up before he went into the store," the clerk explained, licking his dry lips. "Didn't get gas or nothin'. Just parked there. Miller got out of his car and into the other one for a few minutes. Talked to someone, then came in here to pay for gas and buy some snacks. The other car left while he was inside."

Jack's jaw clenched as Blair's eyes flickered with suspicion. An accomplice. Someone was helping Cayde Miller, and from the grim look on Blair's face, Jack knew she already had a pretty good idea who it was.

Before they could ask more, an officer poked his head around the corner from a small back room. "We've got the security camera's footage."

Jack and Blair followed the officer inside, where grainy black-and-white footage played on a tiny monitor. It was rough quality, but it clearly showed Cayde's car pulling up. Cayde's wife's side of the vehicle was angled out of view, so they couldn't see her. The footage showed Cayde getting out of the car, entering another vehicle that had pulled up moments before, staying inside for several minutes, then coming into the gas station. The second car pulled away as Cayde browsed the aisles, picking up snacks like he didn't have a care in the world.

The officer paused the footage, zooming in on the departing car's license plate. "We've got the plate."

"Run it," Jack said sharply, his voice hard. The officer left immediately, leaving Jack and Blair to study the footage in silence.

Blair tapped her phone screen, scrolling through recent calls. "Myers, look at the timestamp." She held the phone up. "This was almost two hours after we contacted Veronica."

"Veronica?" The officer returned, his face grim. "Same name. The plate's registered to a Veronica Webb."

Blair raised an eyebrow, not surprised in the least. "There you have it. So, what's the plan, Myers?"

Jack exhaled, rubbing the back of his neck. "Cayde Miller could be anywhere by now. But *she* knows something—either where he's going or what he's already done. She's an official suspect now."

Blair nodded, the tension between them electric with anticipation. "Let's go get her, then."

CHAPTER 44

SOPHIE

Sophie's run-down Toyota bounced more than was comfortable on the highway roads. Noah and Charlie were quieter than usual in the back seat.

"Mom, I thought you were dropping us off at Dad's," Noah said.

"Actually..." Sophie checked the rearview mirror. But she wasn't looking at Charlie, who sat in the back seat; she was checking the cars behind her. "The three of us are going on a little road trip! We are going to Virginia."

"Does Dad know?" Noah's voice sounded suspicious.

"Yup." A blatant lie.

"Well, what about school?"

"Noah." Sophie smiled at him. "Relax, honey. Tell you what, we can get some snacks for the road. We have to stop at a gas station anyway."

Sophie's phone buzzed on the car console. Cayde. She declined the call, and he called again. Four times. Finally, Sophie turned up the music to overpower the vibrations. Cayde had bought her the brand-new smartphone after hers had broken. He claimed it was a wedding present, not apologizing for the damage he'd done to the last one. But, in all honesty, her last phone had truly kicked the bucket only after *she'd* thrown it.

They drove twelve or so miles before stopping, and Sophie handed Noah her card after she scanned the gas pump. "Two things each! But they both must be under five bucks, okay?"

"Okay!" Charlie said and bolted for the store. Noah hesitated, looking at his mom a moment longer, then followed Charlie. He knew something was up.

As soon as their backs were turned, her smile dropped. She filled the car up with gas and then decided to grab herself something to drink. She entered the little food mart and found Noah and Charlie discussing if they wanted to share all four items or keep the two for themselves.

Sophie grabbed the largest water bottle she could find and brought it up to the counter.

"That's one heck of a bruise!" the cashier said. "How'd you get that?"

Sophie's hand went up to her jaw, where an ugly splotch of yellow and blue painted the place left of her chin. "Tripped up the stairs while carrying groceries. Couldn't catch myself."

The cashier whistled. "Looks like it hurts."

It certainly had.

"Boys, come on!" Sophie called. "Bring your things up here!"

* * *

"There is only one bed." Noah looked at the motel room with a frown.

"Sorry, kiddo." Sophie wrapped her arms around him from behind, resting her chin on his forehead. "It's only one night."

Charlie flopped on the bed. "I love this place!" he said. "I like hotels."

"It's a *motel*," Noah corrected.

Sophie turned Noah around to face her. "What kind of pizza should we order? You get to pick."

"Me?" He still looked suspicious. "Even Hawaiian?"

Charlie spouted a long and drawn-out, "Eww!"

Sophie nodded. "Even Hawaiian."

Noah thought about this for a moment, the corner of his mouth pulling into a smirk at the new power granted to him by his mother. But in the end, he chose Charlie's favorite. "Let's get pepperoni."

The act of kindness made Sophie wrap her arms around Noah and plant a dozen kisses on his face. He protested and pushed her away, but she got in a few more. "You," she said, "are the world's bestest big brother."

Noah wiped his blushing cheeks with his sleeve. "Even better than Uncle Tanner?"

Sophie thought for a moment, then nodded. "Uncle Tanner *is* pretty cool, huh?"

Charlie, who was celebrating the pizza choice by jumping up and down on the bed, asked, "Is Uncle Tanner coming with us to Virginia?"

"No, he's not."

"Does he know we're going?" Noah asked. The boy was shrewd.

"No," Sophie said, unable to tell him any more lies.

"Does Cayde know?"

Her husband's name made her ribs, jaw, and skull ache. "No."

Noah nodded at this. "Good." It was all he said.

He stopped asking questions after that, but Sophie knew he understood the situation wasn't as it seemed. Maybe he knew the truth: Sophie was running. And by God, she would not leave her children behind where that man could get to them.

They ordered their pizza and turned on the television. Both the boys wanted to watch a rerun of *The X-Files*. Sophie claimed it was too scary, but in the end, she gave in. They all crammed onto the bed, the boys on either side of her. They held onto one another tightly during the scarier scenes. All three of them jumped as there was a knock on the door.

Sophie laughed, getting up from the bed. "It's just the pizza." She unlocked the chain latch, the deadbolt, and the knob, then swung it open. The second she did, she wished the motel had peepholes in the door. More than that, she wished she hadn't opened the door at all.

Two police officers stared back at her. One man and one woman. The man looked into the room, saw Noah and Charlie staring back at them with wide eyes, and then made a motion to move forward into the room.

"Got 'em," he said. He pushed past Sophie.

"Hey!" Sophie reached out, but the other officer caught her hands and pushed her up against the door.

"Mom!" Charlie screamed. It broke everything within Sophie.

"Sophie Miller, you are under arrest for custodial interference. You have the right to remain silent. Anything you say can and will be used against you in a court of law. You have the right to an attorney. If you cannot afford an attorney, one will be provided for you—"

"Mom?" Noah was dodging the other officer, his eyes wide and face pale. "What's happening?!"

"Wait, let my kids come with me," Sophie begged. "You don't understand!" Now both of her kids were screaming. Sophie's voice turned just as shrill. "Leave them alone!"

Chaos ensued, but the woman officer held tight to Sophie. "Ma'am, do not resist!" She pulled her out into the hallway. They began to march her toward the police car.

Sophie saw a familiar figure leaning against a black Corvette, watching. Cayde. He smirked. Sophie felt a rage deep within her. He'd turned her in. He'd followed them all. Cayde would rather see her in jail than let her leave him.

"Listen to me," Sophie spoke quietly to the officer arresting her. She could still hear her children crying and yelling. "The man who turned me in is their stepfather. I don't know what he told you, but *please listen*."

The officer opened the car door. "Watch your head, ma'am."

Sophie turned. Faced the woman directly. "Do not let them get into his car."

The officer placed her hand on Sophie's shoulder, about to push her down into the vehicle, but hesitated.

"I'm begging you. Call their father, Mark. Only let him take them home."

The officer stared at her and then nodded. "Your head, ma'am."

Sophie sat down in the police car, handcuffs around her wrists, and watched helplessly as the handleless door slammed shut.

Behind it, Cayde grinned viciously.

CHAPTER 45

WENDY

Wendy yanked down the suitcase from the storage closet the second Cayde left for work. She tossed in a few things for herself but stuffed the rest with Archie's things—clothes, diapers, essentials. He "helped" by pulling out folded items and placing them back in, completely out of order.

She slipped the cash into a Ziplock bag and tucked it into the suitcase's outer pocket. Then she grabbed a pen and started scribbling a note for Cayde. Short and direct. She and Archie were leaving. She'd take the car, fill it with gas, and drive north for hours—until she found a motel where they could lay low for a night. Then she'd call her mom to say they were safe but wouldn't be in touch for a while. No locations. No contact.

Friends, family—all off-limits for now. Running to them was the first thing Cayde would expect. If she really wanted to shake him, she'd have to put Nashville and everyone she knew in her rearview mirror. Far behind. One day, when it was safe, maybe she'd circle back. But not now.

It would cost more than she wanted, but there was a reason she'd endured all those months of rage and pain. She'd been building toward this. Planning. Saving. Now, finally, she had enough to keep her and Archie going for a while. If she was careful. She'd need to find work quickly.

Her phone buzzed. She ignored it and stayed focused on rifling through the desk drawers. Birth certificates, social security cards, everything they'd need to start over. The phone buzzed again, then a text from Cayde lit up the screen: "Wendy, pick up!"

Cayde always called to check in, making sure she was where she should be, doing what she was supposed to—but not this early. He'd barely been gone an hour. She scrambled and dialed him back, forcing her voice to stay steady. "Cayde?"

"I got a flat." He sounded furious. "Had to switch it out for the spare. I'm comin' back to the apartment. I'm around the corner. Start another pot of coffee."

Her pulse went wild. She didn't have time to even buckle Archie in, let alone drive off. Minutes, that's all she had. "Of course," she chirped, forcing a sweetness she didn't feel. "See you in a bit." She hung up and bolted into the bedroom.

She zipped the suitcase up. No idea where to stash it. She tried to just stick it back in the storage closet— it was too full. Bulging with Archie's stuff. So she dragged it into the laundry room and heaped a pile of dirty clothes over it. A rush job, but it'd have to do. Cayde never did housework anyway.

The front door rattled. Wendy sucked in a breath and tried to keep the panic off her face as she stepped out, praying the mess in the laundry stayed hidden.

Cayde stormed in. Wendy poked her head out of the laundry room, trailing him. "What happened to the tire?"

"Ran over a fuckin' construction nail." He threw his briefcase on the floor. He brushed past the note she'd left on the counter. She held her breath, watching as he strode by, not sparing it a glance. With a quick swipe, she snatched it up and shoved it into her pocket.

He headed into the bedroom, stepping around Archie, who was still surrounded by clothes he'd pulled from the suitcase. "He's makin' a mess, Wendy."

She scooped Archie up, grabbing a few items in one hand, forcing a smile. "He was helping me with laundry."

"And diggin' through drawers," Cayde said, nodding at the desk, where the bottom drawer was left wide open, exposing folders stuffed with important documents. Wendy's gut twisted. She hadn't shut it.

Cayde dropped to one knee, rifling through it.

"I don't think he took anything out," Wendy blurted, throat dry.

"I'm not worried about that," Cayde snapped, shoving papers aside. "Lookin' for my damn tire warranty."

"Oh." Wendy backed out. Her smile strained her cheeks. "Come on, Archie, let's get you dressed for the day." The moment she turned, the false smile dropped into a glare. Bastard was fucking up everything. Her eyes darted around, scanning the house, double-checking for anything that might tip him off.

Cayde finally found his warranty, but the shop didn't have any openings until tomorrow. Which meant he'd be home all day, watching TV, complaining, eating everything in the fridge. Hovering. Watching. Days like that were always tense. Now, it felt like a noose tightening.

Archie seemed to sense the tension. He always cried more when Cayde was around. Today, he was worse—flinging his toys, throwing himself to the floor, faking cries to get her attention. Making dinner was nearly impossible with him in her arms. He squirmed and whined.

Normally, Wendy would let him cry it out. Teach him it wouldn't work. But not with Cayde here. Keeping Archie quiet, out of sight, that was the priority. She'd learned the hard way that Cayde's frustration turned brutal when Archie got too loud. Half her bruises came from trying to shield their son. The less attention he got from Cayde, the better.

"Can you get him to shut the fuck up?" Cayde snapped, jabbing the remote to turn the TV up. "You just baby him."

Wendy started bouncing Archie gently. "Shh, it's okay, honey. Want a snack?" Archie's cries rose. He pounded his tiny fists, throwing his head back. "Or maybe a nap?"

"He *needs* discipline," Cayde barked. "Give him to me."

"No!" The word shot out before she could stop it.

Cayde's eyes narrowed. He stood up. "Bring him here. Now."

Panic rose in her stomach. Her thumb hooked into Archie's waistband, tugging back as if checking something. She scrunched her nose, forcing a look of disgust. "He's had an accident."

Cayde paused, then sat back down. He was more than ready to spank the kid, but a dirty diaper? No thanks. Wendy whisked Archie into the nursery, heart pounding. She murmured soft words in his ear, rocking him gently until the sobs quieted and his head slumped onto her shoulder. He'd tired himself out.

Cayde's demand had shaken her to the core. She had to leave tonight. If she took her car, Cayde wouldn't be able to follow her—not until he got that spare replaced. It was risky to move while he was here, but Wendy felt she had no choice.

There was a delicate line she'd have to walk. She took away his empty beer can, replaced it with another. Alcohol sharpened his temper, but it knocked him out cold too. She'd endure whatever she had to tonight if it meant a better chance of sneaking out.

Time dragged. Archie woke from his nap. Dinner was made. Eaten. Evening settled in. Cayde watched TV, made a few phone calls. He never went into the laundry room. Each second stretched thin, vibrating like a wire. So close now. So damn close. She'd kept his temper reined in, but he was already irritable over the flat tire. She couldn't afford one wrong move.

Dishes done, kitchen cleaned. She pretended to read until, finally, around midnight, Cayde turned in. Wendy slid into bed next to him, heart hammering as she focused on every move. Pajamas were chosen for function—sweatpants and a black crewneck. Easy to move in, hard to spot in the dark. Sneakers were already stashed in the laundry room, hidden under the pile of clothes masking the suitcase.

She waited. Listened. Tracked his breathing until it settled into a deep rhythm. Then waited longer. Hours, maybe.

When she finally moved, it was slow. She turned the handle inch by inch, easing the door open. A glance back. His form was still. She felt nothing—not guilt, not fear. Just the hard certainty that she was doing the right thing.

She crept into Archie's room. Scooped him up from his crib. He stirred, little fists rubbing at his eyes, but didn't fully wake. She paused, letting him nestle into her shoulder, then slipped out toward the front door.

The hard part now. One-handed, she reached for the deadbolt. Click. She froze, pulse hammering in her ears. The clock ticked. The AC hummed. She waited. Nothing. Slowly, she turned the knob, easing the door open as the weather strip dragged against the mat. She stretched out, fingers brushing the car keys hanging beside the door. She wrapped her fingers around the keys before lifting them. No jingle.

Then she stepped outside.

The air hit her like a slap, sharp and cool. She hurried down the stairs. She unlocked the car and set Archie into his seat. He mumbled but settled. That weight on her shoulders—it lightened, just a bit. She'd actually done it. The worst part was over. She just needed to grab the suitcase.

She turned back up the stairs, careful, silent. Eased the door open, slipping inside—Cayde was standing right behind it.

Wendy barely had time to draw breath before his hand lashed out, grabbing a fistful of her hair. Pain shot through her scalp as he yanked her inside. She was no better than a ragdoll—thrown forward, body skidding on the floor, belly first. Panic surged through her, but she forced herself to roll, eyes locking onto him as he loomed. The door slammed shut behind him, sealing them inside.

"Where the hell do you think you're goin'?" His voice was low, almost calm, but the rage radiated off him in waves.

She scrambled to push herself up, knees scraping against the floor, but his socked foot drove into her ribs, knocking the air out of her lungs. She gasped, curling in, but he wasn't done. Another kick—this time to her jaw. Her vision exploded in a flash of white, and for a terrifying second, she couldn't tell up from down.

Rough fingers clamped onto the back of her neck and hauled her up. He drove her into the kitchen bar. Pain shot through her spine as her body slammed against the counter's edge. *Move*, her brain screamed. She twisted, legs kicking blindly. One knee caught him in the stomach, and he doubled over with a sharp "*Oof*!"

But it only bought her a second. She spun, lunging for the door. Almost there—almost free—

His hand slammed between her shoulder blades, sending her crashing forward. Her face collided with the door, and the world exploded in a burst of blinding pain. Her skull reverberated with the impact. She crumpled to the floor.

Get up! Get up! She fought through the stars in her vision, willed herself to move, but he was on her again, jerking her up by her arm. Instinct kicked in. She lashed out, her open palm cracking against his face with every ounce of strength she had left. His head snapped to the side, and his grip loosened just enough for her to wrench free.

She staggered back, heart hammering, and rounded the kitchen bar. She placed it between them. He recovered, eyes wild. They moved in tandem—he stepped left, she shifted right. Eyes locked on each other. The muscles in his jaw twitched, rage building. The only way this ended was with blood. Hers or his.

He feinted to the left, and she turned—hand closing around the biggest knife in the block.

"*Back off!*" she screamed, spinning around, the blade flashing in the dim light. The serrated edge sliced across Cayde's palm, and he jerked back.

He bellowed, clutching his bleeding hand, but he didn't retreat. Didn't break eye contact. Just stood there. Glaring.

"Stay back!" Wendy shouted again, voice shaking but fierce. Blood dripped from her nose down past her lips. She could taste it—metallic, hot, and maddening. "I'll kill you!" She slashed again, wild and desperate, forcing him to step back.

Somewhere below them, a loud noise sounded. Someone was awake. Listening. If anyone called the cops, it might be enough to stall him, buy her time.

But Cayde just tilted his head, eyes narrowing. "Give me the knife, Wendy," he murmured, voice low and coaxing. The same voice he'd used when they were dating. The same one that used to make her heart flutter. Now it only fueled her hatred. "You're not goin' anywhere." His lips curled, too calm, too collected. It sent chills racing down her spine.

"Aren't I?" Her voice was raw. "Archie's in the car. I will stab you if you try to stop me." She backed toward the door, hand fumbling behind her. *Find the knob. Open it. Get out. Run.* But her fingers shook too hard, slipping over the cold metal. She turned the knob.

He saw it. The moment of weakness. He lunged.

She twisted, the knife swinging wide—but she was off balance, and he was faster. His hand clamped around her wrist, crushing her bone. He pushed her arm forward through the open crack of the door, then he slammed it shut against her limb. Wendy cried out. He did it a second time. She pulled her arm back through and dropped the knife. He scrambled for it.

But the door—*the door was open.* Wendy didn't think. She turned and threw herself outside. She could see the car, parked just down the stairs. Archie inside it, his head tilted to the side as he slept in his car seat. Suitcase and money be damned—she just had to leave! It was all so close.

A mass slammed into her back, and Wendy staggered forward, right over the stairs. The car, Archie, the plan to escape, all of it whirled and spun from view in a kaleidoscope of failure until there was a crack against her skull, and everything went black.

CHAPTER 46

AUTUMN

Autumn's fingers tightened around the phone as the shout blasted through the receiver.

"Why the hell have you not been answerin' my phone calls?"

She froze, glancing around the kitchen. Her mother moved in and out of the doorway, balancing bags from their recent outing. If she heard Cayde's rage, she gave no sign.

"I was out with my mom," Autumn murmured, lowering her voice.

"Where?"

"Just running errands." She tried to sound casual, not dismissive. Too light, and he'd think she was brushing him off. Too firm, and he'd call it disrespect. "My phone died."

"We haven't spoken in days," he snapped. "First, you move back to your mom's, I'm breakin' my back workin' overtime so we can afford a bigger place, and now you ignore me? Autumn, do you have any idea how that makes me feel?"

"I'm sorry, Cayde. I didn't mean—"

"You need to be available when I call. What am I to you? A stranger? I've changed everythin' in my life to take care of you, to build the future we talked about, and you can't even pick up the damn phone?"

Guilt clawed at her chest. "I'm sorry," she whispered, hating the sincerity in her voice.

It seemed to deflate his fury, if only a little. "We need to talk. I'm comin' to get you."

She didn't argue, and soon enough, he was pulling up to her parents' house, leading her to his car without another word. The drive was tense. He wasn't speaking—just fuming in silence. He took her all the way back to the cramped mobile home, that suffocating space she'd thought she was free from. He parked, led her inside, and they sat at the tiny kitchen table.

Strands of her red hair were still on the floor. Her hand floated up to her head, running her fingers through the choppy few inches she had left.

Cayde paced back and forth, each step tightening the knot in her stomach. "You're not goin' to like this," he finally said, throwing her a quick, assessing glance. "I got a letter in the mail today. From my ex-wife."

Autumn felt the room tilt, her mind struggling to catch up. Ex-wife? He never mentioned being married before. "Your what?"

"Before I met you, I got married. I was really young—it was annulled ages ago. Or at least, I thought it was. Apparently, we never finalized it. I thought we did—I signed the papers and everythin'."

Autumn's mouth dropped open. She stared, trying to make sense of what he was saying. He was still married? So what—*their* marriage wasn't even real? What about their vows? The marriage license they signed together? None of it would be legal if he was still married to someone else.

"I can't believe it," Cayde said, taking a seat beside her. His voice softened, taking on that pleading, almost broken tone he used when he wanted her sympathy. "I don't want you to be mad. It's not my fault. I talked to a lawyer—he says I have to divorce you *and* her. Then we can remarry. Make it right between us. You know I love you, Autumn. I swear I didn't know. I'd never hurt you—"

Autumn yanked her hand from his. "You told me you'd never been married before. And now you're saying you have to divorce *me* to divorce *her*? I might be pregnant, Cayde! And now our marriage might not even be legal?" Her mind whirled with her brother's voice—what if there was another woman? Another life he was hiding? "How can I even believe you? How do I know you're not lying about everything?"

His eyes went dark, a familiar flicker of something dangerous sparking behind them. Before she could react, his arm swept across the table, sending everything—cups, papers, a ceramic dish—crashing to the floor. She stumbled back, heart hammering.

"Don't you dare put this on me!" He lunged, shoving the table over with a roar. It crashed onto its side, the clatter deafening in the small space. He pointed a finger, inches from her face, eyes blazing with fury. "You *will* sign those divorce papers, or I'll tell everyone that you knew. That you married me knowin' I was still married. We'll both go to jail, Autumn. Is that what you want? You think I'm goin' to jail?" His voice dropped, a low, deadly growl. "You're gonna sign that damn paper. You even think about goin' to the police, or gettin' a lawyer—" He leaned in, his breath hot against her skin. "No one can help you. Not a soul. Cross me, and I'll make sure you're beggin' for death."

Autumn's heart felt like it was beating out of her chest. He was too close, his presence suffocating. She shrank back, tears spilling down her cheeks.

He kept going. "I'll kill you, Autumn. You. Your family. Your mother, your father, your brothers—" His hand dropped, fingers brushing lightly against her stomach. "I'll save you for last. After the baby's born, I'll kill them all. And I'll make sure you watch."

The words, so calm, so measured—they hit her harder than any punch ever could. She stood there, trembling, unable to speak, or even to breathe. The tears streamed down unchecked, hot and humiliating.

"I'll sign," she finally choked out, the words nearly strangling her.

"Good." He straightened, his face relaxing into a satisfied sneer. "Get in the car. I'm takin' you back to your parents."

* * *

"Now, I don't want you askin' the lawyer any questions. The sooner this is over with, the faster we can fix it."

Autumn didn't answer. He'd found a lawyer to get them to sign together. It was apparently going to be a much quicker process than she'd expected. They were driving to his office now.

"I don't need you sayin' anythin' you shouldn't to put this off," Cayde continued. He glanced toward her. "Do you still think you're pregnant?"

"I'll need to take a pregnancy test to know for sure," she said. She didn't vomit as much in the mornings as usual. Either her morning sickness was subsiding, or it had merely been symptoms of anxiety from living with Cayde.

"We'll do that after the court finalizes it. If they find out you're pregnant, they may not grant it." He seemed on edge with her lack of responses and placed a hand on her knee. His voice and gaze softened. "I promise I'll marry you again after I fix this mess with my ex-wife."

When they finally met with his lawyer, Autumn did exactly as Cayde wanted. She sat quietly through the discussions, the advice, the legal formalities—barely paying attention.

"Mrs. Miller?"

"Yes?" Autumn's attention snapped to the lawyer. "I'm sorry, what?"

"I asked if you had any questions for me."

She could feel Cayde's eyes on her, practically burning into the side of her skull.

"None at all," she gave a grim smile. "Thank you." Part of her silence was to keep Cayde's temper in check. But another part of her had changed her mind about being angry. In fact, there was a chance this situation could benefit her if she chose to split from Cayde permanently. The thought gave her a bit of hope.

She smiled again. "Where do I sign?"

CHAPTER 47

CLAIRE

Paige insisted on visiting for Christmas. Claire couldn't refuse this time. She had tried to persuade her, but she couldn't do so without arousing too much suspicion. When her daughter finally walked into the house, Claire felt a surge of relief and anxiety. She hadn't realized just how lonely she'd been until she wrapped her arms around her girl. But that comfort brought even sharper fear—fear that Cayde might hurt her.

Strangely enough, he ended up being on his best behavior, so Claire allowed Paige to spend the night. She was happier than she expected to be, waking up to have her child near on Christmas morning. Somehow, Claire had convinced Cayde—who had unfortunately recovered quickly from his tumble down the stairs—to let her buy some presents, explaining that if she didn't, Paige would get suspicious, and things would become complicated.

"Here you go, Sweetie," Claire handed Paige her wrapped gift. Cayde watched, eyes narrowed, but in front of Paige, he kept his anger in check. She'd gotten Paige a new pair of shoes, some jewelry, and a gift card for clothes.

Claire fixed brunch for everyone. Pancakes, bacon, orange juice. Cayde kept mostly to himself. Paige caught Claire up with all the events in her life that she'd missed the past few months. When it came time to leave, Claire held Paige tighter than ever before.

"Tell your Dad Merry Christmas for me," Claire murmured, hoping to keep the farewell light.

"You could come with me." Paige's voice dropped low. "Dad would understand." She knew something was wrong.

Claire pulled back, a sudden spike of fear shooting through her. She didn't dare turn to see if Cayde was close by, listening. "Not this time, honey." She gave her daughter a particular kind of look, hoping Paige wouldn't push it.

"I'll be back tomorrow," Paige promised, glancing at Cayde. "I'll bring Seth over too. Dad's making some Christmas pies. He said he'd make one for you."

Claire hugged her goodbye, torn between sadness and relief. Once the door shut, she exhaled softly, unsure if Cayde would revert to his usual hot-tempered self now that Paige was gone. She busied herself with dishes and cleaned up the remnants of their Christmas brunch, wondering if Cayde would leave to spend the holiday with his own daughters. She'd rather be alone for Christmas than share it with him, but he didn't seem to have any intention of packing up.

Disappointing, as always.

"Why would she suggest you spend the holiday with your ex-husband?" Cayde's voice cut through the quiet from the living room, where he sat on the couch, toying with the fringe of a pillow.

Claire wiped her hands on a towel as she loaded the last of the plates into the dishwasher. "She's still young. Probably just misses the days when her dad and I were together."

"Do *you* miss it?" Cayde asked.

Claire kept her eyes on her work. She didn't like where this conversation was going. "She only suggested it because this is our first Christmas apart. Zach and I split on good terms. We're still friends." The words tasted bitter. She missed him more than she'd ever admit.

"Men and women can't be friends. But I wouldn't expect you to understand loyalty." He muttered the last part, just loud enough to sting.

This, Claire couldn't let pass. "Excuse me? I don't know what makes you think that." She scrubbed the countertop harder, forcing the words out. "I'm allowed to be friends with who I want. You and I aren't together."

She was on dangerous ground. She knew it. But it was too late to take it back.

"And what about Seth comin' over tomorrow?" Cayde narrowed his eyes. "How many men are you 'friends' with?"

Claire blinked, trying to process what he was insinuating. "Seth? My daughter's *boyfriend*?" Fucking hell. The kid was sixteen.

Cayde stood, crossing the room in a few quick strides until he was blocking the kitchen doorway. He folded his arms, eyes boring into her. "Not just Seth. I know you probably slept with your ex-husband."

She cursed under her breath, shaking her head. *Psycho.* "No, Cayde. I didn't." There was no use arguing. He'd believe what he wanted. Fighting back only made it worse.

"Zach," Cayde spat her ex's name. "Paige can't even be bothered to spend Christmas Day with us. She'd rather be with him."

The urge to defend her daughter pulled at her. Paige had just spent Christmas Eve and the morning with them. Going to her father's for the rest of the day made perfect sense. But none of that would register with Cayde. It was always a battle. And then his hypocrisy annoyed her.

"Children *should* spend time with their fathers on Christmas," she said quietly. "But I guess that's not something you'd care about."

She regretted the words the moment they left her mouth.

Cayde's hand shot out, grabbing a mug off the rack. Claire ducked just in time as it flew past her head, shattering against the wall. She flinched at the explosion of glass beside her.

He stormed out of the kitchen, and Claire slowly straightened, her breath catching as a warm trickle slid down her cheek. Gingerly, she touched the skin beneath her eye. A shard from the mug had embedded there. She pulled it free, wincing as blood oozed from the cut. It dripped onto the floor, streaming red down her face in place of the tears she couldn't cry.

CHAPTER 48

SOPHIE

Sophie placed the plastic handset of the jail's phone against her ear. Already, she'd turned down phone calls from her parents and Tanner. She knew they wanted to help. But she refused to involve them. They didn't know what they were dealing with. Didn't know what kind of monster Cayde Miller had become. Sophie refused to involve them.

About a week after the wedding, during a particularly violent fight, Cayde had backhanded her across the face, probably cracked already-sore ribs, then bent down and whispered a horrific threat against her boys.

Sophie knew she had to protect them. Put as much distance as possible between Cayde and her kids. Everything had been strange since the wedding. Maybe even since the divorce with Mark started. Every choice she'd made—everything she felt—was trapped in misery and confusion. As if she navigated through a fog, unable to see the paths before her. Forced to step forward anyway. Her boys were all she cared about now.

When they said her attorney, Mr. Tom Marvin, was on the line, she picked up.

"Hello?"

"Hi, Sophie. I need to talk to you about something important."

"What is it?"

"The court has made a decision regarding your custody case. Because of your recent arrest and previous failures to appear, the judge has decided to revoke your custody rights. This means you no longer have legal custody of your children."

Sophie didn't speak. She wasn't sure she could.

"I know this is difficult news," Tom continued, his voice gentler. "But I'm here to help you understand what it means and discuss the next steps we can take."

"I don't understand," she finally said, the words trembling out. "So, Mark won? All of it? I don't have any custody?"

"I'm afraid not. Right now, I'd advise against an appeal. The priority should be to work on your legal standing, and then we can apply for visitation rights."

"So, I lost them, anyway," she whispered.

"I'm so sorry, Sophie." He sounded genuine. "But in light of recent events..." He didn't have to finish the thought. He didn't have to say it was her fault for missing court hearings. Didn't have to remind her she'd practically kidnapped her own kids. She knew.

"Thank you for calling, Tom," she said, voice lifeless.

"When things settle down, we can discuss filing for visitation, okay? Don't lose hope. Good luck, Sophie."

She held the phone against her head for a moment, tapping it lightly against her temple after the line clicked dead.

There was nothing left. Nothing but the growing shadow of Cayde Miller.

CHAPTER 49

KATE

Extended-stay hotels had turned into motels, and motels had turned into parking lots. Cayde's SUV was parked in a sprawling grocery store lot. A few semi-trucks had settled for the night, their engines grumbling low, unable to find proper rest stops off the highway. Kate shivered in the cold, pulling her blanket tighter around herself and Bella, who had curled up on her lap in the passenger seat. She tried to focus on a new crime novel, but her hands wouldn't stop shaking.

Winter had settled in Tennessee. Cayde wanted to save money for when it *really* got cold. And tonight, he was out there somewhere, doing whatever it was he did when he left her alone. He said he had a "meeting," but she knew better. If he did any real work, it was never so eventful. Most of his cases, if he even got them, were petty: cheating spouses, tracking down runaway teens, digging up dirt on some poor soul for a few bucks. The money never lasted.

Kate's eyes drifted to a figure near the semi-trucks—a man talking with a driver. Even from here, she could tell it was him. He was all charm, that slick smile, drawing people in like moths to a flame. It didn't matter who it was, didn't matter if they could do anything for him. He loved to win people over.

The thought made her grumble, the sound swallowed up by the emptiness around her.

She tried to read, but a strange unease prickled under her skin. Her nerves, already stretched thin, buzzed with something she couldn't quite name. Everything felt wrong. She gave up on the novel and tried reading her Bible instead. Still, her eyes slid over the words, her brain refusing to take them in. Frustration built, anxiety gnawing at her bones.

Enough. She gently moved Bella off her lap and got out of the car. The night air bit through her blanket, raising goosebumps along her arms. Cayde kept a small box cutter in the glovebox. He'd kill her if he knew she'd touched it, but the creeps lurking around here gave her a different kind of chill. She grabbed it and slipped it into her pocket, the thin weight reassuring against her thigh. Cayde was all the way across the lot.

Three men's eyes followed her as she moved, each one giving her that look. The look that snakes under your clothes, crawls along your skin, makes you want to shrink away and vanish. Her throat tightened. Maybe she should've stayed in the car. But it was too cold, and the waiting made her skin itch.

She spotted Cayde waving her over, a broad grin splitting his face. He leaned in and whispered something to the trucker he'd been talking to, a greasy, hulking man who shot a brief glance her way before nodding and turning back to his rig.

Her stomach twisted. She crossed her arms tighter around herself and walked faster. Whatever charm Cayde had turned on for that man made her insides recoil. This place, the dark, the strangers—she wanted to bolt.

Cayde didn't move, even though the conversation seemed over. Instead, he waved her closer. "Come here," he said. Something in his tone made her skin crawl.

Kate stopped, keeping a good ten paces between them. "Let's go back to the car. Turn on the heater."

He stood in the dark, the only light catching the faint outline of his body from the distant lamp posts. That, and the gleam of his eyes and teeth. "I want to show you something."

Kate's gaze shifted from Cayde to the truck, then back to him. "What?"

"You have to see it for yourself."

A sickening pit formed in her stomach. A gut-deep certainty. A warning.

"I'm not getting in the truck," Kate said, her voice flat.

"Come *here*." He stepped closer. Kate stepped back. He frowned. "He just wants to show you what the inside looks like."

"No!" Kate snapped. She gritted her teeth, sucked in a long, hissing breath. A shadow moved across the truck's windshield. Then another. There were *two* men waiting! Her heart hammered. She was going to run. "I'm not getting in there!"

They stared at each other, frozen in the dark. She couldn't see his face, but she knew he wasn't smiling anymore. He wasn't asking anymore. Something shifted between them.

He moved first.

Cayde sprung from the darkness like a snake striking its prey.

Kate turned, legs churning, pushing hard, but she was too tired. Too stiff from the cold. Too slow. Cayde closed the gap easily, grabbing a fistful of her sweater. He yanked her back. One hand slammed over her mouth, cutting off her scream.

He wrenched her body to his, dragging her backward into the shadows. Back toward the truckers.

"Quiet," he hissed, breath hot in her ear. "Be calm."

She kicked and twisted. His hand crushed against her mouth. Pain shot up her jaw, jarring her nose—the same nose he'd broken weeks ago during her daughter's visit. His other arm braced between her breasts, pinning her against him. His fingers creeped toward her throat.

"You don't have to feel anything," he whispered, voice low, rough. "I know exactly how long it takes to strangle a woman without killing her." His grip tightened. "You'll just go to sleep."

Her tears streamed over his fingers. She stopped clawing at him. Her hand slid into her pocket, trembling, and found the box cutter. She pressed the button, feeling the blade click into place, then drove it backward as hard as she could.

The blade punched into his side.

Cayde howled, releasing her in shock. She stumbled forward, spinning, arm flailing wildly, the tiny blade flashing in the dark as she swung it back and forth. Then she turned and ran, legs pumping furiously.

"Help!" Her voice rang out, echoing across the empty lot. And this time, she didn't stop running.

Someone! Anyone! Another truck driver (no—not one of them), a late-night shopper—*God, anyone!* Kate sobbed as she sprinted for the building's lights. Cayde's voice echoed behind her. She didn't look back. Didn't stop running. Didn't let go of the box cutter.

The store's double doors slid open, and she nearly collapsed in relief. They were still open. Maybe just for a few more minutes. Beyond them, the fluorescent lights blazed, the floors gleamed. A stark contrast to the darkness she'd escaped. It may as well have been heaven.

Kate charged up a few aisles and ducked behind a row of canned goods just as Cayde strode in. He clutched his side, shirt stained red. The wound wasn't deep. Probably hurt like hell, but it wouldn't slow him down. He was still dangerous. He was still coming.

"Where is she?" he hissed, eyes wild, movements sharp. He looked like a man possessed. Sometimes, Kate genuinely wondered if he was. The only employee Kate could see took one glance at him and promptly found somewhere else to be.

Cayde's head whipped left and right, gaze sweeping the aisles, every step radiating fury. Kate pressed herself tighter against the metal shelving. She couldn't let him catch her. Not this time.

Moving silently, she crawled on her hands and knees, slipping between aisles. She peeked through the shelves, watching him through gaps between boxes and bags. He stomped up and down the lanes, cursing. He'd pause, suddenly lunging into an aisle, scanning it from end to end, his eyes burning with rage.

Kate crept further back. Her gaze flicked to the yard department. The aisles stretched out, lined with tools and bags of soil. She edged toward it, crouching low, using the towering shelves to keep out of his line of sight. She peered through gaps between the rakes and shovels, holding her breath. *Where was he?* Her pulse pounded so hard it felt like it would burst out of her chest. She tightened her grip on the box cutter. Took a step back. Then another. Waiting for his head to bob around the corner. For him to come charging out from the shadows.

Her spine collided with something solid, and she spun around. The box cutter slipped from her grasp as two hands gripped her shoulders.

CHAPTER 50

AUTUMN

Autumn's mother impatiently tapped her foot. They'd only been waiting for ten minutes, but her mother seemed anxious to get through the doctor's visit. Today, Autumn would find out if she was really pregnant or not.

"Are you sure you don't want me to go back with you?" her mother asked.

"Whatever the news, I think I just need a few minutes to adjust to it on my own. I promise I'll be fine."

"It's very odd, though, not having someone there." Her mother gave a disapproving *tsk*. "At least Cayde should be—"

"Autumn?" A nurse called out from the door, glancing around. "Autumn Miller?"

"Right here." Autumn stood up, handing her purse to her mother. "I'll be fine. Just wait for me."

What Autumn said was true. She did want to be alone to process whatever news came her way. But she also didn't want her mother hearing exactly how many weeks along she might be. Especially if it stretched back six weeks before the wedding.

"Remove your jacket and hop up on the bed, dear," the nurse instructed. "We'll start the ultrasound."

Autumn had already provided a urine sample that was sent to the lab for testing, just in case the ultrasound came up empty. Sometimes, they'd explained, they couldn't find what was there. The urine sample would be the definitive answer.

"Goodness, what have you done to your arms?" The technician's eyes widened at the bruises marking Autumn's skin. Cayde's fits of rage often left traces—shoving her into walls, clamping his fingers too tightly around her, slapping and punching.

Autumn laughed lightly. "Well, this one's from slipping on black ice. This one's from bumping into a door. This one's from building furniture—" She waved her hand dismissively. "I'm completely disaster-prone." She tried to laugh again, but the nurse and technician didn't.

"You ought to be rolled up in bubble wrap," the technician murmured. She then instructed Autumn to lift her shirt. Inwardly, Autumn thought being wrapped up in protective bubbles sounded nice.

As the technician spread the cold gel over her abdomen and started the search, Autumn took deep breaths and prayed.

"Well, there it is!" The nurse smiled, turning the screen so Autumn could see. "There's the head right there, the arm... Oh, honey, don't cry!"

Autumn wasn't sobbing. Her face was expressionless as stone, eyes glued to the screen. But fat, heavy tears streamed down her cheeks, steady and silent. Yes. There it was. A baby.

The nurse offered a few words of comfort, ones Autumn barely registered. Then she handed Autumn a tiny pair of knitted baby booties. She turned them over in her hands, feeling the soft fabric, hardly listening as the nurse spoke about options.

Pregnant.

Even though they hadn't told her how far along she was, she was praying over and over in her head, *Please, God, let this baby come nine months after the wedding.* She prayed it hadn't happened the night Cayde drove her to the park. She might be able to hide it from her family, friends, and church. But she would know. God knew. A shudder ran through her. Maybe everything over the past few months was punishment.

Small tremors ran through her hands. She was going to have a child with Cayde. The thought of bringing an innocent, precious life into the world he was a part of made her stomach twist. She hadn't forgotten the threats he'd made against her family. She could withstand his temper. His violence. But this little being growing inside her—how could she protect it?

"Please, don't cry." The nurse's voice softened as she handed Autumn a tissue. "It's scary for a lot of first-time mothers, but things will turn out, you'll see."

Autumn felt cornered. Trapped. Physically, emotionally, spiritually—it was all wrong. She blew her nose and leaned over to toss the tissue into the trash. What was she going to do?

Above the trash can, on the wall, a bright orange sheet of paper caught her eye. The title read in big, bold letters: *Women's Abuse Hotline.*

And beneath it—a phone number.

CHAPTER 51

CLAIRE

After Paige and Seth returned from Zach's, Claire insisted everyone go out to see a Christmas movie. She wondered if Cayde would protest, but to her surprise, he shrugged and said he'd prefer to stay home.

They took Seth's car, driving up the hill to the nearest theater. Claire kept turning back in the back seat, looking behind to see if Cayde was following in the Mercedes. She never saw him, but her gut told her he wasn't far behind.

"Mom?" Paige looked at her. "What is it?"

"Nothing," Claire said, and sat facing forward until they arrived.

Popcorn, drinks, and a sappy romance movie that Paige loved the most out of the three of them. It seemed to Claire that things were normal, even if for a few hours. She didn't want them to take her home.

Seth opened Claire's door after he'd opened up Paige's—the way Cayde used to treat her. Except it was clear Seth had been raised to be a real gentleman, and she could tell his affection had only grown for her daughter. Claire was at least grateful that Paige had someone who treated her well and cared for her genuinely, even if that was something she'd never again have for herself.

Seth got into the car and started to drive back to the house.

"Are you staying over again?" Claire asked, a bit reluctantly. She wondered how Cayde would take it.

Seth looked at her in the rearview mirror as he pulled out of the theater parking lot and back down the hill. "If you don't mind? I don't want to be a bother."

"You're not a bother," Paige said, then looked back at Claire. "Right mom?"

"Of course, not," Claire said. But her stomach tightened.

Seth made a strange noise, and there was shuffling by his feet.

"Damn, Seth, take the hill a bit slower, will ya?" Paige said, grabbing onto the door for security. The car was only speeding up, cruising down faster than the limit. "*Seth!*"

"I'm trying!" Seth said, and Claire realized he was stomping on the brake. "It won't slow down!"

They were hurtling for a red light. Paige started yelling and Seth yelled back. He started to blare the horn, warning the drivers. They couldn't hear Claire in the back barking orders. She reached up and grabbed the gear, shifting it lower to slow the car down. She reached for the emergency brake, but Seth jerked the steering wheel to avoid rear-ending a car and Claire's body tilted, her hand pulled away from the lever. They hurtled through the intersection, and Paige screamed, throwing her hands over her head as several cars narrowly avoided crashing into them.

"There!" Claire leaned forward again, pointing to a grassy field with rocks next to a gas station. An empty lot that would probably turn into apartments one day. Seth jerked the wheel again, and the car bounced as it went over the curb and then rumbled over the dead grass. Claire grabbed ahold of the emergency brake and slowly pulled it while Seth maneuvered the car so he could get it to circle around and around until it was slow enough that he could force it into park.

The three of them jolted to a stop, breathing hard. Paige was crying, and Claire brought a trembling hand over her daughter's shoulder. "Is everyone okay?"

"Y-yeah," Seth's eyes were wide. "What happened?"

"Your brakes went out," Claire said. "We'll call a tow to get it to the shop."

Seth nodded and got out of the car, not going anywhere in particular. He looked back at the intersection they'd driven through. Luckily for them, no one else had crashed in their panicked attempts to avoid the car running the red light.

Claire tightened her grip on her daughter's shoulder, glad that nothing horrible had happened to her. She realized then that even if her daughter's company was the only current light in her life, nothing was worth endangering her.

CHAPTER 52

WENDY

There was an incessant beeping and a relentless throbbing that pulled Wendy from a deep sleep. She felt the goose egg on her head with stiff fingers before she even opened her eyes.

"Don't touch it," came a voice.

"Ma?" Wendy blinked, looking over to find her mother sitting in a chair, legs crossed, a book resting on her lap.

"You're in the hospital. You fell down the stairs." Her tone was matter-of-fact.

"Archie!" There was no confusion, no need for explanations. She remembered everything. "Where is Archie?"

"He's back at home, with Cayde."

Wendy shook her head, struggling to sit up. "I have to get to him—"

"Archie is *fine,* Wendy," her mother started to say, but stopped when Wendy shot her a deadly look.

She spotted her sweats and crewneck in a hospital bag placed beside the chair her mother sat in. "I'm leaving," Wendy said, voice flat.

"Not until you talk to me," a man's voice sounded from the hallway. A chubby police officer wandered in nonchalantly, flipping through a notepad. "I'm Officer Blake. I'm here to ask you some questions."

Wendy settled back against the bed, breathing out a small sigh of relief. Maybe her failed attempt at escape wasn't in vain. Maybe she was safe, here in the hospital.

"I have it written down here that you were trying to take your child in the middle of the night?"

"Yes," Wendy admitted. "I was leaving my husband."

"Your husband, Cayde Miller, correct?"

"Yes."

"And, Mrs. Miller, have you ever used a knife against your husband before this incident?"

"What?" Wendy gaped. "No!"

"But you did use a knife against him last night?"

She shook her head, voice rising. "I was trying to defend myself. He was trying to stop me from leaving—"

"With his child, correct?"

Wendy glared. "*My* child."

"But Cayde *is* the child's father?"

"Yes." *This is not happening.*

"He has legal rights to him, Mrs. Miller," Officer Blake said, his voice detached. "If you had taken your son away, Mr. Miller could have gone straight to the court, and they would have ordered you to return." He shut his little notebook. "I have to make a report, but nothing is being charged, and no one is getting in trouble, so you don't have to worry."

"*Me*?" Wendy felt like pulling out her hair. "He's the one that should be worried. I went down the stairs, for fuck's sake!"

"Wendy!" her mother hissed, embarrassed by the language.

"In an altercation you started." The officer clicked his tongue. "You took your child from his bed in the middle of the night, came at your husband with a knife when he tried to stop you. He believes you slashed the tires on his vehicle to prevent him from coming after you."

"That wasn't me! He ran over a construction nail—"

The officer put up his hand. "And your neighbors heard you threatening to kill him."

"I was defending myself!" The words were spoken through gritted teeth.

"All I'm saying, Mrs. Miller, is that in the future, keep a wrap on that temper and never, under any circumstances, get violent in a dispute between you and your husband." He gave her a hard look, then nodded goodbye to Wendy's mother. "Ma'am." Then he was gone.

Wendy buried her face in her hands. She thought she might scream otherwise.

Her mother didn't speak for a long time, then asked, "Are you crying?"

"No." Wendy removed her hands, placing them stiffly in her lap. "Why are you even here?"

"My daughter fell down the stairs and cracked her skull." Her mother shrugged. "Isn't it right to be here?"

"You're only concerned with what's right when there's an audience. And I didn't just 'fall.'"

Her mother sighed and looked away, eyes drifting somewhere distant. Wendy's anger flared. She yanked back the covers, pulled out her IV with a painful tug, unhooked herself from the remaining monitors, and snatched her clothes despite her mother's protests.

"Wendy, you are not discharged!"

"You can handle the paperwork," she spat, pulling the sweatpants up under her hospital gown. "I need to see my son."

Dizzy and limping from a sharp pain shooting down her leg, Wendy slowly made her way down the hospital hall and out the main doors. Her mother caught up to her. "Let me drive you, at least."

She paused. Wendy actually hadn't considered how to get home. She'd jumped to the step where she was holding Archie in her arms again. This was one offer Wendy would accept. The drive was mostly silent, mother and daughter with little left to say to one another.

"You should bring Archie around more," her mother finally spoke. "I never get to see him." There was something in her voice that made Wendy wonder if she was suggesting something more.

"Because Cayde never gives me any money for gas, and you never visit my place."

Her mother scoffed softly. "I'm sure he isn't restricting it on purpose—"

"Why?" Wendy threw up her hands. "Why are you taking his side? *I'm* your daughter. You demean everything I say about him."

"I know marriage can be hard, but—"

"Look at me, Ma!" Wendy pointed to her face. "This isn't just hard. This is dangerous." Wendy's mother didn't turn her head from the road. "You can't even look at me. You can't even see what's happening to your daughter." Her voice lowered, her gaze shifting to the passing scenery outside the window. "Afraid you'll finally feel some guilt?"

Eventually, they pulled up to the apartment complex. Wendy unbuckled her seatbelt. "Thanks for the lift," she muttered.

"Wendy, wait." Her mother pressed her lips together. "Let me help you up the stairs—"

"Forget it." Wendy looked back at her mother, her eyes sharp and unyielding. "I don't need your help. I'm on my own. How else will I 'toughen up,' right?"

She slammed the car door shut and turned toward the apartments, fighting back tears. The steps were difficult to climb, but she didn't slow her pace. She pushed forward, ignoring the pain and stiffness coursing through her body. She noticed a small splattering of her blood at the bottom of the stairs, dried and brown. She ignored it. Whatever awaited her beyond that door, she would face it. Better soon than later.

The door was locked. Wendy pounded against it, frustration and fear building. "Open up, Cayde!" Both cars were still parked outside—Cayde's with its flat tire. She knew he was there. "Cayde!"

The door opened. Cayde stood there, calm and collected, his expression unreadable as he stepped aside. Hesitantly, Wendy entered, every nerve on edge, too aware of the door closing softly behind her.

Archie was playing in the living room, surrounded by a mess of toys Cayde had dumped out all at once. It kept him busy, but all Wendy wanted to do was rush over and check if he was okay.

"Hold it." Cayde's voice stopped her in her tracks. He stepped around her, positioning himself between her and

Archie. His eyes were sharp. "The hospital called and said you'd left. What did you tell the officer?"

Wendy glared at him. "I didn't get a chance to say much. It seems like you sweet-talked him into a whole other story."

Cayde shrugged. "It wasn't all untrue. You did come at me with the knife." He raised his palm. A white bandage wrapped tightly around it. "And you did try to kidnap Archie."

"I wasn't kidnapping him. I was leaving you. I still am."

"With a suitcase and a few thousand dollars in cash?" He smirked, raising an eyebrow. "Clever, by the way. I never would have guessed you'd collected all that money. Where had you been hidin' that?"

The air left Wendy's lungs. So, he'd found the suitcase. Found the money. Over a year and a half of scraping, scrounging, and planning. Gone. She glanced at the laundry room. The suitcase lay in the doorway, unzipped, its contents strewn all over the floor.

"The prune jar," Wendy said, the disappointment hidden from her voice.

Cayde laughed. "You belong here, Wendy. This is our home, and you're not leavin' it." His eyes darkened. "And you're definitely not takin' my son away from me."

"You don't care about Archie." Wendy shook her head. "And you don't care about me. All you care about—" She stepped forward, just inches from his face. "—is control."

His gaze hardened, muscles taut with suppressed rage.

"I'm getting out of here," she said. "And I'm taking Archie with me. You can't control me anymore, Cayde. I'm done."

Cayde's expression shifted, calculating. He reached behind himself, then swung his arm around, revealing the pistol she'd bought him for their wedding. "I don't think you are," he said calmly. "You're stayin' here, got it? Say it." He pointed the barrel directly at her head—an inch away. His eyes blazed, a promise in them. He'd do it.

Her chin quivered, eyes flooding with tears, but she gritted her teeth. "No."

"Say it!" He roared.

"No!"

Cayde's hand shook as he lowered the gun, sweat gleaming on his forehead. "Say you'll stay with me." He shifted the gun's aim—pointing it straight at Archie, who looked up at them both with wide, innocent eyes. "Or I *will* pull this trigger."

Wendy slapped a hand over her mouth, biting back a scream. "Don't!"

"I will!" Cayde snarled, dropping to his knees beside Archie. He yanked the toddler closer, pressing the cold metal of the gun against his temple. Archie whimpered, struggling against the rough hold. Wendy's heart shattered. She couldn't take it. "Say you're not leavin'. Say it!"

"Okay, okay!" she screamed, voice breaking. "I'll stay."

"I'm not convinced." His eyes narrowed.

Sobbing, Wendy dropped to her knees. "I'm sorry," she whispered, forcing every ounce of restraint into her voice, fighting the urge to lunge at him. "I'm sorry for trying to leave. I won't do it again—I'll stay right here."

Slowly, Cayde lowered the gun, staring at her with twisted satisfaction. Then, with a shove, he pushed Archie away and rose to his feet. Wendy went to comfort Archie, but Cayde stepped in front of her, grabbing her by the hair. She cried out and stumbled to her feet as Cayde dragged her into the kitchen.

He pulled a knife from the kitchen block, and Wendy's heart jumped into her throat. *Oh my god, he's going to kill me!* She tried desperately to wrench herself free, but Cayde grabbed her wrist and slammed it onto the counter. Using the side of his body, he pressed her into the corner so she couldn't move. Crushed against the wall, she struggled to breathe.

He brought the knife to her wrist. Wendy screamed at him, pounding her free fist into his back.

"Shut the hell up and hold still!" he roared, pressing her harder into the corner of the counter. "Unless you want me to get Archie instead. That what you want? Huh?"

She heard Archie crying from the other room, and all the fight left her.

"That's what I thought."

The tip of the knife sliced into her wrist. Wendy gasped and bit her cheek against the pain as tears ran down her face. Cayde dragged the blade through her flesh. Blood dripped onto the counter.

"You're mine, Wendy," he told her, his voice low and cold. "Don't you ever fuckin' forget it again." Finally, he released her, throwing the knife into the sink with a jarring clatter. "Now clean this mess up." Cayde turned and walked away to the bedroom, taking the gun with him.

Shaking, Wendy went to the sink and turned on the faucet. She ran her hand under the cool water, and as the red cleared from her skin, she saw what he'd carved into her.

"CM."

He'd branded her. Like cattle. Like a possession.

Disbelief and white-hot rage filled her, but Archie's cries took precedent. She grabbed a paper towel and hastily pressed it to her wound. Then she ran to her boy, sitting and gathering him into her arms. The image of the gun against Archie's temple was burned into her mind. Wendy rocked her son, whispering words of comfort as he cried into her chest.

I'm on my own. She'd told her mother that, and it was truer now than ever. The police wouldn't help her, and Cayde was too dangerous for her to involve anyone else—not even her mother. She was back at square one.

No one was coming to save her. She had to figure this out alone. And there wasn't much time. Cayde had escalated. This wasn't just about enduring anymore. It was survival. She glanced at the bedroom door where Cayde had disappeared, feeling the raw fear twist into something colder. Something hateful.

It was kill or be killed.

CHAPTER 53

KATE

Kate sat across the desk, watching the woman scribble details into the paperwork. Her mouth pulled into a hard frown, eyes heavy from the sleepless night. She felt the weight of exhaustion down to her bones.

The woman's name was Mrs. Blanchet. She worked for a women's shelter, handling intakes. Everything after last night felt like a blur. The hide-and-seek horror with Cayde in the department store, the way her heart nearly exploded when she bumped into the security guard. She'd thought it was Cayde, and the panic had almost killed her. He'd seen her distress on the security cameras and called the police, offering her a lifeline she hadn't expected.

But by the time the patrol car arrived, Cayde was gone, the SUV and Bella with him.

Overwhelmed and shaken, Kate didn't want to make a report. The officer had looked at her with that barely-concealed exasperation she'd seen before, but he was polite. Asked if she'd consider a women's shelter. She'd nodded numbly, unsure of what else to do. It felt surreal, ending up in a small dorm with other women—women who bore the same bruises and hollow eyes. Just like hers.

She hadn't slept. Kate just closed her eyes, let tears slide silently down her face, and prayed for morning to come.

Now, here she was. Across the desk from Mrs. Blanchet.

"Kate Moore, is it?" the woman asked gently.

"Miller," Kate corrected softly, hating herself for saying it. Miller. That name tasted foul in her mouth. Kate Moore hadn't been homeless, robbed, and beaten by her husband. Kate Moore still existed somewhere, buried deep. She was the one who smiled. The one who felt hope. "I wrote the wrong name down last night. Moore is my maiden name."

"That's alright." Mrs. Blanchet smiled. The expression softened her severe features. Her eyebrows, too thin and overly penciled, made her look older. Her brown hair, streaked with gray, was pulled back into a bun. Almost everything about her seemed strict and no-nonsense, but her eyes were kind. "Do you mind if I call you Kate?"

"Not at all."

"I wanted to discuss your case," Mrs. Blanchet continued. "This shelter is specifically designed for women suffering from domestic violence. We offer immediate shelter and support."

"My husband has all my cards," Kate cut in, shaking her head. "I can't pay you."

Mrs. Blanchet nodded, like she'd heard that a thousand times before. "That's the case for most women here. Financial abuse is extremely common in situations like this. Our services are free." Her voice remained calm, soothing. "We'll work together to figure out what comes next."

"I don't know what to do." The words fell out of her mouth. How could she think about the future when she couldn't even see tomorrow? For so long, she'd only been able to focus on making it through the day.

"That's okay," Mrs. Blanchet reassured her. She didn't miss a beat. "We have counselors here. Individual and group sessions, if you're interested. They can help you process the trauma you've been through. And help you decide what your next steps should be."

The wording made Kate uneasy. It was like Mrs. Blanchet saw her as a desperate castaway, begging for a handout. "Really, I just want to figure out how to get my cards and dog back from my husband. Maybe stay here a few days until I decide where to go."

"Do you have any family we should contact?" Mrs. Blanchet's gaze was steady. "Someone who can come pick you up?"

"No." Kate's voice was sharp, her head shaking emphatically. The thought of Zoey's grief-stricken face, the sound of Alice's cries—it was too much. "I don't want my family involved in this."

Mrs. Blanchet clasped her hands together on the desk, leaning forward slightly. "Many women feel that way. Their abusers create an atmosphere through threats and violence where the victim voluntarily cuts themselves off from family, isolates themselves from help."

Hearing the very things she'd been feeling spoken aloud, Kate's chest tightened. Tears welled up as she nodded.

"But that's a mistake," Mrs. Blanchet continued softly. "Do not isolate yourself, Kate. If you have family who care about you, who have offered their help, I strongly suggest you take it. It's crucial to have a support system during this time."

"I have a daughter." Kate wiped her cheeks. "But my husband and her—they don't get along. And I don't want anything to happen to her family." She could see it so clearly. Cayde's anger. The way it would focus in on Zoey and little Alice if he thought they were helping her. "He would hurt her. Hurt her child, Mrs. Blanchet. If I stay with her, he'll find me. And he'll be angrier than ever. If I can just get my dog and stay here for a while, I'll figure something out. I'll find another way."

"The dog..." Mrs. Blanchet's expression shifted, a flash of discomfort crossing her face. "This shelter doesn't allow pets. It's policy, I'm afraid."

Kate felt her stomach drop. "I can't stay here?"

"You can!" Mrs. Blanchet leaned forward urgently. "You just can't bring your dog here."

"She's a little Yorkie. Very small. And she's extremely well-behaved," Kate pleaded. "She's old and needs special care. I can't leave her behind. Cayde won't care properly for her. She'll die!" Alarm flared in her chest at the thought. Kate pushed back from the desk.

"Wait, Kate, please listen." Mrs. Blanchet raised her hands gently, trying to soothe her. "Please don't leave. You've already accomplished one of the hardest parts, which is getting out."

"No." Kate shook her head, the panic rising. "No, I—a policeman brought me here. I didn't—I need to call my husband. I have to tell him where I am." Her hand went to her back pocket where her phone was. She'd turned it off after seeing the barrage of texts and missed calls—over a hundred messages, forty calls.

"Kate, please." Mrs. Blanchet's eyes widened, concern etched in every line of her face. "We still have a lot of options to discuss. A lot of women are afraid when they first come here. Other people might not understand, but we do."

"Understand what?" Kate's voice was tight, dismissive. She stood up, her body tense.

"How hard it is to leave the very person who hurts you." Mrs. Blanchet rose too, mirroring her movements.

"He's not..." Kate faltered, voice wavering. "He's not always like that. You know? He doesn't always hurt me." She shrugged helplessly. "I know I should have left him a long time ago. But he has everything. All my money. And I can't go to my family. The only kindness I have left in my life is my dog."

Mrs. Blanchet nodded slowly, her expression understanding. "Many women here know exactly what you're feeling. Sometimes abusers show you glimpses of who they first pretended to be. The dream you fell in love with. When you're going through trauma, that dream is like a bright light. You start craving it more than anything, enough to endure the pain and the abuse, just for a chance to see it again. But Kate, he *will* hurt you again."

Kate didn't want to hear it. Maybe because it scared her. There was something about Cayde that Kate, even after everything, still loved. The man he'd been those first few months. Maybe he wasn't real, but that was the man she'd fallen for. The man she still wanted to believe in. Somewhere inside, she had to believe that version of Cayde still existed. The same way she believed Kate Moore, the strong, vibrant woman she used to be, still existed. Buried deep within, waiting to resurface.

And she just couldn't leave Bella behind. Another sweet, innocent soul trapped in the middle of all this chaos. She didn't deserve that. Kate's heart broke just to think of Cayde neglecting the little Yorkie or leaving her on the side of the road somewhere. She tried to believe he wouldn't hurt Bella, but she didn't know that.

She didn't really know him at all.

"Look, I know you think it's silly, but the one constant happiness I've had through all this is my dog, Bella." She stood, the chair scraping back harshly against the floor. "I can't just abandon her." She turned, starting toward the door.

"Mrs. Moore!" Mrs. Blanchet called after her, and Kate paused. That name. Oh, how she longed to be Kate Moore again. But she wasn't. She was Kate Miller. Mrs. Blanchet's hand lifted slightly, a small gesture. "This is your life we're talking about. She's just a dog."

The words hit like a slap. Bella was more than that. Bella was everything. The only piece of unconditional love she had left.

"I'm sorry," Kate said, and walked out the door.

She moved quickly down the hall, past the other women staring silently at her. She wasn't like them. She wouldn't let herself acknowledge that. But she couldn't meet their eyes, either. She was terrified she'd see the same look she saw in the mirror every morning. As she pushed through the building's exit, tears blurred her vision. She swiped at them violently, frustration and anger tightening her chest.

The doors to the shelter slammed shut behind her. She sucked in a deep breath of the brisk Nashville air, watching people mill about the streets. They laughed, arms linked with friends, smiles bright. Kate refused to think she was like the women she'd just left behind, but she also knew she wasn't like the people before her.

She didn't know what she was anymore.

Pulling out her phone, she turned it on. The calls and messages had tripled. She scrolled past all of them, hit the contact button, and called Cayde.

CHAPTER 54

SOPHIE

Sophie stepped out of the jailhouse to find Cayde waiting. Arms crossed, eyes dark. A look that made her want to backtrack inside. She'd rather stay behind bars.

"You paid the bond?" she asked.

"You're my wife, aren't you?" he growled. "And that brother of yours was breathin' down my neck."

"Leave Tanner alone. Leave all my family alone."

Cayde nodded toward his car. "Get inside, Sophie."

"No."

His jaw tightened. "You want me to leave your family alone? Fine. Me and you are gettin' away from them. For a little while."

"Away?" She squinted, spotting the things packed into his car. "Where?"

"A campin' trip."

Sophie took a step back. "No."

Cayde clicked his tongue, striding toward her. His grip locked around her arm. She opened her mouth, but he yanked her hard enough to jerk her sideways. "Don't you scream," he hissed. "You scream, cause a scene, and we'll really have a problem. Those boys of yours will have a problem." He wrenched the passenger door open and shoved her inside. Slammed it shut. Then he stalked around to the driver's side, threw himself in, and cranked the engine. "Do you even know how much money I spent to get you out? What I had to do?" His voice rose to a shout. "Do you?!"

She shook her head, face white.

"I sold the house my ex-wife and kids were livin' in to get you out. And you want to pretend I'm some horrible man? You want to see how horrible I can be, Sophie? Huh? Should I burn down your parent's house? Maybe pay Tanner's wife a visit, see how much she respects a man? Or maybe I should drop in on your ex-husband. Show him how real men discipline children." His eyes blazed, manic. "Because real men don't coddle kids like you do, Sophie. Real men break 'em down. Make 'em tougher. Teach 'em what it's like to be rebuilt stronger."

The thought of him anywhere near her two boys made her blood run cold.

"No, Cayde," Sophie whispered, tears slipping down her cheeks. "No. You're not a horrible man."

He slammed on the brakes, making the car lurch. "And?"

Every word stung. "And… thank you. For getting me out."

"Better." He nodded, satisfied. The car rolled forward again, easing back onto the road. "Without me, you'd be rottin' in there for a month. So now we're gonna stretch your legs and breathe in some fresh air. Just for a little while."

Sophie glanced at the back seat. It was crammed with bags and clutter. More than anyone would need for just a "little while."

"What about my court hearing?" she asked.

"We'll be back in time."

But the pit in her stomach only grew.

She wondered if she'd ever make it back at all.

CHAPTER 55

JACK

Blair handled the phone records while Jack made a quick call regarding Veronica's recent purchase history. There was a lot to unravel, and time wasn't on their side. Veronica had called Cayde for thirty minutes the morning the kidnapping took place—and several times in the following days. Blair grimaced as she scrolled through the texts Veronica had sent him. It was clear she had a strong dislike for his current wife.

Jack hung up, breaking the tense silence. "That was the tire shop. She bought four new tires the night before our victim disappeared—but guess what? They were placed on the same make and model as our suspect's car."

Blair arched an eyebrow. "So, she bought Cayde tires to help kidnap his wife?" She tapped her chin, processing the details. "She also called him multiple times right before the kidnapping."

"And," Jack added, his expression darkening as he reviewed another report, "she wired him several thousand dollars about a week prior. I'm not sure what for, but it's clear they're still involved." He paused, then frowned. "There's something else. She bought a pistol."

Blair's face fell. "So, she bought tires to help with the kidnapping... and then bought a gun to kill her?"

Jack shook his head. "We've got more than enough to bring her in. Especially with the gas station CCTV footage."

They moved quickly, leaving the hotel and driving in silence as they mentally prepared for the next step. Veronica's house wasn't far, and Blair had already contacted local law enforcement, requesting extra patrol cars in case their suspect tried to run.

When they arrived, the house looked small but well-kept, its manicured yard betraying nothing of the chaos they suspected Veronica had been a part of. Blair and Jack approached calmly, knocking on the door. Their civilian clothes made them look more like neighbors than federal agents. It was exactly what they wanted—except Veronica wasn't stupid. She'd be expecting them.

A moment later, the door creaked open. Veronica stood there, her dark eyes keen. Her long black hair framed a face that might have been beautiful if not for the harshness etched into it.

"Can I help you?" Her voice was flat and guarded.

"Veronica Webb?" Blair asked, locking eyes with her.

Veronica stiffened. She'd been a sheriff once—she knew exactly what was about to happen. "Yes?"

Jack stepped forward, wasting no time. "Veronica Webb, you're under arrest for aiding and abetting a kidnapping." He smoothly cuffed her hands behind her back, reciting her rights. His voice was calm but firm.

As he secured her, Blair slipped past them into the house. Jack shot her a sharp look—she was supposed to wait. Cursing under his breath, he handed Veronica over to the arriving officers and hurried inside, drawing his gun.

"Blair?" His voice echoed through the house as he searched.

"Clear," Blair called from the back and stepped into the living room. She stood with her hands on her hips, eyes scanning the walls. "Cayde and the victim aren't here."

Jack holstered his gun, frustration simmering beneath the surface. Blair began rifling through papers strewn across a table—bills, receipts, junk mail.

"It's all garbage," she muttered, moving toward the bedroom.

Jack's gaze drifted over the walls, where family photos and artwork hung neatly. A fluffy gray cat leapt onto the kitchen counter, hissing when he stepped too close. Ignoring it, he focused on Blair's voice calling from the bedroom.

"Myers! You need to see this!"

Jack rushed in, finding Blair holding two phones—Veronica's main one and a second, cheaper model.

"They're using burners," Jack muttered, grabbing one of the phones. He scrolled through the messages quickly, piecing together the puzzle. "She met him at the gas station. Gave him this burner and warned him we were closing in. He probably took off south as soon as we checked into the hotel. That, or we passed him on the highway."

Blair frowned. "Don't even say that."

"She knew we were watching. She couldn't leave the house." He read aloud the messages he found, then paused, staring at the screen. "Wait... there's a meeting place."

Blair's eyes widened as she glanced over his shoulder, noting the address. She typed it into her phone. "An abandoned warehouse," she said, her voice urgent. "Myers, he's there now."

"But there's nothing here about the victim," Jack said, disappointment weighing down his voice.

Blair sighed, mirroring his frustration. "We have to work with what we've got. Let's not waste time."

Jack gave a tight nod. "Let's catch this asshole."

CHAPTER 56

CLAIRE

"Sit down, Paige," Claire said gently. "We need to talk."

Seth's car had been towed. Paige went with him to the mechanic while Cayde picked Claire up. He'd been quiet in the car—no questions, no concern over Seth's car or their safety. Claire, on the other hand, couldn't stop shaking. The three of them were lucky to have made it out of the intersection alive, let alone without a scratch.

Paige was back now, pacing her room, looking grim. She may have only been a teenager, but she knew what was coming. Claire quietly shut the door, careful not to wake Cayde, who'd fallen asleep on the couch.

"How is Seth's car?" she asked, sitting on the edge of her daughter's bed.

"The mechanic fixed it," Paige said, shaking her head slightly. "He's still waiting there." She paused, meeting Claire's gaze. "Mom, what's going on?" Paige leaned in closer, eyes narrowing at the cut under her mother's eye. She lifted a hand, gently brushing her fingers across it. "Are you going to tell me how you got that?" She had asked earlier, before the movie, but Claire had made up some excuse Paige clearly didn't believe.

"Cayde smashed a glass. A shard cut me under the eye." Claire's voice dropped, almost a whisper. "He's dangerous, Paige. We're still not getting married, but he won't leave." She took a deep breath, fighting the tears that burned her eyes. "I need you to leave."

"I'll call the police," Paige said, jumping up, her face flushed with anger. "We'll remove him and press charges—"

"I *have* called the police, Paige." Claire's mouth set into a tight line. "I don't have any proof he's the one who hurt me, and they can't force him out of the house. I can't even change the locks."

"Then we'll take you somewhere else."

"No, Paige." Claire shook her head. "I have it under control here. Doing anything else would just set him off. This way, I can leave you out of it."

"Mom..." Now Paige looked like she was the one about to cry. "I can't just go. How can I?"

"Because I'm asking you to. I want you to focus on school, get good grades, and have fun with your friends. I don't want you worrying about your mom, okay?"

"Mom," Paige's voice was barely a whisper. "The mechanic said the brakes on Seth's car were cut."

Claire wished the news had shocked her, but it didn't. Cayde had probably followed them—her gut had known it. He'd cut the brakes while they were inside the theater. Her heart sank. Paige and Seth were only sixteen. They shouldn't have to deal with something this dark and dangerous. They didn't deserve to be caught in the crossfire.

"That's why you have to go," Claire said, pulling Paige into a tight embrace. "I need to know you're safe so I can handle things over here, okay?"

It took more convincing, but Paige eventually agreed. She got back in her car before Cayde had even woken up. Claire stood at the front door, heart tightening as her daughter backed out of the driveway. Paige looked through the window, her expression grim. She gave a small, hesitant wave before she drove away down the street.

Claire watched the car disappear, her breath hitching. She sank down in the doorway, covering her face with her hands, weeping as quietly as she could. She was terrified. Terrified to be alone with Cayde again. Terrified that she might not live to see Paige again.

CHAPTER 57

AUTUMN

"The green set is precious," Autumn said, holding up a package of newborn onesies. She and Cayde had spent the afternoon at the mall, buying baby clothes and other necessities. He was driving her back to her parents' house, where she was eager to show her mother the trove of new items. His Corvette sped faster than she would have liked. She thought it best not to suggest slowing down.

"Maybe tomorrow we can look for a crib and a baby bassinet," he suggested, smiling. "We should probably get a start on diapers, too. Babies go through those faster than you think."

"Really?" Autumn glanced at him, surprised. Moreso that he was providing the information. "Good to know, I suppose."

They passed an expanse of trees and a small park, boys around her brothers' age playing in the snow. It seemed peaceful, normal.

"Cayde," she started carefully, banking on his good mood, "Jeremiah said something a few weeks ago that I thought was strange. He said he saw you in the park talking to a woman. That you were—" She hesitated. "—flirting."

The mood changed suddenly. Autumn couldn't pinpoint exactly what he'd done, but the air shifted.

"Well, I wasn't. Jeremiah is a liar," Cayde snapped. "I'm disgusted you'd even believe that."

"No," Autumn said quickly, sensing the rising anger, desperate to defuse it. "I wasn't accusing—"

"And you dare have the audacity to accuse me of flirtin'?" His tone was low, dangerous. "I saw you with that man in the store."

"What man?" Autumn's voice tightened.

"The man who rang up the baby clothes!" Cayde snatched the onesies from her hands and threw them at her feet. The car swerved slightly. "You flirted with him!" His voice, no longer controlled, shot up.

"He just asked if the baby was a boy or girl! It's small talk—"

"Small talk, that's rich. You probably see him often, don't you?" He reached again for the bags of clothes on her lap. Autumn slapped his hand away, her own temper flaring. The car jerked again. "I take you out, buy clothes for the baby, and this is how you repay me? By flirtin' with him right in front of my face?"

"No, Cayde!" she snapped back, shoving his hand. "I've never seen him before!"

"You're lyin'!" His eyes burned, manic. "You go to that mall at least once a week with your mom—it's for him, isn't it?"

Two realizations hit Autumn simultaneously. The first: Cayde had been following her. Stalking her and her mother during their outings. The second: He had just unbuckled her seat belt. Cayde let go of the wheel, leaning over to open her door with one hand and shove her with the other.

"Get out! Whore!" he roared.

Autumn screamed, the car barreling down the road at nearly fifty miles an hour. The black pavement blurred beneath her, and the wind whipped at her hair as the door swung open. The car veered hard, jerking into the next lane. A blaring horn and screech of tires echoed beside them as a driver swerved to avoid a collision. Cayde snapped the car back into their lane, gripping the wheel with both hands.

Autumn slammed the door shut and buckled her seatbelt with shaking hands. She locked the door in a frenzy, then pressed herself against it. Trembling, she tried to make herself small. Every nerve in her body screamed to flee, but all she could do was sit in frozen, horrified silence.

Not a word passed between them the rest of the drive.

He'd completely flown off the handle.

When Cayde finally pulled up to her parents' house, Autumn practically threw herself out of the car, knees buckling as she hit the ground. Cayde hit the gas, tires screeching as he peeled away, throwing bags of baby clothes out the window in a childish rage.

She stood there, numb, staring at the scattered clothes littering the sidewalk. He'd really tried to push her out of the car. He could have killed her. One by one, she gathered the bags, her hands moving on autopilot. The world felt surreal, muted. She moved mechanically, picking up the tiny onesies, the small socks and mittens, stuffing them into bags without really seeing them.

She slipped inside the house as quietly as she could, avoiding the living room where her parents watched TV. In her room, she shut the door softly, then sank against it. Her hands shook violently, but the tears wouldn't come. She pulled out the crumpled paper she'd taken from the hospital, smoothing it flat as if it were made of glass. Her fingers hovered over the numbers, hesitating.

The phone felt heavy in her hand as she dialed.

"Hello, this is the Women's Abuse Hotline. Are you suffering from domestic violence?" The voice on the other end was calm, steady.

"Yes," Autumn whispered, her voice breaking. The admission shattered something inside her, and the tears fell hot and fast.

"Do you need units sent to your location immediately?"

"No." She was sobbing now, shoulders shaking, gasping for breath.

"What's your name?"

The question stopped her cold. Her name? What if Cayde found out she'd called? What if he tracked it back to her? He'd warned her so many times, but tonight—tonight he'd tried to kill her. He'd do it again. He'd go after her parents. Her brothers. He'd threatened them all, and now she knew those threats weren't empty.

Without another word, she hung up.

CHAPTER 58

KATE

A month had crawled by since Kate left the women's shelter. She'd called Cayde to pick her up. She braced herself for the worst, expecting fury. But when he pulled up and stepped out of the car, he swept her into his arms, kissed her, and held on tight. He claimed he'd been frantic, driving around all night, worried something terrible had happened.

She almost reminded him that something terrible had happened—he'd tried to sell her the night before. But she bit her tongue. Didn't want to shatter his calm, didn't want that rare gentleness to slip away. So, she hugged him back. Apologized for making him worry. For a few days after, he was softer, kinder.

"You know I love you, Kate," he kept saying. Over and over. "I love you more than anythin'."

He never tried pulling that stunt again, but he never apologized for it either. Instead, he made a big show of keeping her "safe" anytime they slept at a truck stop or parking lot, like he was her protector. The past month, they'd holed up mostly at the same truck stop just off the highway. It was bigger, close to the city, with large bathroom facilities where Kate could wash up. It wasn't exactly a shower. And every time she dunked her hair under the sink, her cheeks flushed with embarrassment if anyone else came in.

"Weren't you reading a different book yesterday?" A light voice cut through her thoughts.

Kate looked up from her bench. Bella's ears perked up. The little Yorkie was curled beside her, wrapped in a blanket against the cold. The dog had been sleeping more and more these days.

The voice belonged to Bill, an older man in coveralls stained with grease. His hands were rough and blackened from work. A custodian. Someone who didn't bother them for loitering. He and Cayde talked often. When Cayde wasn't around, he'd talk to Kate too.

But he'd learned his boundaries after that one conversation went on too long. Thirty minutes of idle chatter with Kate about Bill's grandkids, and Cayde's jealousy had snapped like a tripwire. She'd paid the price for it—her ribs were still tender, skin still mottled in dark blues and purples beneath her sweater.

Today, though, Cayde was in the city for work. She'd begged to go with him. Even promised to wait in the car. He'd refused. So she'd parked herself on the cold bench outside, a thick novel in hand, and settled in for a long day of killing time.

"I *did* have another one yesterday," Kate replied, smiling at Bill. "Finished it."

Bill raised a brow at the new book in her hands. "But you're already halfway through that one."

Kate gave a small shrug. "What can I say? I'm a fast reader. Always loved a good thriller."

"Maybe I oughta give one a try," Bill muttered, scratching at his thinning scalp.

"I've got a whole stack, if you'd like," Kate offered. "Picked them up at thrift stores back when I could. These days, I get them from the library a few towns over. Cayde works there a lot."

"The library near Blue's Hideaway Motel?" a new voice piped up. Mary, a younger custodian, joined them. Her hair was dyed a rich plum. A cascade of necklaces on her chest and rings across her fingers caught the light. Kate always noticed. She'd once had jewelry like that. Bracelets, pendants, earrings—all locked away in a storage unit back in Virginia. Collecting dust. Part of a life she couldn't reach anymore. Now all she had was the engagement ring that didn't quite fit her finger, and the diamond heart that sat near her throat.

"I think that's the motel," Kate said softly. She and Cayde had crashed there a few times when the temperature dropped too low for sleeping in the car.

"I work there too," Mary replied. "In the mornings. I clean the rooms."

"Really?" Kate blinked, caught off guard.

"Well, if you ever stay there again, say hi." Mary's smile was genuine. The past few weeks, they'd formed an unlikely friendship. Kate normally wouldn't have gone out of her way to befriend a girl with tattoos, piercings, and brightly colored hair, but Mary turned out to be the kindest person Kate had met in a long time. She never pried, never pushed. Just made it clear that if Kate ever needed somewhere to go, her door was open. She'd even taken Kate's phone, inputting her own number with a little rose emoji beside it.

"Just in case," she'd said, eyes serious.

Kate had thought about calling her once or twice. But she couldn't drag Mary into her mess. Couldn't risk her safety. Just like she couldn't risk Zoey's. She was trapped. And dragging anyone else into this meant dragging them into Cayde's crosshairs.

"Maybe *I* should get a second job," Bill muttered, shuffling uncomfortably beside them. "At this rate, I'll be dipping into my retirement fund just to make ends meet."

The word hit Kate like a bolt of lightning: retirement. Her pulse quickened. How had she forgotten? There was still money Cayde hadn't touched, money he didn't know about. She could pull from her retirement. She could get out.

Her eyes darted down the road. Cayde's SUV rounded the corner and rolled back into the truck stop. Mary's face tightened as she spotted Cayde. It was clear she didn't like Cayde from the moment she'd met him. She was one of the few people to see past the charming mask he wore right away. Bill muttered something about heading back to work and shuffled off quickly. Smart move.

Cayde parked and stepped out, a brown bag of fast food in hand. He winked at Mary as he walked by—shameless, even in front of Kate. Mary's face went flat, lips pressed into a tight line, then she turned sharply and walked off without a word.

"How was your day?" Cayde asked.

Kate forced a smile. "Finished my book," she lied. "Maybe we can spend some time at the library tomorrow? I need to pick up another one."

"Sure." Cayde scratched at his stubble. The scruff was turning into a full beard by now, but she doubted he even noticed. "I got some work to catch up on, anyway."

Work. Kate bit back a laugh. She didn't know what he did all day, but it sure as hell wasn't business. The few PI gigs didn't come close to explaining his long absences, his endless meetings with "clients." But none of that mattered anymore. Not right now. Tomorrow, she needed a computer. She needed to access that account.

She'd deal with Cayde being there. She'd have to. This was her shot. Maybe her last one. If she could get that money, she'd have a chance—a *real* chance—to break away from him for good. To be Kate Moore again. To be free.

For the first time in what felt like forever, a flicker of hope lit up the dark space inside her. Maybe, just maybe, she could find herself again.

CHAPTER 59

SOPHIE

Sophie woke up from the car's sudden change in speed. They veered off the main road and pulled into a parking lot. She lifted her head away from the car window and rubbed at her eyes.

"A hardware store?" she asked.

"We need more supplies," Cayde replied, already stepping out of the car. "Extra campin' gear."

It had been several months since he'd gotten her out of jail. Sometimes they went back to the apartment Tanner was loaning her, but when her family asked too many questions, Cayde conveniently whisked her away on another camping trip.

She never answered the phone around him. If she did, it was always on speaker, with Cayde listening to every word. And since he was almost always by her side, the truth was she'd hardly been in contact with her family at all. The worst part was that she hadn't been able to see her boys. Not even once.

The whole ordeal had spooked Mark, and he didn't think it was a good idea for her to see them until things on Sophie's end calmed down. But with Cayde in the picture, they never did. Her court hearing had been missed, and as far as she knew, Sophie was still technically out on bail.

Both she and Cayde eyed the police car that pulled in beside them.

Cayde avoided the police at all costs, despite always boasting that he knew Veronica and everyone on the Nashville force. Sophie, on the other hand, would have preferred being arrested over her current situation.

"Stop lookin' at him," Cayde growled under his breath, grabbing her arm. The guttural tone he used made her skin crawl.

Sophie faltered for a moment but did as she was told and faced forward.

"And pull down your shirt!" he hissed. "I can see your tattoo—you look like a white-trash whore."

"Don't call me that," Sophie snapped, batting his hand away as he tried to pull down her shirt himself. "Stop it."

She'd gotten a swallow tattooed on her lower back after her military days. It was common—and Sophie had always loved it. As far as she knew, Cayde had never minded until now.

He gave her a rough shove toward the doors. Sophie glanced back one last time at the officer. While Cayde browsed the shelves, she followed him around numbly, not really seeing or acknowledging the things he picked out.

Her phone buzzed in her back pocket. She pulled it out as casually as she could, doing her best not to draw Cayde's attention. The caller ID flashed Mark's name—or more likely, it was Noah and Charlie using their dad's phone.

She glanced at Cayde, who crouched by a shelf, absorbed in studying bottles of something she didn't care about, and wandered a few steps away, turning down the next aisle before she answered.

"Hello?" Her voice was as soft as she could make it.

"Mom?"

"Charlie!" Sophie grinned, and her little boy's voice instantly brought tears to her eyes. It was strange how just the sound or sight of her children could do that to her—overwhelming waves of love surged through her chest and poured out in tears. "How are you? Is Noah there?"

"I'm here, Mom," Noah's voice was quieter, more reserved.

"Oh, good!" Sophie's smile widened, tears spilling over. Just their voices had that effect on her. "Are you both doing okay? How was school? Didn't you just start back up?"

"We started three weeks ago," Noah said, his tone flat.

"Right." Sophie winced. "I'm sorry. Do you like your new school?"

"I do!" Charlie piped up, his excitement palpable. "My teacher gave me extra recess time because I did all my assignments on time."

"That's wonderful." She could picture his proud little face, his grin wide and missing a front tooth.

"Hey, buddy, can I talk to your mom for a second?" Mark's voice came through, soft but firm. "Sophie?"

Sophie glanced over her shoulder. Cayde was still browsing the aisles. She lowered her voice. "Mark. What's going on?"

"I was hoping you could tell me." His tone had a sharp edge to it.

"Tell you what?"

Mark scoffed. "I don't know, how about where you've been? Why you haven't settled your court case—or filed for visitation rights?"

"I don't see why I need to file. Can't you just let me see the boys without all that?"

"You know why." There was a pause. "I still don't know the reason you tried to take them out of state."

"I'm not getting into this," Sophie whispered, glancing around the shelves. "You don't understand."

"On the contrary, I think I've been more than understanding. At this point, you just have to take the matter up with the court."

Her chest tightened, frustration bubbling up with every word. "That won't be possible."

"I don't know what to tell you, Sophie. After everything that's happened, it's hard to trust you."

"I'm…" The tears spilled down Sophie's cheeks, hot and fast. "I want to come home," she breathed. "But I can't."

"What do you mean you can't?"

"I *want* to see the boys… but I can't." Sophie glanced around the corner. Cayde wasn't in sight. Her pulse quickened. "I need help."

"Sophie…" Mark's voice was strained.

"I need help." She said it again. The words burst out of her, trembling and raw. She'd refused to talk about it with her parents or brother, knowing what Cayde was capable of, and he reminded her constantly—how easy it would be to hurt her family, her kids. But there was something at its breaking point within her. She hadn't planned on reaching out to anyone, especially not Mark, but she couldn't go on like this. One of these camping trips, she just knew she wouldn't return. "Help me."

"Sophie, I can't." His tone dropped. "Whatever it is you're going through, I hope you figure it out. For the boys' sake, I really hope you do."

It felt like a punch to the gut. This wasn't some mental breakdown! This was true, physical peril. She was finally able to find it within herself to reach out a hand, and he... *hoped she'd figure it out?*

Before she could say anything else, someone grabbed Sophie's shoulder and spun her around. Cayde's face loomed over hers, his eyes blazing, his lips twisted in a vicious snarl. He snatched the phone out of her hand, glanced at the screen, and immediately ended the call.

"We'll talk about this later." His voice was low, vibrating with barely contained rage.

Talk. They'd "talk" about it at the campsite, in the middle of nowhere.

Sophie stepped back, heart racing, but Cayde clamped his hand around her arm and yanked her forward.

"Stop!" she cried out, but he just jerked her harder, his fingers digging painfully into her skin.

His eyes darted around the store, assessing the wandering gazes of passersby, then he leaned in close. "Keep your mouth shut, you cunt," he hissed. His breath was hot against her ear. "Do you want to cause a scene?"

That's exactly what she wanted. But as she struggled in his grip, he tightened his hold and started dragging her toward the exit. Customers glanced their way, some even paused, eyes narrowing in curiosity—then looked away. Moved on. The sight of a man hauling a crying woman away wasn't enough to make them intervene. It wasn't their business.

Her eyes darted frantically around the parking lot as they exited, searching for a lifeline. Where was the police car? Where was the officer? He was gone. Vanished.

Cayde's grip crushed her arm as he shoved her forward. They reached the car, and he flung her against the passenger door.

Once again, Sophie felt that crushing weight settle over her. The weight of absolute helplessness. Of knowing no one would save her.

She was alone. Completely, hopelessly, alone.

CHAPTER 60

JACK

Faster than Jack would have liked, dark thunderous clouds rolled in and rumbled, darkening the sky. He hoped it wouldn't rain. They needed the ground to stay as dry as possible for evidence. If Cayde had done something to his wife, they needed tire tracks, footprints, anything that might lead to where her body was. Jack just prayed that wasn't the outcome. The warehouse was large enough he could have hidden her away.

God, Jack prayed. *Please let her be there.* He didn't believe in God, but this case had him behaving in a way he'd never thought he would.

Blaire was intense and focused in the seat beside him. She had on a Kevlar vest over her shirt and her hair pulled up into a severe ponytail. Still, a few strands of brown hair framed her face. She looked at him, and they didn't need to say a word to one another.

The warehouse loomed in the distance, its shadowed façade a black smudge against the stormy sky. They had a perimeter of patrol cars concealed as far back as possible, hoping not to spook Cayde before they could spring the trap. But no movement had been reported, not a single flicker. In two minutes, the tactical units would seal off every exit, and Jack, Blair, and the entry team would breach.

Detective Jordan, a grizzled veteran with a perpetually irritated scowl, was running point on the local side. Jack didn't care for the man's gruff demeanor or his penchant for barking orders. Jordan had bulldozed through their planning session, barely giving Blair or Jack a chance to lay out the federal angle. The man had even tried to interview Veronica without clearance. Jack had shut that down hard, reminding Jordan that this was an FBI case. But the man's dismissive sneer had stuck with him.

"We're happy to assist, Agent Myers," Jordan had said, the condescension thick as molasses. "Let us go in, get this guy, and then we can iron out the details."

"We could have a potential hostage situation–" Blair had started, but was cut off as Jordan completely disregarded her words and started instructing the men next to him.

"Detective…" Jack stepped up beside his partner, his voice raised. "Need I remind you that Agent McCoy and I are leading this investigation? While we appreciate your cooperation and the support of manpower, this case is under the FBI's jurisdiction."

It had brought a quick end to the conversation.

Now, as they waited for the signal, Jack wondered if Blair held any resentment for the way he'd treated her. She'd often been overlooked, misrepresented, and not taken seriously in the years they'd worked together. She reminded Jack of Jodie Foster's character in *The Silence of the Lambs*: an agent who other men only looked at but otherwise disregarded. Blair never took it to heart. Most of the time, she pretended not to notice. And every single assignment she'd proven how capable and brilliant she was.

"Eyes up," she muttered. Jack followed her gaze. The clock was ticking down. They stepped out of the car, their boots crunching on the gravel, and moved into position. "Hey, Myers," Blair said, staring straight ahead. "About last night…"

"What about it?" Jack swallowed. For some reason, he felt more nervous about whatever she was going to say than he did rushing the warehouse. Their conversation had been one full of vulnerability and emotion. It may have even been borderline inappropriate and unprofessional.

"I don't call you Jack because that was the name of my ex-boyfriend." She wrinkled her nose. "And I hated him."

"What?" Jack hissed. It wasn't at all what he was expecting. But when he saw the smile creep up on her face, he felt his own expression lighten. Even before a situation like this, she had the ability to make light of it. "You never told me that."

"All units, move in."

There was no time for any more antics. They sprang into action, falling in line with the small tactical team as they advanced on the warehouse.

One of them pounded on the warehouse doors. "Police! Come out with your hands up."

There was nothing.

"Ram it," Jack ordered.

The battering ram hit the door with a resounding crash, the echo swallowed by the booming thunder outside. Darkness swallowed them as they entered, flashlights cutting through the dust-filled air. The warehouse was a maze of rusting machinery, stacked crates, and hanging chains. Every creak and groan of the building seemed amplified by the oppressive silence.

"Clear left!" Jack shouted, his voice tight with adrenaline. Blair mirrored him on the right, moving like a shadow. They cleared room after room, their movements synchronized, methodical. Jack's heart hammered in his chest, adrenaline sharpening his senses to a razor's edge.

There was a shuffle, and a dark form darted from one of the rooms, bolting to the end of the hallway where there were stairs.

"Hey!" Blair shouted, her drawn gun lifting toward the form, but it was gone in a flash. "Here!" She tossed the cry behind her, alerting the other police.

Jack was already in motion, taking the stairs two at a time, his pulse thundering in his ears. He caught a glimpse of Cayde at the top of the stairwell, his face pale and desperate in the dim light. Lightning flashed outside, illuminating the raw fear in Cayde's eyes. For a split second, Jack saw it: the terror of a cornered animal, more dangerous because it knew there was no escape.

"Stop! FBI!" Jack roared, but Cayde only pushed harder, his shoes slamming against the metal catwalk. Jack followed, feeling the structure shake beneath their weight. Below, he could see the tactical team fanning out, weapons drawn.

One of them raised their gun toward the both of them. He wasn't going to shoot while Jack was just behind Cayde, was he?

"Hold fire!" Blair shouted from behind Jack, but it was too late. A ringing pop sounded with a flash of light. Jack dove forward, unsure where the bullet went, but it definitely hadn't hit him—nor had it hit Cayde.

Cayde had ducked and looked down, his face a mask of fear. Disgust boiled in Jack's stomach. After everything he'd done to all these women, Cayde was nothing but a coward.

As Jack got to his feet, Blair passed him and threw her body forward, tackling Cayde to the ground just as he exited the catwalk. He twisted his torso around, fingers balled into a fist, and punched Blair square in the nose. For a brief moment, she was stunned. He pulled back his legs and kicked her, throwing her off. It awakened some sort of instinct in Jack, pushing him to move faster as he got to his feet. He couldn't help her, despite wanting to reach down and lift her to her feet, make sure she was okay.

But she was—she'd taken worse hits before, and God knew Jack had witnessed her moving forward as if they were nothing. He forced himself to look away from her, his focus locking onto Cayde, who was already fleeing down the narrow staircase, his footsteps echoing in the hollow space.

Jack took off after him. The chase led them to a cluttered section of the warehouse, a grim, dimly lit area packed with hulking machines and towering stacks of scrap metal. The shadows made the place feel like a twisted maze. Giant serrated wheels loomed like jagged teeth, their edges rusted and sharp, remnants of some heavy-duty industrial equipment meant to tear apart roads or chew through concrete.

Cayde skidded to a halt, realizing he was trapped. Flashlights glanced off the floor and walls as the police hurried toward him. He couldn't go forward, and he couldn't go back. Jack could see the panic in his eyes, the rapid rise and fall of his chest. But then Cayde turned, a desperate snarl twisting his face, and out of options, he came at Jack. His first punch whistled past Jack's ear, missing by a hair. The second one connected hard. Jack's head snapped back as pain exploded along his jaw, the force of the blow sending him reeling into a stack of rusted metal pipes.

Before he could recover, Cayde was on him, grabbing him by the collar and slamming him against a nearby machine. The impact drove the air from Jack's lungs in a sharp gasp. He felt a jagged piece of metal tear through his shirt and into his skin, just above the edge of his bulletproof vest. A searing pain shot through him, but he gritted his teeth, pushing past it. He reached up blindly, his fingers closing around one of the hanging chains.

With a swift motion, Jack looped the chain around Cayde's arm and yanked down hard. Cayde roared in anger, his arm twisting awkwardly as he struggled to break free. Blood oozed down Jack's back from the wound, but he shoved the pain aside, concentrating on restraining the man. Cayde thrashed wildly, his face contorted with rage and fear.

Jack could feel the fury radiating off him, the man's muscles tensing beneath his grip. Cayde's hand, still clenched around Jack's collar, slid up to his throat. The fingers pressed into his windpipe, squeezing tighter, nails digging into flesh. Jack's vision darkened at the edges, his breath coming in gasps as he clawed at Cayde's wrist, trying to break the chokehold.

He wheezed, his voice strangled and barely audible. But Cayde's grip only tightened, his face a mask of frenzied rage, eyes bulging with murderous intent.

In a desperate bid to break free, Jack twisted the chain tighter around Cayde's arm and jerked it with all his strength. Cayde howled, his grip on Jack's throat loosening just enough for Jack to gulp in a ragged breath. But then, with a sudden surge of strength, Cayde lifted Jack off his feet and drove him backward, slamming him down hard against the machine again.

White-hot agony ripped through Jack's shoulder as the sharp metal edge that had already cut him plunged deeper into his flesh. He felt it tear through muscle and sinew, a cold, wet sensation flooding his senses as blood poured from the wound. His head swam, the pain so intense it was almost blinding.

Whatever it was had impaled him.

CHAPTER 61

WENDY

Wendy sat on the couch. A week after leaving the hospital, she stared blankly into space. Archie played on the living room floor, babbling and chattering in that special, indecipherable language toddlers use. He rolled little cars back and forth. Normally, his voice lit up her world. But these days, it was just background noise, drowned out by the unrelenting whirl of thoughts in her head. The "CM" carved into her arm had scabbed over, but it bled now as Wendy picked at it, hardly noticing she'd developed the habit.

She planned. She prepared. Over and over again. Every room, every corner in the apartment. Wendy imagined Cayde advancing on her, and she'd run through a plan. What would she do if he came at her with his fists in Archie's room? If he pulled a gun in the kitchen? If he threw things in the bedroom? Every possibility. Every angle. Every outcome. She'd mapped it all.

For the first few days, Cayde stayed close, his eyes always on her. That night she'd tried to leave had shaken his trust. Even after she'd fallen back into her role of the obedient housewife. Now, any time he came too close, her mind raced, churning out strategies and contingencies. What if he grabbed her from behind? What if he lashed out at Archie?

But as long as Wendy behaved, so did Cayde. She stuck to her role. Played the part. And his temper simmered. Maybe he was lying low, worried the hospital visit had put him on some radar. Maybe he feared police intervention. Not that it mattered—they'd proven useless anyway.

She watched Archie, his tiny hands pushing the toy cars, making his own version of engine sounds. She loved him more than anything. That was what drove her—saving him. But the problem was the damned kidnapping charges. Lying in that hospital bed, battered and bruised, hadn't swayed the cops one bit. But a judge—maybe a judge would see differently. Maybe, if she had enough bruises, enough scars to show what really happened, a judge might just give her what she needed: a protective order, Archie's custody, maybe even a divorce.

The clock chimed. Lunch time. Wendy rose from the couch, moving mechanically to the kitchen. She poured boxed macaroni into boiling water, watching the spirals spin and tumble in the pot. Maybe the bruises could do more than just gain sympathy. Maybe, if she played it right, they could justify something far more final.

She stirred the pasta, lost in thought. If she walked the tightrope carefully enough—showed just enough damage, enough fear, enough proof—she could make a case. If a judge believed her life was truly at risk, maybe she could end it. End him.

There was one option she'd been contemplating since that night he put the gun to Archie's head: manslaughter in the name of self-defense.

The idea wouldn't leave. Evidence of Cayde's abuse would not only secure Archie's safety, it might pave the way to ridding them of him for good. Permanently. Because even if she ran, even if she won custody, Cayde would never let them go. She knew it. She felt it in her bones. She felt it carved in the initials that branded her skin. He'd chase her, haunt her, destroy her—and Archie—if she didn't end it. If she didn't do something soon, she'd be the one who ended up in a body bag.

Wendy kept stirring. Around and around. The noodles swirled, the water bubbled and hissed. Her eyes stared through the steam, vision narrowing.

If she didn't kill him, he'd kill her. It was that simple.

CHAPTER 62

CLAIRE

The hospital waiting room was full of weary, grim faces. Claire sat, tense and miserable, beside Cayde. Her mother was in the E.R. after a nasty fall that morning, and though she'd have preferred to handle it alone, Cayde had insisted on coming along. He was her only transportation, after all. He sat next to her, shifting restlessly in his seat, looking more bored than concerned.

Across from them, Jessie leaned forward, elbows on her knees. She'd rushed over, doing her best to support her friend. Claire suspected it was more to act as a buffer between her and Cayde. Tension coiled tight between the three of them, unspoken but present.

Claire's phone vibrated. She glanced at the screen. The name that flashed made her heart skip a beat—Zach. The last person she'd expected to hear from today.

Before Cayde could peer over her shoulder, she pushed herself up from the seat, muttering something about needing to call the school and arrange a substitute. She moved off a few paces, keeping herself in Cayde's line of sight. The last thing she needed was him following her or, worse, accusing her later of sneaking off. It would look strange for him to trail her in front of a room full of people. But still, she felt his eyes on her back, a prickling heat, like a brand.

"Hey," Claire whispered into the phone, unable to hide her surprise. "I didn't expect you to call." Maybe Paige had told him about her mom's accident.

"Hey, Claire." Zach's voice, soft and familiar, struck a chord deep in her chest. Gentle, soothing. So different from the harshness that had become her reality. "I have some news I need to tell you."

Claire frowned, heartbeat thundering in her ears. "What is it?" Was it Paige? Had something happened?

There was a pause, then: "My father passed away unexpectedly last night."

The world seemed to collapse around her. "No," she breathed. That was all she could say. The air thickened in her throat, refusing to pass through. "No."

Claire's own father had died when she was just fourteen, and in all the years she'd been married to Zach, his father had been a second dad to her. He'd embraced her like a daughter, welcoming her into the family with open arms. A true parent. Someone she could count on. She gasped, breath hitching painfully in her chest as tears blurred her vision. "No," she repeated, voice breaking.

People in the waiting room started to look over, glancing at her with a mix of concern and curiosity as she stood there, clutching the phone, sobbing openly. All the emotions she'd been bottling up surged forth—grief for her father-in-law, fear for her mother, and that ever-present, gnawing regret. The regret that came with every decision, every small hope for change that was crushed under Cayde's heel. Today was supposed to be a new beginning, and yet here she was—spiraling deeper into chaos.

"I'm sorry," Zach murmured, filling in the details in a low, gentle tone as she cried. "I didn't want to tell you like this. I haven't told Paige yet. I thought you should know first."

"Thank you," she choked out, wiping at her face with the back of her hand. "I—" Her voice cracked. "I'm at the hospital. My mom... She's hurt."

"I'm sorry, Claire," he said softly. "I wish I could be there."

She nodded, even though he couldn't see it. "Me too." More tears spilled down her cheeks. "I'm so sorry. I'm so sorry."

They exchanged condolences, Claire's words coming out ragged and broken. She tried to steady herself, forcing her voice to quiet, though every breath felt heavy and painful. Finally, she hung up, clutching the phone so tightly her knuckles ached.

"What happened?" Jessie asked softly.

"Zach's father passed away," Claire managed, her voice barely above a whisper.

Cayde shot her a sharp look, eyes narrowing. "So, I take it that wasn't the school then," he sneered.

Jessie ignored him, moving closer to sit on Claire's other side. She wrapped an arm around Claire's shoulders, her touch gentle. "I know you were close to him."

Claire couldn't hold back the tears. Her chest tightened, squeezing painfully with every breath, and white spots flickered in her vision. The sobs wracked her body, unstoppable.

A doctor emerged from the E.R., speaking in low, calm tones. Claire struggled to focus, her ears ringing. She picked up fragments of the conversation—her mother was stabilized now. That was the only word she clung to, the only thing she could grasp.

Jessie nodded at the doctor, murmured something Claire didn't catch, then turned back to her. "Your mom is sleeping now. Why don't you go home and get some rest?" Her voice was soothing, but the words hardly registered. "Come back later."

Numbly, Claire nodded. She stood up, hugging Jessie tightly before heading to the door, wiping at her eyes with a sleeve that was already soaked with tears. Cayde watched her, his face devoid of any hint of empathy, anger simmering beneath the surface.

The drive home was silent at first. Claire's heart pounded in her chest, pain radiating through her ribs. She closed her eyes, pressing her hands against her face, as if she could hold the pieces of herself together.

"Will you stop it?" Cayde snapped suddenly, his voice grating. He slammed a hand against the steering wheel, making her flinch. "Stop cryin'!"

"My chest hurts." Claire clutched at it, gasping for breath.

"You've been talkin' to your ex-husband this whole time, haven't you?" he accused, his voice dripping with venom. "How many times have you lied to me? How many times was it him on the other end of the phone?"

There was no reasoning with him. Not now. Maybe not ever. "I can't do this anymore, Cayde," she sobbed, the words pouring out uncontrollably. "I'm exhausted. I'm heartbroken. Please."

He scoffed beside her, shaking his head like she was some pathetic, hysterical creature throwing a tantrum.

Claire drew in a shaky breath, trembling. Every inch of her felt frayed, like she was coming apart at the seams. Rock bottom wasn't a place anymore—it was an endless fall, getting deeper and darker every day.

CHAPTER 63

SOPHIE

The campfire splashed sparks into the night sky. Sophie watched Cayde through the flames as he drank beer after beer. In the firelight, his brown eyes looked black, and his handsome features cast angular shadows across his face. It was easy for anyone to fall for a face like his, but she could barely remember the man she thought she loved. That man had seemed like an angel.

Looking at him now, the red light flickering across his features, she quoted Corinthians: *"For Satan himself masquerades as an angel of light."* She was barely aware of whispering it to herself.

"What are you mumblin' about over there?" Cayde asked, taking a swig. He was well past the point of being drunk.

She sat across from the fire, knees to her chest, folded in on herself while sitting on a cheap camping chair. She was waiting, biding her time. He would punish her for talking to Mark at the hardware store, but if she played her cards right, she might be able to lessen the consequences. "I was thinking of the Bible."

"The Bible?" He huffed. "You could have gotten yourself arrested today. You know that?"

"I'm sorry."

"Why did you call Mark?"

"He called me—well, my kids called me." She hugged her legs a little tighter.

"You're lyin'." He raised the can of beer in the air, then tossed it aside. Empty. Then he got up from his chair and staggered over to the supplies sitting out. Probably fishing for another lukewarm beer. "I heard you on the phone."

Sophie said nothing. Anything she could say might make him fly off the handle. As he bent over, she looked at the gun tucked in the back of his pants. He rummaged through the supplies and then brought out a small jug of something.

"You want him to come back to you? You want him to come rescue you from the bad man?" he mocked her.

"No." Sophie tried her best to give a warm, caring smile. "*You're* my husband, Cayde."

"I know what you really are." He pointed at her with his free hand. "Any woman with a tattoo right there is..." He frowned, thought for a minute, and then said, "You're a whore. What you need is to be wiped clean of it."

Sophie started to shake her head, confused. Then she saw the bottle he held in his hands.

"Picked it up today at the hardware store," Cayde said, holding it up. "Highest concentrated mix of sulfuric acid you can buy over the counter."

A noise welled up in her throat. A half shriek and half gasp. She tumbled out of the chair less gracefully than she wanted, and it cost her time. Scrambling to her feet, Sophie started toward the darkness before her. She would rather face the wilderness than what was coming. But even in his drunken state, Cayde was faster.

He merely shoved her forward. She stretched her arms out before her. Her face still slid over the dirt and rocks. And then his weight crushed down on her back, one hand holding down her head as she kicked and screamed. His other hand fumbled with her shirt and the back of her pants. On her belly, she couldn't use her arms and hands the way she needed to. She might have had more luck clawing at the hand placing tremendous pressure on her skull. But fear forced her to swat weakly at her back, trying to pull her shirt down or knock the bottle from his hands.

"And fear not..." Cayde's breath was ragged from the excitement and alcohol. She heard him take off the cap of the bottle with his mouth and spit it somewhere off to the side. He was completely insane.

"Please!" Sophie sobbed into the ground. "Cayde!"

He leaned down, close to her ear. *"For the Lord thy God shall wash away your sins."* And Cayde, in his own, twisted way, did.

CHAPTER 64

AUTUMN

Snowflakes busily drifted about, floating in every direction. Autumn watched as they settled on the grass, slowly dissolving into drops of water. The snow in Nashville wouldn't stick, but toward the end of the year, little white flakes came once or twice.

Autumn watched as they touched the waterfront she stood by. They did not slowly dissolve into nothing but instead were swept instantly away by the water.

It would be fast.

Colored lights decorated the parks and families walked hand in hand, buying presents and enjoying one another's company as they readied themselves for the holidays. College students laughed, sipping warm drinks and shopping with friends during their winter break.

Autumn ached to join them. To be with her family the way she used to be, open and honest. And she missed her friends. She imagined how things would have been, had she not married Cayde. Still living with her old roommates, continuing her education, leading a life with cares so menial it was almost laughable to think about her current stressors.

What she once dreamed and hoped for was now gone, swept away like the snowflakes in the river. Any fight she had left to give, he would crush. She spent her days and nights worried about the safety of her family. Cayde had tried to kill her—instantly making every threat he spoke viable and real. She could never return to the way things were. He had changed—had *taken*—everything from her.

A cold, cutting breeze rattled the dead leaves on the ground. There were no Christmas lights here. She felt just like the trees—naked, stripped bare of everything and exposed to the coldness of the world.

She stepped toward the water. Not even tears stained her cheeks. This was the only way to be rid of him. Like this, there would be no violent struggles she couldn't possibly win, and no danger to her family. She would be gone, and she would be free. In comparison to Cayde, the rushing winter water could have been a warm embrace.

She stepped again and breathed out, sending a prayer to God. She wondered if he would hear her. Another step. This time, her toes went over the edge of the riverbed, the water surging and splashing at her shoes. She closed her eyes, lifted her arms a little, and leaned forward.

A small flutter from within startled her. Autumn stepped back and placed her hands over her stomach. *No—not alone.* Now she cried. Not because of the despair, nor the immense fear, but because for the first time since realizing she'd become pregnant, Autumn had felt her child.

That small flutter changed everything all at once. New emotions flooded out the current ones that plagued her: protectiveness, determination, a type of fierce and all-encompassing love she didn't understand. She was going to be a mother to this little being. It depended on her. Deep inside, Autumn felt it was a sign from God. Maybe he hadn't abandoned her. In turn, she would not abandon her child.

"I promise you," she spoke through her tears. "I will get us out of this mess."

For the sake of her child, her family, and herself, Autumn vowed she would be free of Cayde.

CHAPTER 65

KATE

Kate turned the page of her book about every two minutes. She wasn't really reading. She was waiting. Cayde typed on his laptop across from her. They'd planted themselves at a table in the library next to Blue's Hideaway Motel. He liked it when she sat and read near him on the days he worked there so he could keep an eye on her. They'd left poor Bella in the car with a cracked window. Thankfully, she had a spot in the back seat with blankets to curl up and rest. Kate would check on her in an hour or so.

She'd picked out a book and pretended to read it for a while. Instead, Kate rehearsed in her mind what she needed to do over and over. First, there were several key things she'd already accomplished. She'd called to find out how much retirement she had from her time at the bank. Accounting for penalties and taxes, Kate figured she'd be left with about fifty-eight thousand dollars—enough to get her started somewhere. Then she gathered up some courage and called Zoey.

As much as she didn't want to involve her daughter in this, it was the only way Kate could get the rest of the money *without* Cayde's hands on it. Zoey, brilliant and brave, was more than willing to help.

"You'll have to call in my name. They'll also want my social security number. I'll send that to you as well. Tell them you want to close out the retirement and take a check."

"Okay, Mama," Zoey had said. "What else?"

"You'll have to open a separate account under your name for it. Cayde has access to all of mine. I'm going to send you a document giving you power of attorney. That will allow you to sign the check on my behalf when it gets to your house."

Now Kate just needed to print the POA document to sign and send to her daughter. The library would notarize it for free, which saved Kate a lot of hassle.

She closed her book. "I'm not liking this," Kate said. She'd waited an hour for Cayde to really settle into his work. "I'm going to look for something else."

Cayde, uninterested, didn't even look at her. He only grunted to acknowledge what she'd said.

Kate stood and wandered into the mystery and thriller section of the library but passed through the aisle completely, trying to put as many bookshelves as possible between herself and Cayde. She walked close to the walls and made her way to the public computers.

She logged in with a guest ID and worked as fast as she could. As the browser loaded, she glanced back toward the area where Cayde sat. He was still engrossed in his work. Kate loaded the form she needed, scanning over it to ensure it would work for Zoey. Kate wasn't one to curse, but she swore softly as she realized she would need two witness signatures on the document. To state that she was of sound mind in transferring power of attorney rights to Zoey.

She would ask Bill and Mary, the two custodians at the truck stop, tonight. Mary would do it—but Bill was a gamble. He and Cayde talked often. Maybe enough to have formed a friendship–enough to warn him that she was trying to escape. But there was no one else to sign. She would have to risk it.

She looked back at Cayde once again. He was no longer at the table; he was walking around the shelves, clearly looking for her. She glanced at the printer located at an information desk not too far from the computers. There was a sign that read: "First 10 pages free." Good thing she didn't need any more than that. Kate clicked "Print" and stood up from the computer, not bothering to log off. She ducked behind a shelf and watched where he went. He passed the information desk, his head swiveling back and forth.

Her document was printed out right beside him.

Kate took a deep breath, balled up her fists, and began to pray to God. She said sorry for things that weren't her fault, sorry for things that were, and promised she'd do better if he granted her mercy. Let her get that document safely, let her get it notarized, and let her leave him. She repeated the prayer three times before Cayde set off in the other direction of the library.

Kate breathed out and walked as fast as she could to the information desk. She snatched the document from the printer with more intensity than she intended, slightly frightening the woman behind the counter.

"Hi, I need this notarized." Kate slid it toward her. "Is there someone available to do it?"

"I can do it for you, dear," the older woman said, taking off her glasses to look over the paper. "Do you have ID on you? A driver's license or a passport?"

"Yes." Kate offered up her driver's license.

The woman took it and set it aside, gathering her own tools for the process. "Do you have your witnesses here?"

"No," Kate started, "but I—"

"I can't notarize or sign this until I have all three signatures. I must witness every single one."

Kate wanted to stomp her foot like a child, the fear and frustration boiling up in her body and ready to burst out like steam. "I know!" she said, then looked around. Cayde was still out of sight. He could show up any minute. "I know." She was sweating now. If Cayde caught her, he'd beat her senseless tonight. He'd probably take her phone and cut all contact off with her daughter as well. "I was just wondering if maybe you could make an exception. I could sign my portion now, you could sign and notarize it, and I could get the other signatures later?"

The woman put back on her glasses just so she could tilt her head and look up and over them at Kate, as though she were an idiot. "No, honey, I most certainly cannot do that."

Tears threatened to fall, and Kate clenched her teeth. Cayde would find her any moment. He would see her talking to this woman and cut in, demanding to know what it was they were discussing.

"Look," the words started to spill out of Kate's mouth. "I'm doing this so that I can leave the man who stole everything I was worth, beat me, and threatened my family. I'm doing this because my husband is going to kill me."

The two of them stared at one another, surprise marking their expressions. Kate hadn't admitted that aloud before, and she certainly hadn't meant to now. The woman clearly didn't expect to hear such a small but desperate speech. Kate stared at her, really looking past the fine lines and wrinkles caked over with too much concealer; she could see the hidden splotch underneath the woman's eye. Kate covered up her own bruises the same way.

"Kate!" Cayde's voice was like a bark. He was striding toward them. It was too late. "What are you doin'?"

"I'm so sorry, ma'am," the librarian said, and Kate's heart sank. Unexpectedly, the woman placed a piece of copy paper on top of Kate's document and license, hiding it from view. "I can check the back for that or the return pile for you." Kate didn't understand, but the woman suddenly had an intent look in her eyes. "If you want to sit at the table, I'll bring you what you need."

"Bring what?" Cayde asked, now at the desk.

"She's looking for a particular title," the woman said. "I was just saying I would get it for her." She smiled at Kate. "I'll do what I can."

Kate could have burst into tears, but she continued to hold them back. "Thank you."

"Of course." The woman gathered Kate's documents next to her, hidden under the blank paper, and disappeared into the back room.

Kate walked with Cayde back to the table, wondering how she was going to get back her license and POA document without alerting him. He furrowed his brow a little. "What book did you need?"

"Oh, it was something Mary suggested." She was afraid giving any more information would mess up whatever plan the librarian had.

"I couldn't find you," Cayde grumbled.

"I was looking for the book for a long time. In a lot of different sections. I eventually just asked for help."

Kate sat down at the table with Cayde, who started working on whatever it was he was doing but glanced at her now and again. She didn't dare get up and leave. And she refused to turn around to look at the information desk. She was trying to come up with an excuse to go back to the desk when the librarian appeared at their table.

"Found it!" She handed Kate a hefty romance novel. Kate looked at it, noticing that carefully tucked between the pages of the book was her license and a folded document.

"It's exactly what I needed," Kate said and looked the woman in the eyes. "Thank you."

"You're welcome, honey." The librarian looked at Cayde, perhaps a bit scornfully, and returned to her desk.

Cayde snorted. "A romance novel?"

The cover was a bit dramatic, a blond caught in the arms of a dark-haired man without a shirt on. Yet because of what was inside of it, Kate thought it was the most beautiful thing she'd ever seen.

"Thought I'd take a chance," Kate said.

CHAPTER 66

JACK

Pain flared in Jack's shoulder with every jerk of his body, his vision blurring with agony and frustration. Where were the damned officers? He coughed, his throat raw, and tried to lift his knee, aiming to strike Cayde in the groin. But before he could make his move, Cayde's body convulsed violently, his limbs locking up as his eyes rolled back, a guttural sound escaping his throat.

He crumpled to his knees, revealing Blair standing behind him, her stance steady, a taser gun gripped tightly in her hand. Her hair had come loose from its neat ponytail, wild strands sticking to her sweat-slicked forehead. Blood gushed from her nose, streaking down her lips and chin before dripping onto the concrete floor. Her eyes burned with a fierce determination as she moved in quickly, shoving Cayde onto his stomach and yanking his arms behind his back to cuff him.

Jack gasped, feeling the hot agony searing through his shoulder as he tried to push himself away from the equipment. He let out a strangled cry behind clenched teeth as he peeled himself off the jagged piece of metal that had punctured his flesh. Blood poured freely from the wound, soaking his shirt. He clamped his teeth together, fighting to stay conscious.

"Myers?" Blair's voice was rough, strained, as she glanced up at him.

"Just a scratch," Jack muttered, his jaw clenched so tight it felt like it might snap. "I'm okay." He knelt beside them, breath coming in shallow gasps as he fought through the pain.

The officers finally rushed in, surrounding Cayde and Blair, their faces anxious as they awaited orders. Jack's fury blazed white-hot. Where the hell had they been? He could have killed them for taking so long to cover the distance from one side of the warehouse to the other.

He leaned down, forcing himself to meet Cayde's gaze. "Where is she? Is she here?" he rasped, his voice trembling with urgency and fear.

Cayde's breath hitched, his chest heaving as tears mixed with the dust on his face, streaking his cheeks. "No," he choked out, the word a guttural growl that sent a chill down Jack's spine.

Jack looked over his shoulder, his voice rising in desperation. "Check all the rooms again! Clear everything! Find her!" He turned back to Cayde, his voice dropping to a deadly whisper. "Where is she?"

Cayde's eyes were wide and crazed, his lips trembling as he spoke. "She went to be with God."

Blair's face twisted, her eyes narrowing as a wave of raw fury crossed her features. Her body tensed as she hovered over him, and for a moment, Jack thought she might lose control. The muscles in her arm twitched, her fist clenching, as if she was about to strike him down right there on the cold concrete floor. But then, her shoulders slumped, and something in her seemed to break. The fire in her eyes dimmed, replaced by a hollow, cold emptiness. It was the look of defeat, of utter hopelessness.

"Sir?" An officer hovered nearby, his voice hesitant, waiting for orders.

Jack nodded to him. "Get him out of here." As they hauled Cayde off, he reached around to press his fingers into his back. When he pulled them away, they were wet with blood.

"You're hurt," Blair said, her voice monotone. Neither of them got off the floor. She wiped her nose with a sleeve, smearing red across her cheek.

"He broke your nose," Jack said.

She shrugged and spat a little from her mouth. Then she moved slightly closer and placed a hand on Jack's leg. Both should have gone out to the ambulance, but for a moment, in the blood and dust, they just sat with one another in their shared grief.

They both knew what the silence meant. No one shouted back that they'd found her. No radio crackled with good news. No footsteps rushed forward in triumph.

They had failed, and a woman was dead.

CHAPTER 67

SOPHIE

In this part of Kansas, everyone seemed to own long lengths of land. Small ranches and farms lined the streets and surrounded the stores of what was supposedly a town. A few privately owned convenience stores and gas stations were the only semblance of public communities that Sophie could see as she looked out the window. She would be glad to leave.

Cayde and Sophie were still traveling with no real destination in mind, but instead of camping, Cayde had picked out a motel to stay in. She itched at the scars on her neck, anxious to arrive and carry out something she'd been planning to do for a long while.

She had called Tanner yesterday.

It was something she'd sworn never to do. Cayde was Sophie's responsibility, but as the scars on her neck and back healed, something inside her had revived. Especially after hearing her children's voices. That phone call in the hardware store had done wonders for her spirit. Soon, it would be Thanksgiving. She imagined herself at the dinner table with them, laughing, holding their little hands as she said grace. The mild daydream urged her to take a risk.

Sophie had requested a particular fast-food chain for lunch a day back. It was the kind of food she didn't even like her boys, with their iron guts, to eat. Cayde, in a good mood, allowed them to eat there for lunch. As she predicted, he ordered a cheeseburger. She added a milkshake to her meal but insisted it be his favorite flavor. He drank most of it. The quality of the food, combined with the dairy, had sent him pulling over at the nearest gas station within thirty minutes.

The severity of his emergency allowed for a little sloppy work. He left her in the car and took the keys, but that wasn't what she was hoping he'd leave behind. It was her phone. Since her conversation with Mark, he'd been overly strict with its usage, often keeping it on his person if he wasn't right beside her.

So, with Cayde fighting his own battles in the bathroom of a grimy gas station, Sophie ate a fry and called her brother.

She didn't explain much, only that she had a little bit of time to talk and needed his help. Like the protective brother he had always been, he immediately said he would. She said she was leaving Cayde, but it needed to be a secret. And it might be dangerous. Tanner didn't sound surprised. She told him the name of the motel they were driving toward and planning to stay at for the night.

At this very moment, Tanner was driving all the way to Kansas to pick Sophie up. There might not be a better time to call him, so she promised to text him when she could and, if not, to plan for midnight. She would sneak out of the motel and pray that Tanner was waiting in the parking lot like they'd planned.

Everything had gone to plan for the last twenty-four hours.

Until now.

"I think we were supposed to get off there," Sophie said, turning around and pointing. "The motel should be a few miles east of that exit." She grabbed her phone, intending to look it up, but Cayde ripped it out of her hands and tossed it up by the gear shift.

"You don't need that," he said. "We're not goin' to that motel anymore. We'll drive further south and find a place there for the night."

Her heart drummed. Now what would she do? She needed to tell Tanner the location had changed, but she knew if she asked for her phone back, Cayde would get upset or suspicious.

"Can we stop somewhere?" Sophie asked, glancing outside as the buildings grew scarcer and scarcer. Soon they would be in the middle of nowhere, miles away from where her aunt and brother thought she'd be. Miles away from anyone. "I'm hungry."

Cayde cocked his head toward the back seat, where old gas station snacks had been picked over. "We have food there. Besides, the last place you picked to eat gave me food poisonin'."

It wasn't quite food poisoning, but Sophie wouldn't argue.

She chewed on her lip. "How long until the next motel? And how long are we going to stay there?"

"Why?" He narrowed his eyes.

"I just thought we were going to make our way back to Tennessee soon. You know, for the holidays?"

"We are." He added nothing more to prove his claim.

There was a light from Sophie's phone, which sat face up. It vibrated against the car console, the chimes catching Cayde's attention. Both of them looked at the caller ID.

Tanner Hale.

"Oh, Tanner!" Sophie tried to sound casual and reached for the phone. "I haven't spoken to him in ages."

"Leave it," Cayde growled, and he gave her a hard look. Sophie couldn't tell if he knew she was lying or if she was just nervous about him finding out.

The phone rang a few more times, then stopped. He called again, and inwardly, Sophie just wished he'd stop. It was going to make Cayde suspicious.

Then the screen lit up with a ding as a new text message popped up: "I'm two hours away."

The world seemed to stop then. Sophie's heart sank and accelerated at the same time. As she read it, so did Cayde. He inhaled deeply through his nose, and his fingers tightened around the steering wheel.

"Two hours from where?"

Her mind couldn't think. She'd been too panicked and overwhelmed to come up with a good excuse now. "I—" She stuttered and shrugged. It was almost as good as a confirmation to him.

With one hand, he shoved her against the door and then opened the glove box. Inside was his gun. He grabbed it and tapped it against the steering wheel, his expression dark and furious.

"Is Tanner in Kansas, Sophie? And don't lie."

She'd been threatened and hurt by Cayde more times than she could count. But now, tears stung her eyes. Not just because of the danger, but because with every second that passed, her hope slipped further away. This was her one chance.

"Answer me!"

"I just wanted to see him," she explained, fighting to keep her voice controlled. She stared at the gun, carelessly held in his hand. "He was already in Kansas, so we thought—"

"You're lyin' to me. You said you hadn't talked to him recently." The car started to speed up. "Are you gonna tell me the truth or not?"

"Come on, Cayde." She breathed out, glancing at the road in the hopes that anyone would pass by and see the gun on the steering wheel. "If you'd just calm down—"

He pointed the gun toward her. "I am calm."

To Sophie's horror, he was right. There was rage and fury, but it was held together under a calm demeanor. Nothing about shooting her in his car seemed to frighten or bother him.

"We're going to the motel south from here," she said carefully. "And we won't be seeing my brother." It wasn't an answer to his question, but more of a confirmation of the plan he wanted. It seemed to work, a little. He put the gun back on the steering wheel.

She was silent for a long while. They eventually got off the highway to take a back road, Cayde insisting on finding a liquor store. Sophie had to make a choice. She could sit quietly and drive further out of reach of the one person who could help her, or she could try again and risk the consequences.

"Cayde." She eyed a grocery store as they passed it, cars from the little town pulling in and out. "I have to go to the bathroom."

"You'll wait until we get to the motel."

"I drank all of this—" She held up an empty water bottle. "—and the coffee from this morning. I can't hold it any longer."

Cayde glanced back at the grocery store in the rearview mirror and suddenly pulled over. "You can go here, but I'm not takin' you into any stores after the stunt you just pulled."

"You're going to make me squat on the side of the road?"

He flicked the gun toward the door. "Go on."

"Fine," she huffed and began to remove her jacket. She eyed the phone on the console. No way he'd let her touch it. Or her purse. She would have to do this without them. She got out of the car, leaving her jacket behind and tying up her hair.

"Stay where I can see you," he ordered.

"I'm only going right here." She backed up to the back of the car, making eye contact with him in the side mirror as she crouched down, careful to stay where he could only see her head. Instead of pulling down her pants, Sophie tied up the loose laces on her shoes with trembling fingers. She had one chance at this, and she wasn't about to mess it up by tripping herself. A car passed, and she saw Cayde's eyes look over at it.

Now.

Sophie bolted, running down the side of the road toward the store. She heard Cayde shout and the car engine roar as he started it back up. She glanced behind to see him flip the car around and head straight for her. Ahead, a little Toyota was coming in the opposite direction. She crossed the street, waving her arms and shouting. The Toyota swerved and honked but didn't stop for her. Cayde sped up. He would catch her in seconds like this.

She changed course, going off the road and bolting for a cattle fence. The old brown post gave her hand splinters as she grabbed it to leap over, and barbed wire snagged her pants, ripping into the skin on the back of her calf. Awkwardly, she tumbled on the other side and scrambled to her feet. She could cut directly across the field toward the store without the danger of being run over. As she sprinted through the dirt and dead grass, she kept an eye on Cayde's car as he sped across the roads, making his way to the same place. She would simply have to be faster.

She made it to the other edge of the property, this time ducking through the barbed wire instead of over it. Now the back of her shirt ripped. There was a commotion and screeching of tires as Cayde tried to pull into the parking lot at the same time someone was turning in front of him. It bought her the few seconds she needed.

The doors to the store were only a hundred or so yards away, and Sophie ran, aware that Cayde's car was now directly behind her. She looked back to see his angry face behind the steering wheel. She couldn't hear him, but she knew he was screaming her name.

She faced the doors, keeping her eyes on the target. Only a few more yards to go. Fifty—he was so close behind her—twenty—just a little faster—ten—

A gunshot.

Sophie screamed and covered her head, diving to her left behind a large SUV in a handicap parking spot. Other people screamed too. She remained crouched, only looking up at the sound of screeching tires. Cayde had pulled around the lot, now speeding his way back toward the main roads. He was fleeing.

She panted, her legs barely getting her to her feet, and backed into the store. A security guard, wide-eyed, rushed toward the front. "What was that?" he asked.

Sophie looked at him, almost in disbelief that she'd actually made it. "Call the police," she said. "That man just tried to kill me."

She waited. Her hands wrapped around herself while the police took a statement from the security guard. All she could think about was asking one of them to get ahold of her brother. Not too long ago, an officer not only refused to help her but had belittled and encouraged Cayde. Surely, Sophie thought, after a public shooting, someone would listen to her now.

"Your name?"

"Sophie Miller." One of the officers wrote things down slowly. "One moment, please," he said, and started to walk away.

"Wait, can you call my brother for me?" Sophie asked, hugging herself tighter. "His name is Tanner Hale."

The officer looked at her bleakly. "One moment."

"Oh, please," Sophie whimpered, half to herself and half as a prayer to God. Her eyes darted to the woods beyond the windows. What if Cayde came back? He could always smooth-talk his way out of things. "Please, please, please..."

"Ma'am?" The officer returned, his face contorted with concern. "Are you aware there is a warrant out for your arrest?"

Sophie's heart plummeted. All she could do was stare dumbly at him, her mouth gaping open.

"Please put your hands behind your back for me." He moved toward her, grabbing her wrist and rotating her around. "Sophie Miller, you are under arrest for failing to appear in court and violating the terms of your bail."

"Wait!" Sophie cried. Everyone was watching her. They whispered to one another, not a shred of sympathy on their faces. "You don't understand!" She shook her head, her voice a low moan.

The officer listed off her rights, but she didn't hear a word. He guided her to his police car, and at least, Sophie thought, he was gentle about it. The bystanders looked at her, confused as they gave their own statements.

Sophie became very quiet and looked out the window. She looked at the sky, dimming as the sun set. Birds flapped their wings, swooping up and down in the air. She imagined Cayde shooting them, their little bodies exploding in a puff of feathers.

After a while, the officers got back in the car and started to drive away. One of them looked behind, checking on her, but didn't say anything.

"Have you found him?" Sophie asked.

"We'll keep looking," the driver responded.

Sophie stared at his eyes through the rearview mirror. "Promise?"

His eyebrows furrowed at that, but he didn't say anything more.

Sophie leaned against the window, closed her eyes, and silently cried.

CHAPTER 68

KATE

"Bella, what's wrong?" Kate stroked two fingers down Bella's spine. The little dog didn't move. She remained curled up in her blankets in the passenger seat of the car, blinking at nothing and giving small whines now and again. "Are you sick?"

Kate had been so stressed and anxious for the past year and a half. Maybe all of it was catching up to the poor little dog. "Don't worry," Kate whispered. "Very soon, everything is going to be all right."

Speaking of, she felt the weight of the POA document in the pocket of her hoodie. It was tucked into an envelope with Zoey's address already on it. All she needed was the two signatures. Kate placed Bella's little food bowl beside her, which had not been touched in days, and shut the car door. She wrapped her arms around herself, trying to fight off the cold, and looked around for Mary. She found her exiting the bathroom, a "DO NOT ENTER" sign placed in front of it.

"Hi, Kate!" Mary waved at her. "I wanted to ask you if you'd like to use the bathroom before I take down the sign. It's just freshly cleaned. You'd have it all to yourself."

"Please!" Kate could almost sigh in relief. She'd be able to wash up in privacy—for the first time in days. "Also, I wanted to see if you'd do me a favor."

"Of course." Mary's face got serious.

Kate stepped closer and lowered her voice. "I need you and Bill to sign this. I'm mailing it to my daughter to help me get access to some money." She glanced around again. "I want to take Bella and leave, but I'm going to need your help."

Truly, Kate hated to ask. It burned her up to risk the young woman's safety like this.

Mary subtly took the envelope. "Absolutely."

"Do you think Bill will sign it?" Kate knew he and Cayde were talking at this very moment. The old man seemed to enjoy Cayde's witty banter.

"You leave old Bill to me," Mary said, tucking the papers away. "Go ahead and wash up, if you'd like. I'll get it signed and bring it back to you."

"Thank you!" Kate gave Mary a quick hug. "Be careful Cayde doesn't see you."

"Oh, don't worry; he's more afraid of me than I'm afraid of him." She winked at Mary. "He thinks I'm a lesbian."

Kate laughed, and Mary walked away, resuming her cleaning duties but keeping an eye on Bill for when he separated from Cayde. Kate went back to her car, grabbed a tote bag with her soaps and shampoos, and entered the closed bathroom.

It was still harder to do everything she needed to with only a sink, but now she didn't have to worry about anyone else coming inside. Washing her hair without the fear of embarrassment felt good—the actual scrubbing did not. Her skull was so sore. She wondered if she'd have any kind of permanent damage from how often Cayde hit her there.

A knock came at the door. "Kate? It's Mary."

Kate, now dressed in a crewneck and sweats, opened the door. Mary slipped inside, waving the envelope. "Bill signed it. He said he was happy to do it and not to worry. He won't say anything."

Kate wrapped her towel around her hair and breathed out. "Perfect. I just need to send it to Zoey and…" After that, Kate wasn't exactly sure. She should probably find a way to get back to Virginia. Maybe a shuttle.

"You might want to stay at the motel tonight." Mary frowned as Kate shivered with her wet hair. "Figure things out in a warm room."

They chatted a little longer, Kate trying to towel dry her hair and pack up her supplies so Mary could reopen the bathroom.

"Kate," Mary said after a little while, "why don't you take Bella and come back to my house? It'll be safe for you until you figure out your plan to leave—"

No sooner had she said the word than the bathroom door exploded open, and Cayde burst through it.

"I knew you two were up to somethin'!" he snarled. He took one of Kate's unpacked shampoo bottles and chucked it in Mary's direction. It bounced off the sink near her, hit the wall, and then dropped to the floor, the cap flying off and its contents spilling out.

Mary, startled, jumped and backed into a corner. Her hands flew behind her back, hiding the envelope that she still carried for Kate.

"Cayde, wait!" Kate moved forward, trying to keep him from lashing out at Mary. He backhanded her, and in her shock, she couldn't stop him from ripping the towel from her head. He grabbed a fistful of her wet hair and dragged her from the room.

Usually, he'd never been so publicly abusive, but he must have caught the tail end of their conversation.

"Bill!" Mary screamed as she followed them out.

"Hold it, fella!" Bill was there already; the commotion had drawn him quickly. "You let her go. If she doesn't want to come with you, then she's going to stay here, or I will call the police." It seemed Bill would be on Kate's side after all.

Cayde tossed Kate aside, releasing his hold on her. He looked Bill up and down, sizing up the older man. Then he laughed. He could and would beat the poor man to a pulp.

"Stop, it's okay!" Kate said, tears running down her cheeks. The pain of his hand across her face stung more with each passing second.

"It's not okay!" Mary shouted. The envelope was nowhere to be seen. She reached out a hand. "Come back with me. You don't have to go with him."

Cayde laughed again. "Go on, Kate," he said. "I'm leavin' this place now. And I'll take Bella with me."

"No." Bill shook his head, his voice still calm. "You leave this woman and her dog here."

Annoyance replaced Cayde's amusement. "Are you gonna stop me?" Cayde raised a fist. "One hit would have your skull bashed in and your brains bleedin' out your nose all over the concrete."

Bill stood up a little straighter. "You go ahead and try it. Mary, go on now and call the police." But she didn't move.

Kate stepped forward. She held up her hands to de-escalate the situation as she'd done so many times before. "Cayde, I'm coming with you! It's fine! Don't hurt him."

"Mary." Bill's voice drew itself out like a warning. "Call the police."

Mary pulled out her phone.

This deterred Cayde a little. He stepped back and grabbed onto Kate's arm. "Come on, let's go."

"Kate, do not go with him!" Mary said.

Cayde pulled her toward the SUV. She looked behind her at Bill and Mary. She wanted nothing more than to leave with them, but now wasn't the time. Cayde would hurt Bill. And she couldn't leave Bella—especially when she was so sick.

"I'm sorry," Kate said. "I'm sorry."

Cayde piled her in, almost right on top of Bella, and then slammed the door shut. He glared at Bill, who only raised his chin and stood his ground. He absolutely would have died in a match against Cayde, but Kate felt proud of his courage, and more grateful than he would ever know that he stood up to Cayde.

He sped the car away, and both Mary and Bill watched it go, their faces sad. As they grew smaller in the distance, Kate realized with a horrible drop in her stomach that she never got the documents back from Mary.

CHAPTER 69

CLAIRE

Claire sat quietly in the teacher carpool, dazed and detached from the events of the day before. She looked at the three other women in the car, wondering if they could somehow see how devastated she was. Cayde didn't always like driving her to work, and since she'd never gotten her sedan back, Claire was forced to join in the carpool. She didn't mind it, though. She genuinely liked the group. In a time before Cayde, these were the women she was closest to.

Maybe if they looked at her hard enough, stared into her eyes, they would understand what she was screaming on the inside. Claire turned to look out the window. That was silly. How could they know anything if she refused to tell them? How could they help her if she refused to help herself? If all of them knew, maybe he would be less of a threat to them together.

"Can we meet up after the school day?" Claire suddenly said. "There is something I want to talk to you all about."

The car fell quiet. "Definitely," said Allie, the driver, a little surprised.

The past few months, Claire had been eating alone. Cayde would call and check in, making sure she wasn't mingling too much with the other teachers. The isolation had to end. She knew it in her gut. It was the only way to dig herself out of this pit. She decided she would also call Jessie and see if she would drive over.

That morning, Claire allowed her class to work freely on their projects. She watched the clock, trying to come up with what to say. Maybe she didn't have to say much at all.

When the final bell rang, she hurried to the break room, her face pale and her legs weak. The other women were there, talking amongst themselves. Jessie was already there. Though she taught at a different school, she knew a lot of Claire's coworkers from the days Claire used to go out. That life seemed so far away now.

Claire joined them. They smiled at her and asked how her class was, but Claire got straight to the point.

"I need your help," Claire said. She felt that this might be an emotional moment, but instead, she felt drained and tired. She couldn't even cry. "It's Cayde. I'm in trouble, and I don't know if I'm going to survive if he stays in my home."

"We knew something was going on," said Susan, one of the eighth-grade teachers. The group exchanged horrified looks. "But the more we asked you about your life, the more you withdrew from us."

"But we've been praying for you every night," Allie chimed in. "Praying that somehow we could do something."

Jessie looked at Claire squarely. "We're going to get you away from him." There was no question behind her words. She didn't ask Claire what could be done. She was going to do this for Claire with or without her help.

A semblance of feeling returned. Claire had felt so hollow from the night before, but there was light again—hope and comfort in their support.

Jessie glanced at the clock. "We have twenty-five minutes to come up with a plan. We can't do it after school. I'm assuming Cayde would get suspicious?"

Claire nodded. "Sometimes he lets me drive home with you, or he'll come get me. I'm assuming today he'll be coming."

"Right." Susan nodded. "Tell us everything we need to know."

Claire did, as fast as she could. Jessie listened intently, adding her own suggestions as they went.

"We'll both get substitutes tomorrow," Jessie said. "But you'll ride with the girls as usual, so you don't arouse suspicion—in case he follows you." She added that last part, as Claire had mentioned he often stalked her. "We'll go together to fill out an emergency protective order. This time," Jessie emphasized, "we'll do it at the courthouse. You'll need to write down the information beforehand." Claire nodded, trying to recall the documents she needed for it. "Then," Jessie continued, "we're going to the department store to buy you new locks for your house."

"What about the police?" Teresa, one of the seventh-grade teachers asked. "Claire said the police told her she couldn't."

"Does that make sense to anyone here?" Claire asked. When no one spoke up, she nodded. "Then the police be damned. It's my house. I'd rather face the consequences from them than Cayde."

To this, everyone agreed.

"Then it's settled," Jessie said. "Tomorrow, we free Claire from Cayde Miller for good."

CHAPTER 70

SOPHIE

The police left Sophie in the interview room for over an hour. By the time an officer came in, she had brought her knees to her chest and arms around them, tucking her head away and letting her blond hair spill over like a curtain to shield her face.

She lifted her head as a man, maybe ten years younger than her, sat on the other side of the table. His embroidered tag read: "L. Harris."

"Sophie Miller. You requested to talk to an officer during the booking process. Sorry for the wait, but we're pretty swamped in this area."

Sophie thought the excuse was ridiculous. They'd picked her up in some backwater county. What more could they be handling than the shooting and maybe some old woman complaining about local kids plucking a tomato from her garden?

Sophie leaned forward, her voice taut with desperation. "Did you find him? Is he here?"

The officer barely glanced up from his clipboard. "Find who?"

Sophie planted her feet firmly on the ground and leaned harder on the table. "*Cayde Miller.* The guy who shot at me in the parking lot?"

The officer stopped writing but kept his gaze fixed on the paper. "You mean your husband?"

"Yes, him. Did you find him or not?"

"No."

"You know he shot at me, right?" Were they even looking? "He was trying to kill me."

A faint smile tugged at the corner of the officer's mouth. "I've seen a few domestic spats in my time, Mrs. Miller. But it's rare for men to end up shooting their wives. Though, I suppose husbands think about it." Apparently, this was funny to him. "So why did he shoot at you?"

"I was leaving him. Our whole marriage, he always threatened me about leaving."

"Have you ever tried going to the police?"

Sophie shook her head. "No, I was scared. I mean, he had a gun."

"It's not illegal to carry in the state of Virginia." Officer Harris shrugged.

"But I'm saying he used it to threaten me." That had to count for something. "He tried to shoot me in public!"

The officer scoffed and shook his head. "Yet you didn't call the police any of the times he threatened you? Did you ask *anyone* for help?"

"I tried, but—" Her heart started pounding as she ran both hands over her hair and scalp, trying to contain her frustration. "I'm trying to tell you he threatened me and my family! He was going to hurt them!"

"It sounds like you're saying he kidnapped you. Held you against your will," Officer Harris said, his tone skeptical.

"Yes!" Sophie's voice was a sharp edge of conviction. "Exactly."

"Kidnapped you to... where?"

"He liked to go on camping trips."

"He takes you camping?" The officer raised an eyebrow, clearly unconvinced. "He kidnaps you for camping trips?"

Sophie stared at Officer Harris. "Yes."

The officer chuckled. "I guess most women don't exactly jump at the chance to spend some time in the dirt and woods, but—"

"No, that's not what I'm saying!" Sophie's voice rose, her hands gripping the edge of the table. Why wasn't he understanding?

The officer's expression remained unchanged. "Did he ever tie you up? Physically force you to go?"

"Why are you asking me this?" Sophie's temper flared, her voice breaking with emotion. "Why aren't you asking about him?"

"Ma'am, I need you to calm down," Officer Harris said, shrugging slightly. "You requested to speak to an officer, so that's what I'm doing. I'm just trying to get down to the truth."

"I am telling you the truth!" Sophie buried her face in her hands. "You think this is a joke."

"It's just..." The officer leaned back in his chair, checking his watch before fixing his stare on her. "With your current situation..." He trailed off.

After a moment, Sophie snapped at him. "*What*?"

"Trying to put the blame on your husband isn't going to get you out of this."

"You think I'm lying to get out of this?!" Sophie's voice cracked with desperation.

"You've been on the run for months with a warrant out for your arrest."

"I wasn't running! I'm trying to tell you he was going to kill me!" She couldn't believe this was happening. She put her head down and gave way to the sobs that had been threatening to overtake for a while. "He's going to kill me."

Officer Harris sighed. "Mrs. Miller?" After thirty seconds, he tried again. "Mrs. Miller?"

But she would not talk to him anymore about Cayde. None of them cared. She could hear his pen scratching the paperwork he filled out, no doubt explaining the events she relayed as some sort or scheme to get back at her husband or lessen the legal trouble she was in.

After about three minutes of her refusing to lift her head up, he stood and began to exit the interview room. "If you need anything, Mrs. Miller, let us know."

She did look at him then, snot and tears on her face. "I want a pen and paper. I want to write a letter."

CHAPTER 71

AUTUMN

"Autumn, honey," her mother started, "Whatever is happening, you can tell us."

Autumn had sat her parents down in their living room. Jeremiah was out with friends, and her older brother, Isaac, had moved out months ago. She'd decided to take the opportunity to explain things. Maybe not all of it, but if Autumn didn't do something—if she kept this all to herself—she wasn't sure she or her unborn child would make it.

Autumn took a deep breath. "Cayde and I are divorced."

"What?" Her mother grabbed the armrests of her chair.

"He told me that there were complications with a woman he was married to before. We had to get a divorce, or we'd both go to jail." It sounded ridiculous to say out loud. "He wanted to sort it out with her and then make things right with me. We'd remarry without anyone knowing." Her chin began to tremble, and she fought to get the words out. The faces of her parents looking at her as she struggled to get out what had been buried deep inside for so long almost broke her.

"I'm really scared right now. Not just of Cayde but of having this baby; of being a mother. I think of the future, and I just feel so broken and hopeless. But I'm trying to be strong."

She dashed the tears that began to fall. She needed to get this out, because she wasn't sure she'd be able to have the courage to do it later.

"Cayde hurts me," she continued. "And I'm scared of him. I know raising this child without a father will be hard, and I know being a single mother isn't what you wanted for me, but this is the only way I can live because I can't live with Cayde in my life." Sobbing overtook her and she pressed her palms into her eyes but forced the raw words out. "I feel so alone and afraid, and I need your support on this decision because I can't remarry him."

She removed her hands and wiped her nose on her sleeve. She thought back to the day she walked to the river. "I couldn't live."

Both of her parents stared at her. They exchanged a look of grief on their daughter's behalf, and then slowly, her father stood from the couch and made his way over. He sat next to her for a moment, and then reached his arm around her shoulder, pulling her in. Her mother joined on the other side, holding Autumn in her arms and pressing a kiss against her temple.

It was the only answer Autumn needed. Whatever strength or courage she lacked, she knew they would make up the difference. They would be there for her in this decision, in raising this child. And in their embrace, Autumn felt something she hadn't since the day she got married.

Safety.

* * *

The time had come to confront Cayde. As Autumn dialed his number into her parents' landline, she realized she had never called him before. She hadn't needed to—he'd done enough calling for the both of them. She couldn't call him on her cell phone; she'd blocked him.

"Autumn," his voice sounded on the other line.

"I'm leaving you, Cayde."

"Now hold on—" he hissed, but she wouldn't let him finish. Not this time. It was finally her turn to speak.

"No." She sounded stronger than ever before. "I don't care what you say. I'm through listening to your excuses, and I'm done with your manipulation. I'm done with you, Cayde."

She could almost see the shock on his face. A part of her wished she could.

"What are you sayin'?"

"I'm saying I'm not going to remarry you. I know about the abuse charges filed against you. You will never be a part of this child's life—or mine."

"You don't want to marry me? Fine. Then change your name back. You're not worthy of mine." There was a snarl in his voice. "But don't you think for one moment that you can keep me from my child. I'm the father."

"Let me make this clear, Cayde." Autumn had no patience for his threats. "I've told my parents about you, and they agree. You are not to come back here or contact me ever again. Do you understand? And don't worry; I have every intention to change my name back. I don't want yours, or anything to do with you!"

She slammed the phone down on the receiver. It fell off the hook and dangled, but she was too angry to look back.

CHAPTER 72

JACK

Both Jack and Blair wanted to follow Cayde straight to the station, but with his injury, Blair had to be the voice of reason. She suggested, reluctantly, that they head to the hospital first. Her nose hadn't been broken, thankfully, but Jack's shoulder had been pierced nearly two inches deep, and he'd need stitches.

They tried to explain the urgency of their situation to the hospital staff, and to their credit, they were taken care of as quickly as possible. But the process still dragged on, each minute stretching painfully as they alternated between filling out paperwork and writing statements about the night's events.

The waiting room, usually a place for small talk and idle distractions, was a bubble of tense silence. Jack's jaw was set in a rigid line, and Blair's gaze was fixed on the door, her leg bouncing anxiously.

They requested to stay together, hoping it would save some time, and when a doctor finally examined Jack, the prognosis was grim. The wound, deep and ragged, would require a sling and strict instructions to rest his shoulder. Jack started to argue, but Blair, her voice uncharacteristically sharp, cut in. "We'll do whatever's necessary."

Jack shot her a look, then reluctantly peeled off his bloodstained shirt, wincing as the fabric brushed against the raw wound. He glanced at Blair, a flicker of embarrassment crossing his face, but she was busy dabbing at her nose with a wad of tissues, her fingers stained crimson. The doctor worked quickly, cleaning the wound with steady hands before numbing it and stitching it closed. Jack barely flinched as the needle pierced his skin over and over, his eyes locked on the wall, his thoughts far away.

Once the sling was secured and instructions given, they practically burst out of the hospital doors, Jack moving stiffly beside Blair as they rushed to the SUV. The air was cool against his bare skin, goosebumps prickling along his arms as he fumbled for the keys with his free hand.

"Keys," Blair said, holding out a hand expectantly.

Jack frowned, his brows drawing together. "You're not driving."

"You can't drive," she countered, her tone flat. "Unless you want to split your new stitches and waste more time getting them redone?"

He hesitated, exhaustion weighing heavily on him. With a resigned sigh, he tossed the keys over. Blair caught them easily, slipping into the driver's seat and adjusting. "You're so tall," she muttered.

Jack climbed into the passenger seat, his movements slow and deliberate. His shoulder throbbed in time with his heartbeat, but the pain was a distant echo compared to the gnawing ache in his chest. They were so close, and yet they'd come up empty-handed.

"I'm sorry," Blair said suddenly, her voice quiet.

He looked at her, surprised. "That's the second time you've apologized to me during this case," he said lightly, but there was a tiredness beneath her words. "What's it for this time?"

"You know why." Blair's voice was barely above a whisper. She stared out the windshield, the streetlights casting long shadows on her face.

A sigh escaped Jack, and he let the façade fall. He was disappointed. This case had cut him to the quick—and Blair knew it.

"I'm sorry too. I had hoped…" He wouldn't say it. "Let's just get to the station and find out where she is. Her family will want to know."

Blair nodded.

He reached over with his good hand, brushing his fingers against hers where they rested on the gear shift. It wasn't anything more than a gesture of comfort that they both needed. She glanced at him, a sad smile tugging at her lips before she pulled away, turning her focus back to reversing the car.

Blair hadn't even made it a foot out of the parking stall before her phone rang, the name of the local police station flashing on the screen. She practically slammed on the brakes, causing Jack to lurch forward. His hiss of pain was accompanied by a glare, but Blair's attention was already on the call. She answered quickly, putting the phone on speaker.

"Hello?" Her voice was tight with tension.

"Detective Jordan here. We've got the confession. And we know where—"

"You got his what?" Jack's voice cut through the air like a whip. "Who authorized you to interrogate my suspect?"

"With you and your partner off to the hospital, we thought it fit to start. Everything about this case is time sensitive, is it not?" Detective Jordan's arrogance oozed through the phone, making Jack's jaw clench. "He cracked the moment we put any pressure on him. Told us everything."

Jack's heart was pounding so hard he could feel it in his throat. Blair sat beside him, her face a mask of barely controlled fury and shock. They exchanged a glance, a silent communication that spoke volumes of their shared frustration.

"He kidnapped her early yesterday morning," Jordan continued, his tone brisk and matter-of-fact. "Claims she got into the car with him willingly. He shot her three times before leaving the state. Drove about a hundred miles north of here and buried her. Says the car and everything else is still there. We'll send over the location details so you both can head out immediately. We've already contacted local authorities in the area."

Blair pressed her forehead against the steering wheel. "Understood," she said, her voice cold.

The call ended abruptly, Detective Jordan's smugness lingering in the air. Silence fell over the car, heavy and suffocating. They both sat there, processing the information that felt like a punch to the gut. Jack's mind was racing, replaying every moment of the case, every missed clue, every second they'd wasted when they should have been looking for her.

Blair let out a shaky breath, her eyes squeezed shut as if she could block out the reality of what they'd just heard. Jack watched her, his own emotions a chaotic swirl of anger, guilt, and deep disappointment.

So, she *was* dead, then.

Slowly, Blair took a deep breath, her shoulders rising and falling as she exhaled. She opened her eyes, a steely resolve replacing the shock that had momentarily paralyzed her.

"Okay," she said, accepting it all as it came. She shifted the car into gear. "Let's finish this."

CHAPTER 73

WENDY

Wendy had the dishes cleaned and scrubbed before Cayde returned home. He walked in, immediately looked toward the stove as he always did, and frowned.

"Where's dinner?"

"Oh, I already ate," Wendy said. "So did Archie." She'd placed him in his room to play, away from Cayde.

"Well," Cayde huffed, "what do I eat?"

"Make something yourself," Wendy said, drying her hands on the kitchen towel and facing him. She stared right into his eyes, adding to the challenge.

He took the bait. Dropping his briefcase, he took a few aggressive steps toward her. "The fuck did you say?"

Wendy pushed her head forward, speaking slowly as if he were a simpleton. "Make. Something. Yourself."

He slapped her—hard. Her head snapped to the side, but she slowly turned to look at him, a grin pulling at the corners of her mouth. He hit her again. The anger in his face mixed with something else. Almost as if he was unnerved by her sudden combative behavior.

He jabbed a finger at her. "Don't *ever* talk to me that way. I will fuck you up, Wendy."

It wasn't enough. Wendy needed to make him really angry. She reached up and pulled a cast-iron skillet down; this was her choice of weapon for the kitchen. She'd spent the past few days imagining every way she could kill Cayde—in self-defense, of course—and what item in each room would be best to do it with. Since the kitchen knives could be seen as too planned or combative, she chose the iron skillet for this area. She set it on the stove, the handle facing her.

"There you go, cook yourself some food. I'm done."

He picked it up and slammed it back down on the stove, cursing at her. "Damn it, Wendy! Every time there is some peace and unity in this house, you start this shit up!" He stepped toward her, his hand swiping across the counter and knocking the mug rack down. Everything clattered to the floor and shattered, all to frighten her.

Before the hospital, before he threatened Archie, it would have. Now, all Wendy could think about was her plan to be rid of Cayde. Everything he broke, everything he smashed, it all added up in her favor. She smiled again, which only aggravated him more.

"Here." She grabbed a plate from the cupboard and handed it to him. "Fill it up with leftovers from the fridge. Oh wait—we don't have any."

He threw the plate at her, and she dodged it, letting it fly past her into the living room, where it exploded against the coffee table. She backed up toward it, aware she'd moved farther away from the skillet, but there was another thing she needed to accomplish. She had the welts on her cheeks beginning to form and plenty of bruises on her body from the past few days, but if today was going to be the day she was rid of him, there needed to be more evidence than ever. She bent down to pick up the broken plate, holding the shards in her hand while Cayde watched her angrily.

"These could hurt Archie!" she snapped at him. Then, she curled her fingers around the shards and squeezed.

Cayde's face blanked for a second, shock crossing it as she stared at him, her fist shaking from the pressure she applied to the glass. The broken plate dug into her skin, slicing across her palm. Then, she threw the bloodied shards at Cayde. He flinched, ducking away from them, but it pissed him off exactly to the point Wendy needed.

He launched himself toward her with an angry cry. This first part would be tricky—she couldn't dodge him. Not if she wanted the opportunity to get her handprints on him. He started with a punch to the face and then pushed her down, but Wendy grabbed hold of his arms, taking him with her. She stamped crimson prints all over his shirt and skin as they wrestled for control. To her surprise, he ended up grabbing her neck. He squeezed, his face contorted in red.

She kicked and scratched at him, unable to escape his grasp. Careful thoughts of planting evidence left her brain, consumed by the need to breathe and survive. She bunched her fist, pooling the blood in her palm. Then she smeared it across his face.

Cayde made a sound that was half horrified and half disgusted. He relented his grasp around her neck, sitting up to wipe his mouth and face. Wendy kicked and scrambled away, bolting into the bathroom and locking the door behind her. Then she stood on the toilet seat and removed the lid to the tank, lifting it high above her head.

She waited for Cayde to march toward the door, breaking it down with his fists and boots—more evidence in her favor. Her fingers gripped the porcelain lid tightly. Her right hand slipped a little as the blood continued to flow from the cuts. Her legs shook, and her neck throbbed with heat and soreness, but she paid them no mind.

"Come on," she whispered, tasting blood. The punch to the face had reopened a cut on her lip. Excitement and adrenaline pumped through her. "Break it down."

He'd kick the door open, and she'd slam the lid down on his head as hard as she could. But Cayde didn't approach the door. In fact, the apartment shook as the front door slammed shut. Wendy lowered the tank lid and stepped off the toilet, listening. He'd left?

Disappointed and starting to feel the bruises forming, Wendy left the bathroom and checked the house. She glanced into Archie's room—he was still asleep. Wendy washed her hand in the bathroom sink, numbly watching the blood dilute in the water. She plucked out a shard of glass that had remained with some tweezers, then bandaged it. After that, she took disinfecting wipes and scrubbed any surface that she'd marked with her bloodied hand. Lastly, she carefully cleaned up the broken glass in the living room and kitchen, ensuring it was completely safe for Archie to play.

She brought him back out, cleaned even the mess he'd made in his room, and then took her journal into the living room, kneeling to write on the coffee table.

> *Cayde hit me several times again today. He even broke some dishes because I didn't have food ready for him when he*

came home from work. The glass cut my hand. He tackled me to the floor and strangled me, but I got away and locked myself in the bathroom.

Wendy dated it, unsure of the exact reason why she kept the journals. She wrote them specifically in a way that, should she die, they could be used as evidence against Cayde. Or perhaps she could use them in her favor should her plan work out. Either way, it felt good to document everything. It made her feel less alone or crazy.

She shut the journal and reached out toward Archie, rubbing his back.

Today may not have worked in her favor, but Cayde would be back, and she'd have hell to pay for her stunt this evening. Let him come. The way Wendy saw it, he was only providing her another opportunity to get rid of him—permanently.

CHAPTER 74

KATE

A can of Coke exploded on the wall behind Kate, spraying sticky, dark liquid across the room. Fourth one Cayde had thrown. The first three had hit. One smacked her square on the eyebrow, and she felt warmth trickling down her face.

"Stop it!" she screamed. "That's enough!"

He hurled another can. It hit the lamp she ducked in front of. They'd bought a six-pack earlier that day. At least he only had one left.

"You think you can leave me?" Cayde's face twisted, flushed red and purple. "Don't you know what I've done for us? Everythin' I've had to do so that we could survive?" After the truck stop, he'd dragged her to Blue's Hideaway Motel. Paid up for a week, considering the dropping temperatures. Easier, Kate knew, for Cayde to keep her caged.

"You haven't done anything!" she shot back. "We survived because of *my* money. You're a liar, Cayde. And a thief."

"I am not a thief!" His eyes flashed, something unhinged. But Kate couldn't tell if it was because she was finally pushing back, or if the truth of it stung. It didn't matter. The documents were gone. And Cayde would kill her, eventually. Part of her wanted it over with. If this was her last chance to spit it in his face, so be it.

"You stole everything I had!"

"I did not!"

"Then what would you call it?" They circled each other like vultures. Blood dripped from her brow. "You took everything. Every day, I pray that you drop dead. I've prayed to God a thousand times for you to just die!" She meant it. She used to feel sick about it. Not anymore. It was ugly, sure. But not half as ugly as what Cayde had done to her. "And I don't love you. I don't think I ever loved you."

"Shut up!" Cayde struck. He grabbed her by the shoulders and slammed her to the ground. His fists rained down on her head. She kicked and twisted, tried to scream, but he clamped a hand over her mouth. "I'll kill your family! I'll drown your grandbaby and make you and your daughter watch! I'll burn down your mother's home!"

He'd made those threats a hundred times. Knew her weakness. She didn't fear for herself—only for them. Maybe that's why she stayed this long.

Bella mustered a feeble bark and lunged at him. Cayde swatted her away, but she kept yapping, snapping.

Kate swung her hand up, striking Cayde's jaw, but he barely flinched.

A wheeze. Then a whimper. The barking cut off.

Both Cayde and Kate froze, eyes locking on Bella. The dog collapsed, mouth open, eyes empty.

Silence.

"Get off! Get off of me!" Kate shoved him hard.

Cayde blinked, caught off guard, and moved aside.

She scrambled to the little Yorkie. "Oh, Bella!" She sobbed, trembling hands hovering over the little body. "No! Bella, no!"

But the dog was gone. Dead.

"Kate..." Cayde's voice was low, almost gentle. "I'm sorry."

"This is your fault!" She spat the words, venomous.

He recoiled, his face hardening. "Kate, I didn't touch her. She was an old bitch. Tried to bite me. Her heart gave out."

"Don't talk about her like that!" Kate's hands finally settled on Bella's fur, still warm. She lifted her gently, hugging the lifeless weight to her chest. "What am I gonna do now?"

She sobbed. A raw, broken sound. The kind of grief that comes from a place deeper than the heart. She'd lost her money, her escape—everything. And now the one thing that kept her anchored, kept her sane, was gone too. The only joy she had left.

"Look," Cayde murmured, awkward now. "There's a field behind the hotel. We can bury her there."

"*I'll* do it!" Kate snapped, voice thick, her face a mess of snot and tears. "Don't touch her."

"Fine." He growled and stood, yanked the keys off the nightstand, and stomped out. The door slammed shut behind him.

Kate grabbed one of the motel's towels. She didn't care if they charged her for it. All her things—her clothes, her toiletries—had been left behind at the truck stop. She wrapped Bella up gently, cradled her, and stepped outside.

The SUV was still in the lot. So Cayde hadn't ditched her. Probably lurking, keeping watch. Maybe smoothing things over with the front desk in case someone had complained about the yelling. They'd been kicked out of places before, thrown out for shouting and breaking things.

The field out back was barren. Just dead grass and frozen dirt. She kept walking until the lights of the motel were dim, until only the glow of Nashville far off punctured the dark. The sun had set hours ago. Cold. Lonely. A place like this wasn't right for Bella, but what else could she do? If she didn't bury her tonight, Cayde would probably toss her in the trash the second Kate's back was turned.

She laid the little bundle down and clawed at the ground, fingers digging into the frozen soil. She had nothing else to dig with. Snowflakes drifted down, soft and feathery, dissolving on contact with the earth.

Kate sobbed and clawed and tore at the dirt. Each handful came harder than the last. She gritted her teeth against the pain shooting through her fingers. Wondered if she'd end up like Bella. Dead and buried in some godforsaken patch of dirt, a nameless grave nobody would remember.

He's going to kill me, she thought. *Sooner or later.*

By the time the hole was deep enough, her hands were raw and numb. Dirt packed so deep under her nails, it looked black. She wiped at her face, smearing tears, soil, and blood together.

Her phone buzzed. She pulled it out with shaking fingers. Probably Cayde, telling her to get back inside. But it wasn't.

Mary.

> "I mailed the documents to your daughter. The address was written on the envelope. When it's safe, call me. You can still leave him. Let me help you."

Kate looked behind her. The motel was far enough that no one would hear if she spoke softly. It was dark enough that no one would know what she was doing, even if Cayde was watching her.

So there on Bella's grave, with nothing left to lose, Kate called Mary.

CHAPTER 75

SOPHIE

Sophie knew the dreaded words would come. But hearing them invoked a fear she never thought she could feel.

"Mrs. Miller? You're free to go. Your bond has been posted, and you're being released."

"Who posted it?" Sophie asked, but she didn't need to.

"Your husband."

So, in the end, Cayde would get her after all. Sophie stood up, too emotionally exhausted to cry. She didn't know what else to expect.

She filled out the needed paperwork for her release in a blur. When she stepped out of the building, supposedly a free woman, she looked into the eyes of her husband.

"Get in the car, Sophie." His calm demeanor frightened her. He wore his cowboy hat despite it already being dark. Late in the year, the sun was setting earlier and earlier.

"Sophie!" Another voice shouted, and both she and Cayde looked to their left. Tanner was running toward them in the parking lot. "Sophie, don't!"

"Tanner?" Sophie gasped. He was still in Virginia?

He came up to the duo, eyeing Cayde. "Don't go with him. Get in the car with me."

Cayde snorted. "I posted her bond. I'm the one that got her out of there, so I'll be the one who takes her home."

"You didn't buy her, Cayde." Tanner's voice was low and dark. He turned back to Sophie. "You never met me at the motel, and I couldn't get ahold of you. I've been trying to find you for three days."

"Sophie." Cayde stepped toward her. "We're leavin'."

Tanner advanced forward. He put his hands on Cayde's chest and shoved him so hard it almost sent him sprawling onto his back. The cowboy hat on Cayde's head fell to the ground. "Back off."

Sophie froze, backing away from the confrontation. She worried Cayde would pull out his gun and shoot her brother right there. But Cayde's eyes were shocked, his face flustered. Maybe he hadn't thought Tanner would get confrontational.

"Leave." Tanner pointed to the parking lot's exit. "Or I will take Sophie right back in there and make sure the police know everything you've done to her."

To Sophie's surprise, Cayde started to back away. He glared and seethed at Tanner. "You're both dead. Watch your fuckin' back, Tanner Hale. Tell your wife and kids to watch theirs as well."

"Go!" Tanner roared and took another step.

Cayde cursed, spat on the ground, picked up his hat, and got into his car. As he reversed from his parking spot, he rolled down the window. "You might think you're safe, Sophie, but you'll never be rid of me."

Tanner stepped in front of her, his glare firm as he watched Cayde move.

Cayde sped away, and Sophie wondered if that was the wisest exit to make in front of a police station.

Once he was gone, Tanner placed a hand on her back. "Let's get out of here.."

He ushered her quickly to the car, and she looked at him, still not quite believing that he was here. "You shouldn't have done that, Tanner."

He just glanced at her, concern knitting his features. But she couldn't tell what he was thinking. "I didn't know you'd been arrested until this afternoon. I drove straight here to get you out."

The bond must have been a fortune. Sophie knew Cayde didn't have the money. She wasn't sure how he did it, but she thanked God Tanner got to her before she would have left with Cayde. "I wanted to stay in," she admitted. "I haven't felt safe in a long time."

Tanner opened the passenger door of his car for her, helped her in, and then got into the driver's seat. The second the door shut, he pressed the lock button. As he drove them back to the highway, he kept looking at her. "You've lost weight. And what happened to your neck?"

Sophie brought a hand to it, her fingers tracing over scabbed wounds and healed scars. "He always threatened me with a knife. And his gun."

"Sophie, I–" His throat bobbed, and he didn't say anything more for a long time. "I'm sorry."

Sophie shook her head. "I never wanted to involve you in this. After what happened with the boys—" She stopped herself. "Tanner, how are they?"

"They're okay. They miss you. I don't get to see them that much, but Mark sometimes brings them to Mom and Dad's for family dinner or to my house so I can watch them."

Sophie closed her eyes. She missed them so much it ached.

"We didn't—none of us—" The words stuttered from his mouth. "Sophie, why didn't you tell us? None of us knew it was this bad."

She thought of the bubbled and wrinkled scar where her tattoo once was. They still didn't know—not even a quarter of the hell she'd survived. "Where are we going?" she asked.

"I'm taking you to California," Tanner said. "Over a thousand miles between you and that creep."

"And then what?" she breathed. She'd scarcely allowed herself to hope enough to think of the future. When she was constantly fighting for survival, Sophie could only see one day at a time. Tomorrow was never certain.

"And then we figure out how to get rid of him for good."

CHAPTER 76

AUTUMN

"Breathe, just breathe."

"I am!" Autumn groaned. This contraction was the worst one yet. They were regular now. Labor had lasted for hours. She gripped the sides of the hospital bed, waiting for the wave of pain to pass.

Her mother laughed kindly, unfazed by Autumn's snappish mood, and dabbed a wet cloth on her daughter's forehead. "You're doing just fine, honey."

"Very soon, now," the doctor said, checking how dilated Autumn was. Another nurse in the room glanced at her on the bed.

"There's another call," she said, almost hesitantly.

The doctor looked mildly annoyed. "She's in labor. He can come to the hospital or talk to her family like everyone else."

"What calls?" Autumn lifted her head. Sweat plastered her hair. "Who's been calling?"

"Your husband—or maybe your boyfriend? He keeps calling and specifically asks for an update on you."

Since breaking up with Cayde over the phone, she hadn't heard from him. However, strange things had happened. Things that scared her. While she couldn't define it, Autumn sensed more than she could prove that Cayde was still following her.

Another contraction wracked her body. "I can't deal with this right now!" she screamed. She slammed her head back onto the pillow and gritted her teeth. The pain was excruciating, and exhaustion kept creeping in. Sweat beaded on her forehead.

The nurse gave her a sympathetic smile. "You should have thought about that nine months ago, honey."

Autumn snapped her gaze toward the nurse. "I'm not talking about having the baby! I'm talking about *him*! I don't want him here! I don't want him to know anything!"

Autumn's mother nodded, a protective fire in her eyes. "He's not her husband or her boyfriend. Please tell him to stop calling."

Now the nurse looked a bit embarrassed. "Of course," she said, and left the room.

"It's time," the doctor said. "You're ready. On my count: one, two, three! Push!"

* * *

Autumn had never seen anything so beautiful. She held close to her the miracle that was her child. Tiny little fingers, toes, eyelashes—everything about her was perfect.

"Sweet Madeline," Autumn whispered. The labor had been long and hard, but the moment she heard her child's cries, none of the pain or fatigue mattered. All that mattered was her.

"Why don't we let Mama rest?" A nurse reached for Madeline, but Autumn shied away.

"Please don't take her. Can't she stay here with me?"

"We just need to bathe her and do a routine check-up to ensure she's healthy."

"Please," Autumn begged.

The nurse tilted her head sympathetically. Something in her expression seemed understanding. "We'll do it here in the room, alright?"

Once they were finished, the nurses got the room ready for Autumn and the baby to rest for a while. Autumn kept staring down at Madeline, overcome by a swell of emotions. She thought she'd already loved her baby while she was in her belly—and she had—but this new surge of affection took her by surprise. It gave her more confidence and determination than ever before.

"There is a man," Autumn said, looking at the nurse. "The one that kept calling. His name is Cayde Miller. He is not to come anywhere near this child."

The nurse seemed slightly taken aback by the serious request but nodded her head. "Okay, honey. I'll tell the staff."

Her mother stayed in the room for hours, promising to be there all day if she had to. Eventually, Autumn let herself fall asleep. She awoke at some point in the night, glancing over at the baby bed made for Madeline.

She wasn't in it.

Autumn blinked once, twice, trying to rid the blur of sleep from her eyes. Still, Madeline was not there. Something moved in the corner of the room. There she was, being held, bounced, and swayed gently. But it wasn't her mother holding her.

It was Cayde.

"You'd better not call out," Cayde warned, seeing her mouth open. "I'd hate to drop her." He glanced down at their child. "You can't keep me away. I don't know why you try so hard."

"Cayde," Autumn's arms lifted, reaching out in supplication. Her mother was nowhere to be found, probably home for the night. She wished this was a dream, but her senses were on high alert—his suffocating presence was more real than ever. "Give her to me." Her voice was low and soft, speaking the same way you might to a dog getting ready to snap its teeth at you. "Please."

"Madeline Miller." Cayde looked at her, his face an expressionless stone. "Why did you give her my last name?"

Autumn didn't answer. While she had confessed a lot to her parents, she still didn't want anyone to know that Madeline was conceived before their wedding. This way, Autumn could just tell everyone that Cayde had left them and spare herself and Madeline the shame of what he'd really done.

"You're sendin' me mixed signals, Autumn. Do you want me in our child's life or not? Madeline could use a siblin', after all." He walked around the edge of the bed and handed Madeline to Autumn. She reached out to gently take the newborn, but Cayde didn't relinquish his hold on her yet. It was just like when they'd met, and he refused to let go of the frisbee. Only this time, Autumn wouldn't be able to pull. She had to wait for Cayde to let go to keep from harming Madeline.

He leaned in close enough that Autumn could smell his breath. "You can't keep my daughter from me." His point made, he allowed Autumn to fully take Madeline. Without another word, he walked out the door.

Autumn clutched Madeline securely to her thundering heart. Her grip was gentle, but she wanted to hug her tighter and never let go.

CHAPTER 77

CLAIRE

Everything had gone according to plan so far. Claire carpooled to the "school," as they told anyone who asked—but her real destination was the hardware store. There, she met Jessie, and they picked up new locks. It felt both daunting and strangely empowering. The weight of the items in their hands felt like a fragile promise of safety.

Jessie was confident—more resolute than Claire had ever seen her. They returned to the house. Parking a safe distance away, they waited with the windows rolled down just enough to hear the low hum of the street. Cayde would have to leave eventually. It was only a matter of time. Claire's stomach twisted in knots as they watched from the car, the minutes stretching on forever. Finally, after what felt like hours, his car roared to life, pulling out of the driveway.

Jessie exhaled sharply, nodding. "That's our cue."

They moved quickly. Jessie, hands skilled from years of fixing things around her own house, tackled the door to the garage while Claire worked on the front. Her fingers fumbled with the tools as memories flooded back—the night he broke into her room, the sound of the door splintering under his weight. Even as she twisted the screws into the new lock, a part of her wondered if this would be enough. She thought of the night he'd snuck into her locked room, of the sharp weight of the belt pressing into her neck. Could anything really keep him out?

The job took longer than Claire liked. Every sound, every car that passed sent her heart racing, as if at any moment, Cayde might return and catch them in the act. But finally, Jessie stood back, wiping her hands on her jeans, nodding in approval. "That'll do," she said. She gestured toward her car. "Now, pack a quick bag. We're going to the station to get you an emergency protective order. After that, you're coming to my place. I don't want you here when he finds out he can't get in."

Claire didn't argue. There was no time for second-guessing. The mention of a protective order sent a strange wave of hope rushing through her, fueling her tired body as she hurried inside to throw essentials into a bag. Maybe this could work. Maybe this time she could push Cayde out of her life for good.

At the station, the paperwork felt endless. The fluorescent lights overhead buzzed quietly. Jessie stood beside her, a steady presence, as Claire filled in every detail of the nightmare she had been living. The officer helping them was methodical but kind, guiding her through each line of the protective order. It was different from her previous experience. When it was done, Claire handed it over, a sense of finality settling in her chest.

"When is he notified of this?" Claire asked, her voice barely above a whisper. She stared at the officer, feeling the weight of her words as she added, "What happens if he breaks it?"

The officer looked up from the papers. "We'll send this to the judge now. Typically, these are served within a day. He should be notified by tonight. If he comes around, it's grounds for immediate arrest."

Immediate arrest. Claire clung to those words like a lifeline, imagining Cayde in handcuffs, hauled away from her life, from her daughter, from everything he had poisoned. It comforted her, but only slightly. There were no guarantees, her mind reminded her.

"We also got word on the plates you wrote down. There was a complaint filed a while back about that car sitting in an airport for three months. It was towed several weeks ago."

"An airport?" Claire said, surprised. "Can you give me the address it was towed to? Why didn't I hear of this?"

"We'll get it tomorrow," Jessie promised as Claire wrote it down on a sticky note.

As she and Jessie walked out of the station, something lighter tugged at her heart. She breathed in the cool evening air, trying to believe that maybe—just maybe—things could change.

"I think I'll have Paige fill one out too," Claire said, glancing at Jessie as they reached the car. The thought of her daughter at Zach's or staying late at the high school sent a wave of anxiety rippling through her chest. "I want to cover all the bases."

Jessie nodded, ever practical. "Go ahead and call her. Tell her the good news." Her voice softened, though, and she smiled. "But tonight... tonight we're celebrating."

Claire blinked, caught off guard by the word. Celebrating? She hadn't thought of celebrating anything for so long, it felt almost foreign. But looking at Jessie's determined smile, she couldn't help but feel the edges of her own lips curve upward.

"What are we celebrating?" Claire asked, her tone skeptical, but for the first time in a long while, there was a hint of warmth in her voice.

Jessie opened the car door with a wink. "Your freedom. Or at least, the first step toward it."

They drove away from the station, the weight of the past few hours still heavy but not unbearable. Hope fluttered somewhere deep in Claire's chest—small, tentative, but it was there. Tonight was the first night in months she wouldn't spend looking over her shoulder, bracing for the sound of Cayde's car pulling into the driveway, waiting for the inevitable violence he wrought.

Tonight, she would sleep in a house where she was safe.

CHAPTER 78

SOPHIE

The cold saltwater swirled gently around Sophie's ankles, her rolled-up pant legs darkening as the ocean spray kissed the fabric. She wiggled her toes, feeling them sink deeper into the soft, wet sand. With a slow, deliberate breath, she closed her eyes, letting the wind caress her cheeks and sweep through her hair. The world around her felt muted—the sky a soft gray, reflected in the rippling surface of the sea. But there was no heaviness in the stillness, no trace of gloom. Instead, to Sophie, it looked like a clean slate, a vast canvas waiting to be filled with new beginnings.

Tanner had found a lawyer for her. Soon, she'd return to Nashville to settle things legally; an emergency protective order, the start of a divorce, and the FTA charges against her. It would take time, especially without her ID, her purse, or her phone, but for the first time in years, Sophie felt no urgency, only a quiet sense of relief. She was safe.

"Sophie!" Tanner's voice broke the silence, and she turned to see him jogging toward her, the sand shifting beneath his feet. He held out his phone with a smile. "It's for you."

Curious, she took the phone, lifting it to her ear. "Hello?"

"Happy Thanksgiving, Mom!" The joyous chorus of her two boys burst through the speaker, their voices full of energy and love.

Sophie's heart swelled, her smile bright and wide as she cast a grateful glance at Tanner. "Boys!" She laughed softly, tears pricking the corners of her eyes. "I've missed you so much."

"Uncle Tanner told Dad you're coming home soon," Charlie chimed in eagerly.

"That's right," Sophie replied, her voice steady, filled with warmth. "I'll be here a few more days, and then I'm going to stay with Uncle Tanner for a while."

"Will we get to see you?" Noah asked.

"I certainly hope so," she said, pressing her hand against the phone as if she could somehow reach through it and hold them close. "I'll talk to your dad soon, okay? But for now, have a wonderful holiday, and don't eat too much pumpkin pie!"

"Okay!" they shouted together.

"I love you," Sophie whispered, her throat tightening with emotion.

"We love you too, Mom! See you soon!" Their words echoed in her heart long after the call ended.

She handed the phone back to Tanner, her gaze lingering on the sea for a moment before she looked at him. "Thank you."

Tanner nodded, slipping the phone into his pocket. "Mark knows a little about what happened. I don't think he'll try to keep the boys from you."

Sophie hesitated. "You don't think Cayde would... try anything, do you?"

"Against Mark?" Tanner shook his head. "No. Not a chance."

Sophie bit her lip, glancing down at the sand. "What about Melissa and the kids? They're spending Thanksgiving without you."

"They understand, Soph," Tanner said softly, meeting her eyes. For a moment, Sophie saw the same guilt she felt reflected in his face. "At first, we didn't know what was going on. You were distant, and none of us knew how to reach you." He paused, then sighed. "I'm sorry. For everything. It wasn't your fault."

"It's not your fault either," Sophie said gently, her gaze steady on his. "There are a lot of things I regret, a lot I wish I'd done differently, but I don't want to carry that with me anymore. And you shouldn't either. All I want now is to focus on letting it go."

Healing would take time—Sophie understood that. But standing there, with the wind brushing against her skin and the endless horizon stretched out before her, she didn't mind. She could take the time she needed, whether it was weeks, months, or years. For the first time in a long time, Sophie felt the quiet strength of hope blooming inside her. And she knew, in that moment, she would heal.

CHAPTER 79

KATE

Kate deleted certain messages off her phone. Not all of them, but the ones that detailed her plan to escape. It had been three days since Bella's death. Zoey had gotten the documents and was in the process of getting the retirement check. Mary had set up a room at her home for Kate, and tonight she was coming to collect her. She'd stay with her until Zoey could buy Kate a ticket for a shuttle back to Virginia.

From there, Kate wasn't sure what happened next. Perhaps she'd go to her bank in person and get her accounts locked. Cayde had technically stolen all her cards, after all. She'd remove her name from any joint accounts, leaving him with whatever was left. It seemed like he'd been a spider, weaving webs so perfectly into her life that it felt financially impossible to leave him. That was over now.

The biggest problem was that her purse with her driver's license was still in the car. It had been since the incident at the truck stop. Cayde had kept the keys on him at all times. Kate glanced at the time. It was a little past ten at night. Mary would be here in ten minutes.

Everything was being left behind that could. She was only taking the essentials, packing them into a backpack. She chewed on a thumbnail.

She glanced at his side of the bed, looked at his nightstand, and carefully searched one of his bags. She needed those car keys! It occurred to her that he'd showered tonight. She sent a little prayer as she entered the bathroom and pulled back the shower curtain. A miracle. He'd left them behind. They dangled on a hook next to a loofa, and Kate snatched them. She pressed her ear to the door, listening for any footsteps coming toward her. Silence. She opened it up. The door led directly outside. They were on the second floor, and the concrete was quiet enough to hide her steps as she snuck past the other rooms, looking over the iron guard rail toward the main entrance. Cayde was talking to the employee there. He often did that.

Kate had a theory that he needed constant assurance that he was the kind of person people liked. Once the façade failed and his true nature was revealed, he had to find another person to trick. It seemed exhausting.

She only wore her socks. Despite the cold, it was the best way to sneak around without making any noise. She gripped the keys a certain way, making sure they wouldn't jingle, and slowly went down the stone steps to the first floor.

Cayde's back was toward the glass door. A neon sign flashed on and off over it: "VACANT ROOMS." She took a deep breath and walked past, hoping the clerk wouldn't point out he saw her or that Cayde wouldn't turn around. She opened the car door and dug around the back for her purse. So much junk had piled up in the past months. For being homeless, all of it seemed necessary. But at this point, Kate no longer cared about leaving it behind. She grabbed out her wallet, empty of cards or cash, and slipped out her license. She tucked it into her back pocket and slowly closed the car door, leaving it open about an inch. If the battery died, all the better. It would give her some extra time in the coming days.

She crept back up to the hotel room, leaving the car keys in her pocket. Mary would be here in five minutes. Five minutes before she gathered up anything else she needed before starting fresh. She slung her backpack over her shoulder and decided it was better to leave early. She didn't want Cayde to come upstairs and ask questions. If anything, she could start walking down the road and text Mary to pick her up a block away. It would be safer for them both.

She bent down, slipping on her shoes.

The door opened mid-tie, and Cayde furrowed his brows as he looked down at her, hunched over with her backpack.

"The fuck?" He asked, and then his face tightened. "Where do you think you're goin'?"

Kate stood up. He was right between her and the door. "Nowhere. I'm just taking some of this stuff out to the car. The room is too messy."

Cayde's hands went to his pocket, his face sinister. He marched over to the shower and ripped the curtain aside so violently some of the rungs holding it up popped out and clattered to the floor.

He noticed the keys weren't there. Kate spun around and bolted for the door. Cayde was faster. He grabbed her backpack and ripped it backward. Kate squirmed, wrenching her arms free. Cayde threw it aside and caught up to her just as her fingers brushed the door handle.

The back of his hand slammed into her skull, and she smacked the door face-first. The shock sent her to her knees, and Cayde ripped her hair backward, sending her onto the flat of her back. She felt the chain of her heart necklace break, caught in his fingers.

"You think I would ever let you go?" He got on top of her, straddling and pinning her down. Both hands wrapped around her neck, and he squeezed. His face was already purple, as if he was the one that was being suffocated. "You're my wife! Mine!" His grip lifted her head and smacked it down with emphasis.

Kate kicked so hard one of her untied shoes fell off. She wheezed and gasped. She could practically feel each blood vessel bursting. She thought her trachea would collapse in on itself, or maybe he'd yank her head up and her neck would snap under the immense pressure. Her head felt like it would explode if she didn't breathe. Her hands clawed at his shirt, his face. One of her nails cut into the skin on his cheek and raked down it, drawing blood, but Cayde didn't notice. He only shouted over and over.

He wasn't counting. He wasn't testing to see how long it took until she passed out—he was going to kill her.

The pressure in her head lifted with the realization. Spots formed in her vision. Still Cayde squeezed. Her fingers couldn't curl the same way, and her arms flailed nonsensically. She would die just like Bella. He'd carry her body out of here and drive her somewhere secluded, throwing her in a shallow grave.

Kate's arms flapped down to her sides, and she stopped kicking. Instead, she just looked at Cayde and cried. His face was so angry. *What made him like this?* Kate wondered. What had made this man so full of cruelty and malice? Why did violence and power make him tick the way it did? And God, why was this happening to her?

She thought of Zoey. Alice. Bella. She thought of her parents, old and happy, and even thought of Luke, her ex-husband.

She didn't want to die.

But black ebbed her vision, and the last thing Kate was going to see was Cayde Miller's horrid purple face, with his veins popping out and spittle dripping down his chin like an animal.

As her sight disappeared, her hearing gave way to a loud ringing, and her pounding heart slowed. Here, in Blue's Hideaway Motel, Kate was going to die.

CHAPTER 80

WENDY

"Thanks for coming," Wendy said, stepping aside to let Lisa cross the threshold to the apartment. "He's not here," she added, seeing the hesitation in her friend's eyes.

From the living room, Archie glanced up, wide-eyed and curious at the stranger.

"Oh my God," Lisa breathed, unable to stop herself. "He's gotten so big."

Wendy managed a small, strained smile, her eyes softening as she looked at her son. "He's why I called you."

Lisa turned to her, guilt and shame written across her face. "I'm glad you did. But, Wendy—" Her voice faltered as her gaze swept over the bruises, the pain etched in Wendy's face. "I had no idea—"

"I need you to take Archie."

Lisa blinked. "Take him? Where?"

"Anywhere. Once it's over, I'll call. You can bring him back."

Lisa's eyes darted from Wendy to Archie, unease creeping in. "I don't understand."

Wendy ran a hand through her hair, her movements sharp, tense. "I'm kicking Cayde out tonight. I don't want Archie here if things go south. I can't let him be used against me."

Lisa recoiled slightly. "Cayde would do that? His own kid?"

Wendy hardened her voice. "Archie is mine. Not his. Cayde's no father. He's not even a husband."

Lisa looked taken aback. Wendy knew this was all alarming for her. The Wendy Lisa had known was gone. In her place was a woman who had steeled herself to do the impossible.

"Okay." Lisa nodded. "Okay, I'll take him. Or..." Lisa looked behind her at the door, as if she were afraid Cayde would come in. "Why don't you come with me? We'll leave together and find you some other place—"

"I've tried leaving before," Wendy explained. "He won't let me. But if I can convince him it's his choice, and we're both better off for it, things might be different."

This was a lie. Wendy had no intention of convincing Cayde of anything. She hadn't just called Lisa here to take Archie. She had called Lisa here because she needed a witness. By the end of the night, either she or Cayde would be dead. If Wendy survived, it had to look like self-defense. If she didn't, Lisa had to know the truth, had to be able to prove what Cayde was capable of.

"Wendy, are you sure?" Lisa was looking more and more nervous by the second. Wendy knew if she didn't hurry up, her old friend would back out.

"I'm sure." Wendy knelt down, lifting Archie into her arms. She kissed him—once, twice, then again. "I love you so, so much," she whispered, holding him tightly against her. "And I'll see you again."

Her heart squeezed as she breathed in his sweet scent, hoping that this embrace wouldn't be their last.

* * *

Evening had fallen, and Wendy sat motionless on the couch, waiting. The house was eerily silent now that Lisa had left with Archie. She had packed a small bag for her son, complete with written instructions, but Archie had cried when Lisa took him. It nearly shattered her resolve. Still, it had to be done.

Wendy was grateful Lisa had come through. After all these years, after the rift that Cayde had created between them, it was something. Perhaps, once this was over, they could rebuild what had been lost. The thought felt foreign to her—she had been alone for so long, isolated behind walls she wasn't sure anyone could break, not even Lisa.

The front door creaked open. Wendy didn't flinch as Cayde stepped inside. He paused, taking in the sight of her sitting calmly, almost expectantly. His eyes lingered on the diamond necklace that lay neatly on the coffee table. He hated it when she took it off. To Wendy, it felt as though she'd broken her collar. Suspicion flickered across his face. He'd likely started to sense something during their last fight when he stormed out of the house.

She'd taken it as a sign she'd shaken him up enough to get out of the situation. In that moment, he had wanted to leave more than he had wanted to control her. If she planned on killing him, she needed to do it before he grew more and more suspicious.

"Wendy?" Cayde's voice was low, a mixture of curiosity and threat.

Wendy met his gaze, her tone steady. "It's time for you to leave, Cayde." She kept calm, firm. "I'm giving you one chance. Walk away."

He snorted, his face hardening. "Leave? You're my wife. I'm not goin' anywhere."

Well, no one could say she didn't try. Wendy had no intention of dragging this out. She reached for the lamp beside her, locked eyes with him, and hurled it across the room. It missed him by a mile but shattered against the wall, the sound sharp and jarring, echoing through the house.

"What the hell—" Cayde started, but Wendy didn't give him a chance to finish.

She screamed, a raw, piercing wail of terror. "No! Don't hurt me!" Her voice quivered, high-pitched, like prey pleading for mercy.

"Shut up!" Cayde lunged toward her, his face twisting in anger. "Do you want the neighbors to—" He stopped mid-sentence. It clicked.

"Please! No!" she cried again, louder this time, stomping her foot for effect. Her screams, designed to be heard through thin walls, to be picked up by concerned ears, had a desperate, primal energy. She could almost hear the phone calls being made next door or below.

Now Cayde moved with purpose. He was coming to silence her.

Wendy screamed one last time, her voice raw. "Somebody help me!" She straightened, her voice suddenly dropping to a flat calm. "We have five minutes."

Cayde halted in his tracks, his brow furrowing. "Five minutes? Until what?"

"Until the cops arrive. Until one of us is dead."

His eyes widened, and then he laughed, a hollow, mirthless sound. "You think you can kill me?"

Wendy shifted, lowering herself into a fighting stance, hands ready. Her heart hammered in her chest, but her eyes were steely. "I'm not going to stop trying. Not ever."

Cayde's smile faded, replaced with something darker. "All right, Wendy, enough of this—"

Cayde lunged, his hand shooting out to grab her, but Wendy expected it. She batted his arm aside with her left hand, and with a powerful swing, drove her right fist into his jaw. He staggered back, eyes wide with shock. For a moment, he just stared at her, fear and confusion mingling on his face. He probably hadn't believed she'd actually hit him.

"I don't care how many other women you've beaten," Wendy hissed, her voice low and dangerous. "I'm not going to be one of them any longer."

Without hesitation, she swung again, this time landing a brutal punch to his nose. Cayde yelped, his face contorting in pain as his eyes watered. Perfect. She wanted him disoriented. He wouldn't see what was coming next.

She aimed a blow at his throat, but this time, Cayde was ready. His hand shot up, catching her wrist in a vice-like grip. Rage twisted his features, but Wendy wasn't afraid anymore. She *wanted* him furious, blind with anger, sloppy.

"Now you've done it," he snarled, his fingers digging painfully into her arm.

Wendy gritted her teeth, then swung her free hand into the side of his head, slamming her palm against his ear. She didn't pull back. Instead, she pressed her thumb into his eye, pushing hard until he screamed, releasing her arm in reflex. She darted toward the kitchen, her heart pounding but her mind focused.

She grabbed a dinner plate from the counter and smashed it against the floor, the shards scattering across the tiles. "You must have been so mad that you broke the plate," she said, stepping over the pieces. Calmly, she picked up a steak knife from the counter, twirling it once in her hand. "And then you smashed the lamp, started beating me. This time, I really thought you were going to kill me."

Cayde stood frozen for a moment, his hand still covering his eye, staring at her in disbelief.

Wendy waved the knife, her movements deliberate, controlled. "You even came at me with this," she said, then in one swift motion, she slashed her own arm. The blade bit into her skin, blood welling up instantly. The pain barely registered while adrenaline roared through her veins, pushing it away. It had cut a red line right through the initials Cayde had carved into her.

Cayde flinched, visibly recoiling at the sight. "You're insane," he rasped, his voice thick with disbelief.

She pointed the knife at him, her eyes cold and steady. "We fought over the steak knife. In the struggle, it ended up in your neck." Her voice dripped with malice. "That's what I'm going to tell the police."

Cayde's chest heaved, his breaths ragged and furious. Then, with a guttural roar, he lunged at her, desperation and rage fueling his attack. Wendy moved, trying to dodge, but he grabbed her shoulder, his fingers digging in as he wrestled for control.

The struggle became a deadly dance. Wendy swung her arm, trying to drive the knife into his back, but Cayde twisted, their legs tangling. His grip tightened on her wrist, pulling the knife away, but she fought back with everything she had, muscles straining as she resisted.

They crashed to the floor, rolling over each other, both fighting for control of the steak knife. The struggle was chaotic, frantic. Cayde, realizing he couldn't overpower her this way, changed tactics. With a grunt, he pinned Wendy's shoulder to the ground and punched her in the mouth. Her lips split against her teeth, the taste of blood a sharp tang.

Wendy retaliated immediately, driving her knee into his groin. Cayde grunted in pain, but it wasn't enough to throw him off. His free hand seized her wrists, wrenching them above her head as he straddled her torso, locking her beneath him. She struggled, but she couldn't move.

"How about this instead?" Cayde hissed, a cruel sneer curling his lips.

He transferred both of her wrists into one hand, squeezing them so tightly that her grip on the knife weakened. Her movements were restricted, desperate, as she tried to wriggle free.

"I kill you," he continued, his breath hot and ragged, "and pack your body in the car. Then I drive it somewhere no one will ever find you."

Wendy's heart pounded in her ears as she thrashed beneath him, trying to free even one hand. The knife, barely held in her grip, was useless now. Cayde's weight crushed her, and the panic started to creep in. She strained with all her strength but couldn't break his hold.

He leered down at her, his eyes dark with malice. "Bye, Wendy."

His fist shot down toward her head.

CHAPTER 81

CLAIRE

Claire had stayed at Jessie's through the night and almost all of the next day. She told security while at work that Cayde Miller was not to call or enter the school under any circumstances. Luckily, he'd not even tried. Her phone had been ringing off the hook. He'd texted her, angry that he couldn't get in the house, and after two hours of nonstop harassment, she turned off her phone. She and Jessie had driven after work to pick up her car. She had to pay a hefty fee, and Jessie took care of it. Claire promised she'd pay her back. Still, as she opened up her garage and slid her car in, Cayde's car nowhere in sight, she breathed a sigh of relief.

The sun set and the sky darkened. Claire was back home. She turned her new key in her new lock, opened the garage door, and hung up her keys on the hook, just as she'd always done. It was as though her old life was returning.

Tank welcomed her with a wagging tail and a few barks.

"Sorry baby," Claire said, rubbing his head. "Are you hungry?" She let him out and refilled his bowl with food and water. He'd had an accident in the house, but Claire didn't reprimand him and simply cleaned it up. She'd been the one to leave, after all.

Then she took a long, hot shower. Her hair wet and dressed in nothing but a robe, Claire went back downstairs, hunting for her phone. She checked the counter where she'd thought she left it, and frowned. It wasn't there.

A muffled bark caught her attention. Tank was outside in the backyard, the glass door shut. She hadn't let him out. He looked at her, barking to be let back in. And then she saw it, in the glass' reflection, Cayde stood behind her.

She spun around, clutching at her robe.

He stared at her, eyes flashing with anger.

"Leave, Cayde!" she yelled, backing away. "I've given you all the money I have! Take it and go! There isn't anything left for you here."

He glared, acting as if this speech was unwarranted. "You don't tell me what to do, remember?"

Kate tried to steady herself. "Cayde, get out of my house, or I will call the police."

"With this?" Cayde held up her phone. It buzzed, and he looked at it. "Jessie. This is the third time she's called." He laughed a little, then declined the call and put it back in his pocket. "Too bad you're busy at the moment."

"Why are you even here?" Claire shook her head. "You've taken everything you can. We're not in a relationship anymore."

"Claire, you're not well," Cayde said. "You barely eat, all you do is sleep—who's gonna look out for you?"

"*You're* making me sick!" Claire yelled. She marched toward the key rack to grab the keys to her sedan. She would drive to Jessie's house, or maybe the police station.

The keys weren't there.

"Where are they?" Claire demanded, but she didn't wait for an answer. She started to stride to the front door. She'd run to the neighbors in a robe if she had to. But something exploded against the wall beside her, forcing her to freeze. It was a picture of Paige and her, smiling. For one brief, surreal moment, Claire wondered if anyone would recognize her in that photo now; she looked so different compared to what she once was.

He grabbed another photo from the mantle and threw it at her. This time, Claire shielded her face. She jumped over the glass and started toward the garage door.

"Come back here," he seethed and took off after her. He grabbed her arm, and a short struggle ensued. Finally, Claire reared back her free hand and did something she'd always been too afraid to. She slapped him across the face.

He let her go and faltered back a step. It hadn't been a minuscule hit—she'd practically clubbed him.

Claire ran for the door leading to the garage. She smacked her hand across the button, opening up the main garage and running toward the large door as it lifted. She ducked underneath it, bolted outside and around the side of the garage, and pressed herself against the wall. What she needed to do was get him out of the house. She wondered how he'd even gotten in.

As she predicted, she heard Cayde, cursing and swearing, make his way to the driveway to get into his Corvette. He backed up exceedingly fast, his headlights beaming across the yard. She waited for several moments, then ran back inside, closing the garage behind her. She hoped he hadn't looked in the rearview or side mirrors as she slipped around.

The garage closed, the sensor bulb giving her only the dimmest light. She waited and held her breath, wondering if Cayde spotted her. She could sneak back inside and lock him out, but he had her keys. What she really needed was her phone.

The bulb above her clicked off, trapping her in complete darkness. Frustrated, she hit the side of her car with her palm. If only she had her keys! All that trouble to get her car back, and she still couldn't leave!

Claire inched toward the door that led into the house, twisting it open as quietly as she could. The lights were off. As eerie as it was, Claire wouldn't turn them on in case Cayde drove back around and saw that she'd returned home.

She locked the garage door behind her, making sure to twist the deadbolt. Then she crept toward the front door, staying away from the windows, despite the fact the house was dark enough inside she could barely see. She locked the handle, then the deadbolt, peeking out of the peephole as a car drove by.

Her stomach dropped, but it was only the neighbor's car. She let out a sigh of relief, about to step away from the peephole, but froze. Distorted from the dirty glass, she could make out another car parked behind the street. Cayde's Corvette.

He hadn't left.

At the same moment Claire realized, hands grabbed her from behind.

CHAPTER 82

AUTUMN

Autumn's father held Madeline in his arms. Her mother, sitting next to him, grinned down at the baby as she yawned and cooed in her sleep. Autumn watched them both from the couch across the coffee table. The way they both looked at their grandbaby held a softness she'd so dearly missed. Even her brothers seemed to soften up around Madeline. The little angel had a way of bringing out the best in everyone who laid eyes on her. Being here with her whole family made Autumn feel safe and warm on the inside. She cherished those rare moments when they came now.

The doorbell rang, and for a moment, anxiety sparked in Autumn's chest, breaking through her calm. No matter how safe she felt, she never really let her guard down. Not fully. Ever since Cayde's hospital visit months ago, she'd been a nervous wreck.

"I got it." Her brother, Isaac, jumped to answer the door. A few seconds later, he walked back into the living room with Justin in tow.

The tension left Autumn's shoulders as everyone greeted him.

"Justin!" Autumn's mother stood up to give him a hug.

"I'm leaving for the Navy in less than a week, so I thought I'd come and say my goodbyes." Justin looked at Autumn, and a bittersweet smile broke across his face. He came around the coffee table and gave her a side hug before settling down between her and Jeremiah.

The thought of Justin leaving made Autumn's heart hurt. He'd been staying around the house a lot longer than usual these days. Sometimes she caught him looking out the window, and if they ever drove anywhere, he looked up the street for Cayde's car. Anyone could see that he was protecting her, something Autumn appreciated more than he knew.

"What is it?" Justin asked, whispering. He'd caught her staring.

A slow smile spread across her face. "You know what you need before you leave? Shakes," she announced. "And fries to–"

"–dip in the ice cream," Justin finished. It was something they and her brothers had done often while growing up. He looked at the clock. It was well into the evening, and already dark, but he didn't seem to mind. "Should we all go get some tomorrow?" he asked.

"You know what?" Autumn got to her feet, her hands gesturing for Justin to stay seated. "I think I'll go get some shakes and fries for all of us."

"Do you want me to come with you, dear?" her mother asked.

For a moment, Autumn wanted to say yes, but another part of her knew she couldn't stay inside or depend on her family to protect her forever. Maybe it was time. She had to try to embrace life again. Break free from the chains Cayde had locked her in. The ones that felt as though they still remained—even after he'd been missing for months. She never forgot his final threat.

"That's okay, Mom," she answered. "If you all can just watch Madeline, I'll be back soon."

Autumn slid into the car, her hand trembling slightly as she twisted the keys in the ignition. The engine growled to life, breaking the silence of the night as she pulled out of the driveway, her headlights slicing through the darkness. She would get the food, bring it home, and have a perfect end to a perfect night. It was simple. She wouldn't even get out of the car.

The drive was barely five minutes, but her mind churned, replaying the events of the day. Feeding, changing, more feeding, trying to sleep, feeding again. She needed this—just a quick break, a moment to breathe. The night felt still, almost too quiet, the type of silence that made the hairs on the back of your neck stand on end.

She pulled up to the drive-through, her stomach growling. The smell of grease and salt hit her the moment the window slid open, awakening a hunger she hadn't even realized she had. "Just six vanilla milkshakes and six orders of small fries, please." She wondered if postpartum cravings were real.

The boy at the window handed her two trays with the milkshakes and the fries in a white paper bag, the grease staining the bottom. Promising herself she'd drive carefully, she set the full tray of milkshakes in the passenger seat and took the other two out of their tray to secure in the cup holders.

Autumn paid and mumbled a distracted "Thank you," her hand already reaching into the bag to fish out a few fries. She chewed nervously, the back of her mind tugging at her with an uneasy sense of dread. Madeline was back at the house, but the separation anxiety gnawed at her, even for a few stolen minutes away.

Then, headlights flooded her rearview mirror.

A car pulled up behind her. She glanced at it for a moment before turning back to her food. But something about the headlights—the way they lingered—nagged at her. She ignored it, focusing instead on wiping a spill from one of the milkshakes that had tipped over, but the feeling wouldn't leave.

"Here is your receipt." The boy handed it to her with a few more napkins, and Autumn let her foot off the break.

The car behind her skipped the drive-through window, moving forward as if in a hurry, and Autumn shrugged, merging back onto the road. But the headlights followed. And stayed close. Too close.

Her pulse quickened. Was this guy tailgating her? Annoyed, she switched lanes, hoping he'd speed past. Instead, he switched with her, sticking to her bumper like a shadow.

Alarm shot through her chest. This wasn't normal.

She switched lanes again. So did he.

It wasn't just the headlights now—there was something menacing about the way the car moved, creeping up on her, like a predator closing in on its prey. Then, as they passed under a streetlamp, she saw it—a black Corvette.

Autumn's heart lurched in her chest. Cayde.

Her breath caught, and the world seemed to tilt as a jolt of pure adrenaline hit her bloodstream. Why was he here? There was no reason for him to be following her in the dead of night. No *good* reason.

Autumn slammed her foot on the gas. The engine roared, but the Corvette was right there with her, speeding up as if he'd been waiting for this. She yanked the steering wheel, taking a sharp corner, her tires screeching in protest. The fries spilled across the passenger seat, one of the milkshakes splattering across the floor, but she barely noticed. Cayde's car was right beside her now, closing in.

For a split second, their eyes met. His face was twisted in fury, and hers—hers was painted in sheer terror.

Then he jerked his wheel toward her.

Autumn screamed, swerving violently to avoid the collision. Her car careened off the road, the tires bouncing over dirt and rocks. She plowed through someone's yard, narrowly missing a mailbox as she fought to regain control. Her knuckles turned white as she gripped the wheel, her breath coming in ragged gasps.

The tires screeched as she finally managed to steer back onto the road, but Cayde was still there. Relentless. She pressed the gas pedal to the floor, her heart hammering as she tore through the neighborhood. The houses blurred past her as she flew through the narrow streets. She was almost home. Almost safe.

Her horn blared, long and desperate, as she passed familiar houses—hoping, praying someone would hear her. Justin, her parents, *anyone*.

But Cayde was closing in. Fast.

The house was just ahead. Four houses away. Three. Two.

Autumn slammed on the brakes. The car screeched to a halt, smashing over a sprinkler. She parked the car, but she didn't bother turning it off. Completely abandoning the spilled food, she flung the door open and stumbled out, her legs weak, her body shaking. She hit the ground hard, palms sliding over the freshly watered grass as she scrambled to get up.

Cayde's Corvette pulled up beside her, and before she could move, he was out—charging toward her like a bull.

She tried to run, but he was faster. His hand clamped around her waist, yanking her back with a force that knocked the breath from her lungs. She kicked and thrashed, but his grip tightened, his breath hot against her ear.

"Quiet, or I'll shoot," he growled, his voice slurred, thick with the stench of alcohol. The cold barrel of a gun pressed into her back, freezing her in place.

Autumn's mind raced. *No.* This wasn't how it ended. It couldn't be. She thought of Madeline and her family, just across the yard and beyond the door.

But she couldn't move. Couldn't breathe. All she could feel was the metal against her skin and the terror coursing through her veins.

CHAPTER 83

SOPHIE

"I think I'll go for a run this morning." Sophie finished the remains of a berry smoothie Tanner had made for breakfast and set the glass in the sink.

Tanner sat at a granite countertop, working on his laptop. "Do you want me to go with you?"

"No, you're fine. I'd slow you down." She hadn't gone running in over a year, but the smell of the coast and arrangements ahead renewed energy in her bones and muscles she'd forgotten she had. "There's a trail that goes along the coast and up toward a lookout."

"I've run it a few times. It's nice." He still sipped at his smoothie. "Dad called this morning, by the way. He said a letter for me arrived at the house from you?"

"Oh, right." Sophie had forgotten about it. "When I was arrested, I felt the need to write out some things. No one was listening to me, and I knew that somehow, Cayde was going to try to get to me. I just wanted you to know everything, in case he did."

"I see." Tanner nodded sagely. "Well, no need for any of that now. You're safe. And we'll be heading back to Nashville tomorrow."

Sophie could hardly wait. Her nerves became even more giddy, and she bounced on her toes. "Okay, I'm heading out. How long is the trail?"

"You can run the whole thing in thirty minutes," Tanner said.

"See you in thirty minutes." Sophie smiled at him and went out the front door.

The coastal part of the trail was the worst. The sand was difficult to run in, taking more energy than she expected for the rest of the run. By the time she hit the pavement, moving away from the beach, her legs burned. Yet she moved forward, happy to be running at all. She'd never felt so free in her life. The trail weaved in and out of green shrubbery, sometimes blocking her view of the entire world, before briefly letting her out to see the houses and roads a ways in the distance. She made her way up some switchbacks, sweat drenching the front of her shirt. She should have brought some water with her.

The trail evened out, looping toward a main road. There was a horrible moment where her heart skipped a beat because she thought she saw the same model of car that Cayde drove. She placed a hand over her heart and stopped in her tracks. Whatever she thought she saw, it was gone now. How long, she wondered, until seeing any black Corvette wouldn't frighten her?

She'd never told Cayde about the property Tanner owned on the coast. He couldn't possibly know where she was. She continued her run, but there was a blanket of anxiety that made her sluggish. Her legs, once burning with excitement, now shook, and her lungs tightened around the air she gasped in. Sophie looked ahead and slowed to a stop. She didn't want to go to the lookout anymore. She just wanted to go back to Tanner's.

Turning back felt like a defeat, and the energy she'd had before dwindled. Maybe she'd never feel safe again. Maybe the nightmares and dreams would haunt her forever. No. She pushed the thoughts away. Once she was back near her boys, everything would be better. Life would begin anew.

Sophie was aware of a presence to her left. A car parallel to the trail beside her. It was driving slow enough to keep pace with her, and when she turned her head to look, her lost energy returned in the form of soul-gripping fear.

It wasn't just the same model of car that Cayde drove.

It was his car.

And he grinned devilishly at her from the driver's seat, as if he was proud of himself to have found her. So excited.

Time seemed to freeze for Sophie, one leg poised mid-air, the other propelling her forward as her eyes locked onto his. Even from this distance, the malevolent intent was clear in his gaze. Cayde Miller was not a man accustomed to relinquishing control. If he couldn't possess Sophie, he'd ensure that no one else could—not even her.

Reality surged back into motion, and Sophie ran.

Cayde's car roared to life, the engine growling like a predator unleashed. The vehicle hurtled forward, swerving aggressively. Horns blared in protest as Cayde's car cut through traffic, barreling ahead, momentarily vanishing down the road. Sophie's mind raced. The thought of turning back—of running onto the main road and waving frantically for help—was tempting. But after everything she'd endured, she knew that relying on the fickle mercy of strangers was a gamble she couldn't afford.

Her breath came in ragged bursts as her shoes pounded the trail. She swatted at the encroaching foliage, green, leafy tendrils whipping against her legs with each frantic stride. When she reached the switchbacks, she abandoned the conventional path. Instead of zig-zagging, she hurled herself down the steep slopes, her clothes plastered with mud, rocks biting into her skin. She skidded, crashed onto the trail, and plunged over the next edge. A cacophony of flapping wings and shrieking black birds erupted as she plowed through them, their eyes searching the trail for any crumbs left behind.

At the base of the hill, Sophie veered toward the path that led to the beach, her heart pounding in sync with her heavy breaths. A horrific screech shattered the tense rhythm. Cayde's car had reemerged, veering off the tarmac and skidding to a jarring halt on the rough terrain. Cayde leaped from the vehicle and charged toward her, his every step taking him closer to his deadly purpose.

Sophie didn't have a moment to wrestle with her momentum. Turning back was not an option; instead, she turned right, heading toward the coast. A chain-link fence loomed ahead, festooned with glaring "Private Property" signs. They stood like silent sentinels, a physical barrier that could slow her down. Any delay would give Cayde the precious seconds he needed to catch up.

She sprinted toward the fence, her breath coming in panicked bursts. With a cry, she leapt, her hands clawing at the top of the fence. Her shoes found tenuous grips on the diamond-shaped openings as she climbed, each step a desperate gasp. She reached the top, her heart pounding like a war drum, and swung her body over with a jarring thud. She almost tumbled onto her side but managed to catch herself, springing upright just in time to see Cayde slam into the fence behind her. His fingers gripped the chain links with brutal force, shaking them violently in frustration.

For a fleeting moment, Sophie met his furious gaze, then she bolted along the length of the fence. Cayde kept pace, his footsteps echoing ominously behind her. But as he neared his car, he rounded back toward it, his back briefly turned. Seizing the opportunity, Sophie diverted her path, her eyes catching sight of Tanner's house in the distance. Cayde's car was going straight for it.

Desperation clawed at her. She had hoped for a passerby on the beach, but the shore was deserted, littered with abandoned bags and discarded shoes. A few surfers, mere specks in their black wetsuits, carved through the cold, gray water, indifferent to the signs marking the property's edge.

Sophie needed to be seen. Even if no one helped her, being in a public space might deter whatever sinister plans Cayde had. The fence gave way to a double gate, chains wrapped tight through the links. Sophie squeezed through the narrow gap, ducking under the chains as she burst onto the road. Cars sped by, a blur of color and noise. Cayde's car, now a dark shadow in her peripheral vision, ripped around to come back for her.

Sophie's pulse raced as she sprinted toward the road, the roar of Cayde's engine closing in behind her. Her only hope was to reach the road's flow of traffic and blend into the chaos before he could close the trap. Every second counted.

Sophie's arms flailed as she charged toward the road, her cries for help lost in the low roar of tires and engines. One car honked loudly, and another swerved, barely missing her as she leaped onto the pavement. Cayde's car was getting closer.

"Stop! I need help!" Sophie's voice was hoarse, desperate.

The cars zoomed past, indifferent. One driver even had the audacity to flip her off. Panic surged as Sophie glanced back at Cayde's menacing car. She cursed under her breath and bolted across the street, heedless of the blaring horns and screeching brakes. The four lanes and median felt like an endless expanse of danger. She darted forward, but a trailer roared past so close she had to stumble back to avoid being sideswiped.

Finding a narrow window of opportunity, Sophie leaped off the road and onto the mowed grass, which led into a labyrinth of neighborhoods. If she could make it through the streets, she could circle back to Tanner's house. Cayde would be forced to follow her through the winding cul-de-sacs, each yard and towering house offering brief cover.

She wove a frantic path through the yards. Every glance over her shoulder confirmed that Cayde's car was still stalking her through the streets, but with a tinge of relief, she noticed it was falling further behind. Eventually, she'd lost him in the suburban labyrinth. Now she just had to find her own way out.

Minutes felt like hours as she finally glimpsed Tanner's house again. Relief turned to raw emotion, and sobs burst uncontrollably from her. She had to cross one last road to reach the gravel driveway—a long, winding path lined with trees for privacy. As her feet hit the slippery rocks, a gasp escaped her.

Cayde's car was parked out of sight, past the road. The engine was still running, but there was no one in the driver's seat. Sophie's fleeting hope shattered as strong arms wrapped around her from behind.

"Tanner!" she screamed, her voice muffled as Cayde's large hand clamped over her mouth. Her kicks and thrashes were feeble against his relentless strength. The house was so close—a beacon of white wood, stark against the gray ocean stretched beyond it.

"Tanner!" She tried again, but it was drowned out by Cayde's overpowering grip.

Cayde's strength was overwhelming. With one hand, he managed to open the passenger door. Sophie wrenched herself away momentarily, but his arm shot out, seizing her once more. She was dragged closer and closer to the car, her struggles only marginally slowing him down.

Realization hit her like a ton of bricks—she was going to be taken. Desperation clawed at her as she fought against the hand pressing down on her mouth. Her fingers scratched down his palm and caught at her diamond necklace, pulling it from her neck. It tumbled onto the rocks with a tiny clink.

Cayde's determination was unrelenting. The sky above vanished beneath the shadow of the car. Sophie's mind flashed to Noah and Charlie in a final, silent prayer.

CHAPTER 84

JACK

The drive felt both agonizingly long and painfully short. Neither Jack nor Blair said much. The silence stretched between them, heavy with exhaustion and unspoken emotions. The numbing effect of the painkillers had started to wear off for Jack, and every bump in the road sent a dull, throbbing pain through his shoulder. He could see Blair's face swelling as well, the faint bruises darkening beneath her eyes. By tomorrow, her face would be marked with purplish hues.

"Do you think it's our fault?" Blair's voice broke through the silence, startling Jack out of his thoughts.

Jack shifted his gaze to the darkening sky outside. "We did our best. And we can't be sure. He might have killed her before we were even called." The words felt hollow, even as he said them. Two days—forty-eight hours since they'd been handed this case, and now they were driving to a grave. They'd caught the suspect, found the victim, but the bitter taste of failure still lingered.

When they finally arrived at the location, someone from the FBI forensics team was waiting for them, a flashlight bobbing as they approached. The man introduced himself briskly and led them along a rough, uneven path.

"We've uncovered the body," he said, speaking quickly. "Miller drove off-road, but we've preserved his tire tracks. Luckily, the storm didn't reach this far, so we have a lot to work with."

"How far in?" Jack asked, his voice sounding strained even to his own ears.

"His car is parked and hidden under some branches and foliage, about a quarter mile east of the body," the agent said, his steps quick and purposeful. "Forensics and photos are currently being worked on. We've got everything being processed."

Blair's jaw was set, her eyes trained on the beam of the flashlight ahead. "Do you have a timeline?"

"Looks like he buried the body early this morning," the agent replied. "But she's been dead longer than that. About two days. There's a substantial amount of blood in the vehicle as well. It appears he kept her body in the front seat for an extended time."

"Shit." Jack shook his head. It was a grotesque, twisted relief to know that she had been dead before they were even assigned the case. No matter how quickly they had moved or how hard they had pushed, they wouldn't have been able to save her. The weight of that realization was morbid, but it also lifted a sliver of the guilt that had been gnawing at him.

The lights of the forensic team came into view, flickering through the trees like distant stars. They were clustered around a small clearing where the car sat, half-hidden beneath a canopy of branches. Evidence markers dotted the ground, and flashes from the cameras punctuated the darkness.

But the car wasn't their destination. Jack and Blair were led to a shallow grave, the earth freshly turned. A tarp had been cast to the side and marked as evidence. The top layer of soil had been carefully removed, and evidence photos had been taken. The team had recorded everything they needed. In a few minutes, they'd take her out and transport her for her autopsy.

Blair looked into the grave, her eyes slightly glazed over. Jack did the same, a grim frown pulling down his features. There, posed neatly in the grave with a Bible across her chest and under her hands, lay the body of Sophie Miller.

CHAPTER 85

KATE

Something within Cayde's face changed. He let go and sat back. "Kate," he breathed, staring at her broken, tear-stained face. "I'm sorry."

She coughed and held a hand up to her throat. It burned. Breathing in the air hurt more than it should have, not giving her the relief she wanted. Her other hand slipped behind her as she writhed underneath him, fishing in her back pocket.

"Kate?" Cayde's face was strange. He looked upset and confused. "Kate, I love you! I'm so sorry!"

Kate met his eyes again. Her lip quivered and she whimpered. "No." His hesitancy was all she needed. She gripped the car keys in between her fingers, and with all the strength she could muster, she slammed them into his face. They cut across his forehead and eye, and Cayde cried out, grabbing onto his head. Kate scrambled to her feet, jumping toward the door. His hand shot out and grabbed her leg, sending her onto her stomach, but she kicked him in the face with her socked foot, and he let go. She reached for the door handle and flung it open.

"Mary!" she screamed. It had burst out of her unintentionally.

"Kate!" Mary waved in the parking lot, her car on and running. "Come on!" Bill was watching them from the passenger seat, his old face intense and serious.

With one foot socked and the other in an untied shoe, Kate bolted down the concrete walkway and steps. She could hear Cayde's pounding footsteps behind her. The world was full of gray splotches and stars, and each deep, ragged breaths burned like lava down her throat.

Cayde caught her arm only a few steps from the bottom of the stairs. He was trying to get the keys from her. She slapped him across the face with her other hand, desperate to get him off her, and continued toward Mary and her car. Cayde roared and recovered fast. She couldn't outrun him. Her steps were uneven, and her head still felt like it would burst. So she chucked the keys as far as she could into the grass next to the motel.

"Fuck!" Cayde yelled, and she heard the footsteps move in their direction. He dove into the dead grass, his head whipping around wildly. But in the dim light of the cheap motel, he couldn't find them—at least not fast enough.

Mary had opened the back door of her car and was already in the front seat again. Kate dove in, and Mary stomped on the gas pedal before Kate could get up and shut the door.

"Are you okay?" Bill asked, his eyes wide.

Kate didn't answer. She shut the car door and turned around, looking at Cayde through the back windshield. He'd given up on the keys and was chasing after the car.

"Kate!" he roared. "I'll find you! You bitch!" He was pulling at his hair, kicking and punching the air. "I'll find you!" And then, as the car fully left the parking lot, he stopped, staring after it. "Don't leave!"

Kate took shaky breaths, watching him get smaller and smaller in the dark.

"Are you okay?" Bill asked again. Still, Kate didn't answer.

A part of her was being left behind at that motel. She sobbed, unable to tear her eyes away from him. Bill's hand placed itself on her back, but he didn't ask her if she was okay again.

"You're safe," Mary said. "You're safe, Kate. He can't hurt you anymore."

Somehow, Kate knew it was true. She had seen it on Cayde's face as well. They were through, and his threats toward her family meant nothing now.

Soon, through the tears and distance, and the dirt kicked up along the road from Mary's car, Cayde Miller disappeared from sight, left behind in the dark.

CHAPTER 86

CLAIRE

Claire screamed, her voice raw and desperate, as she struggled to break free from Cayde's grip. His fingers dug into her arms, hard and unrelenting, but adrenaline surged through her, giving her the strength she needed. She drove her elbow into his chest with all the force she could muster. Cayde grunted, momentarily stunned, and Claire didn't waste a second. She bolted toward the back door, her hands trembling as she fumbled with the latch, her breath ragged and panicked.

"Tank!" she shouted, her voice cracking as she flung the door open. The large dog bounded inside, barking furiously, his sharp, growling snapping aimed at Cayde. Claire's heart pounded in her ears as she leaned out the door, screaming again for her neighbors. "Help!"

Then, a cold click echoed behind her, freezing her in place. Claire's body stiffened, her breath catching in her throat as she turned slowly. Cayde was there, standing a few feet away, his face twisted with fury. In his hand, the gun was leveled directly at her head, gleaming under the dim light. Tank's growls grew louder, his teeth bared, snapping dangerously at Cayde, but he kept his distance.

For a moment, Claire felt detached, like she was watching the scene unfold from somewhere far away. A part of her was numb to it—the gun, the threat. She had lived through this terror for so long that it no longer paralyzed her the way it once had. But another part of her, the part that realized he was cornered now, knew this was more dangerous than ever. Cayde had lost control, and men like him didn't accept defeat easily. He could pull the trigger without thinking twice.

"It's over, Cayde," she said, her voice steady despite the pounding in her chest. Her hands clenched into fists at her sides. "You can make the choice to leave. Right now."

He sneered at her, his hand twitching slightly as he tightened his grip on the gun. For a long, suffocating moment, neither of them moved. The air between them thickened with tension, Tank's growing more ferocious by the second.

Then, the distant wail of sirens pierced the air, faint but unmistakable. Help was coming. And they both knew it.

Cayde's eyes flickered with something—panic, maybe fear. His mask of bravado slipped for just a second. He took a step back. The gun wavered in his hand. He heard the sirens too, growing louder, closer. The realization sank in. It was over.

Without a word, he lowered the gun, backing away from her. Claire stayed rooted to the spot, her body tense, ready to react if he came at her again. But instead, Cayde turned and ran for the front door. She didn't chase him. She didn't need to.

A moment later, the roar of his Corvette's engine shattered the silence, tires screeching as he sped off. Claire stood frozen, listening to the sound fade into the distance, her heart still racing. The sirens grew louder, and within moments, blue and red lights bathed the front of her house, illuminating the dark corners of the yard. A patrol car tore down the street, pursuing Cayde.

Claire slumped against the wall, the adrenaline beginning to drain from her limbs, leaving her weak. She waited by the front door, her breath coming in shallow gasps as the flashing lights painted the walls around her.

A police officer approached, his voice firm but calm. "Ma'am, are you alright?"

Claire nodded, her voice hoarse as she tried to collect herself. "He—he broke in," she managed, glancing at Tank, who had quieted but still paced nervously, whining. "I have a protective order. He violated it."

The officer gave her a reassuring nod, his face softening. "We'll take care of it. Let's make sure you're safe."

As Claire explained the situation, recounting the moments with as much clarity as she could muster, she was surprised by how attentively the officer listened. For so long, she had been dismissed and ignored, as if her fears were an inconvenience. But not now. Now, someone was listening. And more importantly, someone was acting.

Just as the officer turned to radio his colleagues, another car pulled up fast, skidding slightly as it stopped by the curb. Claire recognized it instantly.

"Jessie," she whispered.

The door flew open, and Jessie leaped out, running across the yard with panic etched on her face. Without hesitation, she threw her arms around Claire, pulling her into a tight embrace. "I was so worried!" Jessie's voice was breathless, her grip fierce. "You weren't picking up your phone, so I called the police to check on you."

Claire closed her eyes, leaning into the embrace, the warmth of Jessie's presence soothing the tremors in her body. "I'm okay," she said softly, her voice muffled against her friend's shoulder. "I'm going to be fine."

The words felt strange on her lips—fine—but for the first time in a long while, Claire allowed herself to believe it. Cayde was gone, the police were here, and she was surrounded by people who cared. The storm that had once been her life was finally breaking.

"I swear," Jessie muttered, pulling back just enough to look Claire in the eyes, "you're not going through this alone. We'll figure this out."

Claire smiled weakly, her eyes glistening with unshed tears. She glanced at the flashing lights of the patrol cars, the officers moving around her house, ensuring her safety. The weight of everything that had happened. The fear, the pain, the fight for survival—it all began to lift.

CHAPTER 87

AUTUMN

"Hold it!" Justin's voice barked from the doorway, sharp as a bullet in the still night. The sound froze everyone in place. Autumn's pulse hammered in her chest. His figure emerged from the shadows of the porch, cutting through the tension like a blade. There was no hesitation in his steps, no fear. He descended from the porch like a man who had nothing to lose.

"The police are being called," Justin said, his tone cold and unyielding, the fury barely masked. "If you don't want this to get worse for you, I suggest you leave." His eyes burned with a ferocity that Autumn had never seen before—dangerous, lethal. The type of rage that didn't come from anger alone, but from love. Fierce, protective love.

Cayde's grip on her tightened, pulling her closer as he backed toward the Corvette, his breathing shallow and quick. Autumn stumbled with him, her mind racing, the cold press of fear crawling up her spine. *Is this it?* she wondered. *Is this where he'll end it, right here in the yard?* The thought sliced through her, raw and terrifying.

"Cayde, please," she begged, her voice trembling. "Think of Madeline. Think of our little girl."

"Shut up!" Cayde snapped, his voice like the crack of a whip, and he jerked her hard enough to send a jolt of pain through her shoulder. He was spiraling, Autumn could see it in his wild eyes, the alcohol-fueled rage that made him unpredictable, dangerous.

Justin's face darkened, his expression hard as stone. He didn't blink, didn't falter. "Let me rephrase that. I'm not suggesting you leave," he said, his voice low, steady, and deadly. "I'm telling you." He reached behind and pulled out a pistol tucked under his shirt. "This isn't a fight you can win, Cayde. Let. Her. Go."

Cayde sneered at him. "You're just a boy. You don't have the guts."

Justin handled the gun with care. He'd drawn it, but it remained pointed at the grass. He probably wouldn't lift it until Autumn was out of the way. "A year in the military would say otherwise," he growled. "But if you wanna stick around and find out, I promise I have no problem pulling the trigger."

Each word was a challenge, a dare. He advanced slowly, his body tense, every step calculated. For every step Justin took, Cayde took one back, dragging Autumn with him. She could hear Cayde's breathing quicken, feel the tremor in his hand as he tried to keep control, but it was slipping. He was unraveling.

Then, a sharp voice cut through the thick tension. "Hey!" Autumn's father appeared at the doorway, her brother right behind him. They moved as one, grim and determined, their faces hard with the same lethal intent that Justin had.

Porch lights flickered on in the neighborhood, doors creaking open as silhouettes filled the doorways. Autumn's frantic honking had done the job. Eyes were on them now—too many witnesses.

Cayde glanced around, his eyes darting from the neighbors to Justin, to Autumn's father and brothers. He was cornered. Beads of sweat trickled down his forehead as the realization dawned: He'd already lost. Now the only question was—what would he do with her?

Autumn's heart seized in her chest as Cayde's grip shifted, his fingers digging into her side. *He's going to take me. Or worse.*

Then, in a savage motion, he shoved her.

Autumn's body jerked violently as she was thrown, her scream ripping through the air. But before she hit the ground, Justin lunged forward, catching her just in time, his arms wrapping around her in a tight, protective grip. She gasped, looking over her shoulder.

Cayde was retreating fast, stumbling back toward the Corvette, a shattered beer bottle in his hand. It wasn't a gun. It had never been a gun.

"Cayde!" Autumn cried, her voice loud enough for the whole street to hear. The neighbors who had peeked out from their homes—the people she'd grown up with, the ones who whispered and watched—were all there to hear what she had to say.

Cayde stopped. His gaze flickered to hers, his expression a twisted mask of anger and defeat.

"Don't you *ever* come back here again," she said, her voice trembling but strong. "You're no longer a part of this family!"

A sneer curled on his lips, but something in his eyes shifted, something like fear. His gaze darted between Justin, her father,

her brother—then back to her, standing there, defiant despite the fear that still coursed through her veins.

Without a word, he turned, got into his car, and slammed the door. The engine roared to life, and with one last glare, Cayde peeled away, disappearing into the night.

CHAPTER 88

WENDY

Cayde leered down, his eyes dark with malice. "Bye, Wendy." His fist shot down toward her head.

In a split second, Wendy twisted her body violently, shifting just enough to avoid the blow. Cayde's fist slammed into the floor beside her, his knuckles cracking against the wood. He howled in pain, momentarily stunned, his grip loosening just enough.

That was all she needed.

With a primal yell, Wendy ripped one wrist free and swung the knife upward with all the strength she could muster. The blade's edge pressed against Cayde's throat, and suddenly, the world stopped. Wendy's breath came in shallow bursts, her hand trembling as she stared up at him. She could end it right now. With just a little more pressure, she could end all the fear, all the pain.

"I could kill you," she seethed, blood staining her teeth. "I *should* kill you."

Cayde's face went ashen, his eyes wide with terror. Was that what she looked like when he had the upper hand? To Wendy, he just looked pitiful now. They had traded places entirely. The same look he had given her so many times—now it was on her face. She saw it in his eyes. He knew she would do it. She could feel his pulse against the knife's edge, see the plea in his expression, though he was too cowardly to voice it.

"Get off me," she growled.

Slowly, cautiously, Cayde backed away, and Wendy pushed herself up from the floor, her gaze never leaving his. They both rose to their feet, locked in a fragile standoff. Blood trickled from the knife's tip, staining his shirt. He glanced at it, panic flickering in his eyes as he looked back at her.

Wendy stepped closer, her voice dropping to a lethal whisper. "Get. Out."

She pressed the blade harder into his skin for emphasis before pulling it away, the threat hanging in the air between them. Her eyes stayed narrow, unflinching, as she stepped back, giving him just enough room to retreat.

Cayde opened his mouth, maybe to say something, to plead or to threaten, but the wail of sirens outside cut him short. His expression shifted; she saw the decision flash across his face. Without a word, he stepped back, his movements jerky and panicked. He grabbed his briefcase and turned toward the door.

"Cayde," Wendy called after him, her voice a cold promise.

He froze, his hand on the doorknob.

"If I ever see you again," she said, each word razor-sharp, "I will kill you."

For a brief moment, he hesitated, turning just slightly to glance back at her. Then, without another word, he stepped out the door and disappeared into the night.

CHAPTER 89

JACK

"What did you find inside the car?" Jack asked, his voice low as he and Blair reached the vehicle buried deep in the woods. Portable flood-lamps filtered through the trees, casting long shadows over the scene. A somber fog drifted through the air, as if the forest itself knew what had happened here.

They stepped carefully around the flagged evidence markers, their eyes scanning the ground. Cayde's shoe prints were still visible, leading away from the car, each step pressed into the damp earth. Jack followed the trail with his eyes, tracing the long walk Cayde had made back to the road.

To their left, a forensics tech bent over the shovel they'd found abandoned by a patch of disturbed soil. Not far from it, Sophie was being carefully zipped into a body bag, the techs working with a solemn efficiency that spoke of too much experience with scenes like this.

One of the techs, a man in his late thirties, stepped back from the open car door, shaking his head. In his gloved hand, he held a small plastic vial, red with blood. "We've got blood all over the front seat. It's soaked through." He gestured toward the interior. Jack leaned in slightly, catching a glimpse of the dark stain. It had pooled in the fabric, nearly black.

Blair moved closer to the car, her sharp eyes picking up on the small details: a phone left on the passenger seat, a Polaroid camera tossed carelessly beside it. And scattered across the seat were photos, their glossy surfaces reflecting back at them. And inside the glove box, a pistol.

"That's the same gun Veronica Webb bought," Jack said. They'd have to run the serial number to be sure, but he didn't see much point in that.

"He took photos?" Blair asked. She put on the gloves handed to her and held the bagged evidence, inspecting it. "Why take photos and then abandon them with the car?"

"More than likely, he was going to lay low and come back for it," Jack said, looking at the haphazard job Cayde had done to hide the vehicle. It wasn't visible from the road, blocked by trees and foliage, but take only a short walk, and you wouldn't miss it during the day.

"Well, we've got the guy," she told the forensics team. "So you can take your time. Make sure we don't miss anything. Thanks, guys."

As they turned and started back toward the SUV, Jack couldn't help but glance over his shoulder at the forensics van. Sophie's body was being carefully loaded inside, ready for transport to the morgue. For some reason, seeing her treated with care and dignity now—a far cry from the way she had been left in the dirt—brought him a sliver of relief. He couldn't shake the thought that they owed her that much, at least. After all they had uncovered about her short, tragic time with Cayde, she deserved some semblance of respect.

There was still the matter of Veronica.

"It just hit me," Jack said, cursing himself for not realizing it sooner. "The several thousand dollars Veronica paid to Cayde. That amount matches up with the bond posted for Sophie last week."

"You think Veronica paid Cayde to get her out of jail so that they could kill her?"

"And paid for new tires to bring her all the way up here, far from the initial kidnapping. Bought the murder weapon as well."

"She was a sheriff in Nashville." Blair shook her head. "A sheriff, for fuck's sake. And then there's the report of the shooting right before her arrest." Blair stopped in her tracks. "If Cayde had been arrested for attempted murder that day, Sophie would still be alive."

"Instead, they arrested her." Jack could feel the disappointment in his voice.

"Myers, the justice system's really fucked up," Blair said. "They completely failed her. Not just Sophie, but all those women before. He never should have been allowed to get this far."

It was a surprising speech to hear Blair make. She'd always been so confident of her morals and trust within the work they did. Jack, on the other hand, believed justice came in many different forms. He just happened to work for one of them. It was almost sad to see the faltering doubt in his partner's face. But he agreed. The system he had joined in order to help women like his mother—and children in the same position he had once been in—had failed. In a way, it felt like *he* had failed.

"I know." It was all he could say. Learning Sophie's story and this case had changed him the past two days. He didn't see things the same way anymore. "I know."

For now, it was all he could say.

CHAPTER 90

CLAIRE

Claire's mother passed away one week after Cayde's break-in. The funeral came around the following Thursday, and Claire wasn't sure she would have the strength to bury another loved one. Paige, who had lost two grandparents in one month, came to stay for a few days. Her presence had been a dear comfort, but not much could be done to help the overwhelming grief they both felt. Claire greeted guests, thanked friends and family for joining, and did her best to remain strong. She'd already gotten through so much—she would get through this.

"Claire?" A voice sounded behind her, warm like honey.

Claire turned, and a sad smile came across her face. "Hello, Zach."

"It was a beautiful service," he said, and hugged her. "I'm glad I could come. How are you doing?"

"Oh, you know." She shrugged and half laughed, half cried. "Probably about the same as you. After all, I'm not the only one that's buried a parent this week."

"Well. We always ended up doing the same things," he said, attempting humor. The dark joke made Claire laugh *and* cry a little harder. He shifted his weight back and forth, glancing at his feet. "But something tells me you're going through a harder time. Bigger than this." His head tilted to the room where the casket awaited to be taken to the hearse. "Paige says you're not engaged anymore."

"No," Claire sniffed. "I'm not."

"Maybe," he said slowly, "if you wanted, we could go out to lunch. Catch up?"

With those few simple words, it suddenly seemed that standing before her was not her ex-husband, but the best friend she'd had for years and could tell anything to. She smiled, wiping away her tears.

"I'd like that."

CHAPTER 91

KATE

The hotel's continental breakfast was a disappointment. The hashbrowns were overly salted, the eggs bland, and the coffee served in a flimsy paper cup was tepid at best. Kate sipped it anyway, using the cup as a shield, holding it close to her face as she glanced at the three women sitting with her.

Almost two years since she'd left Cayde. Kate had thought he was out of her life for good. But then she'd seen his face on the news, along with a beautiful blond woman—the woman he'd kidnapped. Kate had known, then and there, that she wouldn't be found alive. Not long after, she'd been called to testify in court, and accepted. She wasn't the only one.

They had agreed to meet for breakfast: Kate, Autumn, Wendy, and Claire. Strangers bound together by fate, sharing the same hotel as they awaited their turn to testify. When the idea was first suggested, Kate had thought it might be comforting to meet the others who had also been hurt by Cayde. But now, sitting at the table with them—seeing their anxious eyes and unsmiling lips—she wished she had chosen to eat alone. Her face, she suspected, looked just as haunted as theirs.

"What time is it?" Wendy asked, scanning the room for a clock. She had skipped the food and was already working on her second cup of coffee. The first was gone before anyone else had even arrived.

Kate had been the next to show up, early as well, nerves twisting in her stomach, propelling her out of her room. She had gone for a run around five in the morning, trying to shake off the heavy dread that clung to her. The dining room had been empty then, but an hour later, when she returned, Wendy had already been sitting at the table, her eyes dark and hollow as she sipped her coffee.

After showering and dressing, Kate had lasted a whole three minutes sitting in her room before the suffocating stillness drove her back downstairs for breakfast. Wendy had still been there, nursing her second cup. They had exchanged a glance, instantly understanding why the other was there. But Kate, in an effort to appear polite, had asked anyway.

Introductions were brief and polite but heavy with the unspoken weight they all carried. By seven, the agreed-upon time, all four women had gathered at the table, silently recognizing each other, bound by the same man.

The realization unsettled Kate. Could they all see it, the scars left behind? Was it written so plainly on her face? Or was there an unspoken connection between survivors of the same torment? It wasn't just shared pain; they had all suffered at the hands of the same man.

Autumn picked at the ham on her plate. She looked painfully young, barely in her mid-twenties. The exhaustion was evident in the purple shadows under her eyes, but it didn't dim the vibrant blue of her irises or the brightness of her auburn hair. Her youth made Kate ache. She knew logically that they had all endured the same abuse, but seeing someone so young, forced into the same nightmare, made it seem even more tragic.

Wendy, in her early thirties, had a hardness about her, a cold detachment that made her seem older. Claire, about Kate's age, had made the wisest choice—settling for a bagel with cream cheese and a glass of orange juice.

"What time is it?" Claire asked, her eyes darting around the room.

"Half-past," Kate replied, glancing at her phone. "The cab will be here in thirty minutes."

Autumn paled. "Did any of you ask to testify over video?" Her voice was small, hopeful. The others shook their heads.

"They wouldn't let me," she murmured. "I didn't want to come here, but…"

They understood. All of them did.

"It's for the best," Kate said softly. "And I feel like I owe it to Sophie to testify."

Wendy nodded, her eyes darkened by the bags beneath them. Kate suspected she hadn't slept at all.

"You were the one he married before Sophie, right?" Autumn asked, finally lifting her eyes from her plate.

"I was," Kate said quietly. "For a little over a year."

Autumn frowned, nodding. "I did some digging on Cayde over the years. I wanted to be aware of where he was, who he was with. Better to be prepared with a man like him."

"I wanted to forget," Claire admitted.

The conversation shifted as they began to compare timelines, piecing together Cayde's web of lies. There were three women before them, and several others tangled up in Cayde's mess during their own relationships with him. They laughed at the absurdity of it all—the way he had juggled multiple marriages and affairs. He had married Autumn while still entangled with the others, eloped with Wendy after Autumn's child was born, and had an affair with Veronica Webb during it all. Claire had sued him for stealing her money, all while Cayde was still with Kate, lying about his business troubles.

"I let him borrow that money," Kate chuckled darkly. "The money he used to pay you back? That was mine." She laughed, but Claire's face was stricken.

"I never got it all back," Claire said. "I still paid for a Mercedes I never got to keep."

"I *lived* in that car!" Kate covered her face with her hands. "We were homeless for a long time. I never got any of my money back, either."

Wendy, now on her third coffee, shook her head. "He took all my savings before I even knew what had happened."

"He got to my parents," Autumn sighed. "Smooth-talked them into giving him money for his business. We gave up on ever seeing it again."

"Cayde going to prison will be the payback," Claire said. "Too bad it didn't happen sooner."

Kate's voice grew softer. "Did any of you think... it would be you? That he would kill?"

Autumn nodded, sharing a chilling story about a car chase that almost ended in tragedy. Claire recounted the time Cayde had attacked her in her home. Kate shared her own escape from a motel. Wendy, however, remained silent, absently picking at a scar on her wrist.

Claire's eyes lowered to the scar, and a pit formed in her stomach when she realized what it was. Cayde's initials, with another shallow scar through it. She exchanged a quick look with Kate and Autumn, who seemed to have noticed too.

"Did Cayde do that to you?" Claire asked cautiously.

Wendy looked down at her wrist as if just noticing she'd been picking at it. "Yeah," she answered.

"I'm so sorry," Kate said. Cayde had left his mark on all of them in different ways, but those initials were physical, and permanent. They must have been a constant reminder.

"I've heard of people doing coverup tattoos for scars," offered Claire, reaching for positivity. "You know, to turn ugly memories into something beautiful? Maybe you could do something like that?"

Wendy shook her head. "Maybe someday, but for now... it only makes me stronger. I refuse to let it mean what he meant it to—it doesn't mean he owns me." She looked up at each of them intently. "It means that everything I went through was real, and I got the best of him anyway. I survived, and so did my son, Archie."

"That's right—you had a kid with him too," said Autumn. "I'm glad he's safe. Cayde tried to come after my daughter, Madeline, but my family kept him away. I was always afraid. Still am."

Wendy, with a rare softness, nodded. "He'll never hurt you again."

Autumn gave a small, appreciative smile. "Did he ever—"

"No." Wendy's voice was firm. "He never came back. Never saw Archie again."

Claire looked puzzled. "Wait, *he* left? I thought you would have..." She trailed off, realizing the dangerous ground she was treading.

Wendy's face hardened. "I didn't choose to stay, if that's what you're implying."

"No," Claire quickly responded, lowering her eyes.

Autumn, her voice barely above a whisper, asked, "Did he rape any of you?"

Wendy nodded slowly, meeting Autumn's eyes.

Claire's frown deepened. "I didn't fight him, but I knew he'd get violent if I refused. Some might not call it rape."

"It's still rape," Wendy said firmly.

Kate blinked, feeling off balance. "I didn't really think of it like that. We were married—or at least I thought we were. I just did what was expected."

"Even in marriage," Wendy replied, her voice steady, "it's still rape."

Kate frowned, her mind spinning. It didn't change what had happened, but somehow, labeling it made it worse. What she had considered a wife's duty, whether she wanted it or not, now seemed darker, more sinister.

Her phone buzzed, pulling her out of her thoughts. "The cab's here."

They all stood, taking a deep breath, steeling themselves. It was time to face Cayde Miller one last time.

CHAPTER 92

AUTUMN

The California sky stretched wide and clear, but the crispness of January seemed to amplify the chill in Autumn's bones. She had pinned back her auburn hair, yet she wished it would fall around her face, shielding her from the penetrating gaze of the man waiting inside the courthouse. Claire, Kate, and Wendy had already stepped out of the car, their faces set toward the imposing building.

Autumn lingered, mumbling a quiet thanks to the driver. Her shoes felt unstable beneath her, and the hotel breakfast churned uneasily in her stomach. She took a hesitant step forward, but the distance between her and the other three women felt insurmountable, the courthouse rising menacingly above them.

Her breath hitched, and in that instant, she was no longer the woman who had fought to reclaim her life. She was the scared, broken nineteen-year-old who had been married to a monster, her spirit shattered by every small violation of what she'd expected marriage to be. The darkness that had consumed her then seemed to seep from the courthouse walls, threatening to pull her under again.

For six years, Autumn had labored to rebuild herself from the wreckage Cayde had left behind. Her life now brimmed with light and love, a stark contrast to the oppressive gloom currently surrounding her. She wanted to go back to that light now, to be as far away from this crushing darkness as possible. She took a faltering step back, her vision blurring with gray stars.

Wendy was the first to notice, her piercing gaze locking onto Autumn's trembling form. Claire followed, concern etched on her face as she stopped and alerted Kate. Autumn took another step back, her breathing shallow and ragged.

"What's wrong?" Claire's voice cut through the haze.

Autumn struggled to draw in a steady breath, her attempts coming out as strained, whimpering gasps. She shook her head, extending a trembling hand toward the others—not to ask for help, but to keep them at a distance. She wished fervently for everything to disappear.

"She's having a panic attack," Wendy said, her voice calm.

Kate and Claire rushed to Autumn's side, their voices soothing but distant, as if coming from another world. Her body shook violently, tears streaming unchecked down her face.

"I have to leave," she managed to say, her voice a raw whisper. "I'm not going in there."

"Autumn, you can't!" Kate said with firm desperation. "You've come all this way. We owe it to Sophie to see this through."

Wendy pushed past Kate and Claire, tapping on the passenger window and leaning in to speak with the driver. After exchanging a few words and handing him some money, she turned back to Autumn. "Get in. He'll take you back to the hotel."

Autumn looked at her, still gasping for air, her heart pounding; she thought it might burst.

"We'll handle things today," Wendy said softly. Her eyes were filled with an understanding that spoke louder than words. Autumn nodded, relief mingling with her anxiety as she climbed back into the car.

The vehicle pulled away, the driver glancing back at her in the rearview mirror. "You okay, miss?"

Autumn placed a hand over her thudding heart. As the courthouse receded in the distance, a small measure of relief washed over her. She wiped her cheeks, though the tears continued to fall. "Yes," she managed, her voice trembling. "I'm sorry."

She looked back where Wendy, Kate, and Claire remained, their figures growing smaller with each passing moment. Her heart ached with the weight of her retreat. "I'm sorry."

CHAPTER 93

CLAIRE

Agents Jack Myers and Blair McCoy entered the courthouse, their demeanor calm yet purposeful. Blair, with her petite frame and sharp blue eyes, greeted each of the girls with a warm hug, while Jack, ever reserved, offered a polite nod and firm handshakes. Claire, already familiar with them from previous phone conversations, felt like she was meeting an old boss. As the detectives assigned to the case, both Jack and Blair had been thorough, and Claire had willingly cooperated, knowing they would need her to recount the horrors she'd endured.

"Where's Autumn? Mrs. Armstrong?" Blair asked, her tone professional yet concerned. She was younger than Claire had anticipated, her brown hair neatly cut just below her collarbone. In her fitted black suit, Blair exuded an air of quiet confidence, though her bright eyes held a warmth that stood in contrast to the grimness of the day.

"She left," Claire said. "She looked like she was going to be sick."

Jack and Blair exchanged a glance, communicating more than words could. "That's understandable," Jack said. "We likely won't get to witness testimonies today, anyway. But

Autumn's research was instrumental in catching Cayde Miller. We wouldn't have moved so quickly without her work."

Kate, standing beside Claire, asked quietly, "What if she doesn't testify?"

Blair gave a small, resigned shrug. "We'll cross that bridge when we get to it. For now, we still have all of you. Let's take our seats."

They were led to a designated section in the courtroom. Claire's heart raced as she sat between Kate and Blair, her palms clammy with nerves. *Maybe Autumn was right to leave*, she thought. In a few minutes, she would see the man she'd fought so hard to escape. The thought of being in the same room as him again made her stomach churn.

Not too far from them a man sat, not much older than her. He had blond hair and blue eyes that stared straight ahead, fiery with determination.

"Who is that?" Claire whispered.

Kate shrugged. "No idea."

The doors to the left of the courtroom swung open, and Cayde Miller entered with his legal team in tow. Claire and Kate exchanged tense glances. His once-handsome features were now gaunt, his skin sallow and eyes dark. It was as though the cruelty and manipulation could no longer inflict on others had consumed him from the inside out. The charm and charisma that had once masked his true nature were gone, leaving him looking every bit the monster he was on the inside.

Kate shifted nervously in her seat. Claire studied him for a moment longer, her brows furrowing.

As if Cayde knew she was looking, as he sat down, he threw a glance over his shoulder. The air seemed suddenly ten degrees colder as he spotted them. A small, almost imperceptible grin tugged at the corner of his lips. Never taking his eyes off them, he raised his hand and tipped an imaginary hat, tilting his chin down. Then he turned away, settling back into his seat.

Claire felt a chill wrack her spine.

"Bastard," Wendy muttered under her breath, staring daggers at Cayde's back.

Across the room, the prosecution team sat, their faces steely. Claire felt a flicker of hope as she noticed the focus and resolve etched into their expressions. She had talked to one of them on the phone after agreeing to give her testimony. He explained that the defense would ask her harsh questions and to be prepared for their attacks. Then he ran through some practice scenarios with her, coaching on how to respond. At the time, it had calmed her nerves, but now she hoped the court wouldn't make it to testimonies today.

The bailiff's voice rang out, "All rise for the Honorable Judge Harold Grant."

The room stood as the judge, an older man with graying hair and a firm, no-nonsense demeanor, took his place at the bench. Though his appearance was weathered, his voice carried undeniable authority.

"You may be seated," Judge Grant announced. The rustle of movement followed as everyone settled back into their seats. "Good morning. We are here today for the pre-trial hearing in the matter of the State of California versus Cayde Miller, who is charged with the kidnapping and murder of his estranged wife, Sophie Miller. Counsel, please state your appearances for the record."

The lead prosecutor rose from his seat. His voice was steady, betraying no nerves, though a slight sheen of sweat glistened on his forehead. "Good morning, Your Honor. Brandon Keller for the State."

The defense attorney followed suit. "Leroy Sidney, representing Mr. Cayde Miller." His voice carried an arrogant edge, and the smug expression on his face was reminiscent of the one Cayde had once worn. Claire immediately disliked him.

The introductions concluded, and Judge Grant nodded. "Let's proceed. Defense counsel, I understand you've filed a motion?"

Sidney stepped forward, his voice measured and confident. "Yes, Your Honor. The defense moves to suppress the confession of my client, Cayde Miller, on the grounds that it was obtained through coercion."

A ripple of tension spread through the courtroom. Claire felt her chest tighten, her hand instinctively reaching for Kate's arm. Kate, in turn, grabbed Wendy's hand beside her.

"What does that mean?" Kate whispered, her voice barely audible.

Jack, seated a few rows behind them, leaned in. His face was grim. "It means there's a chance Cayde Miller won't be tried for murder."

CHAPTER 94

JACK

Anger pulsed through Jack's veins, his fists clenching tightly on his knees. He caught the exchange of skeptical glances from the women beside him. He knew what they were thinking: With all the evidence stacked against Cayde Miller, did his confession even matter?

How wrong they were.

That confession had led to crucial evidence—the car, the damning contents inside, and Sophie's body. Any evidence collected through coercion would be suppressed along with it. Jack stole a glance at Blair beside him. She took a deep breath, her face mirroring the turmoil inside him. Both of them were haunted by the missteps of the Washington Police. The frustration was easy to aim at them, but Jack knew better. As lead investigators, this was on them. It never should have come to this.

Judge Grant's expression remained impassive as the defense moved forward.

"Your Honor," Sidney began smoothly, "my client's confession was obtained through coercion, in direct violation of his Fifth Amendment rights, as well as his Fourteenth Amendment rights to due process."

Blair's eyes flicked to Jack. The strength he always relied on from her was nowhere to be found. She mouthed the word, "Shit."

A screen was wheeled in by a squeaking cart, and with it, Cayde's taped interrogation. Jack's frustration boiled over. Sidney's voice was calm but laced with precision, priming the court for what they were about to witness.

"Detective Jordan," Sidney continued, "initiated the interrogation prior to the FBI's arrival, despite lacking the proper jurisdiction or authority. Worse, his tactics were coercive, invoking religious pressure to compel a confession."

Sidney's hands moved with subtle authority, his confidence in the case evident. As the video played, Jack felt a tightening in his chest. The room was filled with the sounds of Detective Jordan's voice, and with every word, the case was unraveling before his eyes.

On the screen, Detective Jordan leaned across the interrogation table, his eyes fixed on Cayde, who sat slouched in his chair. "You said your wife was with God? Is she dead, Cayde?" Jordan asked, his voice pressing but not aggressive. "Did something happen to her?"

Cayde remained silent, staring down at his hands.

"If God is taking care of her, her family needs to know," the detective pushed.

Still no answer.

Shifting tactics, Jordan leaned in closer. "You're a religious man, right?"

"Yes," Cayde muttered.

"And you're a private investigator, aren't you?"

"Yes."

Jack shifted uncomfortably in his seat. Jordan was already playing with fire, bringing up religion. But it was the next exchange that sealed their fate.

"So you know about sin and justice, don't you?" Jordan continued. "As a God-fearing man, you understand what happens to those who don't confess. The Bible says, 'The truth will set you free.'" Cayde's eyes flicked up, briefly meeting the detective's. "God commands that we confess our sins. If something happened to your wife, the first step is admitting it. Let the truth free your soul."

Blair lowered her head into her hands. Jack couldn't blame her.

It was smart of Jordan to appeal to Cayde's ego—his private investigator license, his need to feel like a protector. But invoking divine judgment? That crossed a line. The detective's voice shifted to impatience.

"God already knows what you've done. The evidence is piling up, Cayde. I'm giving you a chance here, to clear your conscience, to do what's right in the eyes of God. This is a matter for your soul and what awaits you after all this."

On screen, Cayde Miller hesitated, a crack forming in his silence. Then, he spoke, his voice low and gravelly.

"I picked her up outside her brother's house. She hugged me, kissed me, and got into the car."

"She went with you willingly?" Jordan asked.

"Yes."

"When did you shoot her?" Jordan's question was sharp, skipping the question of whether Cayde had done it all together.

"We argued, and…"

Sidney paused the tape.

"Your Honor," he said, turning to Judge Grant, "as you've seen, my client was subjected to religious coercion by Detective Jordan. The detective's repeated references to divine judgment and eternal damnation were designed to break Mr. Miller's will. This confession was not freely given and was obtained in violation of both his Fifth and Fourteenth Amendment rights. Therefore, we respectfully request that this confession be suppressed."

He hated to admit it, but Sidney was right. Jack's stomach churned.

Cayde Miller might just be the luckiest man alive.

CHAPTER 95

WENDY

"You're kidding!" Autumn's face froze in shock. "They're going to dismiss it?"

Wendy, Claire, Kate, and Autumn sat around a table at a local seafood restaurant. They'd just finished filling Autumn in on most of what had happened. Blair and Jack had explained a lot of it, but even now, everything seemed too unpredictable for Wendy to handle. She hated that about Cayde. He always had some surprise lurking around the corner.

"Not yet," Wendy replied. "The prosecution didn't have much to argue when it came to the confession—that part was a mess. But they fought hard to keep the evidence from being dismissed. They mentioned something about 'inevitable discovery.' The judge decided to take the motion under advisement and continue the pre-trial hearings until he makes a decision."

Claire took a sip from her beer, leaving a thin ring of foam around the glass. "It was more than alarming. I didn't even know that was possible."

"What else happened?" Autumn ran a hand through her hair, swallowing hard. Wendy could almost feel the anxiety radiating off her.

"They reviewed all the evidence," Wendy said. "The defense argued how it was obtained and whether it should be suppressed. It was... a lot."

"Disturbing, really," Kate added with a shudder. "We all knew what he was capable of, but seeing the photo evidence of what happened to Sophie? Hearing the details? It was horrifying. I don't blame you for leaving, Autumn. I'll never forget today."

Wendy nodded to that. She wasn't squeamish, but the images of Sophie's body, the details of how Cayde had buried her—it didn't just disturb her, it made her furious. More than ever, she knew he was a monster. She thought back to the last time she saw him. He'd nearly died that day. He *should* have died. And Sophie would still be alive.

"But you're coming tomorrow, right?" Claire asked Autumn. "We're all giving our testimonies."

Autumn straightened, but her gaze dropped. "No. I've thought about it all day and decided not to."

"Even after everything we told you?" Claire's eyes widened. "There's a real chance the charges could be dropped. We *all* need to testify to make sure that doesn't happen!"

"Claire," Kate said gently, glancing at Autumn, "This is hard for all of us. But if we stick together, we might get through it."

"Let her stay," Wendy said, looking between Claire and Kate. "There's nothing she could say that we won't be able to. At first, this hearing was about whether Cayde could have committed murder. Now it feels like it's only about whether it's legal to charge him because of some detective's mistake. Everyone knows he did it. Our testimonies won't change that.

Why should Autumn go through the questioning if she doesn't have to?"

"It's not the questioning," Autumn murmured, stirring her spoon in the clam chowder she'd ordered. "It's seeing *him*."

"He barely looked at us," Claire said. But the one time he had before the trial—that subtle, arrogant gesture of acknowledgement—had turned her blood to ice.

"He looked terrible," Wendy added with disdain.

"Yeah." Claire nodded, glancing between Autumn and Wendy. "And older than I remember. I used to think he looked young for a man in his thirties, but now... How old did he tell you he was when you married him? How old were you?"

"I was nineteen. He said he was twenty-four. Even then, I thought the age gap was a little much, but..." Autumn gave a small, rueful smile. "I thought I was in love. Turned out he was three years older than that."

"He told me he was twenty-seven," Wendy added. "Seeing him after all this time wasn't as bad as I thought. It's the cross-examination I'm worried about."

"Did they prepare you?" Kate asked. "The lead prosecutor ran through questions with me. What they'd ask and what the defense would ask."

"They did." Wendy nodded. "And I know they're going to try to make us look stupid."

"Do you think we are?" Kate asked quietly.

"You're not stupid, Kate." Wendy gave her a firm look, then turned her gaze to Claire and Autumn. "None of us are. Sure, we can look back now and wish we'd made different choices. We can see the red flags for what they were because we're removed from it all. But at the time, when it happened, we were all under Cayde's control. He knew exactly what he was doing, and he'd done it before. The manipulation, the calculated moves…" Wendy's eyes flicked to Autumn. "The pregnancies. He knew how to trap us. And once he did, it was too late. All we could do was survive." She placed a hand over her arm. Over the scar she still picked at. Maybe it would never heal.

The three women stared at Wendy, their faces a mix of respect, agreement, and maybe even relief. What had felt unbearable at the start of this process now held a strange sense of peace. Their shared trauma bound them together, and bound them to Sophie.

Claire tilted her head, taking another sip of beer. "Damn," she muttered.

Autumn's thoughts seemed to echo Wendy's. "I'm sorry we never got to meet her."

"Sophie?" Kate said softly. "Me too. In some ways, I feel like I have."

"To Sophie," Claire said, raising her glass. Kate, Autumn, and Wendy followed suit, the delicate clink of their glasses ringing softly through the restaurant.

And to justice, Wendy thought. No matter how it came. One way or another, it would. Wendy was sure of that.

CHAPTER 96

KATE

Kate took the stand, swore her oath, and answered the preliminary questions, giving the court a brief introduction to her life. Her hands trembled slightly as she prepared for what was next—the hardest part. From across the room, she glanced at the other women. Claire gave her an encouraging nod, but Wendy, who had confided in them just the night before, was now as cold as stone. Her gaze fixed on Cayde.

Kate took a deep breath. She would not shy away from looking at him. She had survived this. She was strong. And today, she would face the man who had broken her. Cayde stared blankly at the floor, but she knew he could feel her eyes on him.

Brandon Keller stood and approached. His calm, methodical manner brought a sense of control to the chaos. He had prepared her for this, and the sound of his familiar voice helped steady her nerves. Then he slowly but tactfully led the discussion into the abuse. The first time he hit her, the threats he made, and how she felt. The questions started to move into more serious territory.

"Was the abuse a one-time occurrence, or did it happen repeatedly?" Keller asked.

"It was repeated," she said, her voice steady but her grip tightening on the wooden railing. "There were times when things were good, and he didn't hit me for weeks. But then... there were stretches where it happened every day. I got used to it. I stopped being surprised when he flew off the handle."

"Can you describe the nature of the abuse for the court?"

She hesitated for a brief moment, then answered. "Mostly, he punched me. My ribs were constantly sore. I'd get black eyes, especially in the beginning. Eventually, he started hitting me in the head—past the hairline, so no one could see the bruises."

Keller nodded again, allowing a moment of silence to settle over the courtroom before continuing. "Miss Moore, are there any lasting effects from the abuse?"

Kate's breath caught, but she forced herself to keep going. "Emotionally, it took me a long time to recover. I still feel grief. I lost so much—my home, my money, my credit... I'm still rebuilding my life." She paused, then added, "Because of him, I missed my daughter's wedding reception. I wasn't there when my granddaughter was born. He took all that from me."

There was another thing that Keller had prepped her not to mention. There were other lasting effects of his physical abuse. He'd hit her so many times in the head that Kate had recently been experiencing some memory loss. She'd look back on her time with him and knew things were missing. Chunks of time had just vanished from her brain. Maybe, in some twisted silver lining, it was for the best. It was time with Cayde she didn't have to carry with her. However, admitting memory loss might allow the defense to question all of her testimony. It was better left unsaid.

Keller finished it off with the most relevant question to this case: "Miss Moore, at any time during your relationship with Mr. Miller, were you afraid he would kill you?"

Kate's heart felt like it might beat out of her chest. This was it—the moment she'd been dreading, the memory she tried to bury. She lifted her chin, staring across the room at the man who had once held her life in his hands.

"Yes," she said, her voice clear and unwavering.

"Can you explain to the court why?"

Kate's hands trembled slightly on the stand, but her words were steady. "The day I left, he caught me as I was trying to leave the motel we were currently staying at. He beat me and strangled me... held me down. I looked into his eyes, and I knew—knew he would rather see me dead than let me walk out that door. He didn't want to lose control of me."

A heavy silence blanketed the courtroom. Keller's expression didn't change, but there was something in his eyes—a quiet respect for her courage.

"Thank you, Miss Moore," he said, his tone soft but firm. "No further questions, Your Honor."

"Defense," Judge Grant's voice rumbled. His eyes were as sharp as ever, as if weighing every word that had been spoken.

Kate's heart raced, hoping her testimony had some effect on the judge's future decision to suppress Cayde's confession. Telling her story had felt empowering, even healing, but now the defense would have their turn.

Sidney stood up. His confident stride to the lectern was accompanied by a smirk that rattled Kate. It wasn't enough to be overtly disrespectful, but there was a quiet mockery in it—a reminder that everything she had just laid bare was now fodder for him to tear apart. The air in the room felt heavier. Kate's eyes darted to Claire and Wendy, but their encouragement, once a source of strength, now felt distant.

Sidney's voice was smooth as he began, "Miss Moore, would it be true to state that you and Mr. Miller had a... contentious relationship?"

"Yes." The word dripped with attitude. Had she not clearly made that obvious?

Sidney barely reacted to her tone, continuing with the detached precision of a defense attorney performing his duty. "Do you hold any personal grievances against the defendant that might influence your testimony today?"

Kate straightened her chair. "Not that could affect my testimony, no."

Sidney tilted his head slightly. "But you do hold grievances against him?"

She hesitated, feeling the trap closing in. "Yes."

His tone shifted, becoming slightly more insistent. "Miss Moore, you claim to have endured significant abuse at the hands of Mr. Miller throughout your marriage. Yet, there are no police reports. Did you ever report the alleged abuse to law enforcement?"

Kate swallowed. "I filed a restraining order after I left him."

Sidney's smile was thin. "I'm asking specifically about police reports, Miss Moore. Did you ever contact the authorities during the period in which you claim this abuse took place?"

"No," Kate admitted, her voice steady despite the rush of fear and anger rising inside her. She didn't get a chance to explain her reasons. Sidney pounced.

"And aside from the restraining order, is there any documentation? Photos? Medical records? Evidence to support these claims?"

Her breath caught in her throat. "No."

Sidney took a step closer to the witness stand. "So, we have no police reports, no medical evidence, no photographic proof. Isn't it possible, Miss Moore, that you're exaggerating these claims out of anger or resentment over the end of your relationship with Mr. Miller?"

Kate's jaw clenched. "It is not possible, sir," she said, her voice steady but laced with an edge. "I would never lie about this."

Sidney's eyes remained on her, unblinking. "You say you suffered through this alleged abuse for years. Then why stay? Why would anyone remain in a situation like that? Especially when there is no evidence to back up these horrific claims?"

The courtroom felt as if it had gone still, every eye on Kate as the question hung in the air. Sidney's words cut deep, and she felt her breath falter. This was the question that had haunted her for years, the one even her closest friends and family had asked. Her response had never seemed to satisfy anyone. How could it?

Kate took a breath, her voice trembling slightly, but strong. "He threatened to kill my family," she said, her eyes narrowing on Sidney. "He said he'd burn my parents' house down, that he'd kill my daughter and my grandbaby. He told me he'd make me watch him kill everyone I loved, and then I'd be the last." Her hands gripped the stand tightly. "You can't understand that kind of fear unless you've lived it. He was convincing. Sometimes, when you looked into his eyes, you could swear you were looking at the devil himself."

She glanced briefly at Cayde, still staring at the ground, then back at Sidney, her voice gaining strength. "That's why I stayed. And I know people wonder why—why anyone would stay—but until you're in those shoes, you never know what you'll do. And by the time I realized I had to leave, I'd already lost everything—my money, my home, my credit. I was isolated from my family. I'd lost it all." Sidney's smirk twitched slightly, but he remained silent as she added, "At the time, Cayde was all I had left. For a long time, I stayed because I thought maybe, just maybe, I could get some of it back."

Kate's words were thick with raw emotion. It wasn't the answer Sidney had expected, and for a moment, even he seemed unsure of how to proceed. The courtroom was quiet, tension palpable.

Kate exhaled, her chest rising and falling as she let the words settle. Whether they helped or hurt the defense, she didn't know. But they were the truth, and that was all she had to offer.

Sidney flicked his eyebrows up and tightened his mouth into a grim line, clearly showing his scorn and blatant disbelief for her story. It was more than infuriating. "No further questions."

Cayde continued staring at his hands, unmoved by the words spoken against him. A part of Kate wanted to shout at him—wanted him to look her in the eye and see her standing up there, strong, while he sat shackled, no longer free. But he didn't. So she sat back down, feeling the weight of it all as Blair reached across Jack to give her hand a tight squeeze.

"Good job, Kate," Blair whispered.

Kate exhaled, her breath uneven, trying to steady herself. Telling her story had been draining, but it was also therapeutic in its own way. Perhaps, with time, it would get easier. For now, she had done her part, and it was someone else's turn to speak.

Claire was next. As she took the stand, Kate listened, her mind running through the details that had become all too familiar. Claire's story mirrored her own in many ways. Cayde had used the same patterns, the same insidious tactics of control. Like Kate, Claire had been manipulated, isolated, and threatened. She spoke of how Cayde had stalked her daughter, sending photos of her whereabouts and threatening unimaginable horrors if Claire didn't comply.

In the end, Claire had filed multiple charges against him—actions that led to his Glock being taken away. And for the first time, Kate realized something: because of Claire, Cayde had never been able to use the threat of a gun against her. Kate wondered, briefly, if she would have taken Sophie's place had that weapon been available to him. Claire, whether knowingly or not, may have saved Kate's life.

The defense tore into Claire's character the same way they had attacked Kate. Sidney questioned her decisions, her motives, and her credibility, but Claire held her ground. She spoke firmly, as if each answer only solidified her truth.

Then it was Wendy's turn. Kate watched the younger woman take the stand, her posture guarded, her expression unreadable. Wendy seemed different now—hardened, stronger. It was hard to imagine her as the woman Cayde had once manipulated and controlled, but Kate knew better. They had all been different once, and each of them had been changed by Cayde in their own way. Rebuilding oneself after being shattered by someone like him wasn't easy, and it wasn't for Kate to judge how Wendy had pieced herself back together.

Wendy spoke with precision, never offering more than necessary. Her testimony was concise but powerful, revealing the depths of Cayde's cruelty. She shared how he had used their child as leverage, threatening to harm their son if she didn't comply. Every move she made, every decision, had been for her son's safety.

But something shifted when Sidney began his cross-examination. Wendy's demeanor, so composed until now, changed subtly when Sidney approached the topic of reports of violence—violence toward Cayde. The defense attorney, clearly sensing an opening, pressed on.

"Miss Castilo, isn't it true that during your relationship with Mr. Miller, you had moments of violence toward him as well?" Sidney's voice was probing, almost casual, as if the question were a minor detail.

Wendy's eyes narrowed, and for the first time since taking the stand, her carefully maintained calm seemed to waver. "What are you suggesting?" she asked, her voice sharp.

Sidney smirked, just a hint, as if he had expected this reaction. "I'm merely pointing out that there were documented incidents where you were. . . less than restrained in your actions toward Mr. Miller."

Kate's heart sank. She could see it—Sidney was attempting to paint Wendy as an aggressor, to shift the narrative just enough to cast doubt on her testimony.

"Oh, God," Jack muttered to himself.

But Wendy didn't falter. "Anything I did," Wendy said, her voice firm, "was in defense of myself or my son. Cayde had a way of pushing people to their breaking point."

Sidney leaned in, his tone almost mocking. "So, you're saying you were violent, but only when you had to be? Convenient, isn't it, that there's no real documentation to prove that?"

Wendy's eyes blazed, but she didn't lash out. Instead, she leaned forward slightly, her voice low but fierce. "I did what I had to do to survive. You can call it whatever you like, but I will not apologize for protecting my child."

The courtroom was still. Even Sidney seemed momentarily taken aback by the fire in Wendy's words. He shifted his stance, glancing briefly at his notes before attempting to move on. But the damage was done—the subtle shift in Wendy's demeanor had altered the energy in the room, and Sidney's line of questioning had only strengthened her resolve.

Wendy leaned back in her seat, her eyes never leaving Sidney as he wrapped up his questions. Whatever he had been hoping to achieve, it hadn't worked.

Wendy took her seat beside Kate in the designated area, her gaze fixed ahead. She didn't meet anyone's eyes, though both Kate and Claire watched her closely.

The next witness called was Tanner Hale. The blond-haired man stood up, walking with a purposeful stride toward the stand. After swearing his oath, he waited for the questions to begin.

"Who is that?" Kate whispered to Jack.

"Sophie's brother," Jack murmured back. "She was staying with him when it all happened."

Kate's memory clicked. The media had covered Sophie's case—she'd escaped, just like the rest of them had. But Cayde had come back for her, more violent and unhinged than before. Sophie must have been his breaking point, the final straw in his desperate quest to control them.

Keller started his questions the same way he had with the other women, carefully and methodically building up the emotional tension. Each question seemed to peel back another layer of Tanner's pain.

"Did Mrs. Miller's relationship with her family and friends change after she began seeing Mr. Miller?" Keller asked, his voice steady.

Tanner nodded. "She became distant. We'd always been close, and she was close to our parents too. But after she got involved with him, she stopped coming around. Stopped calling. We didn't know what was going on."

"And did anyone in the family try to reach out to her?" Keller inquired.

"Multiple times," Tanner answered firmly. "But we didn't understand the full extent of what was happening. So when she rejected our offers for help or avoided our questions, we didn't know what else to do."

"At what point did you realize how serious Mrs. Miller's situation had become?"

Tanner's hand trembled slightly as he ran it through his hair, beads of sweat forming on his brow. "She called me out of the blue, said she was in Virginia and needed me to come get her. I drove out there, picked her up, and brought her to a rental property I own here, in California. On the drive back, she told me everything. The things he'd done to her..." His voice faltered for a moment, but he continued, "They were horrific."

"Mr. Hale, I could ask you to recount what your sister told you, but I understand the court may hear it from her directly," Keller said, pacing slightly. "Your sister wrote a letter almost a week before her death, which she sent to your parents' home in Tennessee. In it, she details her relationship with Mr. Miller and expresses her belief that he would kill her. Mr. Hale, would you be willing to read that letter to the court?"

"Objection, Your Honor. Hearsay," Sidney interjected swiftly.

Keller barely blinked. He had anticipated this. "Your Honor, I would argue that the letter qualifies as a dying declaration, which is an exception to the hearsay rule. The letter was written when Mrs. Miller believed her death was imminent and directly addressed the cause and circumstances of her death. We respectfully request that the letter be admitted into evidence."

Judge Grant barely paused before making his ruling. "Objection overruled. The letter may be read into evidence."

Keller nodded, and Tanner took a deep breath as he unfolded the letter, his voice strained as he began to read his sister's surviving words aloud.

"Dear Tanner,

> I'm writing to you from a jailhouse in Virginia. I know I was supposed to meet you, but Cayde found out my plan. He held me at gunpoint. I managed to get away... but just when I thought I was free, the police locked me up again. Ironic, right? And yet, I'm not angry. I actually feel safe.

Safer than I've felt in years. Safe enough that I need to tell you some things."

Tanner's voice wavered, the weight of his sister's words sinking into the room. His grip tightened on the paper, his knuckles white, but he kept going.

"I don't know if I'll get another chance to say this, so here it is. Please tell my boys I never meant to leave them. Tell them I love them, more than they'll ever know. Everything I did, I did for them. I can only hope they don't blame me. Even when I gave up, they were always in my thoughts. I trust their dad to look after them. But Tanner, please, don't abandon them. I don't think I have much time. Be there for my boys. I no longer can. I look back to the day I took the boys to the Christmas Fair in Nashville. It was the day I met Cayde—and yet I still see the looks on Charlie and Noah's faces. They were so happy. All I want is for them to be happy."

The paper in Tanner's hands shook violently now, his breath catching in his throat. Kate could feel the pain that radiated off him, heavy and suffocating. Her own heart pounded in her chest. She brought a trembling hand to her mouth, biting back a sob. An overwhelming amount of grief for this woman she'd never met surged over her.

"My husband is going to kill me. If you're reading this, I beg you—don't let him get me out. Don't let him take me. If he does, I won't survive. I know it. I pray it'll be quick. If

I'm lucky, he'll shoot me rather than stab or strangle me. No matter what, I'll fight back. I hope that will bring you some form of comfort. Know that I fought."

The last word fell from his lips like a stone sinking into the deepest part of the ocean. A stifled gasp escaped Kate's lips as her stomach twisted. This was as devastating as it was sickening. Kate could hardly listen anymore. She had no idea how Tanner was still going.

His voice broke completely now, barely able to form the words as he read the last lines of the letter.

"Please don't hate me. Everything I did was to protect my family. My boys. I didn't want Cayde to hurt you, or anyone else. It was my job to handle him. I did the best I could, Tanner. I need you to know that. Tell Mom and Dad I'm sorry. Tell them I love them. You too, Tanner.

I love you,

Soph."

Tanner dropped the letter, burying his face in his hands. He didn't even try to hold back the sobs that wracked his body. The court was frozen, the tragedy too raw, too visceral. Kate felt the tears stream down her cheeks, unbidden, unstoppable. It was impossible not to feel the gravity of Sophie's last plea—a woman trapped, cornered, and fully aware of her own impending death.

Keller approached, his voice low and gentle.

"Thank you, Mr. Hale. I have just one more question."

Tanner wiped his face roughly, his composure hanging by a thread, but there was a fire in his eyes.

"Can you describe for the court the impact your sister's death has had on her children and your family?"

Tanner swallowed hard, the rage rising beneath the pain. He lifted his gaze, his eyes locking onto Cayde Miller, the man sitting calmly at the defense table as if hearing nothing, seeing *nothing*.

"More than anything else, those kids, my nephews, have lost the most." Tanner's voice, raw with grief, cut through the room. "After Sophie died, their father killed himself. He blamed himself for what happened to Sophie. We all do." Tanner's voice shook with fury now, his eyes narrowing. "Those boys lost both their parents. And now... now, they live with me. I'm the one left to try and fix what that man—" Tanner pointed directly at Cayde, his voice hard, venomous. "—destroyed."

The courtroom remained deathly still. Keller glanced toward the court reporter.

"Let the record show that the witness has pointed at the defendant." He paused, a weighted silence settling over them, before he nodded to the judge.

"No further questions, Your Honor."

Tanner aggressively wiped his face with his hands and leaned forward, elbows on his knees. He would face whatever questions the cross-examiner threw at him. He probably wanted this whole thing to be over and done with.

Kate couldn't agree more.

CHAPTER 97

JACK

The courtroom buzzed with anticipation as the final arguments were made, the room stifling with the weight of the unresolved emotion. Jack sat rigid in his seat, his focus unbroken. Occasionally, Blair leaned in to whisper something to him, but her words barely registered. His mind was elsewhere—fixed on the judge. He studied the man's expression, searching for any sign of which way he might lean. Surely, after the evidence laid out over the past two days, the motion to suppress the confession would fail, and Cayde would be sent to trial.

But that confession. That damned confession.

Jack's fists clenched at the thought. He could've throttled the detective who took it. Or maybe he was mad at himself. It didn't matter. Something like this should never have happened on his watch. Jack had been assigned the case, and despite local detectives acting on their own, he couldn't shake the responsibility that weighed on him like an anchor.

Fucking hell. Everything was at risk. It could all crumble because of a technicality. The mere possibility set Jack on edge, an unfamiliar tightness in his chest. He'd handled dozens of homicide cases, but this one was different. It wasn't just a job this time. As he glanced at Blair and remembered her voice, chastising him during the investigation, he realized this case had gotten under his skin in a way none of the others had.

"Your Honor," Keller's voice rang out, crisp and commanding, as he stepped forward for his closing argument. "The defense argues that Cayde Miller's confession was coerced, and as a result, the evidence obtained from it should be suppressed. But we must consider the doctrine of inevitable discovery." Keller paced slowly, his words deliberate, as every eye in the room followed him. "The investigation into Sophie Miller's disappearance was well underway before the confession. The police were already closing in. Cayde's car, the murder weapon, Sophie's body—these would've been found through lawful means. Suppressing this evidence doesn't serve justice, Your Honor. It only lets a guilty man go."

Jack could feel the tension in the room mount as Keller spoke. The prosecutor wasn't just appealing to legal theory—he was calling on the judge's sense of morality. He knew that technicality could be detrimental, but when it came down to it, Keller knew that wasn't what it was about. It was about Sophie.

"We urge the court to allow the evidence to be admitted."

Beside him, Blair held her breath, frozen. Jack subtly nudged her with his elbow, and she let it out in a rush. He didn't blame her. The uncertainty gnawed at him too. In the back of his mind, a dark truth lurked—he didn't know if he would've found Sophie without Cayde's confession. He liked to believe he would have. But in the end, it was too late for that, and no one had called him to the stand. Both the defense and the prosecution had left his testimony untouched, knowing his words could tip the scales in either direction. It was a gamble neither side wanted to take.

Keller returned to his seat, the tension now a living, breathing thing in the courtroom. Jack watched as Kate and Claire whispered urgently to each other. He didn't need to hear them to know what they were saying. They were reassuring themselves—reassuring each other—that Cayde would be sent to trial. The evidence was overwhelming. Surely, the judge had no choice. Jack wanted to believe them, but he knew better. The confession was a landmine. One misstep, and it could blow the entire case apart.

Sidney rose from his chair, adjusting his tie with a smugness that turned Jack's stomach. For a man defending a killer, Sidney seemed too cocky, too sure of himself. His face was an irritating mask of confidence as he addressed the judge.

"Your Honor, the prosecution is desperately clinging to the doctrine of inevitable discovery, but let's not forget the core issue at hand—Cayde Miller's confession was coerced." Sidney's voice oozed self-assurance, his every word crafted to cut the prosecution's argument to pieces.

Jack's blood boiled as he spoke.

"The evidence in question was found because of that confession—obtained through unconstitutional means. The police violated Cayde's rights, and allowing this evidence to stand would only compound that violation." Sidney paused, locking eyes with the judge, his next words calculated. Like twisting in the wound. "Without this tainted evidence, the prosecution's case falls apart.

"We respectfully request—" Sidney's voice dropped to a quiet intensity, almost as if he were speaking directly to the judge's conscience. "—that the court uphold the suppression of this evidence and dismiss the charges. Justice, Your Honor, cannot be served by allowing evidence obtained through such egregious violations."

Silence blanketed the room. The judge's eyes narrowed slightly, a subtle shift in his expression. Jack could feel his pulse pounding in his ears as the judge leaned back in his chair, deliberating. The whole case—the murder, the investigation, Sophie's voice calling for justice—all of it hung on what the judge would say next.

For the first time in a long time, Jack didn't know if the right thing was going to happen. The fate of the case—and Sophie's justice—was in the hands of one man.

A suffocating silence gripped the courtroom. Judge Grant sat grim and serious, his face lined with the weight of the decision before him. He looked down at his notes, then removed his small-framed glasses, the movement slow and deliberate. His eyes swept across the room—first over Cayde and his defense team, then the prosecution, and finally, they settled on Sophie's brother. They lingered there, heavy with unspoken understanding, before passing to the three women sitting beside Jack.

Jack's heart hammered in his chest as the moments stretched on. For a second, he thought Judge Grant might adjourn without a decision, leaving them all in suspense for another agonizing day. But then the judge shook his head, the weariness in his expression deepening. When he spoke, disappointment ran deep in his voice.

"This case, which should have been straightforward, has been complicated by procedural issues." The judge's voice was low, like a father chastising a reckless child. "It is unfortunate that such matters have impeded the pursuit of justice. However, my ruling must adhere strictly to the law and the rights of the defendant."

He glanced at the three women again, and for a moment, Jack saw something in the judge's eyes—genuine sympathy, a recognition of the unbearable pain this decision would cause. Jack's stomach tightened, sensing the inevitable.

"After careful consideration of the arguments presented, I find that the confession was obtained in violation of the defendant's constitutional rights."

The words might as well have been a gunshot.

"Therefore, the motion to suppress the confession is granted, and the charges based on that confession are hereby dismissed."

A horrified, visceral shriek cut through the stillness. Kate. Her hands flew to her mouth, eyes wide and terror-stricken as she muffled her own cry. The room spun into chaos. Tanner Hale, fists clenched and jaw tight, shot up from his seat and stormed out of the courtroom. Jack watched him go, feeling the hot pulse of anger radiating through his own veins. And then—Cayde.

Cayde, who had sat there in silence for so long, his face unreadable, suddenly let out a low, guttural laugh. It was slow at first, bubbling up from his chest, but it grew louder, more deranged until it filled the room like a grotesque melody. He tipped his head back and let it roar, the sound of a man who had escaped death's grip. Jack furrowed his brow and stretched his mouth into a tight line as he watched Tanner walk through the doors, respecting him more than ever for not turning around, for not lunging at the monster who had taken his sister.

Judge Grant's voice cut through the madness, louder, firm. "Order in this court!"

The room stilled again, the judge's gaze hardening as he stared down Cayde and his defense. "However, this does not preclude the prosecution from refiling charges based on other evidence."

The look he gave the prosecution was sharp, a silent directive: *Find something else. Bring him back.* He couldn't say it, but the message was clear in his eyes.

"Mr. Miller," he continued, voice now like steel, "while the charges against you are currently dismissed, the court is aware of the seriousness of the allegations. Therefore, as a condition of your release, you are ordered to remain within the state of California. You are also required to surrender your passport, should you have one, to the court, ensuring you do not leave the country. Any failure to comply will result in immediate re-arrest and further legal consequences. Court is adjourned."

The gavel came down with a sharp crack. It didn't break the tension. Cayde was on his feet, shaking hands with his defense team, grinning as if they were old friends celebrating a job well done. Then, like a predator stalking its prey, he turned his eyes on Kate, Claire, and Wendy. The grin he flashed them was vicious—pure triumph. His eyes said everything his lips didn't. *I won. I always win.*

Before Jack could react, Blair stepped in between the women and Cayde's gaze, her back stiff with fury. "Come on," she hissed, throwing a venomous glare over her shoulder at him. "You don't need to see this."

She gently guided Kate, Claire, and Wendy toward the exit, but Kate, her voice shaking with panic, couldn't hold back. "He's free!" she whispered, trying to stay quiet, though her terror was unmistakable. "What if he comes after us?"

Jack stepped up, placing a firm but comforting hand on her back, gently leading her forward. "That's not going to happen," he assured her, his voice calm and steady, though his mind was racing.

He kept his hand on her back, guiding the group out as Blair led the way. But just before he reached the door, Jack stopped. He turned, his eyes locking onto Cayde from across the room. Cayde was still grinning, energy and arrogance practically radiating off him, as though the courtroom victory had breathed new life into him. Jack's jaw clenched, his hands balled into fists at his sides.

They didn't speak a word. But at that moment, everything was said.

Laugh while you can. Jack's eyes bore into him, full of quiet promise. *This isn't over.*

Cayde's grin faltered for a moment, but he didn't drop his gaze.

And there, standing in the doorway, Jack made a silent oath to himself. He'd make sure Cayde Miller saw justice. For Kate. For Claire. For Autumn. For Wendy. For Sophie and her family. And finally, for himself.

This isn't over.

CHAPTER 98

JACK

Blair broke the news to Autumn, and it wasn't a pretty sight. Wendy had disappeared without a word, and Claire, pale-faced and shaken, called her husband to change her flight. She didn't care that it would be a redeye—she just wanted to leave the state as soon as possible. Kate quietly booked a seat on the same flight. Autumn tried to follow suit, but her airline wouldn't allow it, forcing her to stay one more night.

Now that the trial was over, the state would only cover her hotel for one last evening. She asked Blair if she could move to the same place where she and Jack were staying.

In the end, Blair ordered pizza, and the remaining women gathered in the hotel dining area. Wendy eventually showed up, though she didn't offer any explanation as to where she had been or what she planned to do next. Jack had a feeling she'd already packed her bags, ready to vanish without a trace. She had been guarded, distant these past few days, but now, as she sat down with the others, something in her gaze softened.

"I think it's good they've bonded," Blair said, her eyes lingering on the women seated at the table beside them. "They'll look out for each other back in Tennessee."

"They won't need to," Jack replied, more bitterly than he intended. "He won't be going back there."

"How fast do you think the prosecutors will refile?"

"If we're lucky? A day or two. He'll be arrested again. Interstate stalking, kidnapping—they won't let him slip through their fingers twice."

"That's what I thought, too," Blair said, a sharp edge creeping into her voice. "Things will be set right. Everyone will get what they deserve."

There was an undercurrent of anger, maybe even hatred, in her tone. This case had gotten to her as much as it had to him. Jack glanced over at the women, who were smiling, laughing—already experts at pushing Cayde Miller out of their minds. He wondered how long it would take him to do the same.

Blair had changed, too. He could see it in her eyes.

Jack had thought nothing could break his heart. But seeing the spark fade from Blair's eyes came damn close.

"We'll see this through," Jack said, nodding toward the women. "They'll be okay. And Cayde... He'll get what's coming to him." He hesitated, then added quietly, "We did our best, Blair. What happened with the confession—it was unfortunate. But we learn and we grow, right?"

Blair turned to him, her eyes narrowing slightly as if sizing him up. "Okay, who are you, and what did you do with Myers?"

Jack frowned, leaning back in his chair.

"I'm kidding!" Blair nudged him lightly. "Don't pout."

"I'm not," he muttered, low enough that the women couldn't hear. Blair laughed, the lines around her eyes crinkling, and for a moment, that was enough for Jack.

A gasp echoed from the table beside them, and Autumn shot to her feet, her eyes wide as she looked toward the entrance of the dining area. Jack tensed, his first instinct readying him for the worst—half expecting to see Cayde. But instead, a man with dark blond hair strode in, breathing hard, his eyes scanning the room until they locked onto Autumn. He didn't hesitate. His long strides carried him toward her, arms outstretched as she ran to meet him.

"Justin!" Autumn cried, throwing herself into his embrace.

Justin's massive frame enveloped her, holding her tight like she was the most precious thing he had. "The moment you told me he was released, I got on a plane," he said, his voice low and rough. "I almost missed it."

"Why?" Autumn pulled back slightly, her brow furrowed. "What about the kids?"

"Your mom's got them," he said, gently brushing strands of red hair from her face. "But I didn't want you to be alone."

Autumn laughed through her tears, her voice a mix of relief and disbelief. "Did you even bring any luggage?"

Justin chuckled, shaking his head. "Just me."

He kept his arm around her as she led him to the table, introducing him to Kate, Claire, and Wendy. "This is my husband, Justin Armstrong. And this," she added, turning toward Blair and Jack, "is Blair McCoy and Jack Myers. They're the investigators who helped us through everything."

"Thank you," Justin said, his gratitude palpable as he shook their hands. "For everything."

"We should be thanking you," Blair replied with a soft smile. "The information you gave us in those first few days—it made a real difference."

Autumn's expression darkened slightly. "Do you think I should have testified? Would that have changed anything?"

"No," Jack said, his tone firm, cutting through the uncertainty. "Don't beat yourself up over that. You did everything you could." He looked around the table, letting his gaze fall on each of them. "None of you could've stopped what happened today." It was important to him that they knew that. It was important for him and Blair to know, too.

Blair nodded. "And don't dwell on anything the defense threw at you during cross-examination."

"They *were* brutal," Claire murmured, shaking her head. She glanced at her watch, then turned to Kate. "It's time. Our ride to the airport's here."

Autumn hugged them both, and to Jack's surprise, Wendy did the same. Jack and Blair walked them to the doors, feeling the strange pull of farewell after everything they'd been through together.

"Thank you for what you did," Blair said sincerely. "And for sharing your stories. No matter how today turned out, I hope you know how strong you are." She hugged them—a gesture Jack usually would've considered inappropriate for an FBI agent, but this time, he let it go. It felt right. When his turn came, he opted for a firm handshake, having said everything he needed to already.

After they left, Jack and Blair returned to the lobby, where Autumn and Justin were waiting.

"We're heading to the room," Autumn said. "Our flight leaves early in the morning. I don't think we'll see you again before we go."

"Take care," Blair said, her tone softer now.

Justin smiled down at Autumn, his expression full of quiet devotion. "We will. Thank you, both of you."

"There's one more thing I've been meaning to tell you." Autumn's voice dropped, her face serious. "I'd forgotten about it until I heard that one of Cayde's brothers died. I spoke to him on the phone once, and he told me something that I think I pushed out of my mind for a long time. He insinuated that Cayde had killed one of his wives before. He warned me to stay away. I don't know if that means anything to you, but it's yours now. If it's a lead that can help you put him back behind bars, take it. The sooner the better."

Another potential murder? Jack and Blair exchanged a glance, one of those silent conversations that only partners could have.

"We'll look into it," Blair said, her voice warm but firm. "But I don't want you to worry about it anymore. Leave Cayde to us. I promise you, things will be set right. You don't need to dwell on him any longer."

Autumn's face crumpled, her eyes welling up with unshed tears. She didn't say anything—just nodded, a large, grateful gesture that spoke more than words ever could. Hand in hand, she and Justin walked to the elevator, disappearing to their floor.

All that remained was to say goodbye to Wendy. But when Jack and Blair entered the dining area, she was already gone. On the table where she had been sitting, they found a napkin with a short message scrawled across it:

Thank you.
– W

Blair glanced around. Her brow furrowed. "Did you see her leave?"

"No," Jack replied, frowning as he watched Blair take a step toward the door, her intent clear. She was going to look for her. But Jack gently grabbed her arm. "Let her go," he said softly. "She's moving on, too. In her own way."

Blair paused, her gaze lingering on the door for a moment before she turned back to him. "And what about us? What do we do about all this?"

Jack met her eyes, understanding the depth of her question. "We still have loose ends to tie up," he said. "Veronica's hearing, for one. And once she and Cayde are behind bars, we'll keep going. Just like we always have." It was up to them to make sure those women weren't hurt by Cayde any longer. "If we have to, we can check out the tip Autumn just gave us."

Blair nodded. "You did good, Myers. For all of this. I can't imagine this case was easy for you."

Jack took a deep breath. "It reminded me why I do the work I do." He looked at her. "Why *we* do the work we do."

"I don't want to see the system fail anyone else again," Blair said. "I think I understand you a little better, Myers. I'm grateful you shared your story with me."

"Not grateful enough to call me Jack?"

"No," she said. An exaggerated frown pulled at her features. "I still hate that name."

Jack laughed. In the solemn moment, he felt lucky to have someone like Blair at his side. And with whatever he had to face in the coming days, Jack wouldn't want to do it with anybody else.

CHAPTER 99

CAYDE

Murderer.

He knew that's what people called him. Cayde didn't care. Let them say whatever they wanted. It didn't change the fact that he was walking out a free man.

The sky was dark. It had been a long day. His defense team prepared him for another arrest, but Cayde didn't intend on sticking around for it. Stay in the state? No fuckin' way. He figured he had about three days, at most, for new charges to be filed. By then, he'd be long gone.

Cayde drove up along the coast. He loved Northern California. The dark skies and seas intensified his mood. Fuck. He felt better than he had in years. Part of him still couldn't believe he'd actually been released. He thought of their stunned faces with a burst of satisfaction—Kate, Claire, Wendy. They should have known better than to think he'd go down without a fight. He grinned. Then he laughed.

He pulled his shitty rental car into a shitty Airbnb. The whole street could've used a remodel. The homes were run-down, the yards a mess. Was it even legal to list such a place on Airbnb? The streetlamp next to the home flickered, bugs dancing in the light. A motel would have been cheaper, but he didn't want any security cameras watching him. Better that he made his plans without eyes hovering over his comings and goings.

Cayde glanced into the rearview mirror. The headlights behind him had been there for a while. Was he being followed? Paranoid, he stepped on the gas. The car behind him passed quickly, clearly not giving a rat's ass about him. He needed to relax.

It was a small one-bedroom home. In Nashville, it might've been considered overpriced, but for a place near the coast, it wasn't too bad. He punched in the key code given to him and entered. It certainly wasn't a millionaire's home, but it would do. He just needed a bed for the night and some room to plan.

He had no clothes, no bags, no belongings. He'd bought an oversized shirt and some sweats from Walmart, a pack of beer, and a bag of chips. He stripped off his suit from court and took a shower, scrubbing off the scent of jail. He changed into his new clothes and popped open a can of beer, guzzling it. Before the night's end, he intended to be drunk. It didn't take long to get there. He was thirsty, and his thoughts were dark. Nothing swallowed up alcohol faster than that.

Cayde sat and watched the television without really watching it. He felt strange. Wrong. Unease crept over his skin, and he found himself glancing out of the windows from his seat. The street was quiet. The other homes and their inhabitants had long gone to sleep.

Someone stood in the street, under the flickering lamp. They faced him directly, but the dim light didn't give any clues as to who they were. They wore a black, hooded sweatshirt and remained perfectly still. Cayde set his can of beer down and stood up, squinting. He moved forward but staggered over the bag of chips he'd been eating, his foot completely crushing everything inside.

"Shit!" he shouted, then whipped his head back up toward the streetlamp, but the person in the hoodie was gone.

A detective? An undercover FBI agent? No, they wouldn't be so bold as to break in, would they? He thought of Sophie's brother. Cayde double-checked the door, making sure it was locked. He didn't need a confrontation with Tanner. In fact, he'd gone out of his way to make sure no one would find him—not even that fuck-face of an FBI agent, Jack.

He stripped the bed of the top blanket and went to sleep, doing his best to push down the paranoia. He hated feeling so unsettled. Even in jail, he hadn't felt so exposed. All night, he dreamed of someone pounding on the door, a myriad of voices calling out to him, demanding that he pay for what he'd done. Autumn, Kate, Wendy, Claire—Sophie. Her voice shouted the loudest; haunted the deepest.

* * *

Cayde awoke with a jolt. A scuffling or scratching noise had pulled him from the nightmares. Or had the noise come from the dreams? He laid his head back down and rubbed a hand over his face, glancing at the light that peeked through the closed blinds. Orange and yellow. Evening.

He'd slept through the whole day.

A shadow passed by, and he froze. That, he didn't imagine. Sitting up, he wished he still had the gun Wendy had given him. Or the one Veronica used to carry.

He crept to the window and looked out. No children. No birds. Nothing but stillness outside. And yet, he couldn't shake the uneasy feeling that he was being watched. Cayde opened the door, stepped outside, squared his shoulders, and looked around. The mailbox to the house was open. It hadn't been the night before. A wrapped item had been shoved inside.

He pulled it out, inspecting the brown packaging. It buzzed, making him jump. He glanced around, saw no one, and took the mysterious package inside.

It buzzed again. Ripping off the tape and thick packaging paper, he found a pager. He inspected it curiously. The buzzing was from a message alert:

> *Cayde, we need to talk. Police are monitoring texts and emails. Head to this address as soon as you get this. It's critical. Leave your phone behind. They are tracking it.*
> *– V*

Cayde furrowed his brows. "The fuck is this?"

V? *Veronica?* Written across the packaging paper were coordinates. Cayde recognized the general area it would take him. Almost four hours away, it was past the state border. Sweat itched at the back of his neck. Veronica was in jail, wasn't she? Unless she'd been released. She was the one who'd given him the burner phone. This was her style. A one-way pager was completely undetectable. But how the hell had she gotten out of jail? Maybe the detective that had screwed up his confession did the same with her. He hadn't exactly kept up with the details of her charges.

Cayde dropped the pager on the table and grabbed his keys. He'd be driving to get food—not to the state lines. Veronica could go to hell. It was her fault he'd been arrested in the first place. Her fault he'd even pulled that trigger. Sophie was dead because of her—she never should have bought him that gun.

He left the pager behind, unease sinking into his stomach as he walked away from the house. Placing a hand on the car door, he paused. Not completely sure why, he went back inside, grabbed the pager, and then left.

As he cruised through a fast-food drive-through, the pager buzzed again.

You're not safe. Go to the address.
– V

A one-way pager made it impossible for him to respond. And Cayde didn't dare call Veronica on his cellphone—not while the police were watching both of them like hawks. He got his food, annoyed with the wait time, and hurried back home, eating most of it in the car. The sun had set, and twilight faded into night. He pulled up in front of the little house and got out, noticing that the mailbox was open again. Cayde snapped it shut with his free hand and carried the food and pager inside. He waited for the buzz, but it didn't come.

So, he ate in silence, still uneasy, and sat in the dark. He didn't want to turn on the lights and give anyone the opportunity to see inside.

There was a noise outside, like the crunching of dirt and stones beneath someone's feet. Cayde stopped chewing to listen more carefully, and sure enough, it happened again. It came from the side of the house. Someone was moving along the edges. He slowly stood up and walked to the front door, bursting through it with the idea of surprising whoever it was. He rounded the corner—

—but no one was there.

Cayde sighed and gritted his teeth. *The fuck is goin' on?* Could he be imagining things? A crash sounded from inside the house. He ran back in to find the window blinds mangled and broken glass scattered across the floor. A rock was among the shards. Red letters were painted across it: "MURDERER."

Again, Cayde checked outside to see if he could catch a glimpse of who threw it. Nothing and no one. He cursed and returned indoors, locking the bolt behind him and glancing again at the rock. His eyes slid to the pager.

> *You're not safe. Go to the address.*
> *– V*

Fuck. Maybe Veronica was right. If it even *was* Veronica. The neighbors clearly knew who was renting the place. Or maybe it was just kids playing a prank. Either way, the broken window wasn't something he wanted to pay for.

So Cayde ripped the address from the packaging paper, packed the remaining beer, grabbed the pager, and started the long drive. Whatever Veronica needed to speak to him about, it had better be good. He left his phone behind. He didn't want it to track him over the state lines. Entering the address into the car's GPS was one thing. But Veronica was probably right about the feds monitoring his phone.

The pager buzzed about thirty minutes into the trip. Cayde glanced down, his eyes flicking between the message and the road.

I will meet you there.
– V

About an hour out from the location, Cayde stopped to get gas. It was already past midnight. He didn't want his card information showing where he'd gone, just in case Veronica was up to something, so he went inside and paid cash. He was grateful to find a station open 24/7.

The cashier was a young man with bags under his eyes. He took the money from Cayde for the pump, then scanned a couple bags of food and two energy drinks.

"You and your friend travel late often? I hardly get anyone in the store past eleven these days."

"It's just me," Cayde grumbled.

"Oh." The cashier frowned. "I thought I saw someone else by your car. My bad."

"What?" Cayde had assumed the cashier thought the second energy drink was for another person. He turned his head, but with the harsh lighting glaring off the dirty windows, all he could see was darkness outside.

"My mind plays tricks on me all the time," the young cashier said. "It's what you expect from a night shift."

Cayde didn't answer the man. He refused the receipt, grabbed his bag, and exited the store. There were no other cars nearby, no other people, but the hair rising on his arms and the sweat beading on his forehead told him otherwise.

Was someone following him? Maybe a private investigator, hired by Sophie's family. He looked around the parking lot a second time. A third.

"Hey!" he shouted, "I see you!"

Of course, no one revealed themselves. Shit. He was losing it.

Wherever Veronica was leading him, it had better be secure. He imagined all the things he'd say to her once he got to where he was going. None of them were kind. He was only in this situation because of her. He also imagined all the things he'd like to do to her. He'd been in jail for months, after all—a record for his celibacy. He hoped he wasn't risking everything for a lousy fuck.

Cayde checked the back of his car, just to be safe, filled the tank, and looked around, tapping his fingers against his leg until the pump clicked and the gasoline stopped. As fast as he could, Cayde got in his car and left the gas station.

The pager buzzed again.

Are you almost there?
— V

It was annoying that she'd ask a question when he knew she couldn't see his answer. The last hour, Cayde looked in his rearview mirror a lot, but other than the occasional car that eventually turned off somewhere else, he saw no one.

The turn off the main road was a long, winding gravel trail that took him deep into the trees. Veronica was leading him into the woods, closer to the coast's edge.

"You have arrived," the car's GPS chimed.

Almost three miles into the woods, passing forks and branches, Cayde finally stopped the car. "Where the fuck is this?" There was nothing. The coordinates had led to a bunch of trees. A few paces out was a cliff overlooking the sea. To Cayde, it was nothing but a black void.

The pager buzzed.

When you get there, I'll be by the cliff.
– V

Cayde hesitantly got out of the car, the door dinging as he left it open. Something told him to leave it running, ready for a quick escape.

"Veronica!" he called, approaching the cliff's edge. In the moonlight, he could barely see the ocean crashing into the rocks far, far below. But he could hear it.

There was no sign of another car.

"Veronica!" he called again. This time, his voice was angry and sharp.

Another buzz.

I will be there soon.
– V

There was something uncanny about the timing of the pages—almost as if she'd had eyes on him this whole time. Yet, she'd dragged him all the way out here and wasn't even waiting like she said. Why had she chosen such a random place to meet? After all this, she'd better have a good fuckin' plan to get him out of this mess. If not, she'd regret it.

With his car headlights pointing in his direction, it was hard for Cayde's eyes to adjust fully to the dark. But he didn't want to shut the car off. Maybe he ought to just wait inside of it.

The pager buzzed, startling him.

I'm almost there.
– V

He froze as the loud snap of a twig echoed in the forest beyond, followed by another. He turned his back to the sea, trying to peer through the car's headlights. Someone was close, and they were sneaking.

"Veronica!" Now his voice was a shout, but he realized the ferocity came from fear. The dryness in his mouth and racing heartbeat forced him to accept it.

The pager buzzed again.

I'm not Veronica.

The car roared. Cayde looked into its headlights, too bright to see anything around it. They grew bigger—it was coming right at him. He screamed and dove out of the way, dropping the pager. The car blitzed past him, nearly slamming into his legs. It barreled forward, right off the cliff. He heard the engine and saw the flash of lights as it fell down, down. An insanely loud crash followed.

Cayde scrambled to the cliff's edge, looking as the waves pushed the rental back and forth. Then, under the black waters, it disappeared.

"Holy fucking shit!" Cayde screamed. His head whipped backward. A figure wearing all black stood where his rental car had been. It was the same person he'd seen the night before, staring at him under the streetlight. Yet, he still couldn't glimpse their face. He never should've left the car door open—never should've left the lights on. He hadn't seen them approach. They must have laid a brick or large rock right on top of the gas pedal.

"Who are you?" he yelled, stepping back. He almost fell off the edge, following the rental to its doom.

There was no response, no motion from the figure—save for the rise of an arm, which held a pistol in a gloved hand.

He didn't have time to dive to the side or duck away.

The pistol went off three times, and Cayde fell back from the force of the bullets. His back slammed into the dirt and rocks below him. Choking and sputtering, Cayde heard the crunch of steps as his shooter walked closer. They loomed over him like death. He still couldn't see their face.

The figure bent down, picked up the pager, examined it, then calmly slipped it into their pocket. They turned back to him.

"What—?" He could barely speak. The life was draining out of him. He got to his hands and knees, trembling. Blood dripped below him, black in the night. "You—can't—do—this!"

The figure paused. "*I can.*"

He knew that voice! But realization hit him too late. The figure lifted a booted foot and kicked him—*hard*.

Cayde Miller's world tilted and spun, like he was floating. Only he wasn't. He was falling. Pushed right over the cliff, he caught a final glimpse of his murderer looking down as he disappeared into the waves.

No, he never saw a face.

But he knew she was smiling.

CHAPTER 100

WENDY

Box after box littered Wendy's apartment. She'd packed most of it up, and now was dealing with the leftovers, all set to go to the dump.

Archie was doing a marvelous job unpacking Wendy's work, finding it hard to be entertained with his toys and games placed away. He enjoyed it when Wendy gave him important tasks that "only he could do," but after a while, he simply no longer wanted to work.

"I don't want to go," he huffed.

"You'll have a yard you can play in at the new house. And the neighborhood will have a lot of kids your age. More friends!"

He considered this, then shrugged, unimpressed. "So?"

"*So*, you'll be a lot happier there. So will I." Wendy looked around at the apartment. This was where Archie had grown up all his life, but after all these years, she still remembered it as the place Cayde had taken over. Even when he left for good, even when he'd gone missing, he still haunted these rooms, as if he'd stained the carpet and walls with his darkness.

"Is this pile all of my things?" Archie drummed his hand on a box.

"Yup," Wendy smiled at him. She rolled packing tape along a box, then wrote across it: "Landfill." They were what remained of Cayde's things.

"I get to keep my toys?"

"And your clothes, and your bed, and everything else! You just get a bigger room."

"Bigger?" He sounded excited. "How much bigger?"

"Stretch your arms out wide. Wider. As far as you can!"

Archie wrinkled his nose and showed his teeth at the effort. In a surprise attack, she shot her hands forward and tickled him underneath the armpits. He shrieked with laughter.

"It'll be much bigger than that!" Wendy said with a smile. "A fresh start."

There was a knock on the apartment door. Wendy looked through the peephole, raised her eyebrows, and opened the door. "Agent Myers? Agent McCoy?"

"Hello, Wendy." Blair smiled at her. The two detectives were in casual attire, no longer in the pressed suits Wendy had grown used to seeing on them during the trial.

"Come on in." Wendy stepped aside. "This is my son, Archie."

"Hello, Archie." Blair waved at him.

Archie suddenly became very interested in the corner of the box, picking at it with his nails while offering up a shy, "Hi."

"You're moving?" Jack looked around at the apartment.

"Yeah," Wendy breathed out, putting her hands on her hips. "It's for the best. After everything that happened, I want Archie and I to start a life without looking over our shoulders every day."

"That's actually what we wanted to talk to you about," Blair said, her brows creasing. "Are you aware that Cayde is missing?"

"We all are." Wendy's face became grave. "Hence–" She gestured to the boxes.

"So you haven't heard from him at all?" Jack asked.

Wendy shook her head. "No. But if I do, you'll be my first call." She glanced at Archie, then lowered her voice. "And if you do find out where he is, I expect you'll do the same?"

"We'll let you know," Jack promised.

"You didn't have to come all this way to visit, you know." Wendy smiled a bit at Blair, who looked a little surprised.

"There are a lot of loose ends Cayde left behind. We're in Nashville to turn over every rock he might be hiding under." Jack's face looked determined.

"No rocks here. Autumn did call me the other day. She told me you two might be looking into another woman who went missing. Do you think it was Cayde?"

The two agents looked at one another. "It's possible. First, we just need to find him."

"So what do you think happened?" Wendy folded her arms. "Maybe he left the country?"

"No, he didn't have a passport," Jack said. "It looks like he took his rental car and split. Probably changed the plates. Probably changed his name. It doesn't matter, we'll catch him."

"Can't you just track the rental?" Wendy asked.

"It completely went off the grid," Blair said. "He probably figured out a way to disable it."

"Fuck." Wendy raised her eyebrows. "You two really don't know where he is, do you?" They gave her a bit of a hard look, and she laughed. "Sorry. So, you'll be seeing the other girls, then? Tell them I said hello."

"You seem—" Blair cocked her head to the side a bit. "—different."

Wendy laughed. "On the contrary, I feel more like myself than I have in years. You'd be surprised what a fresh start can do." Wendy looked back at Archie. "We're going to be fine."

"I'm happy for you," Blair said. "Really, I mean it."

"We've got to go," Jack said. "Please, don't hesitate to reach out if you need anything."

The corners of Wendy's mouth twitched upward. It wasn't really her style.

Wendy walked them back to the door, wished both of them good luck, and watched them leave. She shut the door and frowned, wondering if they knew more than what they'd let on.

Archie hopped around the room and began to pick things out of a box. "Are these mine too?"

"No, those are headed for the landfill."

"What's a landfill?"

"It's kind of like a junkyard. Everything in there is garbage." Wendy got to her knees beside him.

Archie pointed to a DVD player that no longer worked. "That's garbage?"

"Yup."

"And this?" He pulled out something small, inspecting it. "A phone?" He pulled out a second one, which was cracked and dirty.

"No." Wendy took them from him and placed them back in the box. "Those are pagers."

"What are pagers?"

Wendy shut the box and taped over it, the pagers sealed inside forevermore. She wrote "Landfill" across the top of it and smiled. "They're garbage, Archie."

Archie, not really caring for her answer, began to wander from box to box, inspecting what was inside and questioning whether the contents were coming to the new home with them.

She lifted the boxes, carefully went down the stairs, and stacked them into the rented moving van. Most of the big things had already been packed, courtesy of a few neighbors and their helping hands.

And then came the drive to their new home. As Wendy left behind the apartment that had held so many painful memories, she felt the last release of worry and anxiety she'd carried with her for so many years.

Because she knew that she'd never have to check over her shoulder for Cayde again. The sight of his body disappearing into the dark ocean was perhaps the most comforting memory she ever had. Those poor FBI agents, searching for someone who wouldn't ever be found. Wendy's only regret was that she hadn't been able to bury his body. She hadn't been able to see his lifeless eyes. No matter. A makeshift watery grave was even more than he deserved.

Justice for Sophie, for all the women Cayde had ever hurt, had been paid.

Milton Keynes UK
Ingram Content Group UK Ltd.
UKHW022344171124
451242UK00007B/138